praise for an offer fae can't refuse

"A cozy fae mafia story? Say less. Add a little pining, angst, and a bunch of mayhem and you've got the perfect recipe. Lou Wilham brings a varied cast of characters together with beautiful chemistry and an intriguing story that will leave you satisfied but ready for more."

- **Stephanie Combs**, Author of *The Stars Couldn't Break Us*

To the friends we made
later in life.

(and anyone who loves a good mafia AU)

content warnings

Hello dear reader,

I want you to take care of yourself, so here's a little forewarning about the contents of this book. An Offer Fae Can't Refuse is a story featuring mobsters and all that entails. That includes: mentions of abuse, mentions of past character death, character death, blood, torture, disembowelment, violence, coarse language.

Thank you,

Lou

FAE OF EVENTIDE: BOOK ONE

AN OFFER FAE CAN'T REFUSE

Lou Wilham

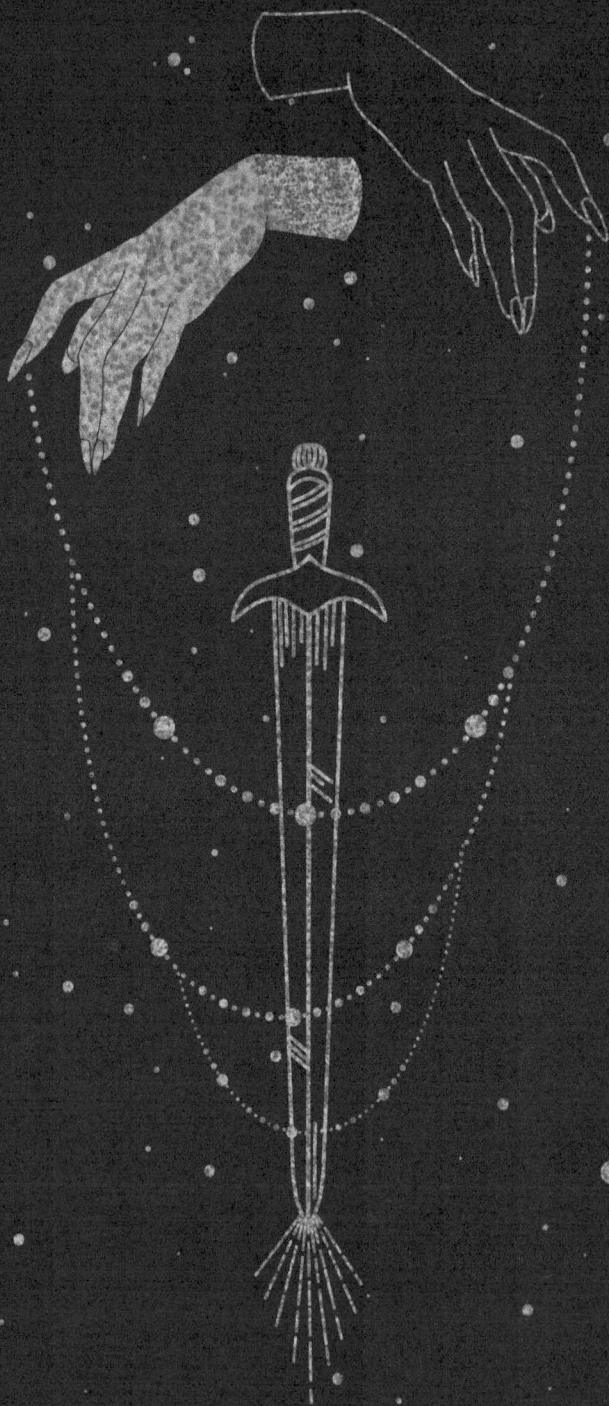

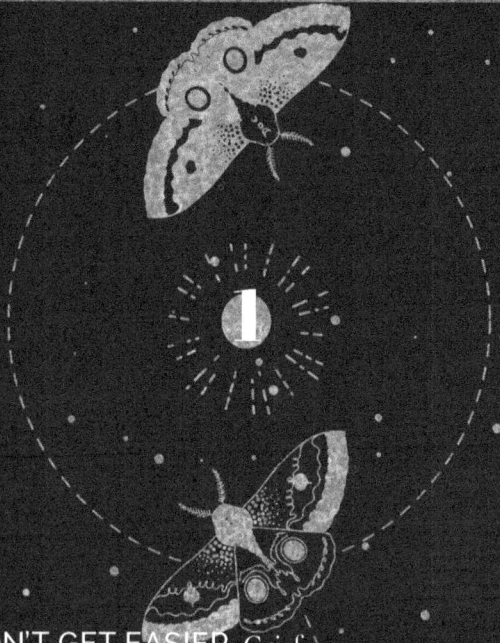

IT DIDN'T GET EASIER. Grief.

Something that had been just out of Mal's reach for so much of his life had been ripped away—like sand slipping between his fingers, the grains lost to the wind—right as he got close enough to *maybe* grasp it.

He'd almost had . . . *everything*.

And then it was gone.

The weight of his grief sat in his chest, every second of every day. Sometimes he could forget about it. Sometimes he could push it to the back of his mind, focus instead on the ebb and flow of life in the District of Eventide, on the way his sister kept him busy, on the blood and sweat and exhaustion that came with running a gang. And then—out of nowhere it seemed—something would remind him of *them*, and everything would ache all over again.

The funny thing was . . . Well. It wasn't really funny so much as sad. But the funny thing was that they—Sage Nocturna—likely hadn't even known Mal existed at all. At the very least, he knew Sage hadn't known his name. Sage had been the heir to a powerful family and all that entailed.

The Night Market. The Faceless Few gang. The property. The money. Ruthless on one hand and kind on the other. The perfect balance. Ethereal in their beauty and vibrant in their violence. So far out of Mal's league that Mal could have played the game for a lifetime and never even have made it out of the minors.

Was that how sports metaphors worked? He wasn't sure. He didn't like sports. That was Mox's thing.

But he *was* sure that after Sage had saved him and Mox from a life of starving on the streets, after he'd made that . . . that promise to Sage, they had probably promptly forgotten about him. Aside from the few moments where they were in the same place at the same time, or where Mal was given orders by one of Sage's underlings, there was no need for the heir to the family to have any contact with someone as low level as Mal. No need for them to ever think about Mal again.

Brushing dark strands of hair back from his face when the night wind of the graveyard threatened to tug more loose, Mal curled further in on himself, the back of his suit jacket pulling as he hunched his shoulders at the onslaught of memories. A life debt never repaid. Stolen glimpses. Smiles that were never meant for him but he hoarded anyway. A few brief conversations between superior and subordinate.

And that one awful, beautiful moment when Mal snuck into Sage's room to haunt their dreams and had been trapped there, sealing his fate for the rest of his life. He knew most didn't adhere to the old laws. They didn't see the traditions of the fae long past as valid anymore. But for a Mare, being trapped by the person they were meant to terrorize was as good as marriage, and while Mal had never been a traditionalist . . . Something clicked into place when he stared down at the person sleeping on the bed, breaths deep. As silly as the tradition was, it was true. Sage was his person, his spouse.

He'd never get the chance to so much as *try*, now. Because Sage was gone. Stolen away by greed and jealousy. Cut down by their own *family*, for fuck's sake.

Mal shook out his hands where they had tightened into fists on his thighs. The grip so intense his knuckles had begun to ache. The wet from the grass had long since soaked into his slacks, but he didn't care. It gave him something to focus on as he smoothed his palms across the wrinkled fabric stretched tight around his quadriceps.

He'd have stains on his knees, barely visible on the dark fabric but there just the same. Proof that he'd once again prostrated himself in the middle of the graveyard before someone who was dead. Who hadn't even known his name. Mox didn't approve. She called it an obsession, but there was little she could do to stop him, even four years later.

"I'm sorry," he murmured, gentle and low, tilting his head back to look up at the statue before him. Soft lights floated around the stone, illuminating the tranquil face of the person who meant so much to Mal that they left a gaping hole in his chest in their absence. "I didn't mean to bring my negativity to you. And I know I promised you I'd live, but sometimes it's just . . . it's so *hard* sometimes."

He frowned, inhaling deeply, trying to regain control of himself where he knelt at the feet of the monument to the one he owed his life. The one he'd loved, to some degree, albeit begrudgingly at times. No. Not *had* loved. Not really. There was no past tense about it, Mal loved Sage still. Would continue to long after the earth had claimed his body. Eternal.

Because Sage saved him and his sister. Pulled them off the streets when they were starving. Sage gave him something to strive for, to live for. Sage was good, and kind, as much as they were vicious and brutal. Mal would never be able to escape his bone-deep admiration.

The monument was a beautiful rendering of Sage — mostly due to Sage's beauty and not Mal's skill — the best he'd ever sculpted. But in the dim light from the moon and the fairy fire drifting through the air like lightning bugs, he could still see where it wasn't quite right. Where it was missing *something*. The shine of life, perhaps.

Still, it was better than nothing and far better than the blur that the sculpture became when the sun shone too brightly and he could hardly see anything at all, just shapes and shadows. It was why Mal always visited at night, haunting the graveyard like a specter in his perfectly tailored black suit, only his white cane flashing in the moonlight. That, and maybe his dress shirt if he'd gone with white instead of black, but that was rarer and rarer these days.

White stained too easily. Running the Faceless Few was a bloody job. And as much money as he'd made over the years since losing Sage, Mal was still an orphan at heart. Aware of the cost of things, the value.

"Chuckles is doing well," he said at last, when he was sure his voice would no longer shake. "Her naming ceremony will be on the solstice. She hasn't told a soul what name she's picked. Says she's keeping it for someone special, whatever that means to her. *Chuckles* will still apply, she claims, though I'm not sure how. But then . . . I'm sure you already knew that. She's here almost as often as I am." Mal pulled in a breath, his next words leaving him on a trembling laugh. "It's hard to keep secrets from the dead, isn't it?"

It would be easy to lean forward and rest his forehead against the outstretched hand of the stone sculpture. To pretend for a moment that it was Sage touching him. To allow himself that small comfort in a sea of darkness. A comfort he'd only experienced once before, when he was a young teen and Sage—in their early twenties then—helped him to his feet in the middle of a crowded street. But the touch would likely only make the ache worse in the end, and what had Mal ever done to deserve such softness? Nothing. Not yet, anyway. He couldn't even wipe out the bastards who'd taken Sage from him.

One got away. Fucking Bentley Nocturna.

"I'm sorry." Mal sighed again, lowering his head. He wasn't worthy of even *looking* at Sage. Why did he think he was? It'd been four years and he still hadn't finished the job. And even if he had . . . he wasn't anything special. Little gutter snipe that he was. He could dress himself in all the finery the Faceless Few could afford, and at his core he'd still be a dirty child who'd killed his way into greatness.

Not greatness.

He wasn't great. He wasn't half the person Sage would have been had they lived long enough to become the head of the family. Mal was just playing pretend. Wearing someone else's shoes that were much too big for him, and hoping no one else noticed when he winced from the blisters.

A rustle of fabric sounded behind him. Mal didn't have to turn to know it was Mox. It was *always* Mox. His sister couldn't leave well enough alone, it seemed. Always had to pick at things like a scabbed-over wound.

Mal released a soft, tense breath and didn't lift his head. "Tell me you've found her."

"'fraid not," Mox said, not even a hint of apology in her tone.

She was lucky she was Mal's twin sister, because if she weren't—if anyone else came to him with that blasé attitude toward their failure—he'd have ripped them apart limb from limb with shadows. Let the darkness and the nightmares he controlled as a Mare tear them into pieces so small only a mouse could feast upon them.

"Then what the fuck, may I ask, are you doing here?" Mal's voice was quiet, deadly. In the years since Sage's death and Mal's subsequent violent takeover of the Faceless Few, he'd learned that sometimes the quietest voices were the most terrifying. Shadows writhed around him, picking up off the ground, hissing in annoyance, threatening even if Mox knew he'd never act against her.

"The Court of Families is being held"—Mal heard Mox shift again, her shoes creaking from the uneven distribution of her weight as she no doubt pulled her phone from her pocket to check the time—"in twenty."

"Fuck the Court." Mal squeezed his eyes shut and clenched his fists again. Hate lit his veins on fire at the mere thought of the group of fae who had benefited from Sage's death. Stood by and let it happen because it wasn't their business. "Fuck the Seelie. Fuck the Unseelie. And fuck the *Court of Families*."

"If only it were that simple," Mox mused, wistful perhaps for the life they lived before Mal decided it was his responsibility as Sage's husband to make those who'd hurt them pay. He couldn't say he blamed her for that. Life was a lot less complicated then. Not easier by any means, but less complicated certainly.

"If only." Mal scrubbed at his eyes, his lips curling at the water that had collected along his lash line without him even realizing it. Thank the Goddess for waterproof eye liner. His chest ached again, the reminder of what he was missing, and how different everything would be were he *not* missing it, so all-encompassing it felt like someone was sitting on his sternum. He wouldn't be the head of the family—that would be Sage's place—but it would be enough to be their underling. To do as they bid. "Give me ten minutes."

"But we have to be at Court in twenty, and it'll take us at least—"

"Ten. Minutes. Mox." Mal's jaw clenched so tightly around the words, his back molars squeaked against one another.

"Yes, sir," Mox murmured, and he could imagine her dipping her head with more deference than she'd ever shown her twin brother in their life before they'd come to the Faceless Few begging for a way to feed themselves. For a home. A family. Before Sage had taken them into the family, protected them with their name, put their own life on the line for two teenagers who'd been begging on the streets days before. He didn't care for it. He knew it was his due, but he didn't have to *like* it.

Mal waited until he heard the car door shut behind her before he returned his attention to the monument in front of him. Sage's visage was carved from a block of pale marble. Each fold of their clothing meticulous. Each feature of their face careful, and kind. Everything in its place, right down to the wrinkles that used to form around their eyes when they were trying to hold back a smile. It was exactly the way they'd looked down at him as his bones ached from the cold hard cement. Exactly the way Sage had looked when they'd saved another dirty child from the wrath of the gangs in Eventide.

Chuckles had gotten just as lucky as Mal and Mox to have had this expression turned toward her. He hoped she realized that.

It had taken far longer than Mal would like to admit, even with his magic to help him along, to get that almost-smile near perfect. And even now, there was a pocket dimension off the basement of his and Mox's old house that led into a cavern full of practice runs. All lacking . . . something.

Still. It wasn't quite right. Like Mal hadn't been able to catch the light in Sage's eyes.

"It's the medium," Mal concluded, running a hand through his long black hair, fingers skimming the undercut on his right side, his dangling diamond earrings tinkling with the movement. "Nothing will ever live up to you. But you know that, don't you?"

The statue looked out across the graveyard, one of those soft, secret almost-smiles carved into their lips, a hand extended to the grave below them. It was the expression Mal remembered the best, even when the other details began to smudge and blur together, like the sound of Sage's voice. The almost-smile stayed.

Perhaps because it was the only expression Sage had ever directed toward Mal outside of vague indifference when they passed one another at Headquarters. Except for one other time.

In the dim light of the crowded hall as they stood over the huddled form of a child who'd been caught stealing from the Night Market, Sage had looked up at Mal, their eyes meeting, and almost smiled. Caught his eye and winked, like they were sharing some secret joke. Only Mal had missed the punchline and instead of laughter, he found his breath lodged in his throat, his lungs burning with . . . *something*. It was so much like a scene a mere decade prior when a twenty-something Sage had looked down at a sixteen-year-old Mox and Mal and extended the same kindness.

The child had been Chuckles. And Sage's care for her was why, even if Mal found Chuckles insufferable—she was nine at the time after all, and it was hard to find any nine-year-old *not* insufferable — he and Mox had taken the pre-teen in when Sage was gone. Protected her as the Faceless Few was torn apart and remolded in Mal's image.

"I miss you," Mal said at last, reaching toward the outstretched hand. He didn't allow himself to touch. He never did. Not since he'd finished the sculpture and paid someone to have it replace the paltry grave marker Sage's family chose for them. But even those words didn't fit quite right. "I miss . . . knowing you were there, if I ever needed you again."

There was only one Nocturna left now to complain about the statue, and it was unlikely Bentley would. And even if she did, Mal wouldn't care. Sage was worthy of more than a cheap headstone. It had been generic and bland when they'd been anything but.

"Until next week." Leaning forward, Mal adjusted the fresh flowers in the vase and rose, the old bouquet in one hand and his cane in the other. He turned for a moment, allowing himself one last glimpse at the face of the person who'd meant so much to him softened by fairy fire and lightning bugs, then headed back the way he'd come, picking carefully across the graveyard to the car where Mox waited.

Mox didn't say anything at first, just pulled away from the curb and out into the busy streets of DE. But Mal knew better than to think that would last.

"It's been four years, Mal," Mox murmured, soft, gentle. It was the only time she ever sounded that way. Most of the time, her tone had a crisp, cutting quality. Biting and acerbic. But when they spoke of Sage, she tried to be kind. It didn't suit her. Neither of them had been built for kindness, to receive nor offer it.

"I'm well aware of how long it's been, Mox." Mal didn't bother to turn and look at her. He kept his eyes forward, watching the lights of the city sweep by them in a twinkling blur. It was almost beautiful. Almost. If he allowed himself to forget the power struggles, and the stink of iron, and the blood coating the streets as the Seelie waged a silent war against the Unseelie. Silent because that's what the Court of Families was for: to keep everyone in line. To keep the peace—the accords. It didn't work. But they all tried to act like it did for whatever reason. Maybe because the quiet battles were more profitable.

"You're not even really married." She winced, likely feeling the way Mal's expression turned cutting without him even fixing her with the glare. "I know . . . Mare tradition. Getting trapped with them when you went to give them night terrors, means you're married. But they didn't sign on for that. They were never as devoted to you as you are to them. Don't you think it's time you—"

"We are not having this discussion," Mal said briskly.

Mox let out a long, slow breath, her fingers drumming against the steering wheel for a moment as the car idled at a stop light. "Okay."

"Tell me what the bastards in the Seelie Court want this time."

"What they always want." Mox laughed a little, the sound hollow, self-deprecating. "Power. Land. Magic. The Night Market."

"Fuck me." Mal sighed, tilting his head back against the headrest. The Night Market. That had been the one thing he hadn't calculated into all his careful scheming in the takeover. Or perhaps not the market itself, but the power struggle over the market that followed the death of the entire family of Nocturna. Everyone wanted a piece of it, wanted control over it because it was the most lucrative business in Eventide. Whoever held the power of the Night

Market held the power of commerce for the folk of Eventide. Capitalism at its most magical.

And then there was the upkeep. Which took a bigger toll on his and Mox's magic than either of them had anticipated. Almost as if the city of Eventide didn't agree with the change in regime.

"My thoughts exactly." The turn signal clicked loudly in the space between them as Mox checked each direction to make sure it was clear. "And there's a new player in town. Or so I've heard. It's got everyone all in a tizzy."

"What kind of new player?" Mal finally tilted his head to look at Mox, his eyes narrowing to try to make out her features and the vibrant blur of her turquoise hair half-hidden by the dark between streetlights. She was mostly a shadow like this, even without the glaring sunshine that turned everything into blurry but colorful shapes.

"A fixer." Mox's cheek twitched, barely visible as they passed under a light, but Mal couldn't tell through the gloom if it was a frown or a smile. "They're making one hell of a stir."

"Do we have anything on them yet?" Mal didn't like a new player in his city. Especially one he was just hearing about.

"No. I wish we did though. Their work is . . ." Mox's form shuddered, and when she next spoke her voice was a little raspy. "*Breathtaking.*"

Mal rolled his eyes and looked back out the windshield. He'd never understand how Mox could jump from one crush to the next without any real thought to the person themself. All while he remained steadfast and true to one person. It was baffling.

"Have they worked with anyone we know yet?"

"Unclear. But I'm going to find out tonight."

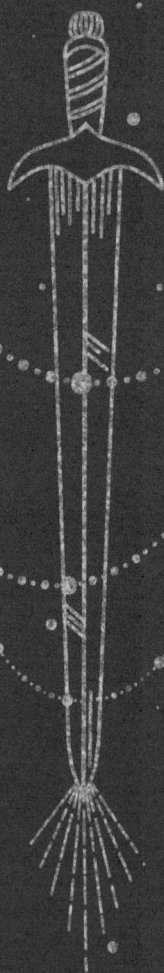

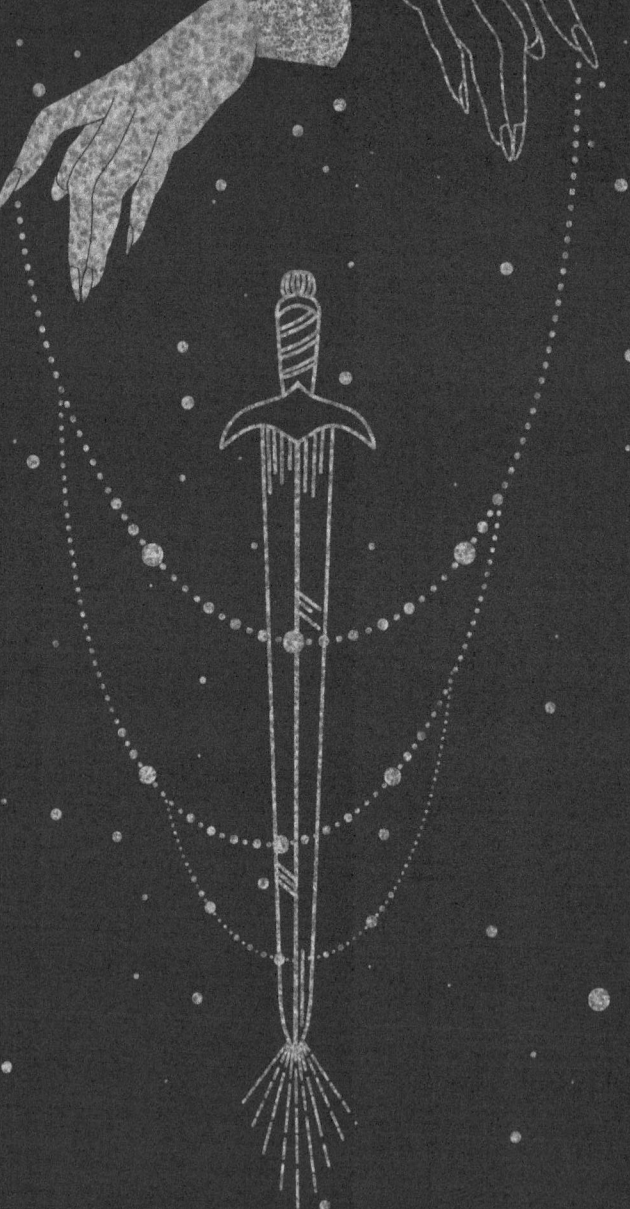

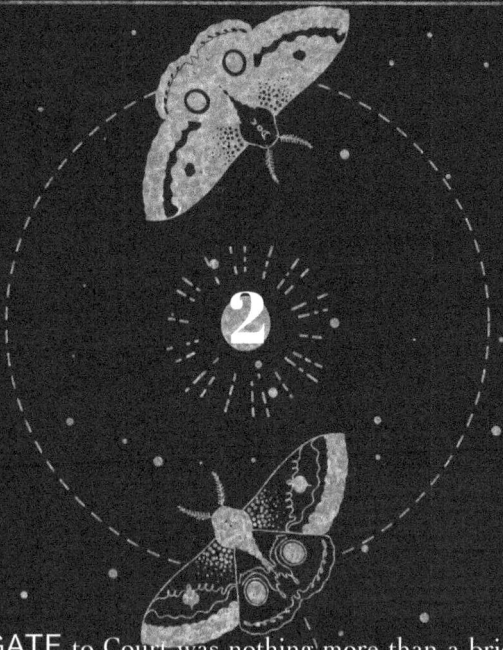

2

THE GATE to Court was nothing more than a brick wall with giant broken pieces of sculpted marble in front of it. It sat just off the walking path that ran between it and the water.

A face, godlike in its size, gleamed in the moonlight. It looked like an art installation by some human, but anyone with any sense for magic — any folk — would know better, would see the way warding spells sizzled around it like heat off pavement. Look-aways. And keep-outs. And camouflages. To make any non-magical peoples walk right past. Maybe they'd take a couple of pictures on their phone, marvel at the broken artistry of a fallen god carved in marble and crumpled to pieces — an eye there, a lip here, a nose that way — before a generic brick wall. But none would get close enough to enter, and that's all that mattered.

A cool, briny breeze coasted across the water behind them, tickling the hairs at the back of Mox's neck where her chin-length turquoise hair was cut high enough to expose sensitive skin. She wanted to grab Mal by the wrist and force him to talk more about Sage and his perpetual widowerhood. To look what he was doing dead in the face and realize how nonsensical it was. Would it make him give up on this insane quest to wipe out anyone and everyone that had anything to do with Sage's death? Maybe. Maybe not. But anything had to be better than this constant *moping*.

She wouldn't though. Because, despite what a lot of people seemed to think of her, she wasn't stupid. She still remembered the fistfight they'd gotten into the last time she'd pushed this. She had a scar along her chin from where he'd shoved her so hard, she cracked it against a tombstone.

So yeah, let the grumpy bastard mope if that's what he wanted.

"You're late," a goblin grumbled from where he perched atop a broken piece of marble cheekbone. "They started without you."

"No, they didn't." Mal didn't even bother to spare the creature a glance. He stepped forward, careful of the small curb and the gravel, and walked straight through the brick wall as his cane tapped lightly against what lay on the other side.

"He's in a mood, innit?"

"Buddy, you've got no idea." Mox rolled her eyes, pulled at the lapels of her plum-colored blazer to straighten it, and followed Mal. Preparing for battle. A shiver rolled down her spine, and she released a quiet curse at the cold, gritty feeling of stepping into a pocket dimension and having all potential glamours stripped away. The room on the other side, if a person could call it that, was more humid than a greenhouse and held twice as many plants. Every one of which shifted subtly as if it were breathing. A vine crawled across the stone walkway at Mox's feet, and she almost tripped over it in her haste to follow Mal to the long stone table at the center of the space. "Sorry. Sorry."

The vine lifted, trembling as if shaking its fist at her, and Mox forced herself to turn away so she could pull out Mal's chair for him. As was proper for the head of their family.

Guin looked up from her phone for a moment, bored already if Mox knew anything about her. She was the head of the Delta Daggers, an Unseelie gang that controlled the docks on the western side of Eventide and seemed perpetually annoyed by the need for bureaucracy in this city. Mox couldn't disagree. She gave her a quick, polite nod. Guin nodded back then returned to her phone, stringy navy hair hiding her face.

"Well, if we're all *finally* here," Alton boomed, "then we can *finally* begin."

Mox tightened her hands on the back of Mal's chair, her perfectly manicured nails digging into the ancient wood as she helped slide it in toward the stone table and resisted the urge to roll her eyes. Alton—the head of the Seelie gang the Divinity of Aquarius—liked to pretend he was king of the castle, high ruler of the Court of Families, even if he was only one of six family heads that ran the District of Eventide.

Three Seelie. Three Unseelie. Balanced.

Mal twitched where he sat in front of her, and she knew he was about to say something they were all going to regret. Something to rile everyone up. Great. Just great. That's what they needed tonight.

"We're *not* all here, are we?" Mal tilted his head, his eyes narrowing as if to better view the people around him and take a head count. Mox winced, already knowing where this was going. She wished Mal wouldn't. He drew too much attention to things they didn't want anyone noticing. "We seem to be missing someone. Alton, where's your dear brother and second? Shouldn't Glyn be here if we're to speak of new business?"

Across the table, Guin's shoulders tightened, her mouth pressing more firmly into a hard line. No one else seemed to notice, but it was Mox's *job* to notice. Likewise, Evy—the leader of Zephyr, one of the three Seelie gangs—lifted her chin from her bored slouch to look around as if Glyn would suddenly appear. Something was going on there, but Mox would have to dig more into it later.

"Glyn is unwell this evening. He has a delicate constitution, you know that." Alton huffed as if this whole thing inconvenienced him most of all. "He'll attend the next Court of Families."

"I see," Mal responded, but there was an undercurrent to the tone that perhaps only his twin would read.

He *did* see, far more than anyone else really. And he knew well enough that Glyn wouldn't be at the next meeting, just the same as Mox did. He couldn't be. But that was a problem for another night.

"Then let us proceed." Mal flapped his wrist as if he were a prince magnanimously allowing his lessers to continue as they were.

These meetings probably wouldn't take half as long if Mal didn't insist on spending so much time winding everyone up. Not that they didn't *deserve* to be wound up, especially the Seelie, but Mox just wanted to go the fuck home, thanks. It was her turn to take Chuckles to school in the morning, and she'd not be caught dead looking hungover and haggard in the drop-off line because she'd been out too late the night before. That led to bitchy PTA moms gossiping, and there was far too much of that going around already. Why Chuckles had to go to Moondale High, Mox was unclear, but Mal insisted. So Mox traded off with a couple of the other execs in the gang to drive her over every day.

"As I was saying." Alton cleared his throat as if he

wanted to say *before I was so rudely interrupted* but was too much of a coward to do anything so stupid. "Let's begin. Old business."

A collective groan went through the room, and Mox tuned out the voices of the six fae at the head of the six gangs that ruled Eventide. Instead, she focused her attention on watching faces, cataloging body language, and noting who looked like their suit needed a little extra attention. It was always easiest to see which gangs were in trouble based on the clothes their seconds wore. Brand names fresh off the summer line, or had someone's jacket been taken in to hide how they were running leaner than they'd been a year ago? The heads, of course, would look impeccable, but the seconds didn't have to try quite so hard. Or at least, *they* didn't think so. And Mal always wanted to know which gangs were running into trouble, which ones would be easiest to pick off. Especially when it came to the Seelie.

Cascade, or Cas, of the Delta Daggers was Guin's second. A tall, dark brown–skinned fae with pointed batlike ears that she hid under a mane of curls that circled her head in a neatly trimmed afro. Mox couldn't see the hems of her pants, but she could see the rest of her. Cas had her sleeves rolled up to the elbows. The liner looked neatly pressed and un-frayed. The crisp white button-up beneath the black suit jacket was ironed to perfection, and the front pleats on her pants were just the same. Neat, tidy, likely professionally taken care of. The Delta Daggers were doing fine, even if Guin herself was fucking around with things she likely shouldn't. Good. They were the Faceless Few's best allies, and the Few couldn't afford a weakness there.

Beside her, keeping a careful distance of about six feet, stood a short, lanky creature, limbs spindly and awkward. Damascus, Dam for short, was the second and elder sibling to Fluonia—Flo, to those who didn't want to get their head bitten off by a bitchy redcap. She led the Blood Moons, an Unseelie gang made up mostly of other redcaps. Dam had never put much stock in dressing, so it was always harder to tell if their gang was doing well. Except . . . Well, except Dam was sporting a thick gold chain around their neck. New, if the way they kept fiddling with it was anything to go by.

Curious. Why were the Blood Moons suddenly flush enough for Dam to start investing in gawdy jewelry?

There was an empty spot beside Dam where Glyn would be standing if he'd been able to attend. His absence made his older brother look smaller. Unprotected. Mox wondered how long it would be before Alton caught on to what was happening right under his nose. But it was none of her business. At least, not until Guin *made* it her business.

Beside Mox stood Celeste. She was a tall, full-figured woman, nothing at all like her name might suggest. She, just like her leader, Evy, was dressed immaculately in all white. Not a stain or a wrinkle in sight. Mox felt smaller standing next to her, but she wasn't worried about the Zephyr gang. Evy and her people had never posed a problem for the Faceless Few, and as far as Mox knew, they weren't harboring Mal's fugitive either.

That left the Wildlings. Mox couldn't get a good look at their second, not from this angle. Silva was a slender young man, probably too young for the position he'd been given. He was the son of the head of the family, a woman who went by Mata. They both had long dark green hair and light brown skin. And although Mata's hair looked freshly styled, that didn't mean anything. As guardians of the forest at the heart of Eventide, and the few blocks that surrounded it, they were a well-respected family. Maybe one of the first that had settled there and taken root, so to speak. Mata had always stayed out of the politics and mudslinging, but Mox could never tell if she thought herself above it or if she was just too damn old for such childishness.

Either way, they probably weren't harboring Bentley Nocturna. That left the Blood Moons and the Divinity of Aquarius. One would think narrowing it down like this would make it easier for Mox to determine which of their enemies had taken in the woman who'd killed Mal's spouse —his words, not Mox's. But four years later, the little rat was keeping herself perfectly hidden. Annoying, is what it was. And Mal was growing increasingly impatient.

"The fixer," Mata said, after someone else must have prompted a call for new business. Mox tuned back into the conversation so fast, the words almost seemed to echo in her ears. "What do we know?"

Mox watched a few of them shift uncomfortably at the question. Most notably, Alton, who had run a hand through his curly blond hair as if it would hide his unease. It just made it more obvious.

Interesting. Alton knew something. Either he'd been the one to hire this fixer first, or there was something else going on. Mox would have to speak to Guin about that.

"They go by the Phantom," Evy volunteered. When everyone turned to look at her, she gave a dainty shrug, lavender hair brushed carefully behind one ear. "They cleaned up a pack of bargheist in my territory. Left a calling card. It was good work, very tidy."

Mox had seen that cleanup job. Evy was right, it was tidy. Almost too tidy. The bargheist, a pack of three giant wild black fairy hounds, had been making a mess of Zephyr territory lately. Digging through trash, killing outdoor cats, the usual antics wild dogs got up to. But they all knew it was only a matter of time before the creatures turned their attention toward bigger prey, their gleaming red eyes hungry. The Phantom had left nothing behind but their hides—so clean and neatly cut that someone could have turned them into rugs—and a sharp, crisp, white business card bespelled to stay in place and weather the elements. The curling font showed the word *Phantom* and a phone number to a burner phone—Mox knew because she'd gone digging.

"Do we think they're for hire?" Flo asked, a gleam in her eyes that Mox decided immediately she didn't care for. Redcaps were much too bloodthirsty by half, and Mox didn't want to think about what kind of work Flo and her cohorts would want a fixer for. "Or are they just going to act as a vigilante?"

"They're for hire," Alton said with too much certainty. Then he tried to lessen the statement by saying, "I believe so, anyway."

Silence followed the declaration, every family head debating what to do with this information. A new fixer meant the rates of those previously helping the families clean up their messes might go down. But it also meant there was someone dangerous and unaligned in their territory. Only time would tell if this Phantom would become a problem that needed to be cleaned up.

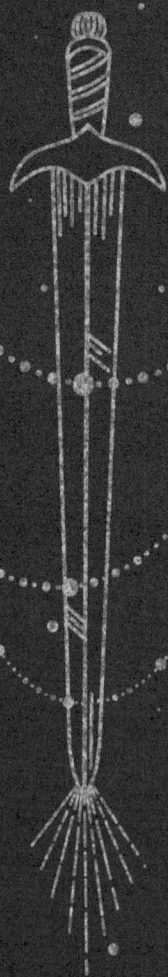

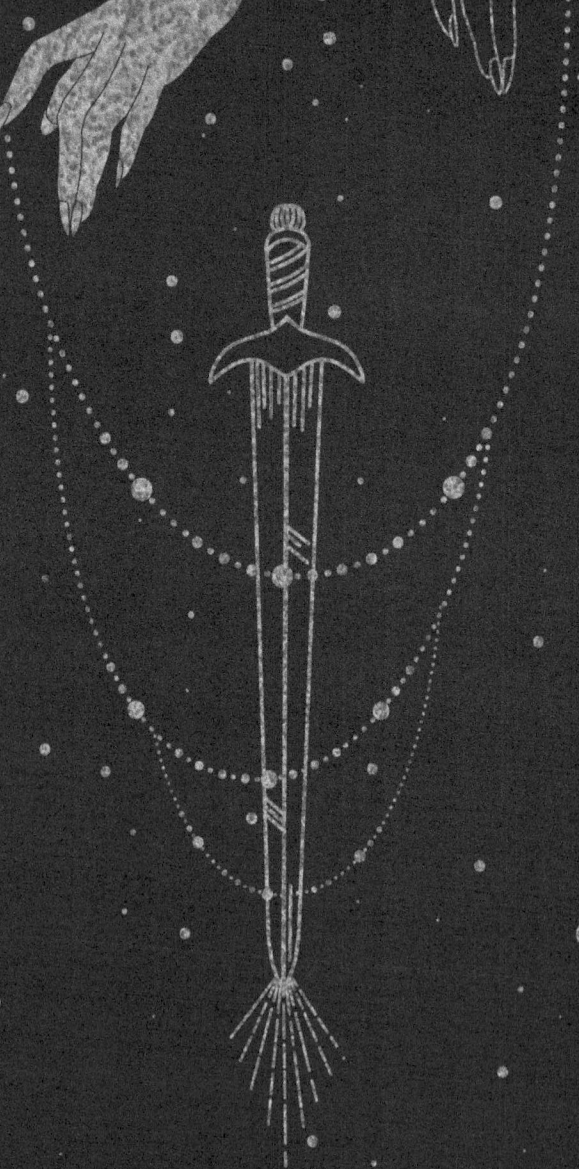

3

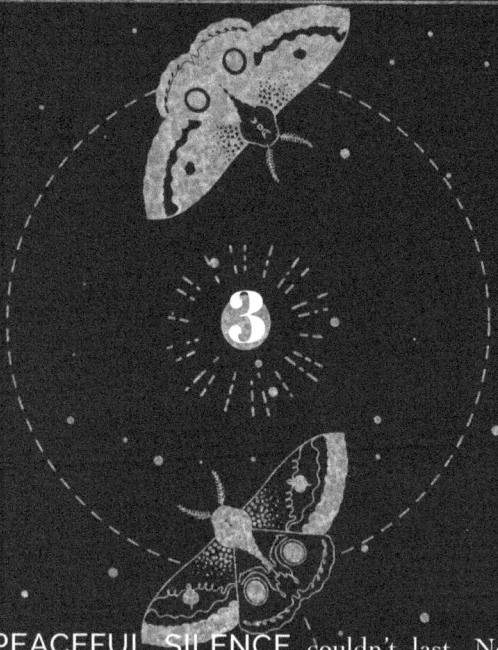

THE PEACEFUL SILENCE couldn't last. Not in a place as blood-soaked and festering as Eventide, Maryland. Corey knew that perhaps better than anyone else in the city. She knew the ins and the outs of the gangs and their violence. She knew the creatures that lurked the streets at night hunting for their next victim in the dark. And she knew, above all else, that she was one of them. Even though she was half human—a halfling—she was one of those monsters.

Bloodthirsty and full of rage.

It was why she'd done so well in the gangs when she'd been a part of them. Why she'd made a name for herself for a short while there, a few years back. It was also why she'd had to disappear. Why she'd taken the chance provided by a dead family heir and enough money to buy her way out and run with it.

The problem was . . . the money ran out.

About six months ago.

And while she wanted to keep her head down, run her bakery, and pretend the underworld of Eventide didn't exist, she couldn't. Because it was the fastest way to make a buck in this Goddess-forsaken place. It wasn't that she was greedy. It wasn't that the money was for her. It was her stepsisters. One of them in medical school, of all things. The other was studying to be . . . She wasn't quite sure what Clancy was planning to do with her degree, but the youngest of them had been at it for only a year at this point, so she had time to sort herself out.

Corey had no such time. Never had.

With a gusty sigh, Corey brushed the back of her wrist over the tip of her nose, scratching an itch, and tried to pretend it wasn't some kind of sign, an ill omen. Her nose always itched when shit was about to hit the fan. Grammy Corwin said Corey was a bit psychic, just like her. Said it was a part of her bean-nighe lineage. Corey thought that was a crock load of shit—she was half human and there was no way she'd gotten anything from her fae side except an annoyingly long lifespan and the ability to see through glamours—but one didn't call Grammy Corwin on things. Even if fae genetics didn't work like that. The woman had been all teeth and had smelled like blood up until the day she died.

Gods, but Corey missed her, the crotchety old biddy.

If only she'd been half as rich as she was bitter, maybe Corey wouldn't be in this predicament. But no, any money Grammy Corwin had before she passed had long since been gambled away by Corey's delinquent father. Not that there had been much anyway.

Wherever Carlin Corwin had disappeared to shortly after Grammy Corwin died and willed what little she had left to her son—mostly just the house—Corey hoped he stayed there. Neither she nor her sisters needed that man in their lives. He'd only bring them down.

The dough squished between her fingers, sticking to her

knuckles in her agitation. Flour. She needed more flour, or this shit was going to wind up glued to her and then she'd never get on with the other five loaves she had to make before morning.

That was one good thing about running a bakery: the late nights. The hours she worked lined up almost perfectly with the hours of her . . . side hustle.

Was it a side hustle when it paid more than her day job?

Maybe that meant the baking was the side hustle. She wasn't sure. The only person who might know—because she knew shit like that—was Clancy, and Corey couldn't ask. She didn't want Clancy or Cassidy figuring out that she had gone back to that life to support them. Not after she'd promised them both she was done with it. She said all the money came from the bakery. Swore up and down that none of the Corwin sisters would ever set foot on Aquarius territory again, not so long as she lived.

She'd kept *part* of the promise, at least. Her home and her bakery weren't situated in Aquarius territory. They were nowhere near Seelie territory at all, in fact. Instead, they were smack dab in the middle of the streets the Faceless Few controlled. Whether that was better or worse than returning to her old stomping grounds was yet to be seen. But she'd kept her promise!

Likewise, the job she'd done a handful of days ago had been on Zephyr land. Which abutted Aquarius lines, but still, it *wasn't* in Aquarius territory. And if she played her cards right, maybe Alton wouldn't even realize she was "back."

Doubtful. But maybe.

Just as that thought flitted through her mind, the phone in her left back pocket buzzed. Someone calling for Corey then, as the Phantom's burner was in the right.

"Please don't be someone from the Aquarius. Please

don't be someone from the Aquarius. Please don't be someone from the Aquarius," Corey muttered to herself like a mantra as she cleaned off her hands on her frilly apron, careful of her floral blouse and corduroy pants. She pulled the phone from her pocket. Her heart sank at the number on the screen.

"Fuck!"

It *would* be Alton, wouldn't it? Bastard. Why was he bothering her? She'd made a clean break. Couldn't he leave well enough alone?

"Did you think you could come back into my city and I wouldn't *notice*, Corwin?" Alton hissed into the phone, his voice lowered like he was trying not to be overheard. It was probably only a matter of time before he started screaming at her. He liked to do that.

Corey rolled her eyes and resisted the urge to remind Alton that Eventide didn't belong to him. There was no single owner of the misty island city. Which was likely for the best as there were far too many fae there and no one being should rule them all without some kind of check and balance. Alton wasn't fucking Sauron. She also did not tell him that she'd never really left "his" city. She'd simply stepped out of his borders and thus disappeared into the hustle and bustle of Eventide. It was easy enough to do when one had the right contacts. When one knew how to disappear, or rather make someone *else* disappear, which Corey had had to do enough times it was almost second nature.

Still, it was amazing it had taken him this long to notice. She wondered what had tipped him off, or who . . . She'd have to check into that at some point.

"Hello to you too, Alton."

"The Phantom," he said, cutting right to the chase.

"What about them?" Sweat trickled down Corey's spine.

He hadn't figured it out yet, had he? She'd been careful. Had left no obvious signs that might connect the Phantom to her. She forced herself to breathe. There was no reason for him to think she was the Phantom. None at all.

"I want to know who they are. Now."

A hysterical laugh burbled up from Corey's chest, and she had to clear her throat to keep it from finishing its journey into the air. "And what would you like me to do about that, Alton? You have people for that, why don't you just —"

"No one as good as you." That would be flattering if it didn't mean there was probably no way to get rid of Alton without giving him what he wanted. "You already know who they are, don't you?"

Biting down hard on her tongue, Corey drew in a short breath and hoped it didn't ring through to the other end of the line. She couldn't lie to Alton. She'd tried a hundred times over. But she was a terrible fucking liar — which had nothing to do with her fae lineage. And besides, he'd practically raised her for a time. At least until she'd grown into her usefulness and been inducted into the Divinity of Aquarius. Then she became just another underling for him to order around. He knew her too damn well. Maybe better than anyone else. And if she was being honest with herself, the way he weaponized that knowing hurt.

He'd been an older brother to her once upon a time. The only person she felt she could rely on after she'd lost her grandmother and only guardian. He'd even paid for her to go to patisserie school. But all of it had been an act. A way to keep her close, to make her feel indebted to him and the family because of her strange affinity for ferreting out lies and people who were in hiding. Her gift, as Grammy Corwin would call it. So that when he needed her, he could call in those favors.

"You do. Of course you do," he said. He didn't sound surprised by the revelation. "I want them, however you can get them for me. On my payroll—"

"They're freelance." Corey shook her head even though he couldn't see her. She sat on the metal stool tucked under the counter, hooking the toes of her loafers into the bottom rung. "They won't accept an offer to be on someone's payroll, no matter what the salary is."

That was not a lie. Corey *was* freelance, and she wouldn't be beholden to one of the gangs, not ever again. She'd learned that lesson the hard way.

"Then get me something I can use to *force* them to accept my offer." It sounded like Alton was gritting his teeth, the words strained and annoyed. Corey wondered why he wanted this so badly. Because it would be something to lord over the other family heads? Because he didn't like not knowing? Or was there another reason? "Blackmail. Family members. Whatever. Just find me *something*."

"And if I don't?" Corey challenged, although she thought she already knew the answer to that question. Alton was not one to trifle with. He'd get what he wanted. He always did.

"Then I'll have to send someone to visit those sisters of yours. I haven't seen Clancy and Cassidy in a long while, you know, and I'm sure they'd be more than happy to come home. To Eventide. To the family."

Bile rose in Corey's throat. It was not a threat, nor an idle speculation. It was a promise. Cassidy and Clancy had never been a part of this life, but they'd met Alton and for a time he'd helped raise them when Corey needed him. He would drag them into this if he had to. He would dig into their deepest, darkest secrets and he would force them. The same way he wanted to force the Phantom. Corey couldn't let that happen. She'd worked too hard and too long to keep them out of this to fail now.

"I've got something better," Corey said, not even thinking, because she was an idiot and a coward and she was going to try to wiggle her way out of this by any means necessary.

"What." It wasn't a question, more a demand. Corey hadn't seen him in four years by this point, but she could picture him raising one blond brow, looking down his nose at her as if she were nothing more than a slug. She'd railed against that look once upon a time. Fought to prove herself worthy of more. She wouldn't do it now.

But she also didn't know what the fuck she was going to tell him to get him to back down . . . "What if I told you the heir to the Nocturna family wasn't dead?"

Fuck a duck. That was *not* what she was supposed to say. She didn't know what she had been planning to give Alton instead, but it definitely hadn't been *that*. That wasn't her secret to barter with.

"What?" This time it *was* a question, a note of surprise in the short, sharp sound, the *t* enunciated in a way that was almost pointed. Corey had heard him say that word in that exact way enough times to know that if she didn't spill her guts in short order, he'd hunt her down and beat it out of her. Didn't matter that she was on another gang's territory. Didn't matter that she'd left Aquarius years ago. Alton would have his answers.

"Sage Nocturna is alive." Or . . . as alive as they could be, considering someone slit their throat and left them to bleed out in an alley four years ago.

"And you came by this information how?"

"Doesn't matter." She couldn't tell him that she'd come by it by being the one to find Sage in that alley. That she'd come by it by promising to resurrect the little shit for a price and following through with that by . . . Well, it was better not to think too much about that night. It'd only give her nightmares to dredge up images of Icarus Ashthorne covered in blood, handing over the still-beating heart of a newly dead fae for Corey to— She shook herself. "Point is, Sage Nocturna is alive and well. Not sure where they're at exactly. They hightailed it out of Eventide, last I'd heard."

Not that they'd had much choice. They were supposed to be *dead*.

"Who else knows this?"

"No one." Well, Icarus, but she wasn't going to tell anyone. It would raise too many questions. Corey was sure the necromancer didn't exactly want word getting around that she'd brought the heir to a fae Mafia family back to life —if she'd even connected the dots about Sage's identity. She might not have. Stuff like that tended to get a witch in some serious shit, and without a coven or clan at Icarus's back to protect her—without one at *Corey's* back to protect *her* . . . Better not to drag Icarus into this.

"Not even Mal and Mox?"

"No." Corey's heart hammered in her chest. She'd promised to never tell another living soul about Sage. To protect their secret until she died. It was the best way to keep Sage safe. But . . . Sage wouldn't have to know, would they? They were in fucking Florida or somewhere thereabouts, the furthest they could get from Eventide, Maryland, without leaving the East Coast. Alton wasn't going to scour the country looking for them, but it would allow him to feel superior to Mal, the head of the Faceless Few, Sage's old gang. Corey knew how much Alton hated Mal, so this would distract him from the Phantom.

Hopefully for a while.

Long enough for her to come up with something else.

"Well then," Alton said, a laugh in his voice, smugness

curling the edges. "So Sage could just . . . come *back* one day. And take over?"

"Yeah. I suppose they could." They weren't going to, not as far as Corey knew. Sage had wanted a clean break, just like Corey. And playing dead was the best way to get it. Sage's relatives had done them both a favor when they'd decided to turn on the rightful heir to the family and try to off them once the old head of the gang died.

"Then they'd rip the gang right out from under that pretentious Mare." Alton was muttering to himself now, content in whatever misery he was fantasizing this would inflict upon Mal. It was all imagined since Sage wasn't coming back to Eventide. It wasn't safe for them here, not with so many enemies still lurking in the shadows. But let Alton get his rocks off on the idea of them returning and stealing back their proverbial throne from Mal. "All right then," he said finally. "You may keep the Phantom's secret, for now. But if they prove to be a problem for me . . ."

"You'll want their head. I know." Corey would have to figure out what being a "problem" for Alton entailed later. For now, she wanted to get off the fucking phone before she said something *else* stupid. Maybe she should call Sage and warn them—

Nah. They'd be fine so long as they stayed far away from Eventide.

"Good night, Corwin," Alton said, then hung up without another word.

The breath whooshed out of Corey in a long stream, and she slumped back against the counter. "That was close."

She'd somehow made it out unscathed. For the moment.

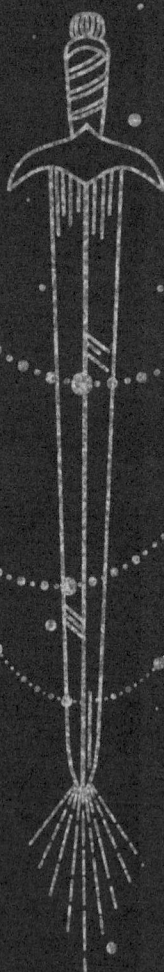

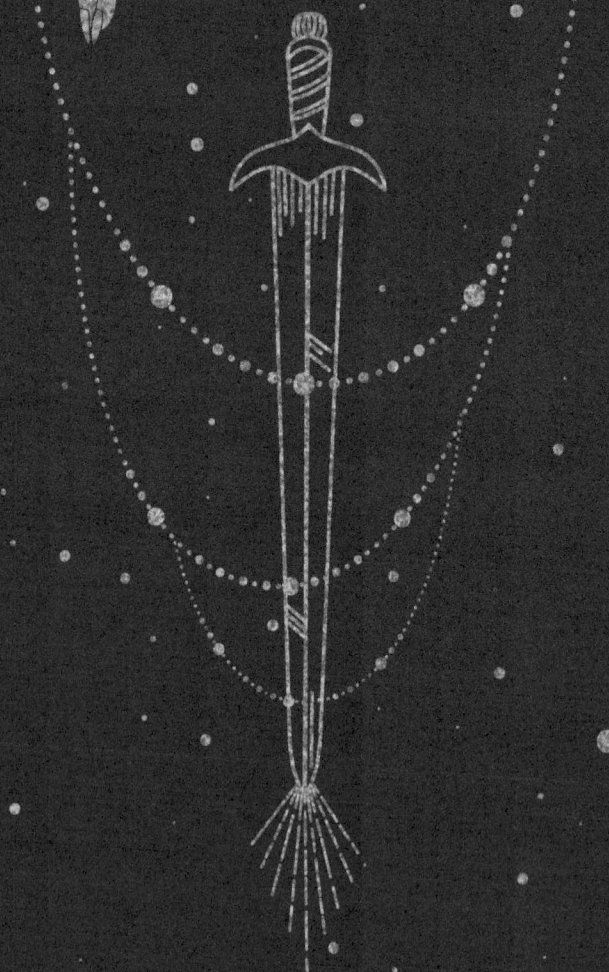

4

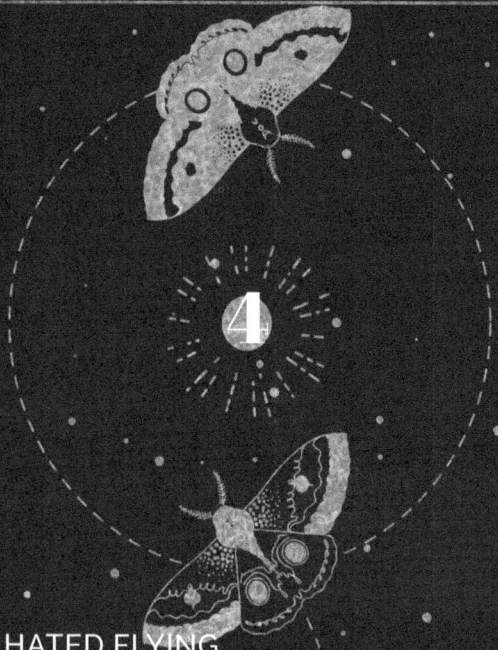

SAGE HATED FLYING.

Something about the change in air pressure fucked up their undead equilibrium. They couldn't remember hating it quite so much before they'd died. Sure, there had always been anxiety. Flying was a stressful situation for anyone with even the most minor amount of anxiety. From the intrusive thoughts about being that high in the air with only a tin can between them and certain death to trying to put all their shit back in their bag post-TSA while also being quick and getting the fuck out of everyone else's way . . . It was a lot.

But ever since having their throat slit in a dirty alley and waking up a few days later in a heavily warded basement covered in someone else's blood, things had only gotten worse.

Now, it wasn't just the constant worry of, *Who will tell your pet if you die? What will happen to your social media? What about your projects? Who will finish them? Will anyone even* care? Those things were definitely enough to make Sage want to avoid flying for life (death? unlife? whatever) but had never stopped them because flying was just so damn *convenient*. But now there was the added irritation of their inner ear aching and causing a massive migraine to the point of tunnel vision, light sensitivity enough that Sage wore sunglasses through the airport at fucking midnight, and the need to pack their own snacks because the packet of pretzels the airline provided was nowhere near enough to keep their blood sugar from dipping.

Either way, it was a relief when they flopped into the cool, dark backseat of an Uber and could shut their eyes for a bit while someone else took care of getting them from DC to the District of Eventide.

They couldn't nap. They hadn't been able to nap since they'd come back . . . different. Didn't sleep much really. A couple hours a night, if that. As if their body felt it would be wasting time if it shut down for even a few hours. As if it needed to seize every single moment it had in case that moment was its last. A fun side effect of being necromanced (necromancied? realived? brought back? Goddess, why was there no solid language for this kind of thing?) that led to a constant case of dark circles under their eyes.

So napping was out of the question, not that they would have even if they had been able to. Sage learned early in life not to fall asleep with someone close by. Not even someone they trusted. And even if that thought hadn't been drilled into their head by their father, passing out in an alley gasping for breath as blood soaked into their clothes was enough of a reminder not to trust *anyone*. They pulled out their phone instead, and tapped on the messenger app.

Sage: How are things?

They didn't exactly expect Tony to answer. He'd been reticent recently, more so than usual. But they needed to keep their mind off what a shitshow returning to Eventide was going to be, if only for a moment, and it'd been a couple of days since they'd heard from their friend.

His move up north with his sister hadn't changed much between them. Sage had always had the habit of disappearing off the map, Tony was used to that. But Tony finding a new boyfriend and then getting turned into a fucking werewolf sure had.

Tony: Stop worrying mom

Sage: Oh good, you're alive, and in good enough shape to be a bitch. Must mean you're fine.

Tony: -middle finger emoji-

Sage huffed a laugh and leaned back into their seat again. The lights of the bridge leading from Ironport to Eventide blurred through the rain-slicked window, and Sage took another dose of aspirin, swallowing the pills dry. All they could hope was that Corey's shop was where it'd been before they'd left Eventide four years ago.

Faceless Few territory wasn't high on the list of places they wanted to be right at that moment, but it was late enough—and dark enough, thanks to a new moon—that hopefully no one would even see them as they crept through the backstreets and alleys to the little bakery. Besides, Corey was the only one in Eventide who knew they were alive, and they couldn't head into Ironport just yet.

"Let me off here," Sage called to the driver when they stopped at a four-way just inside Faceless territory. They tugged self-consciously on the choker around their neck as the driver looked at them in the rearview mirror.

"This isn't where the app said—"

"It's fine. I'll leave you a tip to cover the rest and then some." They didn't particularly want to pull up in a strange car right outside of the bakery and have Corey's neighbors notice. There would be questions, and neither of them needed that. *Who was visiting the bakery in the middle of the night? Is Corey into something shady? Should we report this? Should we be worried?* Corey would be fucking furious, and Sage didn't need that either. She was likely already going to be pissed when she saw them regardless. Best not to add to that.

Throwing the single duffle they'd brought with them over their shoulder, they slid out of the backseat, phone in hand, already sending off a tip to the driver, and shut the door as quietly as they could behind them. The car pulled away and Sage stood for a moment, their eyes closed, one hand on their throat covering the scar there as if it could protect them from further injury, and inhaled deeply. They picked through the scents of the city: garbage, rain runoff, and mildewed leaves. Sought out anyone who might be spying on them. Anyone who might be nearby that could do them harm.

Another fun side effect of being dead (quite literally) for an entire week and some change before being reanimated was a heightened sense of paranoia. Being back in Eventide wasn't helping with that at all. Not when they didn't know exactly who had ordered the hit on them four years ago, and if they were still around. They'd made a conscious effort to stay away from any news of gang politics in Eventide, but now they wished they'd at least checked in with Corey before they boarded the plane.

"Too late now." Sage sighed, their shoulders only relaxing slightly when they found nothing by way of threats for at least a mile radius. Just the muzzy smell of sleeping humans and the grime of mortal critters lingering in alleys. It wasn't much, but it was something. Still, they needed to get out of the open. They were too easy a target like this, and that reminder made their heart beat harder in their chest.

Hunching and pulling the hood of their sweatshirt over the gleam of their white hair in the dark, Sage started down the alley that would lead them to the back parking of the shops on Redwood Boulevard. It wasn't a long walk to Corey's bakery, but Sage felt every step. Unease crawled along their veins, every inch a trudge as they divided their attention between sniffing the air for threats, listening for any signs of life, and not tripping over their well-worn sneakers on the uneven cobbles.

The lights inside the bakery were still on and Corey's car was parked outside, but she didn't answer when they knocked. So either she was getting ready to close up for the night, she couldn't hear, or she'd walked home after forgetting to shut off the lights. Sage didn't like those odds, but they didn't have a lot of other choices.

Oh sure, they could head to Corey's apartment and knock on her door, beg to be taken in like a stray cat if she was even there. But in all probability, Corey would slam the door in their face. Which wasn't something Sage had the time nor the energy for. Not after the flight. Not after the long drive. Not after the weeks of worrying about Tony and his condition. He said he was fine. Sage wouldn't believe him until they'd seen it for themself.

So they knelt down beside the rear passenger side door of Corey's car—the side that couldn't be seen from the windows of the other businesses—and set to work.

Life would have been easier if their first stop could have been Ironport. If they could have shown up on Tony's stoop instead of going to Corey. But Sage's 'script for iron intolerance had run out a while back, and getting refills when they were technically dead was a bitch and a half. The only folk who made the good stuff was the Zephyr, and getting their hands on it was tough without contacts in Eventide exporting.

Sage had managed to reroute a few shipments a couple of times and sell the excess they wouldn't be able to use before it expired, but there was only so much they could do before someone noticed and started sniffing around. They hadn't been on bad terms with the head of the Zephyr family before they died, but Goddess only knew who was in charge now and how they'd react to hearing from a corpse.

Better not push their luck. Thus, going straight to Ironport—a notoriously iron-heavy city—was out of the question. Which left Sage with their knees digging into the hard cobblestone street, working a pick into the lock on Corey's car. Thankfully, she had an older vehicle, and the spell Sage had learned as a teenage delinquent to aid the pick along worked.

They slipped into the back seat, shut the door behind them, and let out a long breath. The iron from the vehicle made their throat itchy, but Sage felt better having steel between them and the streets of Eventide.

They must have dozed off because the next thing they knew, the door was opening and shutting with a slam, they had slumped over in the seat, and the smell of blood burned their nose.

"Are you bleeding?" Sage asked, sitting up abruptly to look at Corey.

Corey screamed.

Sage screamed back.

Corey screamed some more. Then she sucked in a breath, twisted around to get a better look at who the fuck was in the back of her car, and glared. "Why are *you* screaming?"

Sage shrugged. "Seemed the thing to do."

A huff, and the car rocked as Corey shifted around more to better face them in the back seat. She wore a black mask over the lower half of her face, and her hair was in long cobalt blue braids, rings in the strands glittering in the golden light of the car. The whole look shimmered with the signs of a glamour, and if Sage squinted, they'd be able to see through it. There wasn't much point in that as a second later the light kicked off, basking them both in darkness.

"What are you doing here?" she asked, pulling the mask down so she could scowl at them. "The last I heard, you went south. You were supposed to be enjoying the sun and the sand—"

"I hate sand, actually," Sage said primly. "It's gritty and it gets everywhere."

"Who are you? Anakin Skywalker?"

"Could be. He dies and comes back as someone else. I could totally rock the Vader thing. Corey, I am your father." Sage made their voice breathy and growly as they cupped their hands over their mouth, doing a decent impression of Vader if they did say so themself. "What do you think?"

Corey didn't look impressed, just annoyed. "I think you're supposed to be dead."

"A llama?!"

"You were never supposed to show your pretty face around these parts again," Corey continued, plowing right over Sage's snark and their epic *The Emperor's New Groove* reference. Rude.

"Awww," Sage cooed, delighting in the way it made Corey's eyebrow twitch. She really was too easy. "You think I'm pretty?"

"Shut the fuck up, Sage, and answer the question! What are you *doing* here?"

"Well, which is it? I can't both shut up *and* answer the question."

The eyebrow twitch was quickly turning into a full out facial spasm. Sage was reasonably sure Corey was fighting every instinct to lunge over the back seat and throttle them.

"Sage," Corey hedged, and Sage didn't think they cared at all for the threat lingering in her tone.

"Danny," Sage replied, a reminder that Sage wasn't the one at a disadvantage here. As far as the power balance went, Sage held the winning hand: Corey's true name. And it worked just as well on her—half human as she was—as it did on every other fae. Corey's light brown face paled, and Sage instantly felt bad about the threat. They deflated into their seat, their arms crossed over their chest as they turned to look out the window. "A friend of mine in Ironport got themself into trouble. I'm here to check in and keep an eye on them till they're settled."

"Then why are you *here*? In *Eventide*. In *my* car." Most of the bite had gone out of her tone, and Sage winced at the realization that they'd shaken her that badly.

There was no love lost between them. They hated each other, that much was true. Sage had no idea why. They'd been friends once upon a time, then things had . . . changed. But as much as Sage could have once played the part of the snarky, biting, vicious gangster, it had been years since they had. The mold didn't quite fit anymore. They'd outgrown it, or maybe it had outgrown them. Goddess, could they even use a blade anymore? Hopefully they'd be out of here before they had to find out.

"I don't have any anti-iron. And you're the only one on this Goddess-forsaken island who knows I'm alive."

"Not by choice," Corey muttered. The car rocked some more, and when Sage looked back, they saw Corey's glamour melting away. Her face structure was pretty much the same. That was always the hardest to fake, hence the mask. But the long dark blue braids were replaced with shoulder length hair in two tones, the ends lighter than the roots like she'd bleached it and it had grown out. But Sage knew it grew that way. A consequence of her lineage. And her eyes looked a touch lighter.

"Look," Sage said, running their hands through their own hair, the shorter ends flopping into their face, "I just need somewhere to crash for a bit until I can get my hands on some more. Then I'll be out of your hair. Promise."

Corey let out a long slow breath, leaning forward to press her forehead into the steering wheel. She mumbled something. Sage couldn't be sure, but they thought it might have been, "I'm going to regret this." Then she sat up again and faced them. "Two weeks. I can give you two. Weeks. And you don't leave my apartment for *anything*. Am I understood?"

"Yup. Got it." Sage nodded firmly. Not like they'd want to leave the apartment anyway. Probably.

"Except," she said holding up her hand, one finger raised, "to help out at the bakery."

"What? But someone might—"

"You'll be in the back, working after close. I lost my baking assistant last month, and I've been strapped for help. You still know how to work a piping bag, right?"

"I haven't decorated a cake in—"

"Don't want to hear it. You had the prettiest cupcakes at Big Phil's. It's just like riding a bike." Corey's lips ticked up at the corners. Not a smile, she wouldn't smile at Sage. They weren't friends. But she was pleased with herself.

"That was at least a decade ago."

"Those are my terms, Sage. Take 'em or leave 'em. And none of this"—she wiggled her fingers at them distastefully —"true name shit. You use my name, and you're on the streets without my contacts for anti-iron. Mutually assured destruction."

"Fine. Fine." Sage huffed, slouching down more in their seat. The headache had returned full force, and all they wanted now was to sleep for a week, get their meds, and go see Tony. "Deal."

"Great. Buckle up. I'm not getting pulled over because your undead ass has a death wish."

Sage grumbled but did as told while Corey got the car started, and they were off.

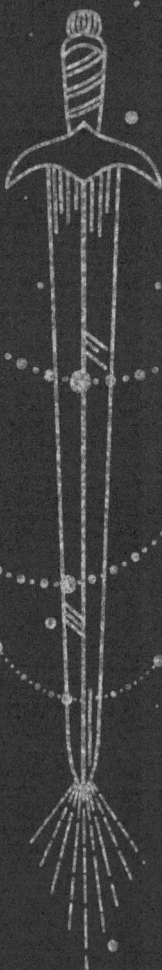

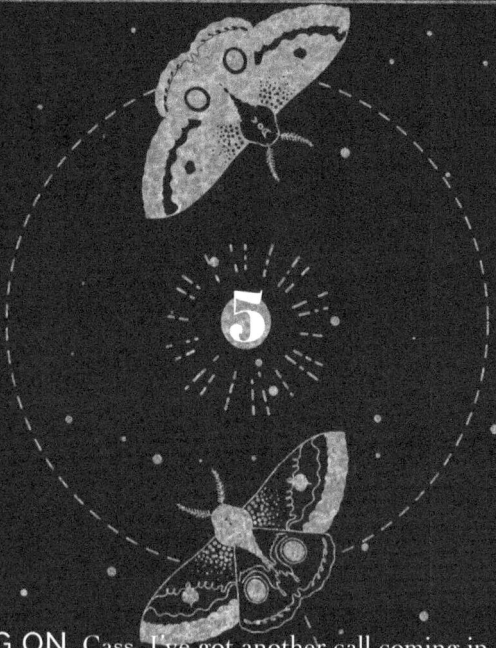

5

"HANG ON, Cass, I've got another call coming in." Corey sighed, picking up her burner phone from next to her on the counter. She didn't recognize the number, which was a relief. If she never got any calls from Aquarius members, it would be too soon.

"She just doesn't listen. I mean, I try to tell her—"

"Right, I know. I'm sorry Clancy is being a pain. But I really will have to call you back." Then she hung up because she knew her stepsister well enough to know that Cassidy would just keep going. There was no end to her bitching about their baby sister. She didn't think she'd ever get used to being the oldest of three girls. Even nearly thirty years after her father remarried and she was introduced to her younger sisters, she still found it strange to not be an only child.

Tucking her personal phone away, she hit the green button on her burner, trusting the voice amplifier to do its thing. "The Phantom."

"This is Dani, from the Blood Moons," the person on

the other end of the line growled into the phone. They were too close to the mic, their voice grating through the speaker.

Corey turned down the volume and waited. Dam would get to what they wanted eventually, she didn't have to prompt them.

"We've got a problem with some graffiti."

Graffiti? Really? Was that what she was reduced to? She wasn't a janitor! Except being a fixer for the families meant she kind of was, actually. Scrubbing at her itchy nose, she waited for the other shoe to drop. There had to be a catch, right?

"We think it's a local group of kids just messing around. We want you to hunt them down and shake them up a bit. Discourage them from painting nonsense on the side of our place over on Birch. How much would you charge for something like that?"

Corey bit her lip, trying to think. This was easy money, a job that shouldn't take more than a couple of hours. But she didn't want to lowball herself either and get into a situation where everyone expected her rates to be so cheap. "A grand, depending on how many there are. I'll expect half up front."

"Send the invoice to this number," Dam said before they hung up.

She breathed easier once she was off the phone, stuffing it into her pocket and heading back through the small apartment toward her room.

"Sage! I'm going out!" she called, not sure why she was bothering. They hadn't come out of their fucking room in almost seventy-two hours at this point. Why would they bother now? With no response, she headed to her own room to get ready for the job.

Blood dripped hot from the injury close to Corey's elbow then cooled and turned slimy as her skin grew clammy. A graze. Not even anything serious, but definitely annoying.

"Always bringing a knife to a gun fight," she muttered to herself, tilting so she could peer around the corner and see if anyone was following her. The job was supposed to be a simple one: put the fear of the Goddess into the person spray painting sigils in Blood Moon territory. Honestly, it was easy work. Too easy. Below her even. But the price was right, and Corey wasn't about to turn her nose up at easy money. Not anymore. Not with the cost of tuition going up every fucking semester.

Except fucking Dam hadn't told her everything.

Except what should have just been a couple of stupid kids turned out to be a coven of five witches who were really pissed when Corey burst into their hideout. Oh yeah, and they had fucking *guns*. What kind of witches carried *guns*?

"Never trust a redcap," Corey reminded herself, the words echoing in her head in a voice that sounded eerily like Grammy Corwin.

Whatever. She'd done the job and then some. The witches in question wouldn't spray paint anything for at least a few months, even with healing magic. And Dam better pay up.

"It's done," she said into the phone, grinding her teeth to keep the wince from her voice as the motion of holding the device to her ear pulled on her injury. "I expect full payment by midnight tomorrow."

"That was quick," Dam growled in surprise, but Corey

didn't give them a chance to say anything else. She hung up a moment later and checked that the coast was clear one more time before trekking back to her car.

THE DOOR TO COREY'S SPARE ROOM SLAMMED AGAINST the wall beside it. Light filtered in from the hall, bright and glaring if the scrunched expression Sage turned on her was anything to go by. That didn't say much though. Since returning to Eventide, Sage had locked themself in Corey's spare room, pulled the curtains closed, and only exited to use the bathroom. Corey wasn't even sure they were eating.

"All right," Corey said, stomping across the room, heedless of the clothes that had formed small mountains on the floor and what might be hidden within them. How Sage had made such a mess in just a couple of days, she didn't think she wanted to know. "You've been here for three days. You've settled in. Time to get to work."

"Work." Sage repeated the word as if it were foreign to them, still squinting at Corey from behind a pair of thick glasses. The frames were made of metal, square and so large that the bottoms of them touched Sage's cheeks. Sage took an exaggerated sniff of the air, no doubt scenting the blood of the bandage she'd hastily slapped into place. "Up to your old tricks I see, Corwin."

"Yes. Work." Corey flung the shades open, letting the streetlights in, and ignored Sage's offhanded comment about her side hustle. The stars were just visible through the mist that always lingered over Eventide, and dawn was coming, though it was still a ways off. "That was the agreement."

"You know, the whole point of me paying you to bring me back was so you could get *out* of the life."

"I know what I'm doing, Sage."

"Of course you do." Sage watched her for a long moment, their glowing green eyes narrowed through white lashes, seeing too much. Corey hated that most about them —their cait sidhe nature. It made them far too observant. What with their excellent sense of smell, enhanced hearing, and the way they could see in the dark. "Can't stay out of it, can you? You adrenaline junky, you. Always looking for an easy fix. An easy way out."

When she didn't respond to the accusation—it wasn't like Sage had room to talk, they'd been worse once upon a time—Sage groaned, their head flopping back against the wheely chair they sat in. Corey wasn't sure where the office furniture inside the room had come from. The last she'd been in there, her spare room had only a daybed and a stack of boxes in the corner she still hadn't unpacked since her move four years ago. But when she turned to face Sage fully now, she found them sitting at a long, narrow desk with three monitors standing side by side on the surface. Which made no logical sense, because Sage had shown up with a half-filled duffle and no other luggage. But Corey had learned a long time ago that one didn't ask questions they didn't really want the answer to. Especially where the fae were concerned. So she didn't bother.

"Can't I just pay you?" Sage asked, clearly deciding to let the other subject lie. Good. Corey didn't have the energy for that particular argument right now, nor for the self-reflection it would spawn. "I'd really rather cut you a check, honestly."

Corey bit her tongue to keep herself from asking Sage how they were planning to cut her a check. They were dead as far as anyone else was concerned, and dead people didn't have bank accounts. That raised another question, actually. How the fuck had a dead person gotten on an airplane without raising any red flags? Were they still using the fake ID she'd had made for them four years ago? That was supposed to be temporary. But again, some questions were better going unasked.

"I don't need money." Which was complete and utter bullshit. She most definitely *did* need money, but that was neither here nor there because she sure as shit wasn't going to take anymore off Sage and find herself further in their debt. Plus, money wouldn't help the bakery, not right now, and the bakery was her priority. It was . . . the only thing she had that was truly her own. She wasn't giving it up. "What I need is someone who can crumb coat a cake in under five minutes. Especially with *this* . . . thing." She held up the arm she'd had to sling to keep from aggravating her injured arm further. It tugged on the stitches she'd hastily applied to the bullet graze and made her wince, which made Sage raise their brows in something that felt distinctly mocking. "You'll have to help in the shop too, at least for a few days until it heals."

She was taking chances she shouldn't take, especially with Alton already knowing Sage wasn't dead. But what other choice did she have? Close the bakery until she was better? Not going to happen. And besides, they'd be working in the back, mostly at night.

"I reiterate, I will *pay* you." Sage scrubbed their face. "With that money you can hire someone else to come here and help. And then I can get back to—" They cut themself off, and Corey was grateful. She didn't want to know what Sage did for work, or how they'd managed to maintain their lifestyle after leaving the gang without the inheritance that should have been theirs and instead had gone to their cousin Bentley. "Plus, I'm in hiding, remember?"

"I don't want your money. And you'll be in the back during work hours, no one will even notice." Corey grunted, kicking their chair. "Get your ass up. You need to be ready in ten, or I'm flipping the breaker." She whirled around and left Sage, ignoring the muttered threats that followed her down the hall.

"YOU SAID YOU NEEDED SOMEONE TO DO CRUMB coating," Sage said, narrowing their eyes at the chilled piping bags as Corey laid them on the steel table, and resisting the catlike urge to knock them off in their irritation. They were already pre-colored in a muted rainbow. Sage itched to grab the pale green and squirt it all over Corey's freshly washed hair. She still smelled like blood. They wondered if she knew that and how much blood she'd spilled to have it linger on her. Sharp and metallic. Embedded in her scent.

"It's a figure of speech." Corey slid an already crumb coated cake over to them.

"I'm pretty sure it's not." Maybe if they did a sloppy job, she wouldn't ask them to help again. But then they'd have to deal with all the bitching and moaning that went along with that action. Besides, Corey was right. If they were going to stay with her, they should help out at least, and neither of them wanted Sage to try their hand at cooking.

"Then I lied." Corey shrugged. A binder of designs joined the undecorated cake. "Get to piping."

"You need five of these?" Sage asked, frowning at the picture Corey pointed at in the binder. It was a pretty simple design, actually. A drip glaze in a contrasting color over the top with a swirl border along the top and bottom edges in the original icing color. Sage had done much more complicated designs when they both worked at Phil's back in the day. "What? Are you the only bakery in Eventide?"

"The only one in Faceless territory."

Sage stilled, their eyes jerking up to watch Corey as she pulled a tub of icing from the fridge, also pre-colored. "What?"

"Phil died." Corey had gone somber, quiet. "A year ago."

Something heavy, like grief, curled Sage's shoulders forward. They hadn't spoken to Phil for a while, even before they left Eventide. Not much at all since that summer when Sage and Corey had worked together. Sage to make a little extra cash for a new computer their father refused to fund, and Corey for . . . They'd never asked Corey what she was saving for. But they'd worked side by side, the entire summer, in the back of Phil's bakery. Bitching, and bickering, and flicking icing sugar at each other when Phil left the room.

Sage had never felt so normal in all their life. Phil hadn't treated them like they were the child of a mobster. To Phil, Sage was just another snot-nosed brat looking to make an hourly wage while school was out. And now Phil was dead. A piece of Sage's childhood ripped away from them, like so many others.

"What happened?" Sage forced their tone to remain steady, to sound curious instead of sorrowful as they slapped dusty blue icing onto the first cake.

"What happens to all humans eventually. He got old."

Right. Sage had forgotten that Phil was human. He'd always seemed larger than life when Sage was growing up. Voice loud and booming. Shoulders wide as he carted delicately decorated cakes around like they were nothing. But he was just . . . he was just a human. Short lived. Frail. And in the end, that had killed him.

Sage swallowed thickly, breathing in through their nose for a moment to suck back the tears that threatened to spill. It was stupid to cry over someone they hadn't even seen in more than a decade. But it wasn't only Phil that they were mourning. It was that stupid kid, shoulder to shoulder with another stupid kid, as Phil showed them how to pipe rosettes. Which was *also* stupid, because that stupid kid had been dead for far longer than Phil.

"His kids didn't want the bakery," Corey continued.

"Right." Sage nodded, rubbing the back of their wrist across their eyes to try to relieve some of the burn. "So you're the only bakery in this part of town."

"At least for now."

The repetitive movements of smoothing and evening out icing lulled Sage a little in a way not much else could. They'd never thought of themself as particularly good at this, but being good at it didn't mean much when it unhitched their shoulders and steadied their breathing. Why hadn't they done any baking since putting Eventide behind them? Why had they left so much of themself here instead of taking it with them?

"Lots of stuff changed," Corey said after a long moment as she passed them a squirt bottle of cream-colored ganache. "I think the only family heads in charge from before you left are Alton and Mata."

The words were the reminder Sage needed. *That* was why they'd left so much of themself behind. Why they'd cut all ties. Why they didn't do any of the things that had once brought them joy in Eventide. Because if they did then they'd have to think about everything else that was still here.

The gangs. The violence. The blood that still seemed caked under their nails.

"Yeah?" they asked, not really wanting an answer. But

Corey seemed to want to talk. And besides, if they were sticking around for a while, it'd be better to know who they needed to avoid from their old life. So they listened. Making noises and asking questions at all the right spots to keep Corey going while they worked shoulder to shoulder, just like that summer and not at all like that summer at the same time.

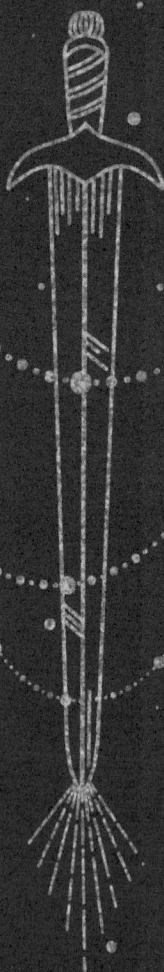

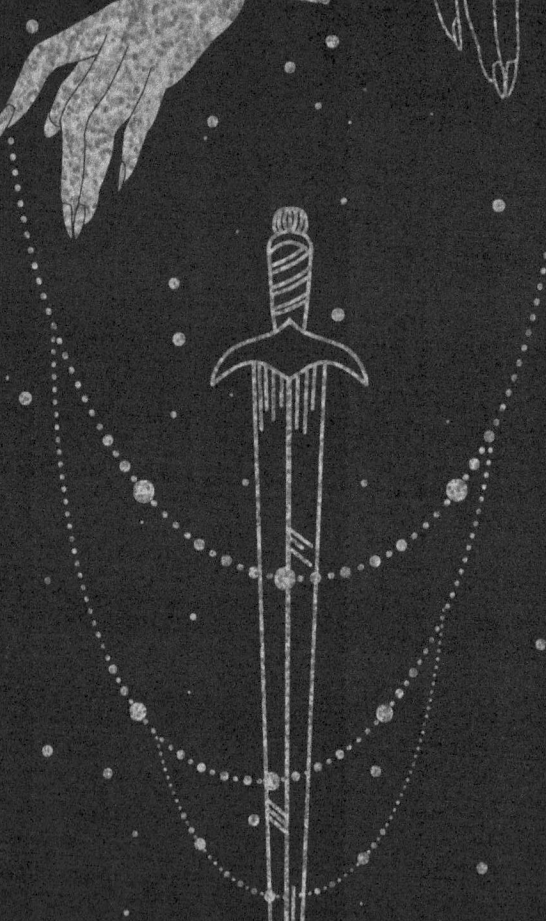

6

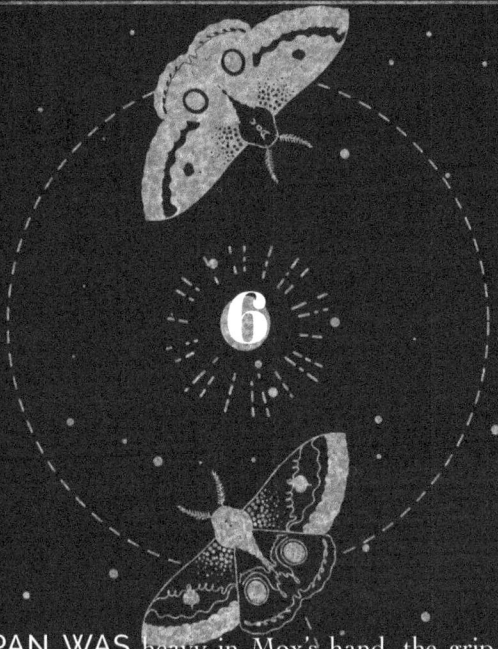

THE PAN WAS heavy in Mox's hand, the grip cutting into the meat of her palm as she tiptoed up the stairs toward the second floor of the house she shared with Mal and Chuckles. It was bigger than any place she and her brother had ever been able to afford before, *much* bigger. Large enough that Mal had hired a cleaning crew. A cleaning *crew*, not just a cleaning person. Like they lived in a mansion or something. She guessed they did, in a way. Things were different now that they had Faceless Few exec money.

Mox was still unsure if she liked it. It was better than sleeping on the streets and in halfway houses like they'd done when they were teens and ran out on their foster home of the week. But it was just so . . . *much*. There were rooms that Mox hadn't set foot inside in months. That couldn't be normal.

The only good thing about having all this money — aside from the clothes, which Mox absolutely relished — was that it gave her the freedom to finally be who she was. The resources to get bottom and top surgery when she decided that's a thing she wanted. And the ability to never have to worry that she wouldn't be able to afford the estrogen—and other medications she could hardly pronounce—that made her body look the way she knew it was meant to. So she supposed she shouldn't complain too much, especially with the top surgery. She had a great rack, if she did say so herself, these days.

And it was a decent place to grow up for Chuckles. Not that Mox thought the thirteen-year-old appreciated it. As evident by the fact that Mox had been up for an hour already and had yet to hear a peep from Chuckles's bedroom. No shower running. No slamming of dresser drawers. Nothing. Which was why Mox was on her way toward Chuckles's room, frying pan and wooden spoon in hand. If the brat wasn't going to set an alarm and get up at a decent fucking time so they could make it to school before first bell, Mox was going to make her regret it.

The door swung open on silent hinges—because like everything else in this fucking place, they were well maintained—and Mox didn't wait a beat before she started banging the spoon against the pan as hard as she could. Filling the room with the clangs and bangs of wood on metal.

Chuckles shot up in bed, her bright eyes wide, curly red hair a gnarled mess where it was stacked on top of her head in a loose bun. It was amazing that the light through the curtains hadn't woken her yet with how it streamed directly onto the canopied four-poster.

Mox continued banging.

"What the fuck!" Chuckles shouted, clamping her hands over her ears and fixing Mox with a cold glare.

"Wakey wakey, eggs and bakey, sunshine!" Mox yelled over the noise, her smile wide. She could have stopped banging on the pan now that she'd gotten Chuckles up, but honestly, she was having too much fun making a Goddess-awful racket and annoying the living shit out of the little brat who was sitting up now but still hadn't bothered to get out of bed. "And you're too young to use the word *fuck*."

"Bite me, Mox!" Chuckles let go of her ears just long enough to grab a pillow and hurl it across the room at Mox.

Mox ducked but it did get her to stop banging on the pan, so Mox supposed Chuckles won this round.

"What time is it?" Chuckles leaned over to look at her phone.

"You've got enough time to roll out of bed, throw on some clothes, and eat breakfast in the car. If you're downstairs in ten, I'll get you Necromancer's on the road." A peace offering, because as annoying as Mox found her teenage charge, they were still family in a loose sort of way. In the way that Mal had brought her home one day after Sage Nocturna died four years ago, and she'd been with them ever since. In the way that they never really defined what they were to each other, but Mox bemoaned sometimes having gained a sibling, and a pre-teen one at that. In the way that they all sometimes resented each other, but the missing of someone long gone kept Mal and Chuckles from gutting each other in the pristine white marble kitchen.

An "I hate you" was hurled at Mox as she turned her back, alongside a loud groan. But Mox wasn't going to take it personally. She'd been thirteen once. She knew how it was.

"Ten minutes, Chuckie. Twenty if you don't want breakfast," she called over her shoulder on the way back to the office to finish gathering what she'd need for the day. It wasn't normal to bring a set of enchanted daggers to the drop-off line, she reminded herself as the safe swung open, but what she had planned after dropping off Chuckles at school would require it.

EVENTIDE WAS ONE OF THOSE PLACES THAT DIDN'T ROLL out the sidewalks until at least early evening, and nothing interesting happened until sundown. But that didn't mean Mox could rest on her laurels, or however that saying went.

Someone needed to go out and make sure the Night Market portals were working properly, and that no one was fucking around where they shouldn't be while the majority of the Faceless Few were sleeping. It was a job Mox usually traded off with whoever was taking Chuckles to school that day, but one she didn't mind all that much. It was nice to get out and get some sun every once in a while, even as the heat of early summer crawled across her skin and had her sweating in her suit.

She pulled at the lapels of the maroon blazer she'd tugged on over a lacey black tank top that morning and seriously considered ditching it. It would help with the heat, but then her outfit would be incomplete. And someone might notice the holster tucked underneath the jacket carrying her daggers. That wasn't something she needed, even if Mal paid the cops in the city plenty to look the other way when there was folk-on-folk violence.

The first five or so portals to the Night Market had turned up nothing, but what were the chances that Mox's luck would hold? Slim.

As she came up on the sixth portal of the day, she realized she was right. It was the one closest to the docks run by the Divinity of Aquarius, and there was something off about it, because of course there was. Of *course* the portal closest to Alton's territory would have something wonky going on with it. Because when had Alton and his crew ever been known to leave well enough alone?

Mox inhaled deeply, eyeing the door at the end of the dock that led to nowhere. The dock itself was clearly run-down and abandoned, by human standards. And the door at the end of it was disintegrating so much that Mox could see the Chesapeake on the other side in between the boards. It might have been made by humans at one point in time. Maybe built as the entrance to some grand marina. But the project had either gone belly up or been abandoned in favor of something else. Leaving the door, and the empty space beyond, as the perfect place to set an entrance to the Night Market. Especially with its adjacence to the east side of Eventide and the docks.

The parking lot around it was empty, but that didn't mean no one was watching. Mox took a moment to close her eyes and slip on a look-away glamour that wouldn't make her invisible but *would* keep any mortal eyes from noticing her. It made it that much warmer—will-o'-wisp magic always ran hot—to the point that she was suffocating in her blazer now, but she'd suck it up and deal.

A wince left her as she stepped onto the pier and it rattled under her weight.

"Might have to see about finding a new spot for this one soon," she murmured to herself, stepping carefully over rotting boards so she didn't fall through or get her stilettos stuck. With one more glance over her shoulder to make sure no one was watching, Mox squatted to look at the carvings in the wood that grounded the portal magic to this spot. Nothing looked amiss. But the magic didn't feel quite right. A residue lingered around the portal, not visible to the naked eye but it cast a chill up Mox's spine that felt really nice, actually. If, you know, it wasn't attached to someone fucking around with one of her portals.

Pulling out her phone, she fired off a quick text to Mal.

Mox: Portal 6 has been messed with

Can't tell how or who
Mal: I'll send someone out to look at it
Cordon it off

Like she didn't already know that's what she needed to do. Mox scoffed. Pushing to her feet, she made her way carefully back to the end of the dock and pulled one of the daggers from their holsters. Normally she would burn the characters into the wood, but her will-o'-wisp magic had been acting up since —Well, that didn't matter. She scratched the symbols into the wood, creating a barrier at the beginning of the dock to block it off, a warning to any passing folk that this portal was closed.

That done, she headed back toward the parking lot and the sidewalk that wound its way through the streets of Eventide. There were four more portals to check out then she could go home for a nap, and she intended to get to them before the day really heated up.

Mox: It's probably Alton nosing around

Alton wasn't exactly shy about his desire to take over the Night Market. It wasn't like he didn't already have his own source of income. His import business into Eventide made a killing. Add to that the export fees he charged Evy to get her drugs out of Eventide, and he should be well taken care of. But greed was an ugly emotion. Ugly and foolish. It made people stupid. One would think that Mal almost wiping out an entire organization would be enough to put people off from crossing the new Faceless Few, but Alton had never been the type to see his own weaknesses. Brash and overconfident. It was going to get him killed.

Mox shook her head and turned down one of the many streets in Eventide just as her phone buzzed in her pocket again. Not the single buzz of a text either. A call.

"Ugh, what do you want now?" she grumbled to herself, digging the device from the bottom of her pocket to glare at her brother's name on the screen. The thought to ignore it flitted through her head. It would be so easy, just push the button and pretend she hadn't seen it. But Mal wasn't going to stop, she knew that.

"Don't go after Alton" was the first thing Mal said after she picked up, not even leaving room for a greeting.

"I'm not going to." Mox clenched her teeth. "I'm not stupid."

"We have no proof that it was him," Mal continued as if Mox hadn't spoken. "Just because it's the portal closest to his territory doesn't mean it's him."

"I know."

"Even if it was, I want to know what he was trying to do before we start a turf war with him."

Mal did this sometimes; he got on a tirade and went on and on. It was typically brought on by the idiocy of the other family heads. Usually Mox tuned him out, but it was hot and she was irritable, so his voice was grating on her ears instead.

"And I want a sanctioned war. If we're going to do it, I want to bring it before the Court and have him kicked the fuck out for going against the accords. It would mean that his territory would either go to one of his underlings or they'd split it between us, but that'd be far less—"

"Hang on," Mox said, stopping where she'd been all but trudging down the sidewalk to blink across the street at a brightly lit bakery. Well, not exactly at the *bakery*, more at the person standing outside of it who had an ass like a peach, scrawling something on a chalkboard sign beside the door. *Holy shit*.

"Mox, are you listening to me? Don't you dare—"

"Fuck off, Mal. I've gotta go." She hung up, put her phone in her pocket, and crossed the street without even bothering to look for traffic. Let them hit her. It would be worth it.

It was only after she got closer that she noticed the two people standing next to her target. They appeared to be heckling them, although Mox couldn't make out what they were saying.

"Hey, honey," she said, slinging her arm over the shorter person's shoulders and fixing the two men with a sharp-toothed smile. "Sorry I'm late. There's still time to grab breakfast before your shift, right?"

Mox's breath lodged in her throat when she looked down and was met with a startling pair of hazel eyes set into a rich terra-cotta-toned face with high cheekbones, a perfectly kissable mouth, and dark brows that were pinched together in confusion. Goddess. Who *was* this woman?

"I uh—" Her voice was slightly husky, sending a shiver down Mox's spine.

"So about that number," one of the hecklers said, clearly not taking the hint.

"She's not giving you her number," Mox answered, her eyes flashing with will-o'-wisp fire as she shifted slightly so both the hecklers could see the glint of fae steel stashed under her blazer. They blinked for a moment, unsure what they were seeing, then it dawned on them. "You guys have a nice day."

They nodded, spun on their heels, and left.

The woman huffed an annoyed sound and slid out from under Mox's arm to return to writing on the sign out front. It was then that Mox noticed the bright blue sling sitting glaringly against her outfit. A floral corset tied tight over a white peasant blouse, with an orange cardigan thrown over top, the sleeves pushed back. An A-line mint-green skirt swished around her hips. Goddess, who knew Mox could be into cottagecore girlies? Not her!

"Looks like they're gone," Mox said, moving to lean against the door next to the chalkboard.

The woman didn't pause, didn't look away from her work, just kept her long, graceful fingers moving as she said, "What do you want, Mox?"

Mox gasped, holding her chest just over her heart. "See now, that's not fair. You know my name, but I don't know yours."

She could probably find out the woman's name. If she worked at one of the businesses in Faceless Few territory, then her name was on a list somewhere back at the house. But finding it that way would take all the fun out of the chase, wouldn't it?

"Let's try this again." Mox stood up straight, ran her hands through her hair, sent up a prayer to the Goddess that sweating had made her look dewy instead of gross, and extended a hand. "Hi. I'm Mox."

The woman stopped what she was doing finally and turned to fix Mox with a look of annoyance. Her gaze flicked down to the extended hand and back up to Mox. "I know who you are."

"Great. And you are . . . ?" Mox had never struck out this hard before. Weird. Especially not with people who knew who she was. Normally people fawned all over her to win her favor, wanting to get in good with the second in command of the Faceless Few.

"Busy," she said. "Do you mind?"

"Do I mind?" Mox blinked, her brows pulled together in confusion.

The woman nodded to the door Mox still stood in front of.

"Oh. Right. Sorry." Heat crawled up her neck that had nothing to do with the summer sun. She took one too-big step away from the door, leaving room for the woman to head in and pull the door closed, locking it before Mox could reach for the handle to enter behind her.

The woman glared at her and pointed to the vinyl letters on the door that said their store hours. "Come back later," she said, then turned and left Mox standing on the sidewalk gaping at her back.

What the actual *fuck*?

Mox took another step back so she could watch the woman through the big front window of the shop. The whole storefront was painted powder blue, but someone had put planter boxes above the front window. Trailing vines hung down from them, framing the glass. The place was. . . *cute*. Which didn't fit the reception of the woman Mox had met out front. Maybe she was a worker and not the owner?

Mox had probably walked past the bakery a hundred times since living in Eventide and never noticed before. Funny how all it took was one really great ass to draw her attention.

Tilting her head, Mox flicked her dark gaze to the handwritten "help wanted" sign in the window before going back to watching the woman and—

No.

That couldn't be who Mox thought it was. Right?

She took a step forward, narrowed her eyes, and looked more closely at the person helping the woman load the pastries into the front case.

It had to be a trick of the light. She had to be seeing things.

She turned away, rubbed at her eyes, tried again.

No. They were still there.

The hair was different, dyed a gray-white with an ombre to a rainbow of colors at the tips. They wore glasses now. But Mox had seen that face enough over the last four years to know exactly who it was. She remembered that face from the day she and Mox had been caught pickpocketing someone in the Faceless Few. It was the kindest face in the entire gang. It was the face of their savior.

How could it *not* be burned into her mind?

Sage Nocturna.

Sage Nocturna was alive.

Sage Nocturna was alive, and in Eventide.

She had to tell Mal!

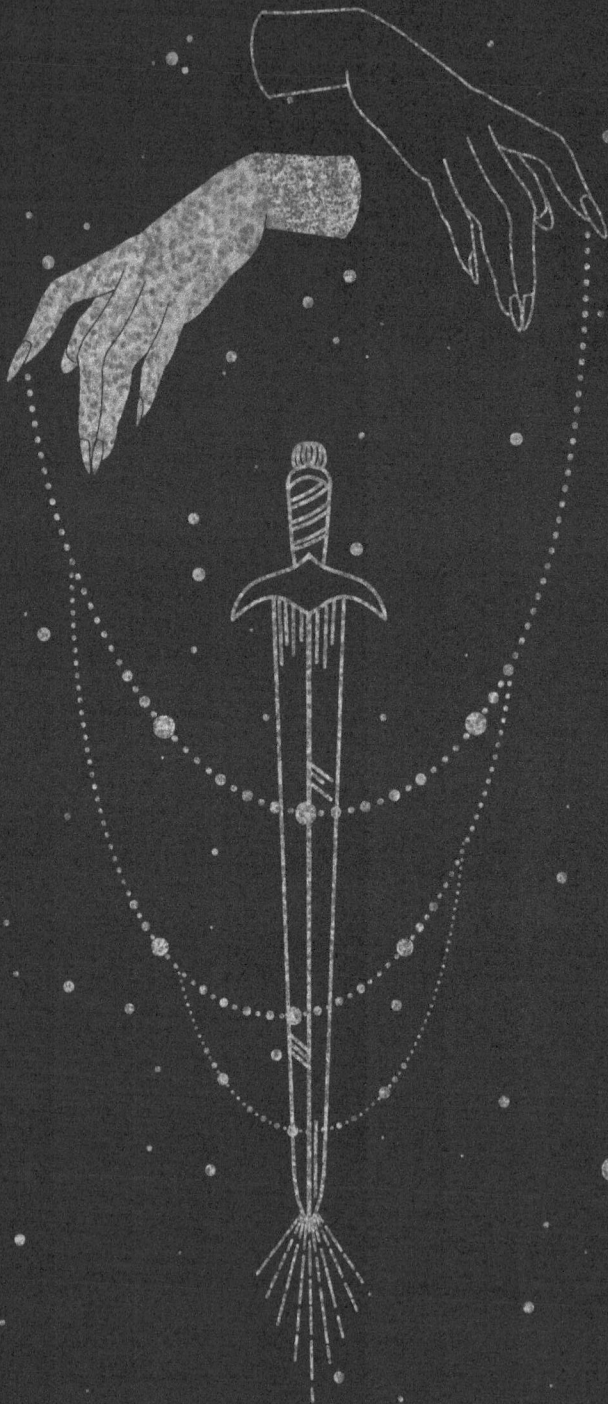

7

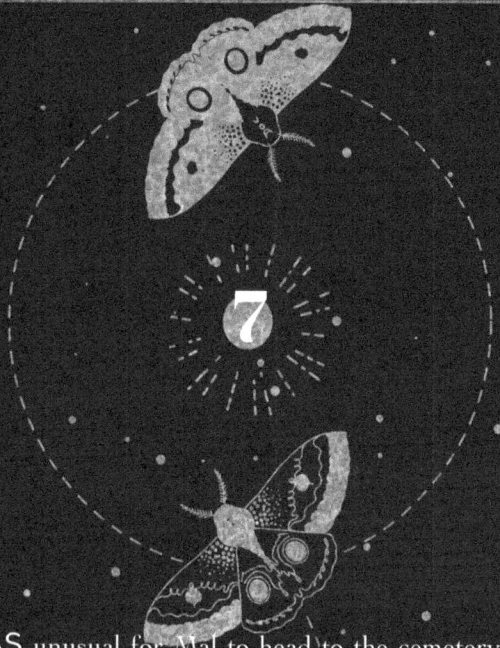

IT WAS unusual for Mal to head to the cemetery during the day. He preferred visiting Sage's grave at night when there would be no one to interrupt his mourning and the sun wasn't glaring down through the mists that surrounded Eventide. When he could actually see Sage's face.

But there was something about that day. Something that crawled under his skin and made a home for itself there. It didn't help that Mox had texted him while he was sitting down to do his paperwork and told him someone had been fucking with one of the portals to the Night Market. But that wasn't the whole reason for the unsettled, unsure feeling buzzing through his veins.

He couldn't put a name to it, but he knew why it was there. It was the anniversary.

Four years.

Sage had been gone for four years.

It wasn't that long in the grand scheme of things. Compared to how long Mal would live with the grief that weighed him down almost every day, it was nothing. Just the beginning. But it felt like it had been decades already. Every hour ticking by sunk deep into his bones, threatening to make his back bow under the weight. And yet, he kept going. He kept trying.

"I'm doing my best," Mal said, lifting his chin but still unable to meet the soft stare of the statue. The statement tasted like a lie on his tongue. Sour and slightly bitter. Acrid in his mouth. Burning at his gums. He'd promised Sage once upon a time to build a life they'd be proud of, to learn to be happy. He'd been unable to do that. "I could do more," he conceded. "I *should* do more. There's no excuse for why Bentley has slipped through my fingers this long."

Not when he had an entire organization at his disposal. Not when he knew she hadn't left the city. Not when everyone he'd killed so far had pointed their finger at her as the original instigator of the assassination. Mal couldn't let her get away with it. He couldn't reach the fifth anniversary of Sage's death without exacting vengeance on the person who'd planned it all.

"I'll try harder this year," he vowed. "I'll avenge you."

"Are you sure that's what he'd want?" someone asked from just behind Mal. He didn't turn around to see who it was, though he did reach out through the shadows that lingered on the ground to feel their magic. Not a threat, but someone old. Someone powerful. Someone not of Eventide.

"They," Mal corrected gently.

"Apologies," they said, and Mal heard them step across the damp earth so he could see their shape from the corner of his eye.

They were short in stature, hardly even reaching Mal's mid-section. A fact made more pronounced by the way they leaned heavily against their own cane. But aside from that, Mal couldn't see enough of them in the bright light to know what kind of folk he was dealing with, although he knew they *were* folk. Water folk, specifically, based off the saltwater scent that drifted through the air around them. And far older than Mal. Maybe as old as Eventide herself.

"But the question stands."

"They're dead." Mal let the words burn at his throat, scrape raw and cutting down his sternum, and settle into his lungs heavy like a stone. "There's nothing else I can do for them, and the ones who hurt them should be punished."

"That might be."

Mal couldn't shake the feeling that this person was speaking from experience. A tone in their voice sounded strangely like sadness and defeat. A quiet companionship, as if they understood what Mal was going through far better than anyone else had.

"Who are you visiting?" Mal asked, hoping to change the subject. He didn't particularly want to question his motivations now. Not with so much blood already on his hands.

They made a sound like they knew exactly what he was doing but they were going to let it go, at least for the moment. "My wife," they said without any hesitation. "She got sick on the journey from our homeland to Moondale."

"But she's buried in Eventide?" It wasn't terribly uncommon—the two locations were close enough together. All it would take was a ferry ride from Eventide to get to Moondale. Still, it seemed strange that their wife wouldn't want to be close to them.

"She wanted to be buried with her clan." The blur that was their shape shifted out of the corner of his eye. It may have been a shrug, or a readjusting of joints that were sore from standing. He couldn't tell. "She was a forest nymph from the clan that eventually turned into the Wildings family. One of Mata's siblings, I believe, in fact."

Mal fought the urge to question them further, even as his brows raised high on his face. Mox would love to know that her theories about Mata being one of the original fae in Eventide were true. She could add it to her database of information she'd collected about the family heads over the years. Although Mal wasn't sure what purpose the information would serve in what he was trying to do. Knowing that Mata was one of the original forest nymphs to settle in Eventide didn't tell him whether she and her gang were hiding Bentley Nocturna on their territory or not, and that was all he was concerned with. The whole of Eventide could burn for all he cared, so long as he found the last name on his list.

"I'm Nixie Vernan," they offered after a long moment of silence, drawing Mal away from his dark thoughts. Not out of them. They lingered, always, at the corners of his mind. Threatening to swallow him whole if he didn't stay one step ahead of them. He liked to think it was because of what he was—a mare, a creature of nightmares—but it likely had more to do with the violence he'd inflicted on others and how it had tainted him than the night terrors and darkness he had control over.

"Mal," he said simply, not offering them his hand.

"Well," Nixie said with a little nod, "it was a pleasure chatting with you, Mal."

He was sure that wasn't true, but he dipped his head in respect anyway, because one did not go around disrespecting creatures that had walked the world long before even their grandparents were around. "Likewise."

Nixie spun and started toward the street that looped around this section of the graveyard, and Mal watched them go over his shoulder for a moment. They stopped and turned once more to face him. "Bear in mind what I said. Perhaps the vengeance you're after isn't for the person you lost, but for yourself instead. And as much as it might seem like it, it likely won't make you any less lonely."

With a long exhale that kept him from saying something stupid, Mal said, "I'll give it some thought."

"You do that." Then they were off again, and Mal returned to his ritual.

He bent before the statue of Sage and pulled the flowers from the vase, replacing them with fresh lilies. They wilted faster in the summer than they did in the cooler months, and no amount of magic would keep them fresh for more than a couple of days. Likely for the best that he'd stopped in sooner rather than later. He knelt at the statue's feet and allowed himself the small comfort of being close to Sage, if only in body, for a quiet moment.

"I suppose you'll tell me they were right," he said, and hated himself a little for it. Because he knew the truth in Nixie's words. "You'll tell me not to sully myself for your sake." Mal's voice cracked around the honesty in the words. "I know what you'd want."

Tears burned at the backs of his eyes, making them itch, and he scrubbed at them, hoping there was no one else around to witness the weakness.

Four years.

He couldn't . . . He didn't think he'd *make* it four more.

"But I'm not as good as you. I don't have the capacity to be a part of this organization and not get my hands dirty like you did. You were just—" A sob crept up Mal's throat and he swallowed around it, coughing when it choked him. "You were too good for all of this. And I was—"

"Oh good! I found you!" Mox called from somewhere behind Mal, her voice a breathy huff as if she'd been running.

Mal scrubbed at his eyes again and turned to face his sister. "What's happened?"

"You're never gonna believe it." Mox bent over to brace herself on her knees, trying to catch her breath. She had her jacket tied around her waist, and at some point she'd managed to pull her short cerulean hair up out of her face.

"Never going to believe what?" If he sounded irritable, it was because he was. Being interrupted twice in a row was a fucking nuisance and a half. And if Mox thought she could come out here and kick up a fuss about him saying she couldn't go after Alton, then she had another thing—

"Sage is alive."

Mal's heart stopped in his chest for a second, then kicked up so hard he was dizzy with the sudden change in blood pressure. "What?" He had to lock his knees to keep them from crumpling under him.

"Yeah, I saw them—"

The rage took over not even a whole beat later, burning through Mal so fast his vision tunneled. "That's not funny, Mox. Don't fucking joke about shit like that. You know they're—"

"I would never joke about something like this," Mox pled. "Please just—Here, I'll give you the address to the bakery and you can scope it out yourself. If I'm wrong, you're free to scream at me until you pass out. But just—just check first, yeah?"

"Fine." Mal grunted, but his hand shook where it was clenched around his cane.

"You might want to glamour yourself before you go over there though." Mox shifted back on her heels, and Mal recognized the posture for what it was. His sister was uncomfortable. Although she hadn't been when she'd given him the news about Sage. She'd been confident, sure of herself. Now she looked like she was puffing her chest out to make herself seem bigger. An attempt that was wholly unnecessary as she was almost as tall as he was, and she was wearing fucking heels that made her slightly *taller* than him.

Mal raised a brow in her direction. "What did you do?"

"Nothing. Nothing." She scrubbed at the back of her neck. "Can I give you a lift back to the house?"

"Fine."

THERE WAS NO REASON TO THINK MOX WAS CORRECT about her assertion that Sage was alive, well, and in Eventide. But Mal knew if she were lying, she wasn't doing so maliciously. His sister was a lot of things. Spiteful. Vindictive. Bloodthirsty. But she'd never do something to intentionally hurt him or Chuckles.

So he dragged himself through showering the morning's sweat away and changing into something Mox deemed more appropriate.

"You want to look less like a mob boss," Mox said.

"I hate to break it to you, Moxxie. I *am* a mob boss." Mal tugged at his jeans, pulling them up a bit to hide the roll just below his belly button. They weren't nearly high waisted enough. He definitely needed a new pair, and to go up a size. He didn't usually wear jeans. It was all perfectly tailored suits these days, and with the Faceless Few doing as well as they were, he was able to keep a tailor on staff. So whenever he needed something adjusted, he just went and got it done.

"You look fine," Mox hissed, reaching over to swat at him from where she walked at his side, nearly knocking his cane from his opposite hand in her admonishment. "Stop tugging on them."

"Remind me, why can't I look like a mob boss?"

Although she'd said it at least three times since leaving the house about ten minutes ago, she'd yet to explain why. He could only assume there was something she wasn't telling him. Granted, if he knew anything about his sister, there was probably a *lot* she wasn't telling him. She had always been an on-a-need-to-know-basis kind of person.

A strange sluggishness filled his veins. Anticipation, nervousness, both bogged down by the certainty that he was about to be disappointed. He couldn't help but hope though, foolish as it was. Mox's inane chatter and her frenetic energy made it easier for him to focus on that hope.

"She really wouldn't like it."

"She who?" Mal turned to narrow his gaze on her. It didn't make the blur of maroon clothing and teal hair any clearer, but he got the sense that Mox was trying to shrink in on herself. Her shoulders hunched forward more.

"No one."

"There's a girl, isn't there?" Of course there was a girl. There was *always* a girl with Mox. And there was little doubt in Mal's mind that this girl was going to get them both into a buttload of trouble. Because every girl Mox had ever been interested in did.

"What? No!" Mox answered too quickly for it to be anything but a lie.

"Does she own the bakery or work at it?" He tried not to let the laugh burbling up in his throat free. Laughing at Mox and her antics, and her ability to constantly find a new crush, never ended well for anyone. He wasn't about to start a fight in the middle of the street.

"I don't know." Mox huffed, the exhalation making her hair flutter around her. She picked up the pace, clearly trying to outstep him so she didn't have to talk about this, but he wasn't going to let her get away so easily.

"What's her name?"

Mox grunted and walked even faster.

"Moxxie," he hedged carefully. She sped up again, refusing to so much as turn her head to look at him, and then, right there, he understood. Mox hadn't *gotten* this girl's name. She hadn't gotten her name, and she hadn't gotten her position at the bakery. She maybe hadn't even spoken to her. Oh. Oh, this was bad. So very bad. And also, so very funny. "What *do* you know about her then?"

"I know she doesn't like the family," Mox mumbled under her breath, running a hand through her hair.

"And how do you know that?" Raising one dark brow, Mal tilted his head. He may not have been able to see the expression playing across Mox's face, but he could read her tone well enough. He'd grown adept at reading people's emotions via their voice over the years. It had been paramount to survival when he'd lived on the streets.

"Because she called me by name and then refused to tell me hers. So obviously she knows who we are, and she isn't a fan." Mox's shoulders slumped further, and her pace slowed again.

"Her loss then." Mal bumped her lightly with his shoulder, a companionable gesture he wouldn't do in front of anyone else. It felt nice to be like this with her if only for a moment. It was so rare they got time alone where they could be brother and sister anymore. Not outside the walls of their home, and sometimes not even inside them.

"All right, this is the place," Mox said, stopping and turning to face a shop on the other side of the street. It was a light blue color, with a large bay window in the front through which Mal could make out a steady blur of people heading inside to fill up on their favorites.

"You know, you never did tell me," Mal started, leaning his cane against his side so he could straighten his hair, "why am I the only one in civvies?"

"Because there's a *help wanted* sign out front, and I thought there was no better way for you to get close to Sage again than to apply for a job." She sounded desperately proud of herself, her tone rising as if she were smiling. Mal could tell her no. He could tell her to stuff it and head back to the house and forget this whole thing had ever happened. Wallow in his misery for another four years.

But.

But what if she was right?

What if Sage was alive?

What if they were working at this bakery?

And what was the harm in checking, just to be sure?

"She doesn't like mobsters, you said so yourself."

"Then you won't be a mobster. You'll wear a glamour and pretend to be some kid who needs a part-time gig. I can cover the day shift with the Few." She tilted her head, her short turquoise hair falling in front of her eyes, and Mal could imagine the expression on her face. It would be something soft and understanding. The kind of expression she had likely worn the day he learned Sage was dead. Although then he'd been too grief stricken to appreciate it.

Now though, now he was grateful to have a sibling who understood him.

A friend who stood by him even when it was hard. A partner who joined a gang when she didn't want to. A sister who took in a child someone else had sworn to protect. And above all else, someone who wasn't afraid to get her hands dirty when it was necessary. She was the only person in this entire world Mal could have imagined doing this with, and he was grateful for her.

He didn't tell her that enough.

He should probably buy her flowers.

"Go on then." She gave him a nudge.

"What if you're wrong?" The anxiety returned full

force, gnawing at his bones, making his knees sag. Hope fleeing him in one quick breath of panic.

"Then I'm wrong." He hated her a bit for how okay she sounded with that.

"I can't just —" Mal swallowed around a lump of anxiety in his throat. He took a step forward and stopped, shifting back on his heels to stand next to his sister again.

"What is it?"

"I can't just go in there and ask to see the person in the kitchen."

Mox let out a long, slow exhale. "Then do your shadow thing to check before you head in."

"I really wish you'd stop calling it that," Mal grumbled, rolling his eyes. He knew exactly what she was talking about, of course he did. But that didn't mean he had to like it when she diminished the ability gifted to him by his mare nature by calling it a "thing."

"Whatever." Mox scoffed. "Just do it."

"I need a good long shadow, you know that."

Mox didn't give him any time to argue. She grabbed him by the wrist and pulled him down an alley into the darkness he'd need to perform this particular trick. Without the sun shining directly in his eyes, he almost didn't need his sunglasses. But it felt weird not wearing them during the day, so he left them on.

A deep breath. Mal closed his eyes and called forth the shadows. They writhed and chittered like insects in the night, answering the call of their master. And when he lifted a hand to touch them, they wound cold and biting around his fingers, threatening to leave marks. They wouldn't dare, not if they knew what was good for them. Even shadows could be destroyed, and any mare worth their salt knew how to do just that.

As they slithered up his arm, Mal fought against the menacing chill creeping toward his spine. It shook off some of the worst of the early summer heat but replaced it with something worse. A cold that threatened to give him frostbite.

He breathed through it, fighting off the shivers and the trembling that would make his teeth chatter. There was no point showing this weakness to Mox. She knew what this did to him, what it would cost him. That's why he could only do something like this for a short period of time, and only in proximity to a target.

With a few clicks of his tongue, a response to the questioning sounds of the darkness, the shadows rushed up his arm to his face. Settling there in a way that made his eyes burn. But moments later, they showed him what he wanted to see.

The angle was all off, the kitchen so brightly lit that the shadows had to find him a viewpoint from somewhere down low, tucked behind an oven so that he could only make out the person's legs as they moved about the kitchen. Still, he waited, breath held, for them to move in a way that would let him see, would give him even a—

Shit.

He'd know that face anywhere.

Even hidden behind thick glasses and far too many white eyelashes, those seafoam green eyes were so achingly familiar. The button nose. The plush lower lip. The strong jaw. Mal *knew* them.

His heart lodged in his throat and he coughed, choked on it. A little whine left him. He needed a better angle. He needed to be able to see more. There had to be a place where he could get a better sight line. Behind the fridge? Above the cabinets?

Nothing.

The shadows would offer him nothing else. The kitchen had too many lights, no good places for them to hide. And already the biting cold was starting to freeze him too much, too close to the bone.

"Enough," Mox said, and a bright flash of light overtook the alley, chasing away the shadows. Her hands were on his wrists, warmth spreading along his skin from the fire she carried in her own blood.

"They're alive, Mox," Mal rasped, throat tight with some emotion he didn't think he wanted a name for. "They're alive. They're here."

"I know." Mox pulled him into a tight hug, rubbing the feeling back into his arms where the shadows had eaten away at it. "I know."

"What do I do?" he croaked. If Sage wasn't dead, what did that mean? Why hadn't they told anyone? Why hadn't they come for their place at the head of the family?

"First, take a breath," Mox advised then worked by example, taking a deep inhale then exhaling slowly.

She didn't stop until Mal followed her directions.

"Next, go get your person!" She shoved him toward the mouth of the alley without any warning, and he stumbled to right himself. It took him a minute, but once he did, he knew what came next.

"I'm going to need a distraction for the other baker," he called over his shoulder.

Mox laughed, loud and bright. "I got this."

"And a glamour," Mal said, letting out a slow breath. He didn't like the idea of going to meet Sage finally with his face hidden, but he couldn't run the risk of someone noticing the leader of the Faceless Few paying special attention to this bakery. If anyone noticed, it would put Sage in danger. Or at least, that was the rational reasoning.

He also worried that Sage would want nothing to do with the head of the gang they'd run from.

Mox squinted at him, a frown marring her face. "If you insist."

"I do."

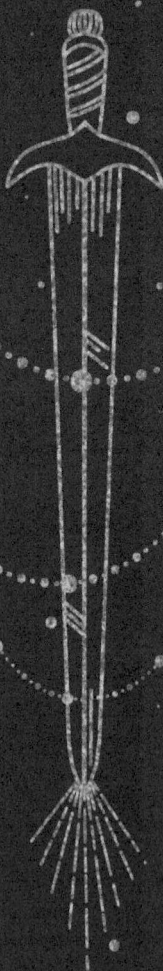

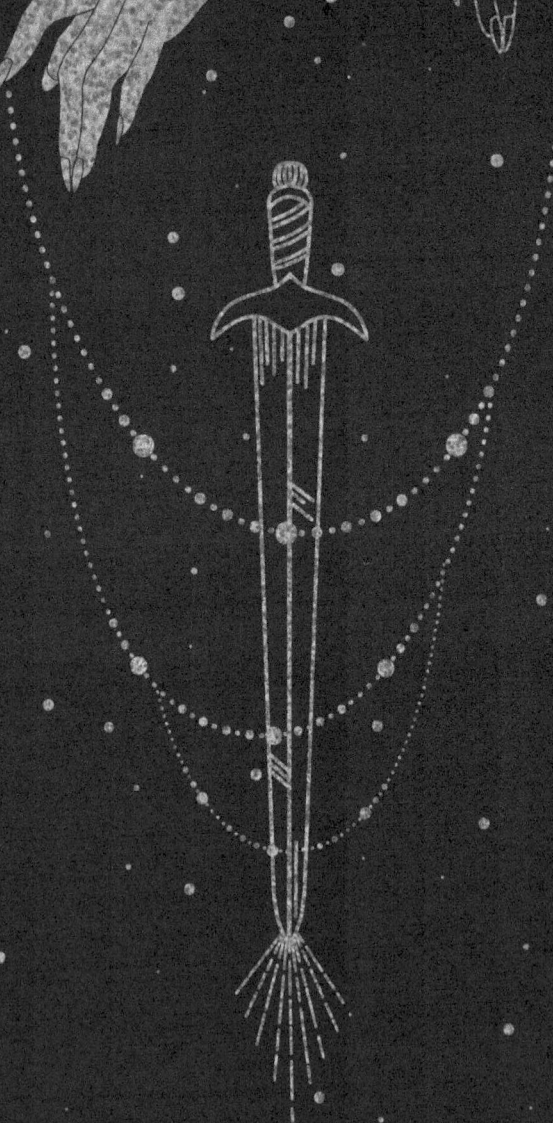

8

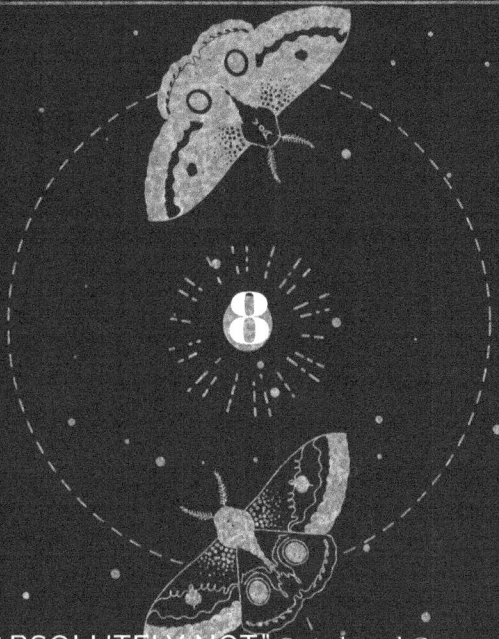

"NO. ABSOLUTELY NOT," Sage heard Corey say from the back. There was a growl in her voice the likes of which they'd only heard when directed at them. To everyone else Corey tended to be polite, cordial even. Especially when it came to her shop and her customers. There was something about Sage, and this other person apparently, that set her off.

Sage looked up from their phone where they were checking on their text thread with Tony again. He hadn't messaged back in a couple of days, and Sage was starting to worry. What if something had happened? What if his werewolf transformation had caused something to go wrong with his T? Should Sage look up Tony's boyfriend and try to get into contact?

"Absolutely not what? I'm not even doing anything?" another voice asked.

Sage scooted closer to the little window that led from the kitchen into the front of the bakery. If they could move onto their tiptoes, they could peek around the edge of the window without anyone seeing them. Probably. No one would be the wiser, most likely. And besides, the shop was almost closed anyway, mostly empty. It wasn't like—

"Hello there!" A face popped up, blocking Sage's view.

Sage yelped. They wobbled, arms cartwheeling to regain their balance and put some distance between themself and the person. Panic lodged in their chest. They couldn't let anyone look too closely. Couldn't be recognized. No one was supposed to know that the heir to the Nocturna family wasn't only alive but also back in Eventide.

Fuck. Corey was going to skin them alive.

Clearing their throat, Sage did their best to put some distance between themself and the other person. "Hi."

"You okay back there?"

"Yup. All good." Sage gave a shaky thumbs-up and ducked their head back to the cupcakes they had been decorating before an errant thought had drawn them to their phone. "Just trying to get these done for tomorrow."

Were Corey and the other person still arguing? And what the fuck was someone doing behind the counter, poking their head into the kitchen? That wasn't normal behavior.

Sage spun to tell them that. "You shouldn't be back—" Another yelp escaped Sage and they almost put their hand into one of the cupcakes, the other clutching their tweed vest.

The person was in the kitchen now, almost close enough that they could lean over Sage's shoulder and see what they were doing. Glamour glittered around their appearance, the lights blinking off the magic.

"Sorry. I didn't mean to scare you." They took a giant step back, their dark brows pinching together in a manner that could only be called apologetic. When Sage squinted to see through the glamour, they looked familiar, a hazy memory of a dark-haired teen that Sage couldn't pin down.

And when Sage finally took a moment to meet their mismatched eyes — one icy blue, one a rich, warm brown — something in their chest jolted, like a line pulled taut. "I'm Ianthe."

They didn't *look* like an Ianthe, and that wasn't the name that sat at the tip of Sage's tongue when they got a better look at the face beneath the glamour. But what did an Ianthe look like anyway?

"Nice to meet you." Sage curled their shoulders further forward to hide their own face. At least until they could pull on a glamour. It was hastily done, shoddy work, and they knew that. They hadn't been able to get a glamour right since coming back. One more thing to add to the I-came-back-wrong list. But it was better than nothing. Even if Sage didn't know this person, even if they weren't a part of one of the Eventide families, it paid to be careful.

When they glanced at their reflection on the oven door, their nose was a little crooked, their eyes a dark brown instead of the normal seafoam green, and their lips were thinner. They'd also taken care to hide the long horizontal scar that stretched almost the entirety of their throat — even if the choker did most of the work for them — but that was mainly out of self-consciousness. Small changes. That would have to do. They hadn't been able to change the overall structure of their face, their magic too limited from the whole being dead thing, and even this much was a strain. Already their muscles burned with overuse. They didn't know how long they could hold it in place before it gave up under the weight of their exhaustion. Hopefully long enough to get Ianthe out of the kitchen.

They turned and held out their hand, their name on the tip of their tongue before they could think better of it. "Sage."

Shit. Probably should have given a fake name. Or at least

something that wasn't likely to connect Sage back to their previous life. Another part of their true name perhaps. Or even just an initial. Though how weird would it be to say they went by S?

It was definitely too late now. All Sage could hope was that they weren't the only Sage living in Eventide. They couldn't be, right? The city was big enough to house at least a few hundred thousand people. What were the chances that there wasn't another Sage floating around there? Then again, they were in Faceless Few territory. Standing on the very land that once should have belonged to them.

Fuck it.

"Sage," Ianthe repeated, a smile splitting their face, their teeth sharp. It was a nice smile, even still. Threatening, bold, handsome. "Nice."

"You're really not supposed to be back here. It's for staff only." A halfhearted protest, and by the way Ianthe's smile twitched at the corners, they heard it too.

"I won't tell anyone if you won't." Ianthe winked.

Sage couldn't help the chuckle that burbled up their throat. They tried to choke it back, but there was no holding it in. There was something effortlessly charming about Ianthe. "I use they/them," they offered, tapping the pin Corey had stuck to their apron before they got to work. Needless, since she already knew, but it was nice just the same.

Ianthe nodded, in approval it seemed, before offering, "He/him. Now that that's out of the way, what are you making back here? Anything good?" Ianthe's hands were stuffed deep into the back pockets of his black stone-wash jeans. They were practically painted on, leaving very little to the imagination, and Sage had to admit, it was working for Ianthe. Whether Sage liked it or not.

"Cupcakes," Sage offered, reaching back, unable to tear

their eyes from him. They held the tray up so Ianthe could see. "Red velvet."

"My favorite." Ianthe gave an appreciative murmur, his nose crinkling in delight.

Fuck, was he cute. So cute that Sage could hardly be held responsible for what came out of their mouth next. "Do you want to go out sometime?"

Ianthe's smile fell to leave room for his jaw to fall slack in surprise. His dark neatly sculpted brows rose high. "Me?" he squeaked.

"Yes, you." Could he get any more adorable?

Color flamed bright on Ianthe's cheeks, and yes, yes he *could* get more adorable. Sage wanted to lean in closer, feel that warmth on the tip of their nose, see how different it was in temperature from the rest of Ianthe's skin. An urge they hadn't felt in a long while. Maybe not since before they'd died.

Ianthe opened his mouth. Closed it. Opened it again to make a vague croaking sound. Snapped his jaw shut. Averted his eyes, his hand lifting to cover his mouth, likely to hide his embarrassment.

"You can say no," Sage offered kindly. "No pressure."

"No!" Ianthe all but shouted, then flushed further. "I— I'd love to."

"Wonderful." A contented feeling Sage was unfamiliar with curled up in their chest. Like a cat purring low and pleased, which seemed largely impossible as they hadn't been in touch with their panther in . . . They shook the thought aside. Now was not the time. Now was a time for something happier, something better.

They shouldn't go out. They needed to keep a low profile. They needed to go unseen until they could get the fuck out of Eventide, far away from the gangs and the violence that they thought they'd left behind. So many reasons not to. Good reasons. Sensible reasons. *Valid* fucking reasons. Not one of them could drown out the gnawing feeling in Sage's gut that if they didn't do this, if they didn't make this move, they'd regret it for the rest of their life. Unlife? Whatever. Point was, they would look upon this months—years—from now and see all the missed opportunity one sees in a seed never sprouted.

"Yeah?" Ianthe asked, a grin tugging at his lips again, small and sweet.

"What time do you want to pick me up?"

The grin that spread across Ianthe's face could have rivaled the sun, it was so bright and beautiful. Sage's heart skipped along in their chest, and they had to lean back against the metal table to keep their legs from buckling under them.

SAGE HAD ASKED HIM OUT . . .

They'd . . . they'd asked him to dinner.

Was it a date? Could it be a date?

Even if it wasn't, it would be enough. To get to speak to Sage one-on-one. To get to know them in a way he never had before.

Mal was unable to believe his luck. Fate had dealt him some bad hands in the past. Forced him into some truly shitty situations. But if that was the price he had to pay for *this*? For a Sage who was alive, well, and inviting him to dinner? Mal would pay it a hundred times over.

Not that he deserved this. He wasn't worthy. But if Sage was willing to spend time with him, to get to know him? Well, Mal was a greedy man. Greedy and selfish. He'd take whatever he was offered. Even if it was just a few hours of Sage's time.

"I'll um . . . I'll pick you up at eight. Friday?" Two days. That gave Mal two days to plan the best fucking evening anyone had ever experienced in their life. It wasn't near enough time, not really. But Mal couldn't chance that Sage would change their mind if he left it for too long.

"Eight on Friday is good."

"What the fuck are you doing in my kitchen?!" the woman Mox was currently infatuated with screeched. Mal thought her name might start with a *c*, but he hadn't been paying attention to her. Why would he when Sage was tucked back in the kitchen like a hidden treasure?

"Saying hello?" Mal blinked at her. She was wielding what must have been a broom in the hand that wasn't tucked against her abdomen in a bright blue sling. Fucking hell, what had Mox done to this woman to get her so pissed that she was willing to chase Faceless Few execs with a broom?

"Out! Now! This space is for employees only. There was a sign!" She looped around behind him and started herding him toward the swinging door into the front of the bakery.

"Corey," Sage said, taking a step forward as if to stop their boss. Partner? Whatever. Ah, Corey. That was it. Good to know. "It's all right—"

"No, it's not! This is a business in the food industry! We can't have—" She cut herself off, her shoulders jerking in the way that meant someone had gone rigid all of the sudden. Mal was well acquainted with that gesture. It usually accompanied someone trying to keep themself from saying something they knew they ought not to lest it bring down the wrath of the Faceless Few.

He tilted his head, curious. Did Corey know who he

was? He supposed some assumptions could be made because he was with Mox, but he'd put on a glamour. There was no reason for her to recognize him. And if she did, why was she keeping his identity from Sage? Interesting.

"Weirdos," she said at last, "back here in the kitchen."

"Very well." Mal held up his hands, cane under his arm for a moment so he could appear the picture of innocence. "I'm going." He took a step backward toward the door, allowing Corey to shoo him a bit. "Eight?"

"Eight," Sage responded with another nod. "Friday."

"Eight. Friday," Mal repeated, half breathless with his excitement. "What do you like to eat?"

"Dealer's choice." Sage laughed, and Mal's heart soared.

He spun on his heel and allowed Corey to chase him through the bakery and back out onto the street. She followed him, shutting the door behind her, and when he turned back toward her, she was barring the entrance.

"What now?"

"I know you," Corey hissed. She had the broom slung over her uninjured shoulder now, as if she intended to use it as a bat. Mox was mysteriously absent, like she'd left Mal to deal with this shitshow all by himself. Asshole.

"You do?" Mal tilted his head. Most people, fae included, couldn't see through glamours.

"Yes. You're Mal. The leader of the Faceless Few."

Ah. So Corey *could* see through glamours. Mal leaned back on his heels, the picture of nonchalance as his magic reached out from him, crawling from his shadow to hers, tapping it lightly. What it found there was fae magic, but it was dulled by mortality, by humanity. A halfling then. That explained the glamour thing. No wonder Mox had bounced.

"I suppose you're going to tell me to stay away from your friend." Mal crossed his arms over his chest and lifted a brow mockingly. He'd never received a shovel talk before. It was almost amusing how this small halfling thought she was going to boss him around. She'd said it herself—he was the leader of the Faceless Few, for Goddess's sake. "If you know who I am, then you also know how I came by that position, do you not?"

"I do." But it didn't seem like she was backing down. If anything, she gripped the broom handle harder based on the slight squeak of her hand on colored metal. He had to admit, it was impressive.

"Do you think it wise to be so adversarial toward me then?" Maybe Mal could see what Mox saw in this Corey. If anything, she wasn't cowed by their position. That would make things interesting. Mox always did love a good chase. She tended to get bored once the chase itself was done. Maybe she'd finally met someone who would give her a run for her money. Not that Mal was going to let Corey get away with this behavior just because she might be a match for his sister.

"That is my meal ticket in there," Corey continued, undeterred. "If you fuck with what I've got going on, they will never find the body. I don't care what gang you're running with, what fae runs through your blood. They. Will. Never. *Find*. The. Body."

Scratch that, Mal could *definitely* see what Mox saw in this one. He didn't particularly care for Sage being termed a meal ticket, but if that meant they were protected by this fierce little thing, so be it. "I mean them no harm."

"You know who they are." It was not a question, it was a statement of fact. Mal wondered what had given him away. "And if you know that, then you know that no one can know they're here."

Ah. So that was it then. Mal dipped his head forward, his hand to his chest in the motion of a vow. Binding and true. "I will tell no one what I've seen here. And I will not let anyone else know they're here either. So long as it is within my power, I will protect this information with my life."

"Good." Corey sniffed, her posture relaxing. "Now get the fuck out of here. I've got work to do."

Mal fell into a dramatic bow, bending deeply over his arm, then righted himself and spun, his cane tapping merrily as he started the familiar route home, mind still reeling from being near Sage again. He hadn't been able to see them with the too-bright LED lights of the kitchen. But they smelled the same, they sounded the same. That was enough.

And they'd asked him out!

In the meantime, Mal had work to do. If he was going to keep his promise to Corey and ensure that nothing could possibly hurt Sage again, Mal had to find that bitch Bentley. He had to eliminate her and any other threat that might arise.

He pulled his phone from his pocket, tapping the side button so he could speak into it. "Call Mox."

The phone rang loudly in his ear as he thought more about this problem. He had much to do and not a lot of time to do it. First, he'd find Bentley Nocturna. Then he'd make sure she hadn't been working with anyone else.

"How'd it go?" Mox asked when she finally picked up.

"We need to go over all the shit you've been compiling again. I want Bentley's head on a fucking platter before my date this Friday."

"I'll get everything together." Mox hung up, hopefully to set to work.

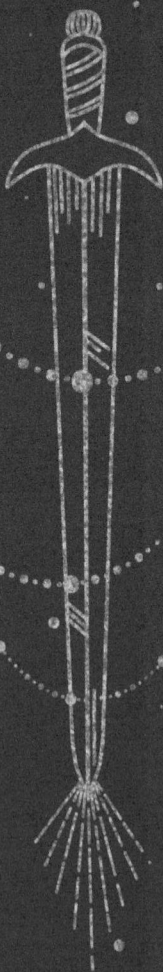

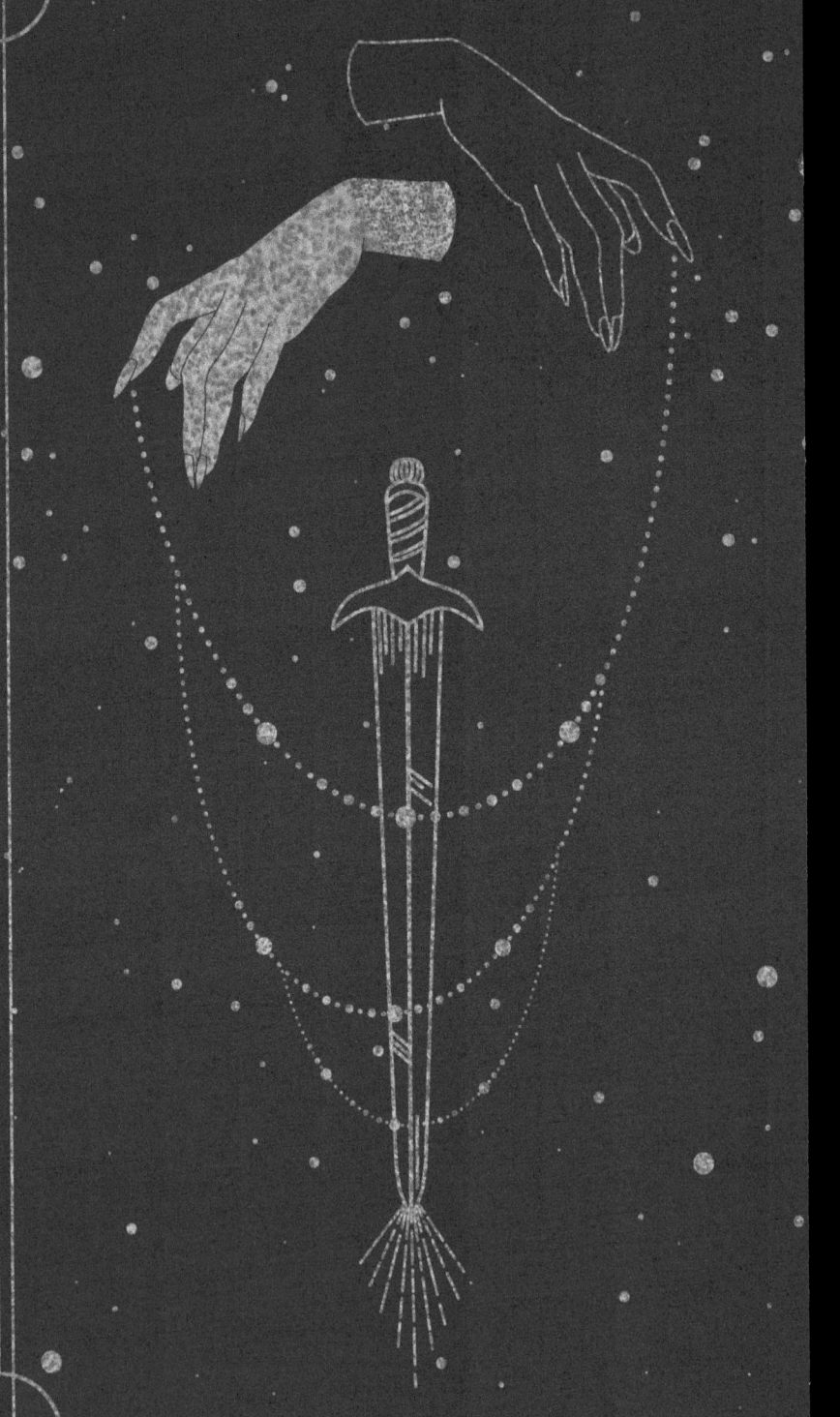

9

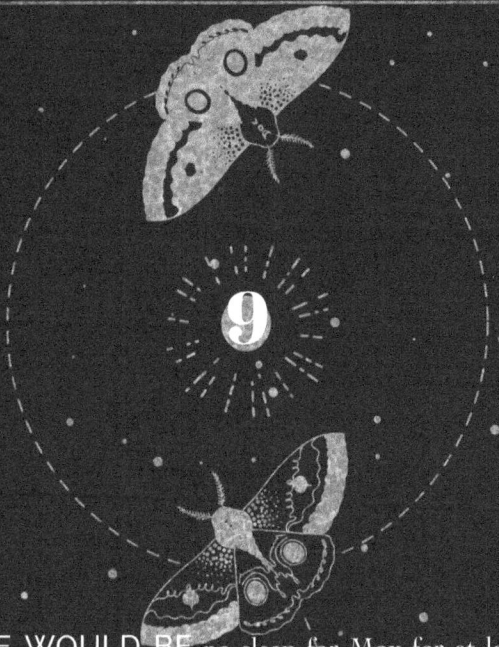

THERE WOULD BE no sleep for Mox for at least the next couple of days. It had been evident in the tone of her brother's voice when he called.

No sleep. No rest. No time off.

They would find Bentley Nocturna before Mal's date with Sage if it killed them.

Which it very well might.

Not that Mox could begrudge her brother this. He had mourned for four years for someone who barely knew he existed. Dedicated his life to avenging their death. Now that he had a chance at the thing he'd wanted so much for so long? It only made sense that he'd do anything to get it. She'd do the exact same if she was in his position.

Which, honestly? She was kind of glad she wasn't. She had enough problems. She didn't need to add all the disastrous pining that seemed to come along with loving someone to everything else. Even if Corey from the bakery was objectively *very* hot.

"What do you have for me?" Mal asked as soon as he

walked into her office. He hadn't even bothered to take off his shoes.

"Not much, unfortunately." Mox frowned at the notebook sitting on top of her desk. She had been collecting information on the gangs of Eventide for years now, trying to weasel out who would be hiding Bentley. But so far there was nothing. "The Blood Moons looked a little flush at Court the other day, but they were the only ones who really stood out."

"Do we have anyone in their territory?" Mal dropped into one of the chairs on the other side of the heavy oak desk from Mox, crossing one leg over the other. He looked strange sitting there in jeans, without his custom-tailored suit, in the crushed red velvet of Mox's office chair. But she wasn't going to bring it up to him. She hadn't seen him this happy in . . . well, maybe ever. She'd be hard-pressed to ruin it by poking fun at him for how he didn't look an inch the crime boss he was in that moment.

"No. But I think Guin does. Her spy network runs deeper than ours."

Mal scoffed. "Only because she's been at this twice as long as we have."

That wasn't the only reason, but Mox wasn't going to bring up how Mal's approach to things was usually *the bloodier the better*. He'd made a name for himself when he'd taken over, and people weren't going to soon forget the twins who'd killed everyone who'd stood in their way of the throne of the Faceless Few. Which made it hard to gain loyalty through anything but fear. And even harder to get people to trust that they wouldn't turn around and slit the throats of their informants. Being bloodthirsty helped in some instances, but in others . . .

"Either way, Guin will have a better handle on what's

going on with whom." Mox tapped her fingers on the desk, her nails clicking in a slow rhythm.

"Why haven't you gone to her then?"

"You damn well know why not, Mal. She's currently in our debt, meaning we own her. If we call in a favor of this magnitude, it's likely she'll try to call us square." Mal may have gotten to where he was in this life by leaving a trail of blood in his wake, but Mox had gotten here by being a bit smarter, a bit more conniving. There was plenty of blood on her hands, but she preferred if people owed her rather than killing them outright. It was more entertaining and more useful.

"I would like to see her try." Mal sat up, a slow, cruel smile on his face. "We both know so long as she's masquerading as Alton's little brother, and we're the only ones who know about it, we can call in any favors we want of her." Pressing his fingertips together, he lifted them to his lips like some kind of Bond villain. "Set a meet. Tonight."

"Let me handle this."

Mal raised a dark brow, his lips pursed. She could tell he wanted to argue, maybe even pull rank. It was his way.

"Seriously, let me take care of it. I think this needs more finesse than—"

"I can finesse!"

"Please, you have all the finesse of a bulldozer." Mox laughed, shaking her head. "This needs more tact. Let me handle it. Besides, don't you have a date to plan?"

The smile that bloomed on Mal's face could put even the DE botanical gardens to shame. It was absolutely effervescent. Mox wondered for a moment if this happiness would make Mal softer, if it would smooth his edges.

"It's not technically a date, but while we're on the topic of that . . ." Mal said, the smile turning sharper.

Ah, there it is. There was the Mal who obliterated an

entire gang in the name of a person who didn't even know they were married. No, if anything, having Sage back in his life would make him more vicious. Good. Mox couldn't work with a Mal who'd gone soft.

"Call off your attack dog girlfriend."

"Corey isn't my girlfriend."

"So I can go out for a nice night with my spouse."

Mox fought the urge to roll her eyes. "You know you don't have to refer to them that way. They don't even know you're married. I mean, technically you're *not* married."

Mal growled, and the shadows in the room shivered as if readying to leap forward at their master's will.

"Seriously, Mal, don't make it a thing." She didn't want him to get hurt, that was all. He had been through enough —they both had. It was about time he got to be happy. "If you make it a thing, if you put too much pressure on them, you'll likely lose them."

"But we're—"

"Only by mare tradition." Mox sighed, running a hand through her hair. "Yes, you snuck into their room to plague them with night terrors. Yes, they trapped you there, so by mare tradition you're married, I know. But that's not legally binding. Literally no other fae abides by those—"

"The selkies still give away their coats."

"*Willingly*. They're no longer forced into a marriage just because someone steals it. All the old traditions are just that: traditions. You know that."

Mal grunted, crossing his arms over his chest.

"Don't sulk. I know you think of Sage as your spouse, and I'm fully in support of you building a relationship with them, if they're amenable. I want you to be happy, trust me, I do. Goddess knows, we'll *all* be a lot happier if you are."

He cut her a hard look, and she offered him a smile before letting it slip into something more serious.

"But don't frontload this thing with baggage. Okay? It's not fair to you—"

Another huff came from Mal, and Mox half expected him to argue further.

"And it's not fair to them either, is it? Take the time to get to know each other. See if that's what you really want. If it is? You've got my blessing, and I'll fight off anyone who stands in your way," Mox vowed.

Mal blinked at her for a long moment, his lips not parting, but she could tell his jaw had gone slack. As if he was surprised by her declaration. "Even your latest crush?"

"Even my latest crush." She nodded firmly.

"You really are the best sister anyone could ask for. You know that, right?"

"Oh. I know." Mox sat up, preening and flipping her hair over her shoulder. "And don't you dare forget it. Also, you owe me—*big*—for this one."

"Yeah." Mal grinned, soft and kind—an expression most rarely saw. One he reserved for his family. "I guess I do."

"Definitely, and you can start by being in charge of dinner for the gremlin tonight." Mox rose from her desk, the chair wheeling across the floor.

"Nooooo." Mal groaned, leaning his head back so he was staring at the ceiling over the back of the chair.

"Yup. If I'm going to be out, then you're in charge of dinner. Order takeout, I don't care. But make sure she eats something that's not cereal." Mox moved to his side and pressed a kiss to her brother's cheek as he chuckled lightly. "I'm serious. If she eats Froot Loops for dinner again, I'm going to skin you alive and turn you into a fucking crossbody purse."

"That's eerily specific. You've been giving this some thought, haven't you?" He didn't sound as offended or scared by it as he perhaps should have been. But then again, they were twins. He knew her well enough to know when to duck right before an actual strike.

"What can I say? I've got a fondness for good quality handbags." Mox shrugged and headed for the door.

"You're so weird."

"Pot, kettle, dear Mal. Pot, kettle." Mox blew him a kiss and trotted off to make some calls. If she was going to force people to do her favors, she'd need a bit of muscle to scare them into behaving.

"IS ALL OF THIS REALLY NECESSARY?" GUIN ASKED, gesturing to the three grunts standing behind Mox.

They were armed to the teeth. One even had a broadsword. Lewis was definitely compensating for something, but Mox didn't know what, and she wasn't going to call him on it. Everyone had their thing, right? And who was she to judge.

"Just thought a little reminder of who I am wouldn't go amiss." Mox shrugged, settling back into the chair she'd claimed upon walking into the outdoor café Guin chose as their meeting spot. It was right on the border of Delta Dagger territory, far too close to a three-way meeting of the lines between them, the Faceless, and the Wildlings. Even without being on enemy turf, Mox would have brought backup to a spot like this. She wasn't stupid. An ambush would be all too easy.

"And, if my brother has taught me anything, it's how easy it would be for someone to slit my throat in public without any *witnesses*." Witnesses was said with air quotes around it, because although there might be citizens of Eventide around to see such a thing go down, no one would ever step forward. Not if it meant getting in the middle of feuding gangs. Mox couldn't blame the people for that. They just wanted to live their lives. They didn't want to be bothered. She'd be the same way if she wasn't already a part of this.

Guin scoffed and rolled her eyes, brushing a strand of stringy blue hair back from her face. She, unlike Mox, had come without backup and looked to be unarmed. But the café she'd chosen was right on the water, and all it would take was a little concentration for her to dip into her fauthon magic and use the water to gut Mox like a fish. Fauthon were water fae, a strange blend of fae and ghost that Mox didn't particularly want to understand better than she already did.

"What do you want, anyhow?" she asked when Mox didn't reply to her obvious displeasure.

"You have contacts in the Blood Moons, yes?" Mox leaned forward, purposefully invading Guin's space, and making her lean backward to keep her at a safe distance.

"Of course I do. I have contacts everywhere." Guin's dark blue eyes narrowed on Mox, and the water just over the sea wall grew choppier. As if she thought Mox doubted her skills.

"See?" Mox pointed across the table at her and then turned to look at one of the grunts, Harold, who didn't even react. "That's what I told Mal. I told Mal she was just the person for the job. Didn't I, Harold?" she crowed dramatically, pretending to ignore the way Guin seemed to sit up straighter as if she were preening. Mox had her now, she was hooked. She probably wouldn't even ask for a favor in return. "What we need is to know if Bentley Nocturna is hanging out around Flo and Dam's territory."

Guin went still, her eyes jerking from Mox to the goons she'd brought along and back. "I have someone in their territory, but they're not high enough in the food chain to know if the execs are hiding your fugitive." Guin frowned as if she was upset she was disappointing Mox. "But I can give you the name of someone who *would* know." She reached into her purse and pulled out a pad of paper and a pen. "I can also give you where they'll be, so you and your brother can . . . have a *chat* with them."

"That would be very much appreciated." Mox smiled pointedly and took the torn sheet without glancing at it. "Well." She stood, stuffing the paper into her back pocket where no one could take it off her without the risk of losing a hand. "As always, it's been a delight."

"Yes. A delight." Guin grunted, sipping her coffee. "Don't cause any trouble on the way out of my territory."

"Please, I'd never."

"Of course not. And don't tell anyone I gave you that."

Mox grinned in return before taking her leave. "Come along, dears. We need to pick up some food on the way back."

"I thought you told Mal he was in charge of dinner?" Lewis asked.

"I did." Mox shrugged and stepped out onto the street.

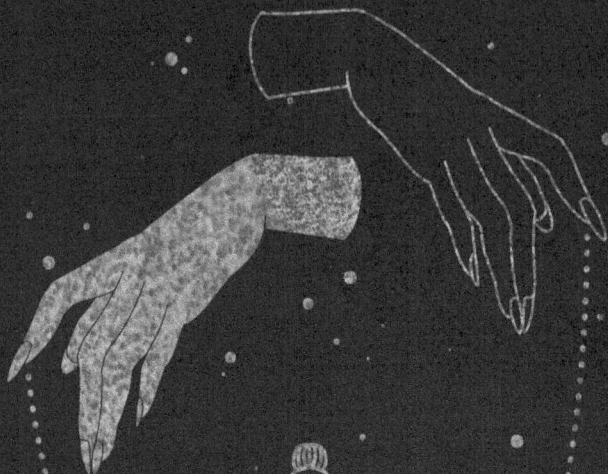

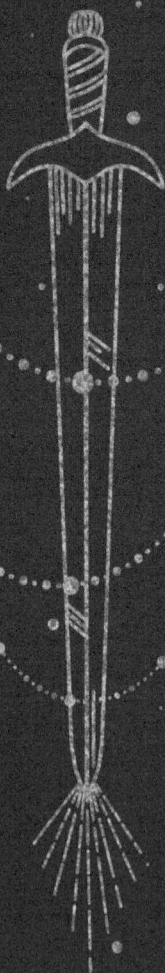

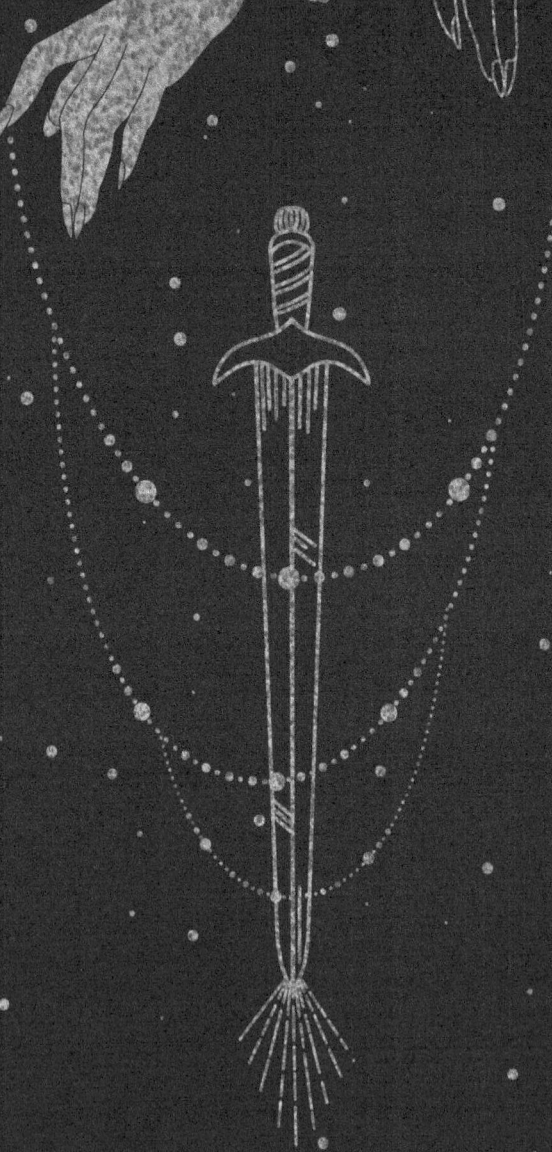

10

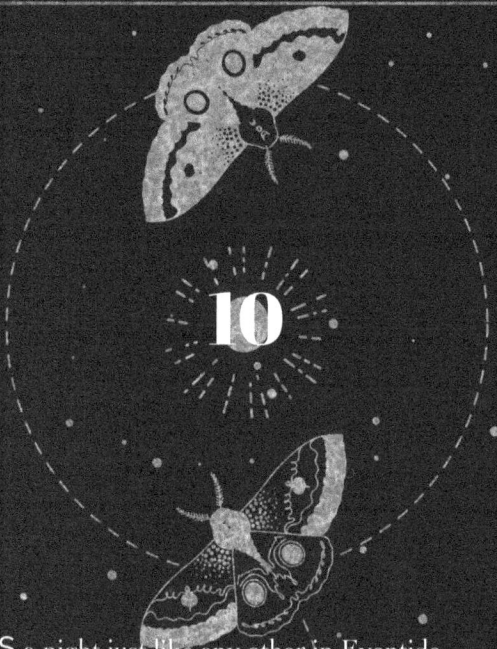

IT WAS a night just like any other in Eventide.

The darkness was alive with the sounds of magic and mayhem of folk and human alike, and Sage was happy enough to be among their numbers.

More than happy, actually, as it got them out from under the watchful eye of their father and the other Faceless Few execs. And with the way they'd dressed down that night, their long dark hair pulled into a messy bun, and slipped a glamour on, no one had even recognized them so far.

Out on the street of Eventide, among the hustle and the bustle of a late summer evening, Sage Nocturna, heir to the Faceless Few, only child of Nocturna, was just another person. Just another face in the crowd.

They were old enough to see the beauty in that now. To realize that while being the heir to one of the gangs in Eventide had its perks, it also had its drawbacks. There had been a time, in their twenties, when they had relished the attention. When the fear their name struck in people's hearts was the best high they could get. That was no longer the case.

But still, they walked with a kind of swagger. Still, they did not fear going down dark alleys by themselves and traipsing the streets at night. Why should they? They were the heir of Nocturna. They would be the head of the Faceless Few in a few short years. There was nothing for them to fear.

With their hands stuffed into their pockets, Sage ducked into the alley that was the best shortcut from their apartment to the epicenter of Eventide where all the businesses and bars were opening for the night. The plan was a quick dinner then they'd settle in at one of the bars that was on the calmer side, have a beer, and unwind after a long week of playing the dutiful child, the violent mobster.

They could practically hear the soft chatter now—the perfect white noise to act as a soundtrack to catch up on some reading. Because sometimes Sage wanted to be around people without actually *talking* to anyone. And there was no better way to do that than to—

A shoe scuffed behind them. The hairs on their neck lifted at the knowledge that someone was following them. Sage had been born and raised in a gang. Brought up to be the head of a family of violent mobsters. They had paranoia beat into them.

Increasing their pace to put distance between themself and whoever it was, they glanced over their shoulder but saw nothing. Just a yawning darkness. They picked up their pace further. Better safe than sorry, even if the person meant them no harm. The alley stretched on forever into the night. The end growing further and further away, warping around the edges.

A dream, they realized. This was a dream. *The* dream. And they knew what came next.

The first slice of the knife didn't hurt.

It burned.

Sage almost immediately grew dizzy as they tried to press their hand to hold in the blood dribbling from their wrist. How had someone even wounded them *there*? The cut wasn't deep. Or it didn't *feel* deep. But it didn't *need* to be to nick an artery—they knew that well enough from their own training.

They reached for their magic, calling upon the large black cat that lived under their skin. The panther. She would slow the bleeding, enough maybe to get them away from their attacker, and she had claws and teeth to defend them. But she wasn't . . . she wasn't there. She wasn't sleeping. She wasn't quiet. She was *missing*. Absent. Dead?

"Quick, before someone sees us," someone said, their voice warbly and indistinct like it was coming through glass, the only indication they weren't alone. Sage couldn't *see* anyone. Couldn't smell them.

Sage lifted an arm to swipe blindly for their attacker, their balance wobbling. But the blade bit into the thin skin of their neck, carving a smile-like slice below their chin, draining them of more blood.

The world grew darker, narrowing to a pinprick.

The summer heat faded away, a chill racing down Sage's spine.

They lifted their head from the ground to growl, feral and broken, at their attacker.

But the assailants were gone already, a mere clomping of footsteps in the dark. A pair of white sneakers disappearing around the corner.

Sage was choking, gasping. The blood on their hands grew cold and sticky, mixing with the blood from their wrists. And they were alone.

Goddess.

Another chill wracked their body, sending pain shooting along their nerves. They'd finally registered that they'd been hurt now that the initial burn had faded away.

They were going to die.

They were going to die in a dark alley, and no one would ever be the wiser.

Someone would find their body in the morning, and that would be it. That would be the end. There would be nothing left. And what was it all for? Their father had been right. They should have stayed home. They should have stayed hidden away. Safe. They shouldn't have tried to be normal. They shouldn't—

Sage woke with a gasp, their hands flying to their throat where the scar from the attack rested. The coroner had stitched the wound closed when they were still dead, but he'd done a sloppy job and no amount of healing magic would make the scar go away.

Just like no amount of healing magic could fix the ever-present chill that had sunk into their bones that night. Or the way their cait sidhe nature had been forever altered, the large black cat all but abandoning them in death. Or how their vision was deteriorating the longer they remained undead, their glasses growing thicker every year. Or the way their body didn't process sugar the way it ought to anymore, making them need to be hyper aware of their intake and reliant on artificial means when things got too bad.

None of that held a candle to the nightmares though. It was as if that night had burned itself into the back of Sage's eyelids. Every time they laid down to sleep, the pain and the fear was waiting for them. The empty alley and the *cold*.

It would take at least a couple of hours to ward off the chill.

They scratched at their wrists, the skin reddening and

itching the way it would were it newly healed. Which made no sense, just like the dream didn't. Their wrists hadn't been wounded that night. And when they'd reached for the panther, she'd been there. She'd helped ward off their attackers. But it seemed every time Sage dreamed of that night, they were more and more helpless. Weaker. Easier to take down. With more wounds. And every time they had that dream, it was shorter.

They didn't want to know what that could mean.

Sage pulled their blankets more tightly around themself and wrapped them over their head like a hood.

"A hot shower would be good," they murmured to themself as they forced their stiff joints to move through the ache of the cold. "But then I have to get undressed." Another shiver zipped up their spine, jolting their locked joints and ripping a cry from their lips. "That's out. Tea. We'll start with tea."

With a nod, they slipped their freezing toes into the big fluffy cat slippers Tony bought them before he left Miami and scuffed out to the kitchen. The light over the stove was still on, so Corey was out, either on a job for her "side hustle" or at the bakery.

A quick glance at the clock might have answered that question if Corey were anyone else and *did* anything else, but she ran a bakery and was a hired cleaner for the local Mafia. So at 3:36 in the morning, she could literally be anywhere. Not that it mattered. Sage wasn't getting back to sleep, they never did.

Having to move their arms from the blanket burrito was not ideal, but if they wanted tea, that's what they were going to have to do. Sage heaved a sigh to prepare for the incoming chill, then looped the blanket over their arms more securely and dove for the kettle to get it started. They snatched their arms back under the blanket as quickly as possible.

They were struggling to keep the blanket out of the water as they filled the kettle when Corey slunk through the door, the scent of blood lingering on her.

"Long night?" she asked, kicking off her shoes then coming into the kitchen to nudge Sage out of the way and continue filling the kettle.

"Nightmares." Sage shrugged, curling back into their blanket burrito. Although now that the cold of the kitchen had gotten in, there was no going back.

"Yeah. I can see that." Corey moved to put the kettle on, then pulled down two mugs and the tea without any further questions.

Sage liked that about her. Which was funny because there wasn't a lot they *did* like about Corey. She was abrasive, and crass, and they knew for a fact she'd only saved their life so she'd have an out. But on some level, Sage got it. She was doing what she had to. And wasn't everyone in this city? Sage included.

"You have a job tonight?" Sage asked when the silence stretched on for too long and the dark started to creep in around them. They should have turned on the kitchen light, but the light over the stove had seemed like enough when they were going to make tea and retreat to their bed again.

"I don't think you want me to answer that question." Corey poured water into their mugs and held one out to Sage. A hint of blood lurked underneath her nails, caked into the wrinkles around her knuckles, but she was right. Sage didn't want the answer to that question. They'd left that life behind when they died, and it was better things stayed that way.

"Okay, I can't ask about your side hustle. What can we talk about then?" With their hands wrapped tight around the hot mug, their joints and muscles began to relax, and Sage leaned back against the counter, letting themself slouch. It was always hard after just waking up. They felt like they needed to hold themself even stiffer out of fear of the pain of a body that sometimes forgot it was alive. Rigor mortis was a bitch.

"How about we talk about the fact that you agreed to go on a date when you're supposed to be in hiding?" Corey settled against the counter opposite Sage and fixed them with an unamused expression. "What the fuck are you thinking?"

"I'm thinking I can't spend the entire time I'm here locked up in your apartment." Not that that was much different from when they were living in Miami, but it felt different here. Sage couldn't explain it, but it was like a buzz under their skin demanded they get out and do things, see things. It had been so long since they were home, and they wanted to know all that had changed. The siren call of Eventide. Plus, they really wanted to get laid, so sue them. "I'll wear a glamour."

"A shoddily slapped-together one." Corey scoffed. "My glamours are better and I'm a halfling."

"No, they're not."

"Yes they—" Corey stopped, huffing softly and pinching the bridge of her nose. "Look, you can't go out looking like that. It was okay in the bakery for a brief conversation, but if you go out and about like that someone is going to notice you. And we don't want that, do we?"

"No." Sage curled their shoulders in more. Corey was right, of course. Sage shouldn't be wandering around Eventide flaunting their general aliveness. (Undeadness? Reanimatedness? Fuck, they really needed more friends who'd been brought back from the dead so they could compare notes on terminology.) It was asking for trouble.

But the idea of being stuck inside for the foreseeable future until Corey could get her hands on some extra anti-iron made their skin crawl.

"Don't look like I just washed and dried your favorite sweater. Goddess." Corey rolled her eyes. "You really want to go out with this Ianthe guy?"

"It's not really about that." Although it wasn't *not* about that either. Sage couldn't put words to the instant connection they'd felt with Ianthe. There was something there that they hadn't experienced since before they'd died. Like something had clicked. They didn't want to examine it too much because that way led to insanity and the ruination of what could possibly be something really *good*. Plus, they wanted to understand the strange familiarity that was there. Who *was* Ianthe? How did Sage know them? "I just . . . I want to see what Eventide is like now."

"It sucks. That's what it's like now."

"Corey." Sage rolled their eyes.

"Okay, fine. But we need to work on your glamour. What the fuck is going on with that?"

"No idea. It's not like I can just google *hey I'm undead why is my glamour all wonky?*" Although they'd tried to some degree. There wasn't any information out there about it. Besides, the more pressing matter had always been that their panther had abandoned them, leaving them feeling half of a whole and unable to defend themself if they got in real trouble.

"Hmmm." Corey tapped her fingers against her mug in thought, her eyes narrowing on Sage. "I might know someone who can help."

"Really?"

"Yeah. But they're not going to do it for free."

"No one works for free in Eventide." Sage shrugged. They'd take it.

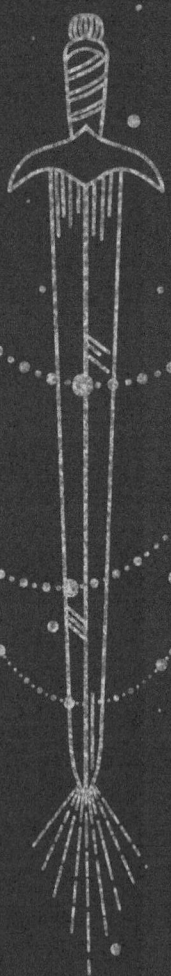

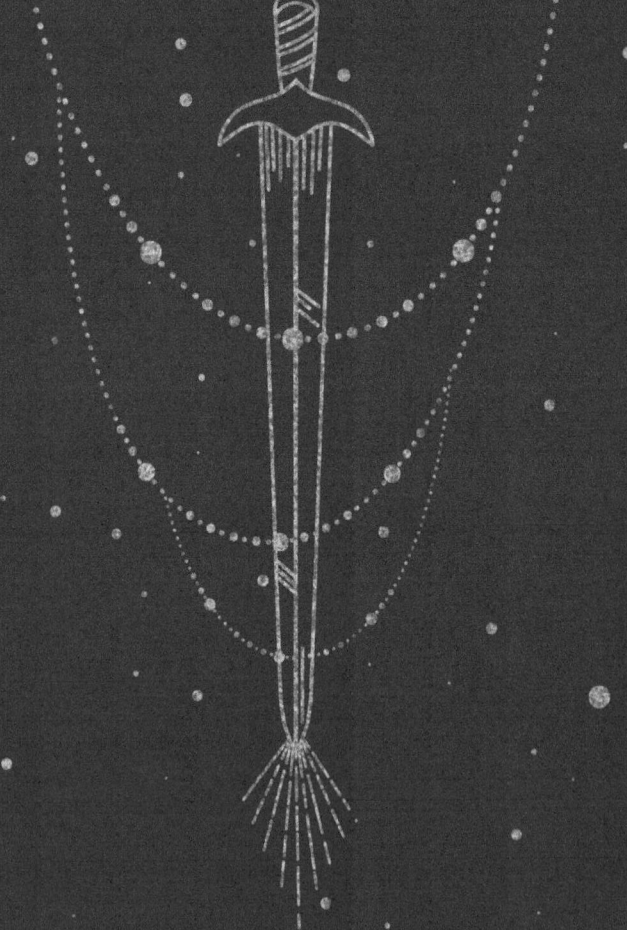

11

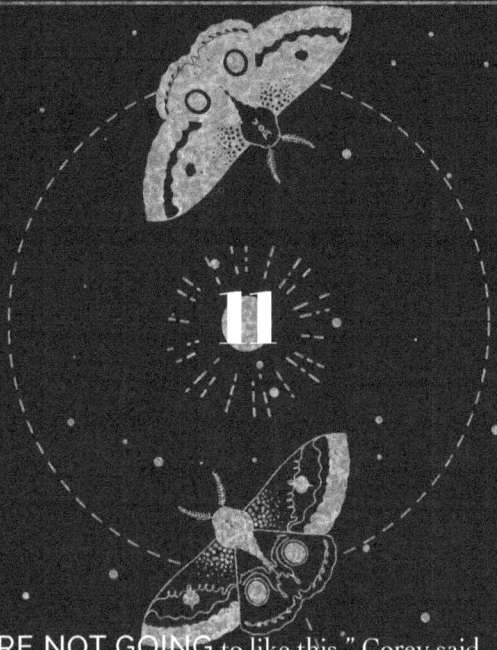

"YOU'RE NOT GOING to like this," Corey said.

"Yes, you've said that. Fifty fucking times since we got in the car." Sage ran a hand down their face and looked up at the house Corey had brought them to. It didn't fit with Eventide, especially this neighborhood. Where most of the residences were either well-kept historical townhouses or newly built apartments, this one was something entirely different. It was certainly old as dirt—though Sage hesitated to use the word *historical*—but it was also decrepit. The tall, crooked townhouse had a wraparound front porch with several missing boards, and gray siding that once might have been green but had gone sun faded, and no one had bothered to paint or replace it.

"I know, I just—"

"Are you going to tell me *why* I'm not going to like this?" Sage narrowed their eyes on the house through the windshield, pushing their glasses further up on their nose.

Corey didn't answer, and when Sage turned to look at her, she couldn't meet their eyes either.

"Fine." They opened the door and before their foot even

touched the ground outside the car, the smell of sulfur hit them in the face. They stilled, their foot hovering above the ground, and turned to fix Corey with a *look*. "Is the reason I'm not going to like this because your contact is a demon, by any chance?"

"Demons need work too, Sage." Corey huffed, slamming the door behind her.

"They also have a tendency to get people in more trouble than they get them out of."

"Don't be racist, Sage."

Sage's eye twitched. They were sure Corey was using their name that way to be purposefully annoying. "I don't think it's racist to be cautious of a creature that's literally from the dark dimensions and likes to make deals with people so it can drag them back to—"

"Are you two just going to stand in front of my house arguing? Or are you coming in?" A woman stood on the front step, her burgundy hair tied in a messy fishtail braid that hung over her shoulder, a pair of cat-eye glasses perched on her nose, and a navy turtleneck clinging to her full frame in spite of the sticky heat.

"Give us a minute, Lucy," Corey called.

"Fine. Fuck me, I guess." Lucy turned back toward the door, stepping on the places where there were missing boards in the porch but not falling through. As if she wasn't sure how gravity worked. Maybe she'd forgotten about it entirely. Or maybe she didn't care. "Tea's gonna go cold."

"It's fine, Luce." Corey rolled her eyes and looked back to Sage, a mousy brown brow raised. "We'll meet you inside."

"Maybe it's fine for *you*." Lucy huffed one more time then slammed the door behind herself.

"A demon? Really? *This* is your solution?" Sage crossed

their arms over their chest and refused to take another step toward the house.

Now that they knew who lived there, they could almost feel the negative energy clogging the air, making the few feet in front of the house—which included the curb they were parked on—about ten degrees colder than it ought to be with summer well on its way. Now that they were looking, they noticed how the air in front of it seemed to ripple with magic—a spell to keep people from looking too closely, they were sure. Because if people looked, they'd see the way the house in the center of the street, the one Lucy had come out of, didn't fit with the others. And if they noticed that, they might try to do something about it.

"Demons have more magic than you and me combined. And Lucy has been around the block. She knows her shit." Corey had crossed her arms over her chest too, mirroring Sage's posture, although they weren't sure if she was mocking them or if she was equally defensive. Defensive. Of a demon. What a day to be alive. Sort of.

"They also have this really ugly tendency to—I don't know—drag people's souls to the darker dimensions, like I was trying to say before, where they're never seen or heard from again." Usually, the body was left alive when they did that, but that wasn't the point in this discussion. The point was demons were fucking trouble. "And you can't trust them. They always have their own agenda."

"Oh, you mean like literally everyone else in this city?" Corey snapped back.

When Sage continued to glare at the house, refusing to move a single muscle, Corey sighed. Her arms dropped from where they were over her chest so she could run her fingers through her hair and slump forward. "Look, I know this isn't ideal—"

"That's putting it fucking lightly." Sage scoffed.

"Fair." Corey nodded. "But hear me out. Lucy does good work. And she's not looking to go back to the dark dimensions anytime soon, much less drag someone there. All she's going to ask from you is cash. Probably a lot of cash, but still, just cash."

Sage tilted their head so they could look at her finally, one white brow raised. "Just cash?"

"That's what she said, isn't it?"

Sage's gaze snapped back to the front porch, but Lucy wasn't standing where she had been a moment ago. She'd somehow exited her house and gotten to the end of the walk without Sage even noticing, and she now stood not more than an arm's length from them. She leaned closer, again ignoring gravity as she pressed all her weight into her toes and didn't stumble forward like a normal person might.

"Only cash," Lucy assured, her nose practically touching Sage's. Sage could smell the sulfur in her hair, the brimstone lingering on her skin. Sage wondered how long she'd been topside if she still smelled like that. Did it linger forever? Or would it eventually fade?

"Fine." Sage huffed.

"So have we got a deal?" Lucy stuck out her hand and the wind picked up around them, making Sage's hair whip against their face. It didn't seem to touch Lucy, who just stood there with her hand outstretched like this was the most normal thing in the world. Her mismatched eyes—one green, one almost black in how dark it was—glowed.

"Lucy," Corey said, her tone a warning.

"Right." Lucy dropped her hand and the wind died away, her eyes ceasing their glowing. "Sorry. Old habits and all that." She waved off Corey's glare then turned on her heel and started back up the walk. "Like I said, come along. Tea's going cold."

"Do you make tea for all of your clients?" Sage followed

her, although at a much more sedate pace. They were in no hurry to step inside whatever hellscape Lucy lived in.

"Only the ones who're mobster royalty." Lucy looked over her shoulder for a moment and winked, then she stepped toward the door.

Sage and Corey had to take more care crossing the porch. For all Lucy seemed to step over thin air as if there were some sort of invisible barrier to hold her up, the porch was very much rotting, and twice Sage felt the boards give under their weight more than they'd like.

"Did you tell her who I was?" Sage muttered to Corey as they stepped over the threshold into a surprisingly tidy foyer.

"Oh please, *everyone* knows who you are," Lucy said. Although she'd disappeared into another room, Sage could still hear her voice perfectly as if she were standing right next to them. Likely because, like with gravity, the laws of sound didn't apply to her. "Heir to Nocturna. Only child of the late Seamus Nocturna. You died, didn't you?"

"I got better." Sage huffed, rubbing their arms as they followed Corey through to a sitting room where Lucy was setting out a shining silver tea tray on a white coffee table that looked antique.

"So I see." Lucy settled back into her seat on the flower-printed settee and took a sip from her teacup, not waiting for them to take their own. She seemed to recognize the unease that had stiffened Sage's shoulders. "Oh, don't you fret, Heir to Nocturna. I'm not going to tell anyone. I stay out of gang politics. They draw too much attention, and I don't particularly want anyone to notice I'm hanging around here if I can help it. They might try to exorcise me, and that is *so* fucking annoying. Not to mention messy."

Sage relaxed a little, their fingers loosening where

they'd been clenching their teacup perhaps a bit too tight. They allowed themself a slow sip, if only for show.

"Seamus means *supplanter*, did you know?" Lucy asked after a moment, as if she were continuing a train of thought the other two hadn't been privy to. "Curious your father chose that name for himself before he married your mother, killed her, and took her place as head of the family."

Sage choked on their mouth full of tea and almost spit it all over the floral rug at their feet. "Excuse me?"

Lucy met their eyes with a smile so sharp it could cut. She had been looking for a reaction, and she'd gotten it. Sage was going to have to ask Corey how they knew each other once they were back at the car. And how long Lucy had been living in Eventide for her to know about Sage's father like that.

"I'm not here to talk about my father," Sage said after a moment, clearing their throat and leaning forward to replace their cup on the tray. If Lucy was going to do things just to see how off balance she could make Sage, it was better they not do a spit take in the middle of her living room.

"No. You're here to ask a favor from a demon." Lucy wiggled her burgundy brows, her nose scrunching in delight. "So, what'll it be? Curse your ex? The name of the fae who killed you?" She leaned forward enough that it looked like her tea might spill, but for some reason it remained perfectly still in the cup. "Ooooh, or do you want me to turn Corey into a goat? I'll do that one for free."

"Fuck you, Lucy," Corey piped up from where she'd been quiet during this whole exchange in the plush armchair opposite the one Sage was in. They noted that she hadn't picked up a cup of tea; she was just sitting slumped in the chair, glaring at them.

"You wish, darling." Lucy winked then returned her

attention to Sage, leaning impossibly closer, enough that it seemed like her neck was stretching so she could put her face too close to Sage's again. "So, what'll it be?"

"I need help with my glamour," they said, trying to put as much space between themself and Lucy as they could with the chair in the way. They didn't get far, and the way Lucy seemed to have no respect at all for physics made Sage uncomfortable. Resisting the urge to pull their knees up to their chest to have a barrier between them, they said, "It hasn't been right since I died."

"Well, of course it hasn't." Lucy scoffed and rolled her eyes, but she eased off, her back hitting the sofa with a soft *oof*. "You died. That tends to screw up the natural energy pathways required for magic use. Let me guess, you also can't access your shifter abilities."

"I'm not completely block—" They bit their lip and sighed. What was the point in lying? Lucy already knew too much. If she wanted to hurt them, she could have the moment they walked through the door. "I can use the enhanced senses sometimes, but I've been unable to shift fully since. That's correct."

"Right." Lucy nodded, setting her teacup on the narrow arm of the settee. It wobbled for a moment as if it might fall off, but she turned to glare at it and it seemed to think better of it. "So, I can give you something to help create a better glamour. But it's not going to solve the source of the problem."

"I understand." It wasn't the best news. Although Sage hadn't come here searching for answers, it was always a bit of a letdown to find they wouldn't be getting them.

"What do you recommend to reopen the pathways?" Corey asked. Sage wasn't sure when, but she'd unfolded herself, leaning on her elbows to fix Lucy with a curious look.

"Months and months of practice and grueling hard work, usually. I can provide you with a training plan for that. But sometimes, if you're lucky, these things right themselves. Magic wants to be used, after all." Lucy shrugged. "Trauma can do it too."

"Is there anything guaranteed that can speed up the process?" Sage frowned. They weren't likely to get lucky, given past experience. Not that they wouldn't do the hard work, but if there was a quick ticket to getting back all that they'd lost? If there was a way to put them back at full power, especially when they were living in Eventide? They'd take it. "Other than more trauma." They already had enough to take a therapist a century to unpack.

"There is. Of course there is!" Lucy's smile grew even wider, seeming to eat up her whole face with teeth and stretched lips, like a python about to unhinge its jaw. "But it'll be spendy."

"*How* . . . spendy . . . exactly?" Curling their shoulders inward to make themself as small a target as possible, Sage fixed their gaze just over Lucy's shoulder so they didn't have to look at that smile any longer than necessary.

"Something more than cash." The words slithered through the air, crawling along Sage's skin, although they swore they hadn't seen her lips move out of the corner of their eye.

"We'll just take the trinket to make the glamour work better," Corey said, butting in. "Then we'll be out of your hair."

"Fine." Lucy huffed, the grin slipping into a pout, but when Sage glanced back, she looked more like an everyday human or folk again. "You always take all the fun out of everything, Corwin."

Corey shrugged. "Give them the amulet or whatever so we can get the fuck out of here."

Rolling her eyes, Lucy reached into what must have been a small pocket dimension, her hand and wrist disappearing as if into a box, but in thin air. When she pulled her hand back out, she was holding a rock. A plain gray rock. Like one might find on the side of the street.

"Here." She tossed it to Sage, and it hit the rug between their outstretched hands.

"A pebble?" Corey scoffed, clearly unimpressed.

"A lucky pebble." Lucy grinned again, her eyes ablaze as if she half expected to have to argue with Corey further. "Keep it on you whenever you need a glamour, and it should limit the effects of your blocked energy. It won't solve it completely, and it's by no means a permanent solution, but it'll do the job."

"What do you mean, it won't solve it completely?" Sage turned the rock over in their hands. It was smooth like it'd been cast about by the tides, and warm where it should have been cold.

"You won't be able to completely change your appearance, not like you used to. But you can make yourself fairly unrecognizable to those looking at a glance, and most won't *want* to look much more than that. It'll also help with the issue of magical strain." Lucy leaned back again, her arms crossed in a gesture of self-satisfaction. "That'll be 3K."

"For a *rock*?" Sage asked.

"You can give it back and leave for all I care, Heir to Nocturna. If you miss your date, that's not my problem."

"Can I Venmo you?"

"Of course."

"HOW DID SHE KNOW ABOUT MY DATE?" SAGE FIDDLED with the rock while they headed back toward the bakery, their hands sweaty from the interaction.

"How does a demon know anything?" Corey tapped her fingers on the steering wheel. A nervous twitch, Sage realized. "Better not to think too hard about it."

"How did you meet her?"

"Better not to think about that either."

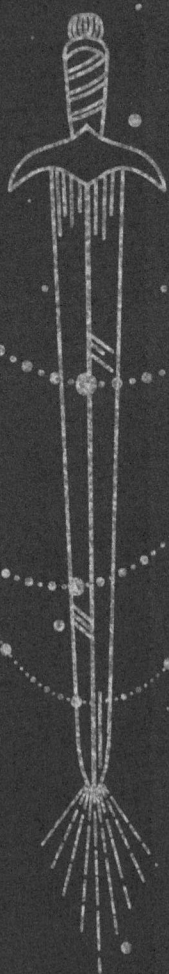

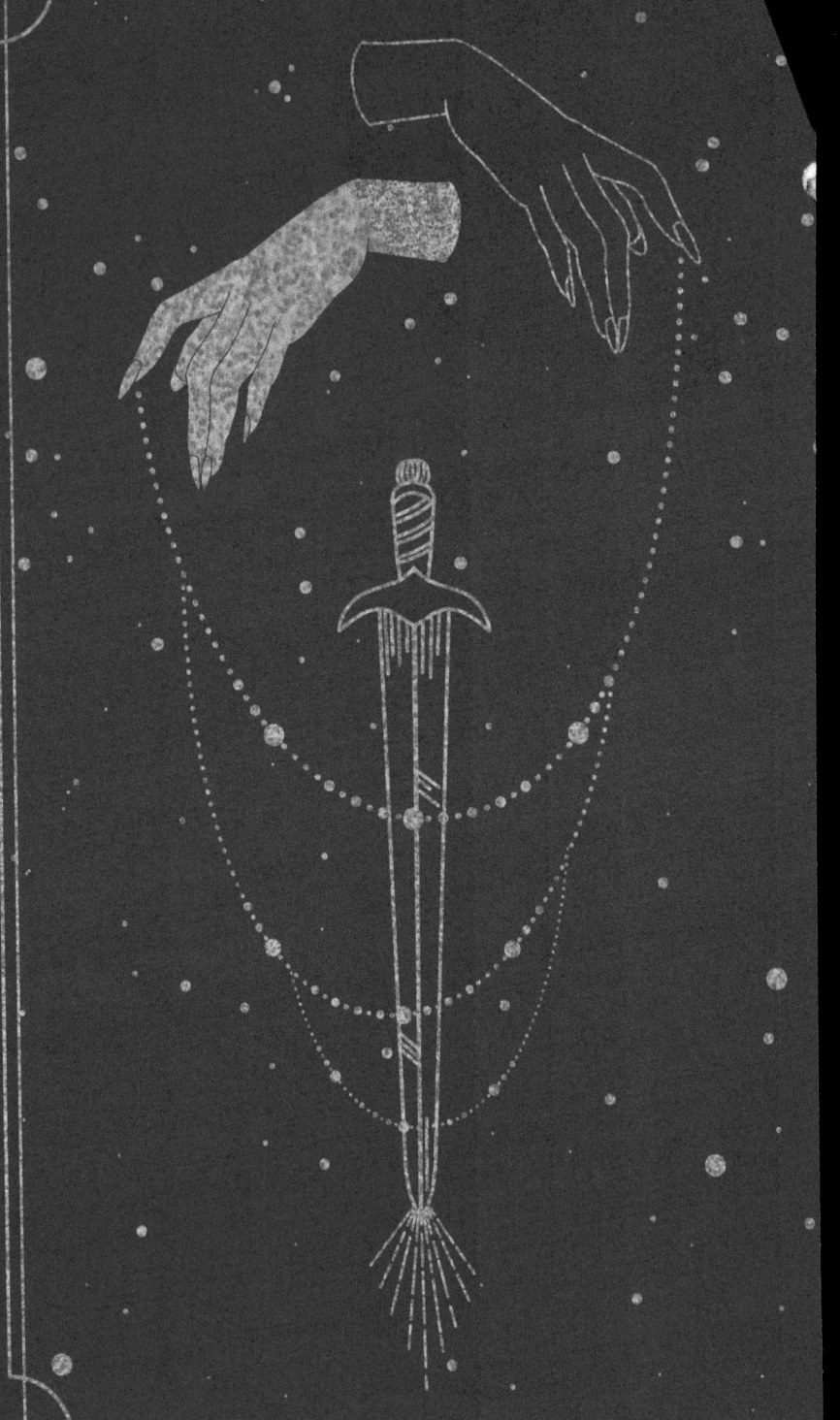

its thing. Not that she thought anyone in Eventide would be good enough to recognize her by her voice, but it paid to be careful.

"No hello?" the person on the other side asked, their voice a husky rasp that was lighter around the edges, like they were smiling.

Weird. Who smiled when they called a fixer?

"No." Corey resisted the urge to roll her eyes, realized they couldn't see her, and rolled them anyway. She'd found early on that it was best to keep her words short and clipped when she dealt with these calls. Less chance of someone recognizing speech patterns if all they got out of her was one- or two-word answers.

"Oh well, that's a shame." They sighed, and Corey thought she recognized the voice now that they'd said more than two words. She just couldn't place it with a face yet.

They fell silent as if they expected Corey to say something else, and Corey went through her mental list of all the people in the Eventide underground. If it wasn't someone in Alton's crew, and it wasn't Dam again, that counted out a few people, but there were still so many more to consider. But this had to be someone she'd spoken to. That list was fairly short. Since she'd left the scene four years ago, a lot of the higher-ups had either died or retired. Although she supposed it didn't necessarily have to be someone higher up. Maybe they were one of the grunts making the call so they could—

Shit. She knew exactly who this was. *Mox*.

"Well, anyway," Mox said, sounding uncomfortable with the long stretch of quiet that had spanned between them.

Corey wondered what she'd expected out of someone who made their money cleaning up the gangs' messes. Did she think Corey was going to be friendly? Act like a barista at Mox's favorite coffee shop? Smile and include a personal message on the invoice she sent? Corey was a fixer. She made people disappear, mostly, and usually that meant killing them. She wasn't going to put on a customer service smile.

Mox cleared her throat. "I have a job."

Corey waited again, refusing to give in to the bait of Mox trying to get her to speak more. Mox would tell her what she wanted eventually. That was something Corey had learned early on in life: If you were quiet long enough, people would fill in the blanks for you. You wouldn't even have to ask questions.

"I need someone picked up. I have their address and want them brought to me largely unharmed." Finally, Mox's tone turned businesslike. Good.

"Text the address." Corey glanced at the clock. She needed to be at the bakery to put bread in the oven by at least three, but she could probably send Sage to do that if this job ran over. Even if she couldn't, that gave her a few hours to play with. A kill order would be easier to fulfill, but she could make this work. She was sure of it.

"What are your rates for something like this?"

Corey blinked, her gaze flicking to the dark of the night. Outside the bay window, Eventide's mists hung heavy around the streetlights, making them look like lightning bugs.

"I expect half up front," she said after a moment, tapping her fingers against the shelf where her plants resided. "I'll send you a bill."

"That's fine, but I want to know how much." Mox sounded uncomfortable in a different way now, though Corey couldn't ferret out the source. Were the Faceless hurting for cash? It didn't seem like they were from what she'd seen of Mox and Mal the day before. They were both dressed to the nines. Even Mal, who was in jeans, wore some designer brand Corey couldn't have afforded in her heyday as a member of Aquarius.

"Five thousand for an extraction."

Mox hummed thoughtfully. "Is that more or less than if this was a kill?"

"More." Why were they having this discussion? Corey shouldn't have to explain her business model to a client. Either they paid for her services, or they fucked off. She didn't have time for this. "Extractions are harder."

"Right."

Corey frowned. Was Mox going to try to haggle with her over this? Her rates were nonnegotiable, and no one had even tried so far. Granted, she'd only done a few jobs, and the first had been for free just to get her name out there. But she wasn't about to give Mox some kind of discount, even if she was pretty. She waited in another long silence. There seemed to be a lot of those, but maybe Mox was used to the push-pull of conversation. She expected this to be like talking to anyone else when it wasn't—it was a business transaction.

"I'll send it over along with the address. Will you send me an invoice?"

"Yes," Corey said, then she hung up, giving Mox no chance to try extending their chat any further. She sent off the invoice. A moment later, her phone dinged with an address and a notification that her full fee had been paid upfront. She blinked at it, shook her head, and headed down the hall, already calling, "Sage! I've got a job!"

"Who for?" Sage asked when she opened their door to find them sitting behind their wall of monitors again.

"Does it matter? If I'm not back by three, head down to the bakery and put the loaves we left to proof into the oven."

"Sure. Sure." Sage flapped their wrist at her over their shoulder, and Corey huffed an annoyed breath before heading further down the hall to her own room so she could get her shit together.

THE ADDRESS MOX PROVIDED COREY WITH WAS TO AN apartment building in Blood Moon territory. She'd also helpfully provided a picture of a young redcap man. Dam and Flo were probably going to be pissed about Corey going into their territory and dragging one of their own back to Faceless execs. Especially so soon after she'd done a job for them. But it would be a good reminder that she didn't belong to any one gang. Her services were bought and paid for, not allegiance bound. Besides, if she did her job correctly, they wouldn't even know it had been her. The guy would just disappear.

Thankfully, the apartment building wasn't one of the new high rises at the center of Eventide, which meant the security wouldn't be as tight.

There will probably still be cameras.

And even if there weren't, it was better she utilize every trick she had to keep from being seen by this guy's neighbors.

Her breath was hot in her mask as she took the time while still across the street and out of any kind of sightlines to double-check she had everything she needed. Stunning powder. Her blades. The necklace Grammy Corwin had gifted her years ago, an innocuous looking peach colored cameo that hid heavy shielding magic. Grammy Corwin didn't know when she'd created it how handy it'd be for the technological age to come, but Corey was grateful for her foresight every day.

She stepped from the alley and glanced at what should have been her reflection in the window of a dark shop. There was nothing there. Just the slight shimmer of an invisibility spell so heavy, if they had an actual ruling magical body in Eventide, it would be illegal. Good thing they didn't. And good thing no one knew Corey had this thing either.

Although the building was older, the front door was locked. There was a pad with numbers to buzz the residents for deliveries, and Corey considered using it. But it was late enough that most people would probably sleep through it. And if they didn't, then they would remember someone buzzing them and waking them up. Not a chance she could take. She'd have to wait for someone to come home from their red-eye shift or leave for their morning shift. Not ideal, but Eventide was the kind of city where that was more common than anywhere else.

She settled in to wait.

It didn't take long, thankfully. The building being an older one meant most of the people residing inside were working class folk. People who worked at bars or had to be up early to get into the office before their boss so they could get the coffee started.

Ten minutes in, and Corey was grabbing the door before it could close behind the harried looking barista with an apron in their hands and slipping inside before letting the door slam behind her. From there, it was a short trip up the stairs—because elevators usually *did* have cameras—to the fifth floor.

The address Mox provided was the first door on the right in a dark part of the hall where the lights had clearly been tampered with. A benefit to not just her, she was sure.

Her target had probably done it himself so his neighbors were less likely to notice if he came home bloody.

She pressed her hand to the door, reaching out with her magic to check for wards. Not that it would matter if they alerted her target to her entry — she'd have him knocked out before he could attack. Probably. It'd been a while since she'd used the stunner powder. But it came from a reputable source, and she wasn't anywhere near the expiration date yet.

Nothing. Huh. Is this guy stupid?

Sure, he was part of the Blood Moons, which would afford him a certain amount of protection within their territory, but not enough to not ward his home. Even she knew that, and to the outside world she was just a baker.

Whatever. If he was going to make this easy for her, she wasn't going to look a gift kelpie in the mouth.

The door opened with a creak, offering Corey a view of a room cast in total darkness aside from the limited light provided by the hallway.

Shit. Should have brought the night glasses.

Too late now. I'll just have to make do.

With a slow breath, she stepped into the abyss and shut the door behind her, determined to stand there until her eyes adjusted.

She didn't get the time for that.

Something slammed into the back of her head, making her stumble forward. Her ears rang, her vision dancing with stars as she rolled across the floor and to her feet to get away from her attacker.

"Thought you could come into my home, did you?!" the man shouted, taking another swing at her, so close she felt it pass her in the dark. Too close. How was he fucking *seeing* her? "Well, I'll be damned if you're taking me back to those fuckers!"

Someone had to have told him she was coming. Someone warned him, and he was prepared.

Corey ducked another swing and pulled a dagger from the holster at her back. She couldn't see him to use the powder, and she couldn't risk wasting it or accidentally knocking herself out. She'd have to do this the old-fashioned way.

When the next swing came her way, accompanied by more cursing, Corey sliced upward with her dagger.

He yowled in pain, and she heard him back away from her, slam against the wall beside the door, and drop whatever he was swinging at her with a dull clatter. Good. It sounded like it might have been a bottle. If she could back him into a corner, he'd be easier to subdue. She just had to make sure she didn't break her fucking ankle tripping over his furniture.

He was still cursing and spitting when she tapped carefully with her toe to find a clear path toward him. She must have cut him deep if he was struggling that much to regain his footing and attack her again. Either that, or he wasn't a fighter. Maybe he held some other position in Flo and Dam's organization. A bookie or something. The Blood Moons ran the racetrack and casinos in Eventide.

When she got closer, she noticed that he was breathing heavily. His pants were loud enough that she could hear them over the ringing in her ears that still hadn't stopped. She pulled the powder from her belt, poured a little on her palm, and blew it directly in his face.

She knew it worked when he sneezed, wheezed, slumped, then slid down the wall onto the floor.

With the target subdued, Corey let herself slump as well. When she reached up to touch the back of her head where he'd hit her, her hand came away wet. Great. She probably had a fucking concussion.

It took some time to find the light switch near the door —she'd gotten turned around in the scuffle—but once she did, she blinked against the burn of the bright LED bulbs.

The apartment was sparsely furnished, which accounted for how she hadn't hit her head a second time when rolling across the floor. And there didn't seem to be anyone else living there. There weren't even any photos around the place. Just one squat three-shelf bookcase that was more full of trinkets than books.

Well, at least she wouldn't have to feel guilty about breaking up a family.

Pulling her phone from her pocket, she hit the number Mox had called from a little over an hour ago and waited for her to pick up.

"That was fast," Mox said with a delighted laugh in her voice.

Corey rolled her eyes. "Open the portal, I'll drag him through."

"Can do!" The line clicked off, and a second later a new door appeared beside the front door, right where the target was leaning. It was old and worn, heavy wood that had aged into yellowed darkness, with a crystal knob.

Corey opened it and let the target flop onto his back on the cold warehouse floor on the other side.

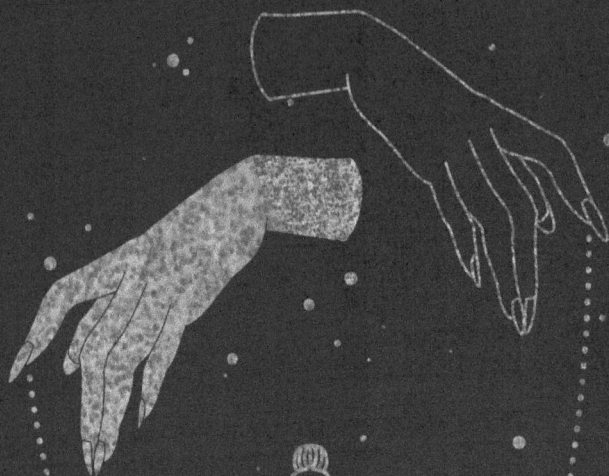

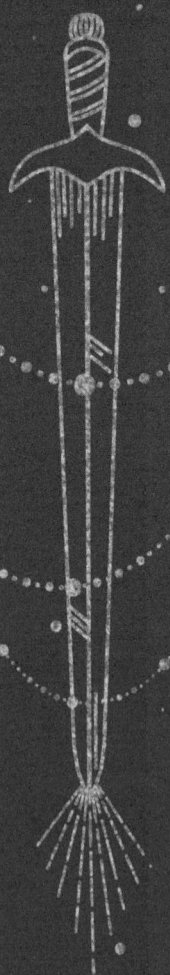

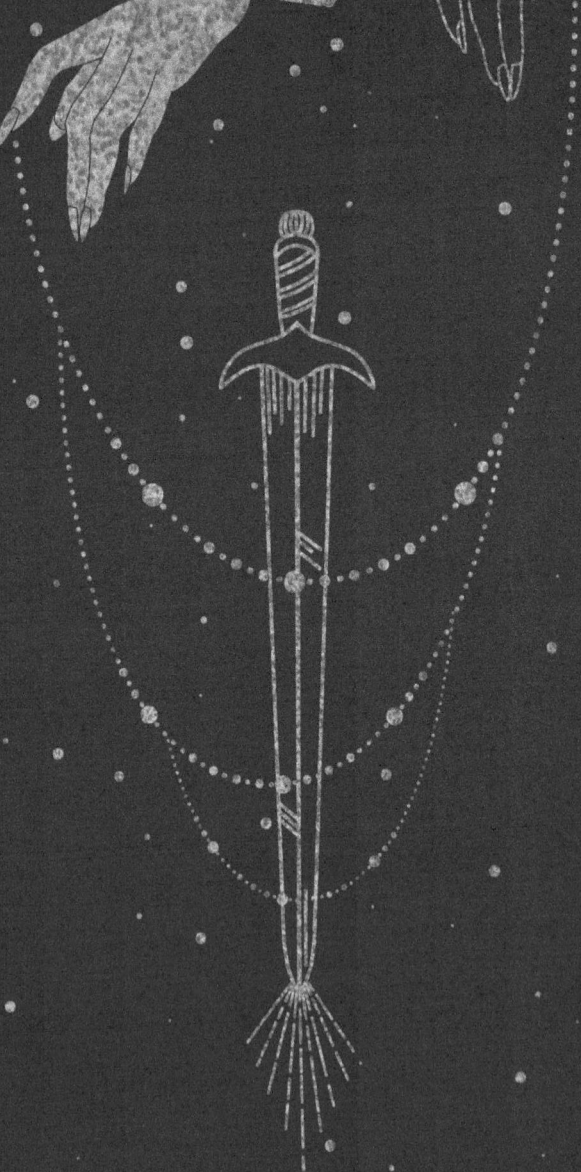

13

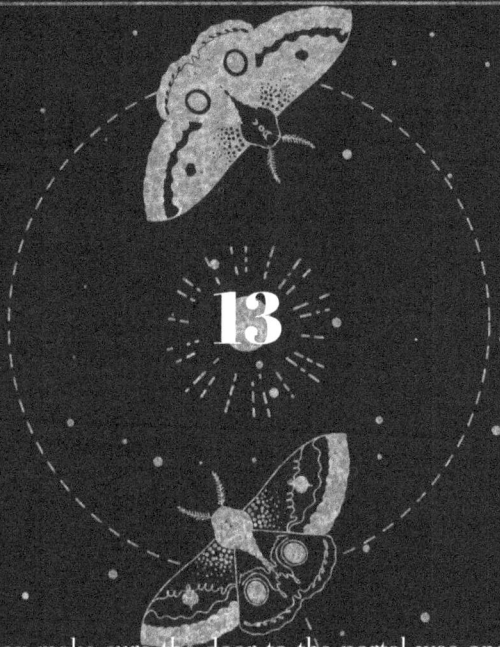

DID Mox make sure the door to the portal was one of the prettier ones available for her use in an attempt to impress the Phantom? Yes, she did.

But really, who could judge her for that?

The Phantom did good, clean work, and Mox had a bit of a crush. So sue her. She had a thing for competent people. Who *didn't*?

But then the door opened, the target slumped through onto the floor with a thud, and a person in all black stepped over him into the warehouse where Mox and Mal stood waiting for the job to finish, and Mox . . .

Her throat ran dry.

It didn't seem right for someone to look that good when they were covered head to toe in black, not an inch of skin showing apart from their forehead, eyes, and wrists. Couple that with the way the Phantom bent over and dragged the target the rest of the way through the portal, and—

Hang on. Mox recognized that ass. Where did she know that peach—

The cute little baker! The one who refused to give Mox her name!

Corey!

She was the Phantom?

Interesting. Very interesting.

"Are you going to stand there gawping or are you going to help them get him into a chair?" Mal asked, his voice soft near her ear, and whatever hope she'd had that he hadn't noticed her momentary gay crisis was out the fucking window. Wonderful. Perfect.

When she focused again, she saw the Phantom standing there with her hands on her hips, watching them expectantly. Mox wondered if she'd said anything, or if she had decided to use her body language. The Phantom's voice was different over the phone, clearly sent through a modulator to keep people from recognizing her.

"Right." Mox nodded and moved to help the Phantom lift the target by his shoulders then drop him into a chair. A moment later, bands made of shadow slithered out of the darkness and secured him there. "I guess that's it then." Mox grinned, clapping her hands as if to remove dust from them.

The Phantom nodded.

"You've been paid in full?" Mal stepped closer to them.

The Phantom turned to meet him and nodded again.

Aside from the mask, she'd slipped on a glamour. Gone was the soft-brown-to-pale-blue ombre, replaced with navy-blue hair that caught the light. Her eyes were a darker shade of hazel, less warm, flatter.

Something glistened on the back of her head, and Mox took a step closer, squinting. Blood. There was blood on the back of the Phantom's head. As if someone had struck her! Mox's gut twisted with concern.

"Are you okay?" Mox took another involuntary step forward, her hand outstretched as if to reach for the wound.

The Phantom's head jerked around, her eyes narrowing, and Mox froze where she stood, her hand still reaching for the wound as if she could do something about it. She couldn't. She had no healing magic, no medical knowledge, nothing. All she could do was press at the wound and see if it made the Phantom wince.

"You're hurt."

Mal frowned at Mox but pushed past her to lean down and inspect their target, leaving Mox to her inability to act like a normal person when faced with someone she found attractive. Traitor.

The Phantom shrugged.

This whole one-sided conversation thing was on the verge of becoming annoying already. But there wasn't much Mox could do about it. She couldn't make the Phantom talk to her. Not when she so clearly wanted to remain anonymous. Why, though? What was she afraid of? The underworld of Eventide was dangerous, sure. But as far as Mox had seen, the Phantom's skills were beyond anything any other cleaner had ever shown. She could take care of herself.

"You should let me look at that," Mox insisted.

The Phantom shook her head and took a step back, keeping a careful distance from Mox's searching hands.

"Did he do that to you?" Rage danced along Mox's nerves, making her warm all over. There was no other explanation for the fresh wound. She'd make him pay for it. Not that they hadn't planned to torture him already, but Mox was sure Mal wouldn't be angry with her if she ensured their current hostage would never make it back to his shitty apartment.

The Phantom's eyes jerked from Mox to the man

strapped to the chair over her shoulder, then back. Seeming unsure how she was meant to answer that.

"He won't hurt you again," Mox swore, and although she couldn't see Mal from where she was standing anymore, she could almost feel him still at the promise in her words. His gaze burned at the back of her neck, heating the skin until it was red. Or maybe she was blushing. Who was to say.

The Phantom raised one cobalt blue eyebrow in question, then rolled her eyes as if to say that she didn't need Mox's protection. Which was fair, she didn't. But that didn't mean Mox wasn't going to offer it.

"We've got work to do, Mox," Mal said from behind her, breaking the moment between them. Mox almost wished he hadn't come with her. She could have tortured the information they needed out of their target. She didn't need her brother to oversee her. But he'd insisted, probably so he could make sure she didn't make an ass of herself in front of the Phantom.

Joke's on him, I did that anyway.

"Right." Mox cleared her throat, finally dropping the hand she'd had extended as if to pull the Phantom in close and shield her from their world. It was foolish to think she could, or even *should*, do such a thing. Even more foolish to think this scrappy little woman would let her when the Phantom had been unwilling to so much as give Mox her name.

The Phantom stood up straighter too, and Mox couldn't be sure, but it looked like her jaw might be clenched as if to keep herself from speaking.

Mox forced herself to relax, to breathe. Fuck, she was off her game. Why was she so off her game? She never had this much trouble talking to women. The teasing and flirting she utilized to get women into bed had always come naturally to her. But now . . .

She shook herself internally. "Well, in the meantime, why don't I give you a lift home?" Mox asked, stepping away from the spotlight where they'd tied up their prisoner toward one of the cement block walls at the back of the warehouse.

The Phantom followed on silent feet, but when they stopped in front of the back wall and Mox turned to look at her again, her cobalt brows were both raised in question.

"You can't expect me to let someone as pretty as you walk all the way home." Mox scoffed, leaning forward on her toes to press into the Phantom's space, one of her more charming smiles curling the corners of her lips. "Can you?"

The Phantom rolled her eyes, her throat working as if she were swallowing a laugh, but she made no noise.

Infuriating. Mox could tell her, of course, that she knew who she was. That there was no point in this charade. But she didn't particularly want to find out what happened to people who knew the Phantom's identity. And besides, this little game of cat and mouse could be fun.

Already, Mox's heart kicked up at the idea of hiring the Phantom for more and more jobs. Seeing how long it would take before she could get the surly baker to come clean about who she was. Or to snap at her in a way that would expose her identity. Or to find Mox as hopelessly charming as everyone else did. Whichever came first, she wasn't picky.

"So, where am I sending you?" With her freshly manicured nails tapping against the cement, she turned back to the Phantom and offered her a charming smile. "Home?"

The Phantom narrowed her eyes again, likely in a scowl,

as if this were a trick question. It was, of course, but Mox wasn't going to back down from it. She waited, her nails continuing to tap against the bricks in a soft beat. Instead of answering, the Phantom pulled a phone from her pocket, typed something on it, and held it out for Mox to see.

An address on the notes app. It wasn't anywhere near the bakery, but Mox would bet her last dollar that it also wasn't the Phantom's home address. She wasn't stupid.

A friend's place, maybe?

No. She wasn't that careless. If Mox looked up the address, she was sure it would lead her nowhere at all. Probably to someplace abandoned.

But it was still in Faceless territory. Curious. So maybe, just maybe, that's where the Phantom lived. Mox would find out.

"Right. Can do." Mox gave her a salute then turned back to the wall. Her magic warmed her from the inside out, making sweat trickle down her neck in a near blistering way. It didn't usually affect her so intensely. She was meant to be more resistant to the flames of a will-o'-wisp, and her lack of resistance wasn't worth thinking of at the moment. Not when there were other things to worry about.

It took more energy to build a door and the pathway beyond it than to use a preexisting door, and Mox staggered under the draw of it. She was practiced in this kind of magic, got better at it every time she did it, but it still took a lot out of her. Even after all the things she'd done to ensure she was more powerful, on the level with her brother.

A narrow oak door with an even narrower window over the knob appeared on the wall when she was finished. It was modern, not as pretty as the other door she'd created, but it would get the Phantom where she wanted to go.

"Ladies first," Mox said with a deep bow, her lips twitching into a smirk.

The Phantom rolled her eyes and stepped through the door. There was a moment when she looked back through the opening to eye Mox closely, as if trying to better understand her. Their gazes connected. Warm, honey hazel met dark brown as the Phantom's glamour slipped slightly, and something seemed to shift between them. Then it passed, and the door swung shut behind the Phantom.

With a pop, the door disappeared, and Mox was left blinking at the dark wall, her heart stuttering in her chest. What the fuck *was* that?

"Mox," Mal called from deeper in the warehouse. "Get the fuck over here. He's waking up."

"He hurt her."

Mal didn't say anything, but when he looked at her, Mox could see understanding in his eyes. He wasn't going to ask why it mattered. He wasn't going to point out that Mox didn't know the Phantom from a hole in the wall. He knew, better than anyone, what it was to like someone from a distance. And shit, Mox really didn't want to have that in common with her twin brother along with all the other shit they shared. Not when she had told him to not get so caught up in his pining that he missed what was right in front of him not even twenty-four hours ago.

"My. How the tables have turned," Mal muttered.

"Shut up." Mox huffed a laugh, her shoulders slumping forward. "Not in front of the hostage."

"Hmmm . . . Later then." Mal's grin turned sharp as they both directed their attention to the redcap muttering to himself as he came to.

"Wakey wakey," Mox sing-songed, kicking the leg of the chair so it jolted its occupant, and their hostage jerked awake with a grunt. "All right, Percival, you're going to tell us everything we want to know."

"Or we're going to make this hurt."

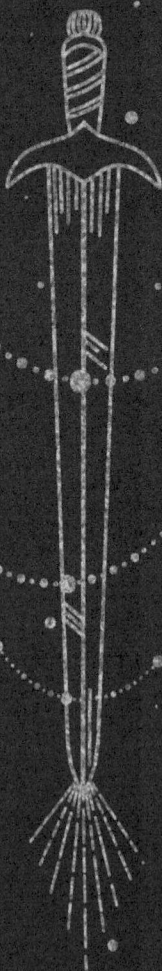

14

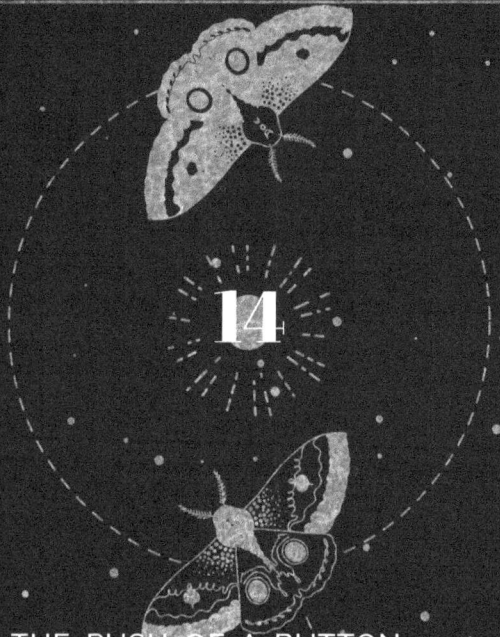

WITH THE PUSH OF A BUTTON, music started. Some annoying-ass song from a kids show or a theme park that Mal had never seen or visited. He hadn't had time to be a child when he was one, and some twisted part of him thought it justice that he reframed the memories of those who did into something horrifying.

"Oh. He's in a mood," Mox cooed, bending over so she could meet their target's eyes.

Percival Rake, from what they'd been able to find in the scant hours since Guin had given them his information, was an accountant for the Blood Moons. One of a handful. He largely worked at the tracks, and he barely ever got his hands dirty. That didn't make him a good person, however, as Mal had learned early on. Just because no blood stained his scent the way it clung to Mal and Mox, thick and metallic, didn't mean he didn't have it on his hands, metaphorically.

Percival Rake had been the driving force in not one, but five expansion projects for the Blood Moon gambling empire that led to people being displaced. And when those people stood their ground? When they refused to be pushed from their homes? Things got violent. And Percival Rake had no qualms about burying someone under the cement slab the Blood Moons used to build their newest casino.

Not that Mal had any room to judge as far as having bloody hands went. But Mal didn't get civilians involved when he could help it, and the Faceless empire didn't require pushing people from their homes. When they wanted to build a new portal to the Night Market, they looked for a place left abandoned by the humans and linked it to the liminal space that was the Night Market. As far as the Faceless Few were concerned, they didn't even need territory in Eventide, but they had it just the same.

"Shall we begin?" Mal asked, tapping his fingers against the glass of his phone where it sat on the wheelie tray table they'd set their tools on.

Percival was fully awake now, his muscles jumping and twitching to the sound of Mal's neatly manicured nails tapping against metal. He and Mox had gone with blood red polish tonight, if only to hide the evidence of what they were up to from Chuckles once they got home. Not that she didn't know, of course. She'd been a member of the family —by virtue of her relation to execs—for years now. She knew what the twins did for a living.

"You really don't have to do this." Percival shook so hard, the chair rattled beneath him. Mal approved of the fear in the redcap's voice. There should be fear there. As violent and vicious as a redcap could be, they had nothing on the trail of blood and viscera Mal's rise to power had left.

"Oh, but I think we do." Mal shrugged. "Don't you think so, Mox?"

"Definitely." There was a smile in Mox's voice, a sharp, toothy one that could rend anyone who stood in her way to pieces. It was not new, she relished the kill as much as he did sometimes, but there was something different about it this time. Something that reeked of the need for vengeance Mal had smelled on himself for the past four years. "Where would you like to start?"

"I'll tell you what you want to know. I swear I will. Just ask me. Just ask." Percival's voice trembled around the words, his head jerking from side to side as he fixed a pleading gaze on first Mox then Mal. "Just ask."

Mal sighed. He hated when they begged. Hated when they tried to make him feel like he was the one in the wrong here. He wasn't, not to his mind. The Blood Moons had something he wanted, and he was going to get it. So what if that meant getting his fresh suit a little bloody.

"That's not the way this game works," Mox said, and Mal heard the soft *shink* of a metal tool being dragged across the cart's top. He wondered where she'd start.

"If you want to get out of this alive," Mal offered. He knew Percival Rake would leave this warehouse in pieces so small, even Percival's nearest and dearest would struggle to identify them. But it was better if Percival didn't know that as well. People tended to be less likely to talk when they knew they were going to die anyway, in Mal's experience. Yes, a person would tell them anything to get the pain to stop, but if it was the truth or death? Well.

"A-alive?" Percival stuttered. His eyes had gone wide, and a note of hope lingered around the edges of the question.

"Yes. Alive." Mal cut a glance to his sister, and she shifted as if confused. "We'll even give you a one-way ticket out of here," Mal continued, still looking at Mox. That clicked, and she nodded her understanding. It was funny the way they had developed shortcuts between themselves, ways to say what they meant without saying anything at all.

"But first, Mox here is going to rip out your index fingernail on your right hand."

Mox's grin twisted to something more sinister, curling up her cheeks like the fucking Grinch in the animated movie. "So specific," Mox teased as she stepped over to Percival, the pliers held aloft in steady hands.

Specifics did two things. They brought fear. The expectation of pain was a powerful force, more powerful than the pain itself. They also brought hope. Hope that after one nail was removed, no more would happen. Hope that the pain would end.

"You really don't—" The words were eaten up by a garbled scream as Mox ripped the nail from the cuticle.

This kind of wound, Mal had learned, didn't gush the way a knife wound would. The pain was intense, yes, but the blood loss not so much that they had to be concerned with their current target passing out right away. He might get dizzy. But he would stay conscious. Plus it would linger, throbbing for hours afterward.

"Now," Mal said when Percival had finally stopped screaming. Tears streamed down his cheeks, and he sniffled loudly as if trying to keep the snot from going into his mouth. No scent of urine yet, so they were still at a good place. "We want to know why the Blood Moons are flush all the sudden."

"F-flush?" Percival's eyes bounced from Mox to Mal, down to the pliers, then back up to Mal.

"Flush," Mox repeated. "They've come into more money than usual, and they're not afraid to show it off." She tapped the pliers against the metal arm of the chair, and Percival jolted at the sound.

"So where did the extra money come from?" Mal had decided not to jump straight into asking if the Blood Moons were hiding Bentley. He wanted to see what else they could get out of Percival before he became desperate enough to tell them *anything*. Plus, there was the slim chance that Percival didn't know. Following the money, at least at the start, was more likely to get them what they wanted. "Mox, the middle finger."

"Yes, sir," Mox crowed cheerfully and grabbed onto the next nail, ripping it out quickly like pulling off a Band-Aid.

Percival screamed, the sound high-pitched and piercing, cutting through the low drone of the music in the background.

"Like I said," Mal tried again, "why have the Blood Moons suddenly come into money?"

"A deal. A deal." Percival panted, trying to curl his fingers inward away from Mox and her seeking pliers. "They made a deal with Aquarius."

"What sort of deal?" Mal frowned. The idea of the Aquarius making deals with Unseelie organizations was unsettling at best, worrisome at worst, but most of all it was fucking annoying. Alton liked to pretend he was too good for something like that, but Mal knew better.

"They've been selling off shares at the new casino." A wince left Percival as Mox tapped the pliers against the top of his hand, a reminder not to lie, not to fuck with them. "Or well, Dam has been. Behind Flo's back."

"Why?"

"Why else?" Percival barked a laugh. "They're a greedy son of a bitch. They're tired of Flo taking most of the pie and want a bigger slice. Alton made them an offer they couldn't refuse. Take your pick!"

"And what does Alton get out of this?"

"Money." Percival shrugged then whimpered when the movement seemed to jostle the sluggishly bleeding wounds. "Buying in means he gets a cut of the profits."

"And Dam doesn't think Flo will notice?" Mox snorted,

likely thinking the exact same thing as Mal. Flo probably already knew, she just hadn't decided what she was going to do about it yet.

"Dam has been paying off the accountants to hide it."

This wasn't the answer Mal was looking for, but he could use it. He wasn't sure how yet, but he'd think of some way to hold this over both Dam's and Alton's heads. "So what is Alton using the money for?"

"I don't know." Percival's voice shook again, the fear returning.

"How much is he making regularly?"

"I don't know." The words trembled out of him, and he tried to slump further in the chair, but the shadows held him tight.

"Mox, the ring finger."

Mox's dark chuckle was almost entirely drowned out by a wail from Percival and his ensuing panted breaths. A thin sheen of sweat had settled onto his skin, making him shimmer slightly in the warm light above them.

"Please. Please. No more. I don't know, I swear I don't know. If I knew, I'd tell you. Please," Percival begged.

Mal rolled his eyes. "Don't be such a baby, they're just fingernails. They grow back."

"Are we almost done here?" Mox looked down at her phone held in her free hand and frowned at the time. "We need to get home."

"Just about, I think. What time is it?"

"4:56."

Mal nodded. They'd get home in enough time to make a big breakfast for Chuckles before she had to be off to school. Which would make for a good wind down after this little adventure.

"Last question." Mal moved back to the tray and turned

off the music, his fingers idling for a moment over the device.

Percival slumped in relief, his eyes drooping. It probably wouldn't have been long before he lost consciousness anyway, so better to get this over with now.

"Are the Blood Moons hiding Bentley Nocturna?" Mal didn't bother looking up from his phone, even though he wasn't doing anything on it, his tone disinterested. Not that it mattered much. Percival wouldn't be telling anyone about this conversation. But there was some concern that if Mal let on how desperate he was for the information, Percival would hold on to it to extend his miserable life.

"Wh-what?" Percival stuttered, choking on another whimper as his eyes grew listless with pain. He wasn't going to be any good to them for much longer.

"Bentley Nocturna. The last remaining Nocturna. Is she on Blood Moon territory?"

"I—" Percival swallowed roughly, and when Mal looked at him, he found Percival's eyes narrowed as if he were trying to sort out what answer would get him out of this alive. "I don't know."

"I see." Mal frowned, picking up his phone and tucking it back into his pocket. "Mox, he's all yours. I'll see you at home."

"Wait!" Percival shouted after Mal, but he didn't care to listen. He'd gotten everything he could, and Bentley Nocturna still eluded him. "I can tell you other things! I know more!" But nothing about where to find the one person Mal most wanted to find. So what was the point?

Mal didn't respond. He moved to the door that led out into the street, Percival's screams at his back, and pulled his phone out to make a call. "Your informant was a dud. Give me something else."

Guin huffed. "I'll see what I can do. Did you get anything useful?"

"Yes, but not what I wanted."

"I don't suppose you're going to share, are you?"

"Not on your life." Then he hung up and got into the waiting car to head back to their house on the hill.

BACON SIZZLED IN THE PAN, POPPING GREASE AT MAL'S bare wrists as he looked over his shoulder to find a sleep-tousled Chuckles clomping down the stairs in her slippers and pajamas.

"Mornin'," he murmured softly, turning his attention back to the breakfast he was preparing for all of them. It was rare they got to have meals like this between Mox's and Mal's work schedules and Chuckles's school, but there were things that needed to be said, and Mal knew his family unit was *less* likely to scream at him with their mouths full.

"There's blood on your neck," Chuckles grumbled. The scrape of a chair at the island was loud in the early morning quiet. "Didn't you shower?"

"Must have missed a spot." Mal shrugged. He wasn't sure how he always got blood on himself even when he wasn't the one doing the torturing. But he never noticed, not that it mattered. The viscus red liquid seemed caked into his every pore these days.

"Where's Mox?"

"Cleanup. She'll be home shortly." He slid the last of the bacon onto a plate and turned to set it on the island in front of where Chuckles had leaned over and rested her forehead on the granite countertops.

Without looking up, she snaked a hand out to snatch a

piece of bacon. Mal swatted at her with the spatula, but she was too fast. With a little crow of victory, she stuffed the entire piece into her mouth, heedless of the fact that it was still crackling.

"Fucking gremlin," he muttered, shaking his head. "Leave some for Mox."

"Fuck Mox. She woke me up with a pan and a wooden spoon yesterday." Chuckles shrugged, unbothered, and snatched a second piece.

Mal sighed and turned back to the stove. "Sandwich or omelet?"

"Sandwich."

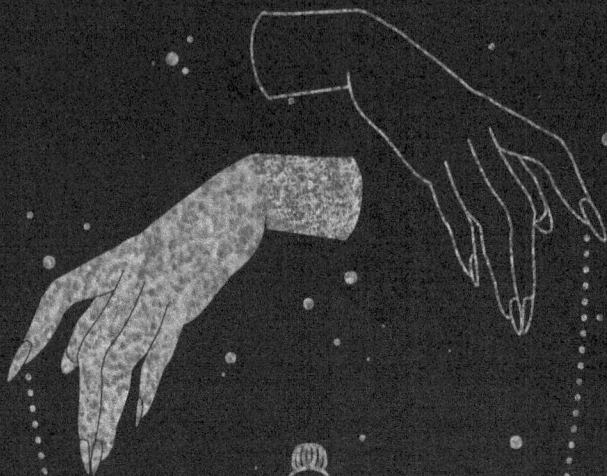

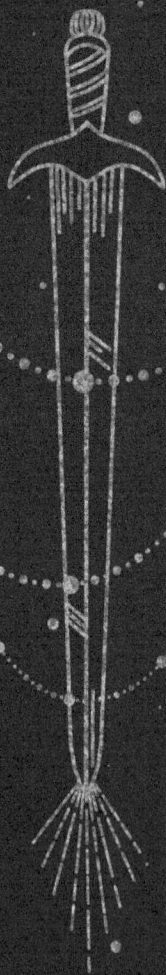

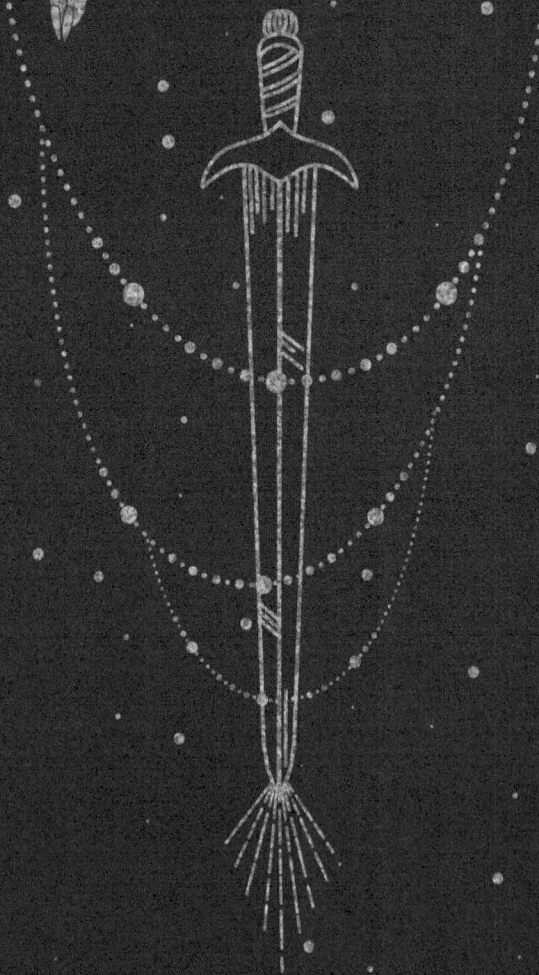

15

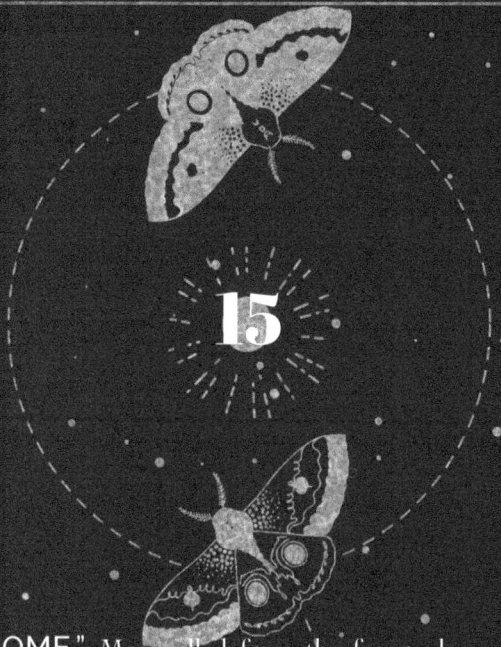

"I'M HOME," Mox called from the foyer, slamming the door behind her.

Mal winced as the sound rubbed harshly against his eardrums, making the dull headache he had by the time he got home from the warehouse give another hollow throb. Fuck. He needed sleep. It had been almost forty-eight hours at this point since he'd slept, and it was starting to take its toll.

"I'm just going to take a quick shower and—"

"Not if you want any bacon!" Chuckles shouted back, and Mal's shoulders twitched with the sound. He took a moment to breathe deeply, stretching his neck first one way then the other in an attempt to make the clenched muscles loosen. It didn't do much good. But Chuckles seemed to notice the discomfort because she murmured a quiet "Sorry."

"It's fine." Mal shook his head. "I just need to get some sleep soon."

"Don't we all." Mox huffed, dragging herself into the kitchen, her feet scuffing against the tile. Over his shoulder,

Mal could see that she'd gotten most of the blood off her hands, but the scent clung to her and the color stained her sleeves.

"I'm still not sharing the bacon." The plate scraped against the countertop as Chuckles pulled it to herself before Mox could snatch a piece of bacon.

"Fine. Be that way," Mox grumbled but didn't break her stride as she moved to Mal's side to look over his shoulder at the eggs he was cooking. "Over easy."

"You'll get what you get. Just be grateful I'm making food," he snapped, cracking another egg into the pan.

"Bitch."

"Asshole."

"Are you two going to be grumpy all morning? Cause I could take my shit and go eat in my bed while I wait for Maurice." The crunching of bacon echoed after Chuckles's words, her feet thumping against the island where they swung in the air.

"Stay," Mal ordered, pointing the spatula at her. "This is a family meeting."

"A family meeting or a *family* meeting?"

Mox pushed past Mal to get to the coffee maker, bumping him with her hip, and when he looked up at her, she was frowning slightly, a question in her eyes. He shook his head. "Do you see any other Faceless Few members here?"

"Ugh, I hate this kind of meeting." Chuckles groaned, slumping forward again. "This isn't about my C in history, is it? Because—"

"You're getting a *C* in history?!" Mal whipped around to glare at her.

Chuckles blinked at him slowly, like a cat. He was pretty sure she'd learned that from Sage before she'd come to live with them.

"If there's a C on your final report card," Mox threatened, motioning with her coffee cup, heedless of the way it made liquid slosh hot and reddening against her skin, "we're going to have to start sitting down and doing study dates with you."

"You won't, like . . . ground me? Isn't that what parents normally do?"

"One. We aren't your parents." Mox took a deep sip from her mug, hissing at the burn.

"Two. It never worked with us when we were your age." Mal shrugged, turning back to the stove. "Punishments don't do anything but make you feel like a failure."

"You're not a failure," Mox added, picking up where Mal left off. "You just need to spend a little extra time on it, and to get a little extra help."

Chuckles blinked at them, her mouth agape for a long moment. She shut it with a click and nodded firmly, her eyes glassy in the soft, warm lights of their kitchen.

Thankfully for all of them—because they were all fucking terrible with emotions—the eggs started to burn, and Mal had to jolt around to save their breakfast.

"What the fuck, Mal?" Mox hissed, starting the water in the sink for Mal to run the pan under while she pulled out another one for him to start over.

WITH PLATES FULL OF FRESH, UNBURNT EGG sandwiches, Mal, Mox, and Chuckles sat around the island on tall chairs, their feet dangling—even Mox and Mal, who were arguably taller than average.

"So," Chuckles said, stuffing a too-big bite into her

cheek so she could speak around it like the gremlin she was, "what's the meeting about?"

Mox shifted beside him, her chair creaking loudly as if she were preparing for a storm. Mal resisted the urge to roll his eyes. He didn't think it was that dramatic, but . . . Well, one never knew with teenagers. Especially teenagers like Chuckles who had practically been raised in a gang. Mal wasn't going to let her volatile nature stop him from telling her the truth. He'd learned enough about raising kids in the last four years to know that honesty was better than hiding something. So he cleared his throat, sat up straighter, and was thankful they weren't eating anything with cutlery. Luck, not foresight, was on his side.

He'd debated over and over again how to tell her this, and still, he wasn't sure the best method. He supposed he'd just have to come out and say it. Rip off the bandage.

"Sage is alive," Mox said, not giving Mal a chance to work up to it.

Mal turned to glare at his sister.

"You were taking too long." Mox shrugged, unbothered.

"What do you mean, Sage is alive?" Chuckles asked, her sandwich halfway to her mouth, her entire body completely stiff. "Sage, like . . . *my* Sage? Like the one who saved me? Sage Nocturna. That Sage?"

"Yes. That Sage." Mal swallowed, the saliva burning his raw throat the whole way down from the emotions he refused to let surface.

"How?" The word was whispered, like Chuckles was almost afraid of the answer. Like she was afraid it might hurt her. Mal could understand that fear and the hurt that went along with it. He doubted Sage had meant to leave anyone behind, but the fact was, they did. The only question that remained to Mal was— "Why?"

"We don't really know." Mal cleared his throat, sitting

up straighter, his own food forgotten and going cold on his plate. He didn't want Chuckles to think this was her fault, that Sage left because of her. He was sure that wasn't the case. Sage cared deeply for her, risked their life to protect her. There was no world in which Sage would have left Chuckles behind if there was any other choice.

"Can I see them?"

Mox shifted beside Mal, clearly uncomfortable. "After schoo—"

"No. *Now*." Chuckles slid her plate away from herself, sandwich half-eaten. "I want to see them now. I have to see —to know for myself."

Mal turned to meet Mox's mirrored expression of raised brows, wide eyes. There was worry there, more than she'd ever put to words, because she wasn't comfortable with how much she cared about Chuckles, and they all seemed to understand that. They weren't lovey dovey types. They looked after each other, they took care of one another, but they'd never been the sort to *hug*.

"I'm not sure that's such a good idea," Mox hedged.

"Where are they?" Chuckles swung down from the chair, already taking her plate to the sink, not seeming to hear Mox's protests.

"Chuckles, you have school." Mox tried to be reasonable, but Mal could see the way Chuckles set her jaw.

"Mox," Mal said, gentle, tone low. "You got some sleep last night, right?"

"Mal, that's not really—"

"There was a 'help wanted' sign in the window." It wouldn't be bad for Chuckles to have a job with summer right around the corner. It would keep her out of trouble. And if Mal could distract her from getting in the middle of Faceless business, he sure as shit would.

"But you said—"

"Mox." Mal shook his head, patting his sister's shoulder lightly. "She needs to do this." He understood that, probably more than anyone else in the world. Definitely more than Mox, who had no connection to Sage outside of Mal and Chuckles. Turning his attention back to Chuckles where she'd frozen beside the sink, her fingers so tight on the lip of her plate that her knuckles were turning white, he nodded. "They'll be wearing a glamour. I think they're in hiding."

Chuckles sucked in a breath, likely to steady her nerves. It was a lot to be faced with the knowledge that someone she thought was dead was not. It had been a lot for Mal too, and he hadn't been as close to Sage as she was. Hadn't been raised by them for three years. Arguably, she'd been with Mox and Mal for longer, but that wasn't the same. They'd taken her in when no one else in the Faceless would. It was never meant to be permanent; they didn't do it out of kindness the way Sage had. Mal did it out of obligation.

Chuckles set her plate in the sink and took a few steadying breaths. "Why are they in hiding?" Her voice shook on the next question. "Is someone still after them?"

"We don't know." Mal's words were far calmer than he felt, the rage and the fear gnawing at his belly and making him nauseous not coming through. *Sometimes it pays to be a bit of a sociopat*h. "What we do know is, you need to be careful when you go to see them. And you can't tell anyone that you have."

Chuckles practically fell forward with her nod. "I can totally do that."

"Perfect. Go get dressed. Mox will take you, and I'll call Maurice to tell him not to pick you up this morning. We'll get you a doctor's note."

Chuckles stood there for a moment longer, not moving, not blinking, just staring at him.

"Go on." Mal shooed her, and she turned on her heels to scurry toward the steps.

"You've gone soft," Mox murmured once Chuckles was out of earshot.

"Fuck off, Mox," Mal hissed as he rose from his chair and went to finish cleaning up their breakfast. "Just take her to see Sage, and don't flirt with the owner so much that she refuses to hire Chuckles for a summer job. Do you think you can manage that?"

"Do you think you can manage that?" Mox repeated, her tone high and nasally, but they both knew it was not a good imitation of Mal's voice at all. "Yeah, I think I can do that."

"Mm-hmm," Mal agreed. He didn't quite believe her, but he also knew how stubborn Chuckles could be. She'd be all right.

SHE COULDN'T DO THIS, MOX REALIZED AS SHE STOOD outside of the bakery, her hands stuffed into the pockets of her well-tailored plum suit. Chuckles had given her only enough time to clean away the last vestiges of blood from her skin, brush her teeth, and change her clothes. Not enough time to straighten her hair and make sure her cat-eye eyeliner was sharp enough to cut.

"How do I look?" Mox asked for perhaps the fifth time, running her fingers over her hair to make sure there were no fly-aways. The messy half ponytail was meant to look effortless and cool, but when she looked at her reflection in the glass, it kind of made her look like a dude from early colonialism. Fuck.

"You're fine." Chuckles brushed her fingers over her T-shirt, clearly as nervous as, if not more than, Mox.

Mox took a deep breath and turned her full attention to her thirteen-year-old charge. Chuckles needed this more than Mox did. "You look great," she said, untucking Chuckles's shirt because what was she? In her thirties? No. No French tuck for Mox's girl. "They're going to be happy to see you."

"Will they? I mean, they—"

"You were important to them, Chuckles. No matter what that brain of yours might be telling you right now." Mox tapped on Chuckles's temple lightly, making her wrinkle her nose. "Sage cared for you. The fact that they left and have had no contact for four years is in no way a reflection on you. Remember, someone tried to kill them and they almost succeeded. It was likely just to protect you."

Fuck, Mox hoped that was true. She didn't think she was equipped to help Chuckles through the heartbreak of losing someone she saw as family again. Not when Mal wasn't also in mourning.

"What if—"

"Then I'll kick their fucking ass and make them *wish* they died." Mox growled, her eyes glowing faintly with the power of a will-o'-wisp.

Chuckles stared at her, blinking, then slowly and all at once, a smile crawled across her face and she was laughing softly. "Thanks, Mox. That's what I needed."

"Uh . . . sure, kid?" Mox wasn't sure what part of that was so funny. She'd killed people for a whole lot less than upsetting her family. But it seemed like it snapped Chuckles out of her own head. "You ready?"

"Yup!"

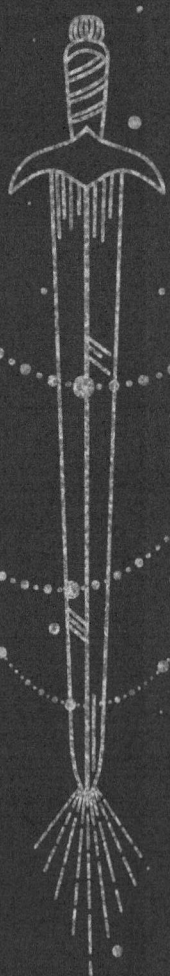

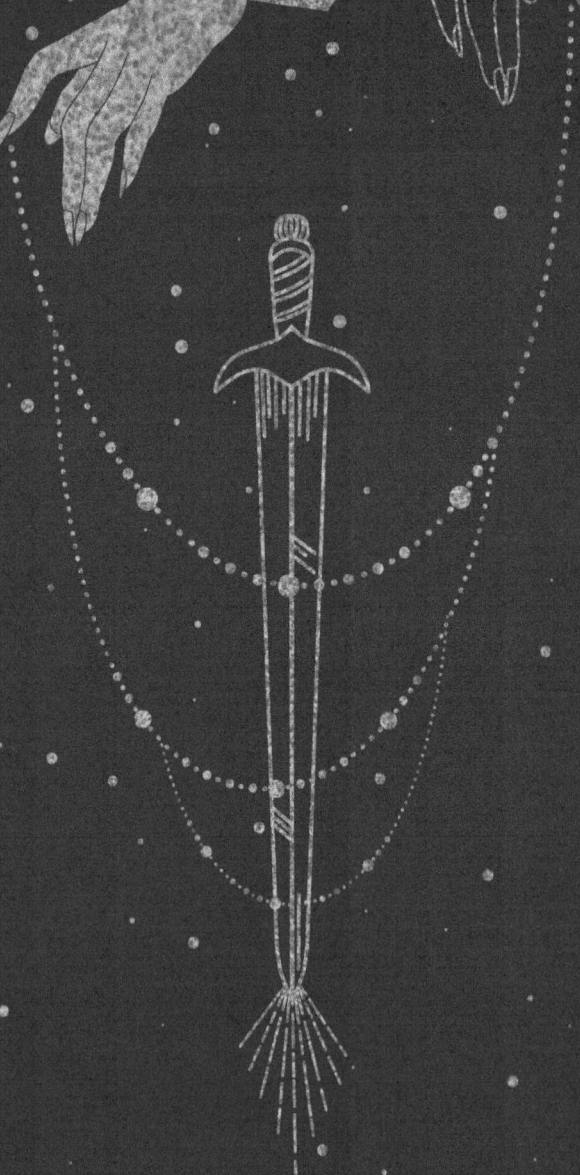

16

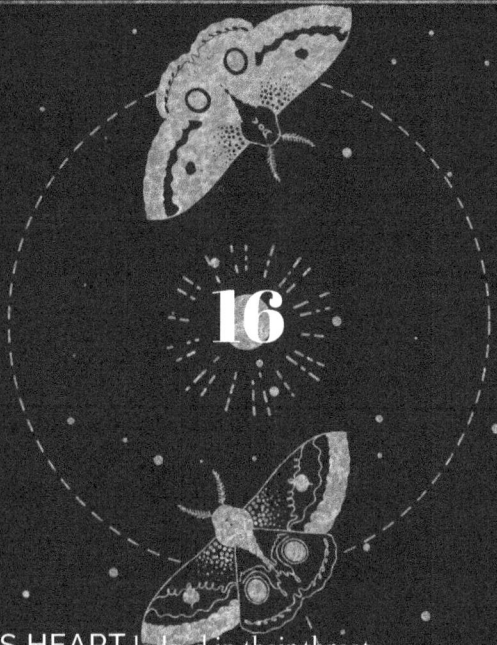

SAGE'S HEART lodged in their throat.

Chuckles was right there. Right in front of them. Her hair was longer, the wild almost carrot-orange curls trailing much further down her back than when she was seven.

Goddess, four years. She'd been nine when Sage left. Just coming into her own with her magic, just starting to understand her power as a cait sidhe. And now, there she was, a teenager.

There were so many things Sage wanted to say to her. Apologies. Explanations. Memories. They all stacked up on the back of their tongue, making it heavy and useless. Fuck. There she was. Sage's . . . Well, Sage didn't know what to call her. She wasn't their child, even for all they'd raised her for a couple of years. And she wasn't their sister. But she was . . . she was *important*.

They would have felt bad about standing there staring, but Chuckles was doing the same. Her mouth agape, her blue eyes wide. Like she was seeing a ghost. Sage supposed, to her, she was. They were glad they hadn't bothered with putting up a glamour yet, as the bakery wouldn't be open for a couple of hours. It made this moment sweeter.

Then Sage shifted, opening their arms for her, and Chuckles started across the bakery timidly at first before breaking into a run, barreling into Sage so hard they stumbled backward into the kitchen again. Chuckles squeezed them, and Sage squeezed back. Not wanting to let go. Never wanting to let go.

Goddess, it was like they had been missing a limb for the last four years, and now that it was back it tingled and ached, but it was so fucking good that Sage wouldn't trade the feeling for anything else.

"You left me," Chuckles accused, but she didn't pull away from Sage's hold. If anything, she seemed to cling tighter. Like she was afraid if she let go, even for a second, Sage would disappear again.

"I know," Sage whispered apologetically. "I know."

"I thought you were dead." The words left her on a sob, and the front of Sage's turtleneck was starting to cling to them where Chuckles's tears soaked into the fabric, her hands fisted in their suspenders.

"I know." Sage's eyes burned. They pressed their nose into the hair on top of Chuckles's head. She didn't smell like a little kid anymore. Like cheap strawberry shampoo and crayons. A pang of regret went through them, aching and hollow. Goddess, they'd missed so much.

"I was scared."

Sage squeezed tighter, probably a little too hard, but Chuckles didn't complain. "I'm sorry," they whispered into her hair. "I'm so sorry."

There was no excuse for leaving her behind. Nothing Sage could say would erase the hurt they had caused this child, and they understood that. All they could do was apologize and be there for her from here on out. Now that she knew they were alive, she could come with them. Or she could at least stay in contact when they went to Ironport.

"Are you going to leave me again?" Chuckles whispered, the words half garbled by Sage's shirt.

"I—" Sage's hands fisted in her T-shirt. They wouldn't make promises they couldn't keep. They knew better than that, but oh how they wanted to in that moment. Oh, how they wanted to tell Chuckles exactly what she wanted to hear. The urge was so strong, Sage had to swallow around the swell of words at the back of their throat. "I don't know."

Chuckles pulled back as if Sage had stung her. Her eyes were red and puffy when she met Sage's gaze, but her jaw was clenched, fists tight at her sides. "Why not? Why don't you *know*?"

Sage sighed, running their fingers through their hair. They wanted to glance around the room and see if Corey or her admirer could help with this. Corey's admirer, who'd brought Chuckles to them. What did that mean? Had they been caring for her? Sage should ask. Then at least they would know for certain she'd been taken care of like she ought.

"Sage," Chuckles pressed, her voice wobbling as if she were afraid of the answer, ripping Sage from their thoughts and back to the moment. "Why don't you know?"

"I—" Sage sucked in a deep breath and stuffed their hands into their pockets to hide the shaking. "It's not safe for me here. In Eventide." The words were stilted, uneven, harsh, but it was the truth. "Someone tried"—succeeded—"to kill me. And they will likely try again if I stay."

"So you're just going to leave." Chuckles snarled, vicious and cutting, and Sage felt every word rip into them down to their very core.

"I don't want to."

"But you *will*!" A sob left her, and suddenly she wouldn't meet their eyes anymore. She looked over their shoulder, directing her fury to whatever was behind them. "You'll leave me again!"

"You could—you could come with me." Sage stepped forward to reach for her, but she stepped back and away. Goddess, they'd fucked this all up. This should have been a happy day. A good reunion. And Sage had ruined it because they couldn't tell Chuckles what she wanted to hear. They understood on some level that she was a teenager, that she'd eventually grow to understand, but it would do nothing for the heartache and abandonment she felt now. It would do nothing to change the hurt that would linger for years to come.

"I don't want to come with you. I like it here. Eventide is home! Eventide is your home too. Or it was. Why— What changed?" Chuckles shook, finally meeting their eyes as if searching for an answer. Whatever she saw there seemed to make her change tack because she sucked in a breath, set her jaw, and said, "Mal and Mox will protect you. They—they got rid of all the old Faceless members. They restructured everything. They can—they can keep you safe."

Sage shook their head, sighing. "I couldn't ask that of them." They reached for her again, pulling her into another hug, this one less tight. Chuckles held on to them as if at any moment she might pull away and run from the bakery, never to turn back. "But I can promise you that I'm here another couple of weeks, at least." They'd have to extend their stay a bit, but if it meant more time with Chuckles, it would be worth it. "And at the end of those weeks, we'll talk."

"Talk about *what*?"

She wasn't going to make this easy, was she? And they couldn't blame her. She had no reason to let Sage off the hook. What they'd done was fucked up. It was necessary. They hadn't been left any kind of choice. But that didn't change how utterly fucked-up it was. They didn't deserve for this reunion to be easy, or for Chuckles to accept what they said.

"About everything." Sage curled more around Chuckles as if they could protect her from the world by simply putting their body in the way of whatever was coming at her. They couldn't, of course. Dying kind of proved that point beyond a shadow of a doubt. But they could try. "I won't leave without talking to you first. We'll revisit the idea of you coming back to Miami with me, or me staying here. Maybe you can visit on breaks. We'll find ways that I can keep in touch with you. I'm not going to disappear off the map again, I promise."

"I want an oath." She pulled back again, scrubbing at her eyes and lifting her chin.

"An oath?" A laugh burbled up their throat but died on their tongue at the way Chuckles met their eyes without a single ounce of hesitation and held out a hand expectantly. "All right." Sage nodded and took the extended hand to shake. "An oath."

"You won't leave Eventide without talking to me first," Chuckles insisted.

Magic buzzed where their hands were connected, waiting to seal the deal. It had been so long since Sage had made an oath. Binding their magic and their will to a promise. Would it even work the same way it once had now that they were no longer alive? Not that it mattered. Even if the magic of the oath didn't bind them to their promise, they wouldn't go against it. Not at the risk of losing Chuckles again.

"I won't leave Eventide without talking to you first," they promised, and the magic zinged up their arm, raising every hair in its wake before traveling down their spine in a shudder.

"Okay." Chuckles sighed, pulling her hand back then wrapping her arms around herself in a hug. "Okay."

"I love you, you know that, Chuckles." Sage couldn't remember if they'd ever told her that before they left. They were sure she knew they were family. They were sure she knew she was important to them. But they didn't know if she knew that they loved her, more than any blood relation they'd ever had. "You're family."

Chuckles colored brightly enough that her skin almost matched her hair. She squeaked, "You too."

Warmth flooded Sage, a grin turning up the corners of their lips. It wasn't exactly the same, but it was likely the best they'd get out of the teenager. And it was enough.

"How—" They swallowed again, their hands opening and closing at their sides, skin still tingling from the lingering magic and the want to hold Chuckles close and keep anything else from harming her.

Goddess, when had Sage become so protective of this little urchin? Ah. Right. When she'd been caught stealing from the Night Market at seven, and they'd saved her from the consequences. Funny how that girl had grown into this young woman who would one day be a strong and capable fae. A force to be reckoned with. Sage couldn't be prouder.

Funny how Sage had a habit of doing that. They wondered what had become of the twins they'd saved from a similar fate nearly two decades ago now . . . They shook themself.

"How have you been? Tell me what I've missed."

Chuckles smiled crookedly. "I've been good." Her shoulders relaxed and she pulled out a stool to sit, so they could talk. So she could tell Sage all of the things they'd missed in the four years since they left Eventide. Pictures included.

It was beautiful.

It hurt.

It ached down to their marrow.

IT WASN'T JUST HER, RIGHT? COREY WASN'T THE ONLY one who found this whole situation awkward, *right*? She didn't know what she thought it would be like to interact with someone who had hired her for a job who didn't know that it had been her, but she didn't think it would be this fucking weird. Although the fact that the person doing the hiring had been Mox really wasn't helping. Nor was it helping that Mox seemed perfectly content to stick around after she dropped Chuckles off to visit with Sage. Which. *Why?*

"Can I get a job application?" Mox asked, leaning over the counter, popping out her ass to put it on full display to absolutely no one because Corey was in front of her, behind the counter, glaring down at her. Although it did have the added benefit of giving Corey a glimpse at her cleavage . . .

"For you? Not a snowball's chance in hell." Corey snorted and swatted her with a rag. "Get your boobs off my countertop, I just cleaned that."

"Not for me." Mox rolled her eyes, but the grin on her face morphed into something sharp and feral as she came around the counter like she owned the place. It was a complete power move, and Corey would be lying if she said her gut didn't twist at the boldness behind it. "Unless you'd like me to stick around, sweetheart. Because I could totally do that. I'm no good at baking, but—"

"The position is for a bakery assistant. Why would I hire someone who isn't good at baking?" Corey wiped the counter again, purposefully ignoring the way Mox stretched herself out against the back of the display case like a languid cat, showing off all her long, lean curves.

The flirting was beginning to get annoying—or so Corey told herself. It wasn't like there was anything behind it. Corey knew Mox's reputation better than the average citizen of Eventide because she'd been up close and personal with some of Mox's castoffs over the years. Mox had a fondness for hearts, and she'd eat Corey's whole if Corey let her. Which she couldn't, because she didn't have fucking time for this nonsense.

"I'm good at . . . *other* things." Mox winked. Corey supposed it was meant to be salacious, but it just looked ridiculous.

"Sure you are." Corey's lips twitched into a smirk at the look of annoyance on Mox's face. Honestly, she was too easy.

"My dear, are you calling me a liar?" Mox gasped, clutching her heart. "I'd never!"

"Either way. No." Corey turned her back to head into the kitchen and grab some of the finished goods to pile into the display case. Sage and their daughter were still back there, murmuring softly to each other. As much as Corey found Sage an insufferable little shit, it was kind of nice to see them like this, happiness rolling their shoulders back more than they'd been the entire time since they returned to Eventide.

"Oh, come on, sweetheart." The pet name made Corey's eye twitch. But she was not giving the second in command of the Faceless Few her name. No way. "I'd be a great asset to this place."

"Don't you have a job already?" Corey asked, shoving a tray of mini tarts into Mox's hands before grabbing another full of petit fours for herself.

"I—well—" Mox's gaze flicked to where Sage was sitting with Chuckles.

"That's what I thought." Corey snorted, brushing past her almost hard enough to make Mox drop the tray in her hands. "And what would Mal do without his right-hand woman?"

"Fine. Be that way." Mox huffed, but she obediently moved up beside Corey and waited as Corey loaded the petit fours into the case before swapping trays with her so Corey could start on the tarts. "You know it's cute when you try to ruffle me."

Corey paused for a moment to blink at her before saying in a tone entirely devoid of emotion, "Try again."

"Oh, come on! How is none of this working?"

"Maybe I'm just not interested." Corey shrugged. It wasn't entirely true, nor was it entirely a lie. Part of Corey was very much interested. That part ached to see what all the fuss was about with Mox. But the sensible, rational side of her knew that Mox would use her up and throw her away, like she did with every person she was interested in. Likely faster, if she was honest, because Corey wasn't half as pretty as the others. Why was Mox even bothering with her?

"That's impossible. Everyone is—"

"Excuse me," Chuckles said. She stood on the other side of the counter, like someone who respected boundaries. Her cheeks were red and Sage stood behind her, a hand on her shoulder, a smile on their lips.

"Yeah?" Corey asked, shoving the now empty trays into

Mox's hands so she could give Chuckles her full attention. Mox huffed, but she took them and returned to the kitchen to set them on the counter. "What is it, kiddo?"

"Sage said you were looking for someone to help around the shop. And . . ." Chuckles shifted on her feet, and Corey caught the way Sage gave her shoulder an encouraging squeeze. "Well, school will be out in a couple weeks, and I'd like — I mean, if you don't mind, I could — "

"Do you have any experience working in a bakery?" Corey raised a brow.

"No. No, I don't. But — "

"How old are you, kiddo?"

"Thirteen." Chuckles huffed.

"We were sixteen when we did that summer at Phil's," Corey said to Sage over the girl's shoulder.

Sage shrugged.

"All right. I'll get you an application. Your guardians will have to sign off on it, and you'll only be part-time. But sure. Why not?" Corey huffed and had to duck behind the counter to hide her smile and grab the application. "Bring this back this evening when your brother comes to pick Sage up for their date, and I'll let you know my final decision by next weekend. Just in time to start training. Good?"

"Perfect." Chuckles's smile blossomed like a flower in the spring across her face as she took the application, holding it to her chest like it was something precious. Sage beamed at Corey from over her shoulder.

Well fuck. Corey sighed. She'd have to give this kid a job, wouldn't she?

Goddess, she was going soft.

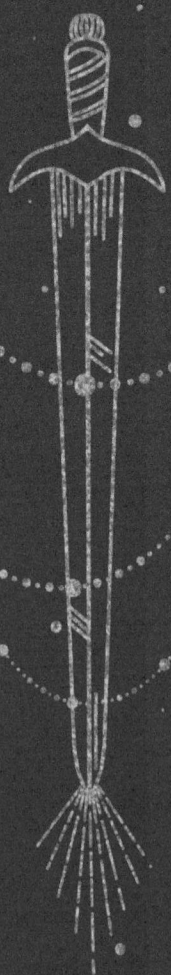

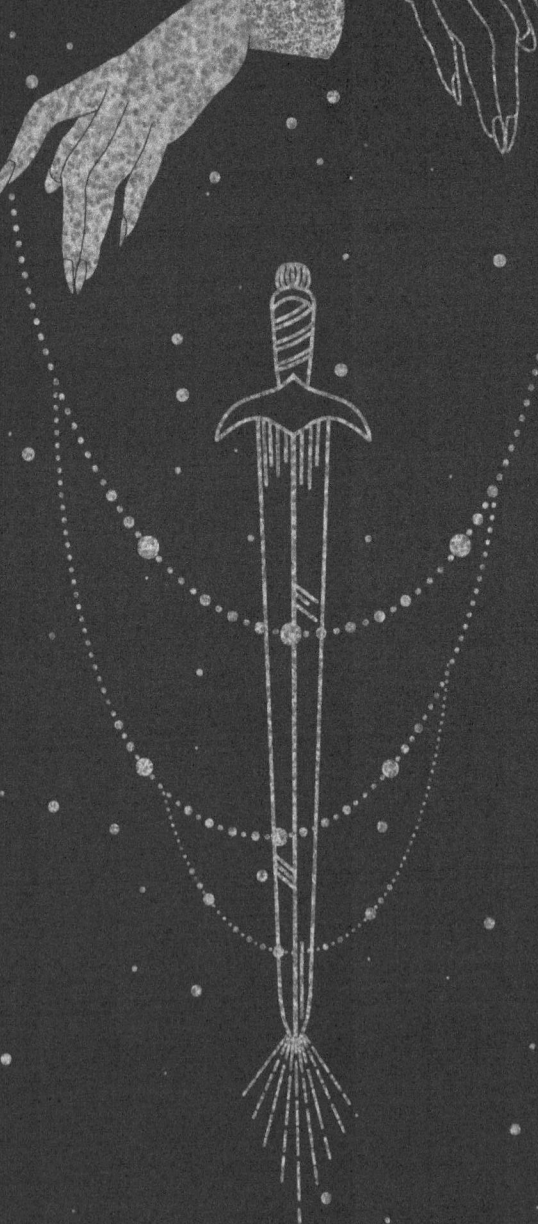

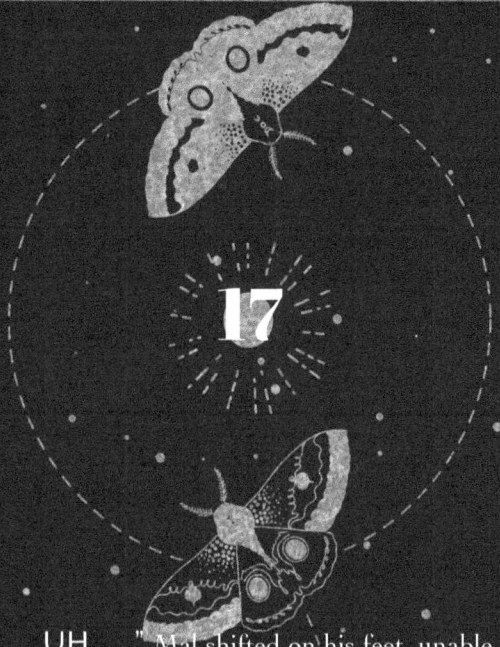

17

"SO I . . . UH . . ." Mal shifted on his feet, unable to meet Sage's eyes, Chuckles's application crinkled in his hands. He could feel the warmth in his cheeks, and no amount of trying to breathe calmly seemed to make it go away. He'd waited how many years for this? To take Sage on a proper date. To prove himself worthy of them. Probably close to twenty, if he was doing his math right. His first run-in with Sage had been when he was just barely sixteen . . .

More child than man. Dirty. Sullen. Starving. And willing to steal to stay alive. Sage had been a shining beacon then. His and Mox's saving grace. And nearly two decades hadn't dimmed their light.

"So I—" Mal swallowed again, trying to gain control of himself. It was a struggle, and although he knew why, he still hated every minute of it. He was fucking powerful. Stronger than most other folk in Eventide, as it happened. Maybe not more than Sage, but he'd burned the very foundation of the Faceless Few to the ground and rebuilt it. He'd killed so many who thought themselves strong. A trail of blood led from his position as an underling in the Faceless to being their leader.

And yet, seeing Sage under those soft lights, even with their glamour hiding them away, making them look just different enough, Mal could hardly speak. It was as if his tongue had grown three sizes, and he couldn't get it to function correctly no matter what he did.

"Ianthe," Sage offered, their voice soft and forgiving. Their eyes glowed faintly in the dim lights of the closed bakery. Goddess, they were even more beautiful today than they'd been the day Mal fell in love with them all those years ago. How was that possible?

"Yes?" Mal asked. The word came out an octave higher than he meant it to, like he'd had to force it out past a throat that threatened to strangle him. Maybe he did—he was having a hard time breathing, going lightheaded in the face of Sage's perfection.

"Just take a breath." Sage's lips twitched into that almost-smile, the one Mal had tried to capture in stone to put over their grave. He hadn't. He hadn't even come close to their beauty. None of his memories, none of his art, could ever stand up to this. He couldn't do this. He couldn't go on a date with Sage Nocturna. He wasn't worthy. He wasn't—
"It's fine. I promise. I like this idea, actually."

"It is? You do?" Mal's eyes jerked to meet Sage's, his dark brows raised high. He hadn't expected Sage to rebuff him, but he hadn't expected the warmth and the wholehearted agreement to his idea—Corey's idea, really, because she was so worried about losing her "investment."

"I do." Sage nodded. "It'll be nice to not have to worry about people being too loud around us, or crowds. It'll be relaxing."

"Relaxing." The word tasted foreign on his tongue. He didn't think he'd ever had a moment he could call relaxing in his life. Especially not since taking over the Faceless. Sure, he had more money than he'd ever dreamed of. A big house. Nice clothes. A luxury car. Arguably a place in the world that would make one think he could have time to relax. He had people to do things for him. Money to throw around. But he was still running a gang, and that took almost every hour of the day to maintain. He couldn't let his control slip, not for a single moment. Because if he did, he knew he'd lose all of it.

"Yes. Relaxing." Sage's almost-smile bloomed into something stronger, their eyes crinkling at the corners. "You know what relaxing is, don't you?"

"I can't say that I do, honestly." Mal huffed a laugh at himself, but he didn't pull away from the gentle chiding in Sage's tone. It was nice.

"Well, you're going to learn. Come." Sage held out a hand to him, and Mal looked at it for a moment too long, unsure if he should allow Sage to sully themself with the blood that still clung to his skin. Sage sighed, letting the hand drop and heading for the small table set up in the corner of the bakery. "You can leave Chuckles's application on the counter."

Mal's shoulders drooped. He didn't want Sage to think he was rejecting them. It was just . . . Well, there was so much to unpack there, and none of it was first date material.

"She wanted to hand deliver it," he told them, amusement curling at the edges. If there was one thing he could talk about, it was Chuckles. He couldn't explain their bond or how she'd wiggled her way into his black heart, but she had. "But she's got a history final she needs to ace."

"It was mostly so Corey has proof that her guardians approved anyway." Sage's smile ticked up another notch, and Mal didn't . . . he didn't know what to say to that. His tongue stuck to the roof of this mouth again.

So instead of stumbling over yet more words, he pulled Sage's chair out and gestured for them to sit before flopping down in the seat across the table.

"So what's on the agenda for the evening?" Sage asked, leaning their elbows on the table, their chin in their hands. The picture of innocence and nonchalance. Mal wanted to kiss them so badly, his jaw ached with it.

"Well first, you're going to sit here and hold that thought."

"What thought?"

"Whatever thought has you smiling like that." Mal lifted a hand so he could draw a circle in the air around Sage's smiling face.

"Hmm. I think I can manage that."

"Perfect." Mal nodded and rose, grabbing his cane as he went. "I'm going to get the first course and the wine."

"First course? *Fancy*," Sage cooed.

Mal's ears heated as he raced through the small café space of the bakery, his cane hitting one of the chairs a little too hard in his rush to get away from Sage's eyes for a moment. Once the swinging door was shut behind him, he huffed a long breath. "Fuck. Get a hold of yourself, Mal. You can do this. You can totally do this. You've just got to be your usual charming self."

Except his usual self wasn't overly charming, was it? Shit.

With a groan, he pressed his forehead against the metal of the island in the middle of the kitchen. The relative coolness on his burning face did little to make him feel better, but it at least woke him up. He would make this date the best one Sage had ever been on, because he didn't have any other choice. That was final.

One last deep inhale that tasted like icing sugar on his tongue, and Mal pushed himself to standing before digging through the takeout bags Mox had so kindly dropped off at the bakery despite her grumbling, "Do you want me to plate it for you too?" Mal loved his sister, really he did.

With the first course—crusty bread covered in vine-ripened tomatoes, mozzarella, and a balsamic reduction—settled onto delicate plates, also provided by his loving sister, Mal balanced the tray in one hand and picked his way carefully across the darkened café area. He could see better in low light, but if he wanted details, he needed to be close to someone. And sometimes the blur of a shadow looked much the same as the blur of a chair.

"This looks really yummy, Ianthe." Sage grinned widely and reached for the tray to help him set it down.

"So," Mal said, settling across from them again and taking his own plate, content to watch Sage pick the best of the bruschetta from the sharing plate.

He wasn't sure what was a safe topic to start on. He knew that Sage didn't want to give away their identity—that much was obvious by the glamour. But Mal desperately wanted to get to know them better. Where should he start in doing that? He fidgeted with his fork, uncomfortable with how hard it was to speak to someone he'd once thought he knew so intimately, even if from afar. But wasn't Mox right at least a bit about that? Mal didn't know Sage at all, that was the point of this whole thing.

"I don't like the beach," Sage said impromptu of nothing. "I left Maryland for Miami some years back, and let me just say, Florida's seafood has nothing on ours. And forget asking for Old Bay down there." Sage barely breathed as they took a bite of bruschetta that crunched loudly between their teeth. "I asked once, and they brought me bay leaves? Like . . . who would put that on mac and cheese?"

"You put Old Bay on mac and cheese?" Mal laughed, startled. His shoulders eased, the grip on his cane loosening.

"Are you really from this state if you don't have at least one food item you'd inappropriately put Old Bay on?" Sage grinned broadly. "What's yours?"

"I don't have one."

"Liar," Sage goaded. "Come on, it's just us. You're allowed to be as weird as you want. I won't tell." They winked, and Mal noticed a bit of sauce lingering at the corner of their grin. He desperately wanted to lick it off.

"Fine." Mal's gaze flicked down to his plate then back up before he looked about the room theatrically as if checking to make sure no one was there to overhear. Then he leaned forward, pressing himself closer to Sage's space than he'd normally dare, all for the sake of the bit, and whispered, "Ice cream."

Sage crowed, delighted. "Yes! That is so wonderfully Maryland."

"You've had it?"

"No, but I would!" Sage laughed, and Goddess, Mal would do anything, absolutely *anything*, to ensure they laughed like that for the rest of their life.

Mal nodded. "What other things about home did you miss while you were in Miami?"

And the floodgates opened.

Sage was happy to fill what had once been an awkward silence with anecdotes and stories and answers to their favorite color—crimson, by the way. And Mal found himself opening up just as much. Answering questions he didn't think anyone had asked him since he was in high school. It was . . . perfect.

And Mal was even more in love with Sage than he'd ever been.

"WHO TAUGHT YOU?" IANTHE ASKED, LEANING BACK IN his chair, looking quite comfortable now. Sage had recognized the tension early on. As if Ianthe was worried what Sage might think of him. As if Sage could find him anything but charming.

"To crochet?" Sage paused their story about the last time they'd tried to create a garment and wound up with a sweater that, although cozy, hung crooked off their shoulders. "Well, when I was young, I had a grandmother who was crafty. She got me started. But for the longest time, I was doing it backward."

"You can crochet backward?" Ianthe laughed softly, disbelieving. He looked lovely like this: out of his shell, free.

"Oh yes." Sage nodded. "I'd show you if I had some yarn and a hook with me. But the point is, I was looping the yarn around the wrong way. Likely because I'd learned by watching her, so I was mirroring her, you know?"

"Right."

"Anyway, when I got a little older, probably my late twenties, I watched a couple of YouTube videos and realized oh hey, I was doing it wrong. Things got a lot easier after that." Sage tilted their head, their nose scrunching as they watched the way the light danced in Ianthe's mismatched eyes. "And I just kept up the practice. I don't make a whole lot. Mostly I get halfway through a project, get bored, frog the whole—"

"Frog?"

"Rip it apart and start over. Although usually I rip it

apart and start something else." Sage shrugged, unbothered. "The point isn't really the completed project most of the time for me."

"No?" Ianthe was so interested, intense. He seemed to lean closer as they spoke, like Sage was drawing him in. It was intoxicating to be the center of someone's attention that way, but for some reason other than their name and the blood they'd once shed.

"No."

"Why bother then?"

"A few reasons. One"—Sage held up a finger—"I find it relaxing, even when I completely mess up. Two, I don't do well sitting still and watching TV. I get bored. Crocheting allows me to actually enjoy a show or movie because my hands are busy, so I'm not tempted to pick up my phone. Three, a few years ago I was in an accident"—that was putting it mildly—"and since then I've had some issues with stiffness. The crocheting helps. A body in motion stays in motion, you know?"

"I suppose so." Ianthe nodded. "So, you wouldn't be interested in teaching anyone, would you?"

"You want to learn?" Sage brightened. "I've never actually taught someone before, but I'd be happy to try."

"Great." Ianthe leaned back again, taking his glass with him and sipping from it. "I should go get our dessert. I got us a cake."

"Could we maybe do ice cream instead?" Sage pushed the remainder of their pasta around the plate. There wasn't much left, and it'd been delicious, but the best part of this whole thing had been the company. The quiet, easy chatter that flowed like water between them. Sage couldn't remember the last time they'd had that. Or maybe they could. A vague memory niggled at the back of their mind. Another dark-haired boy. Sage shook themself.

"I don't—"

"It's a beautiful night outside," Sage pressed. They knew it was a bad idea, logically. They were in hiding, so this date in the bakery had been perfect, especially with the low lighting that helped to cover the weak glamour they'd created with the help of Lucy's pebble. But the stars were shining. The mists of Eventide had thinned to allow them to see them above the lights of the city. It happened so rarely, and Sage missed nights like this in Eventide. Nights when everything seemed possible. "We won't go far. Corey told me about this shop that stays open late. Just down the block."

Ianthe hesitated another moment, his lip twitching as if he were unsure whether he should frown or laugh. Then he sighed, running a hand through his long dark hair, pushing the strands back from his face even as a few escaped to fall into his eyes. He looked beautifully bedraggled. "All right."

"All right." A laugh left Sage unbidden, free. "Come on." They reached across the table, took Ianthe's hand without warning, and pulled him to his feet. Not waiting a second to see if he'd argue further. "I want to try Old Bay ice cream."

"Fine. Fine." Ianthe laughed with them, letting them pull him to the door and out into the streets of Eventide. Without a second thought, Sage looped their arm through his. Ianthe stiffened for a moment before relaxing under the touch.

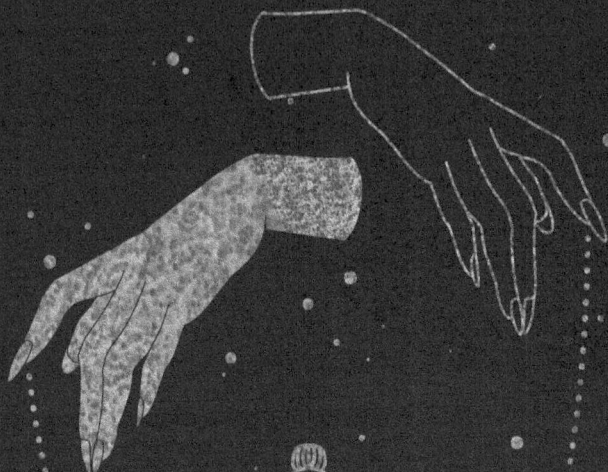

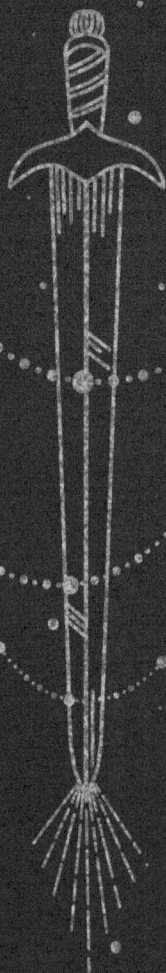

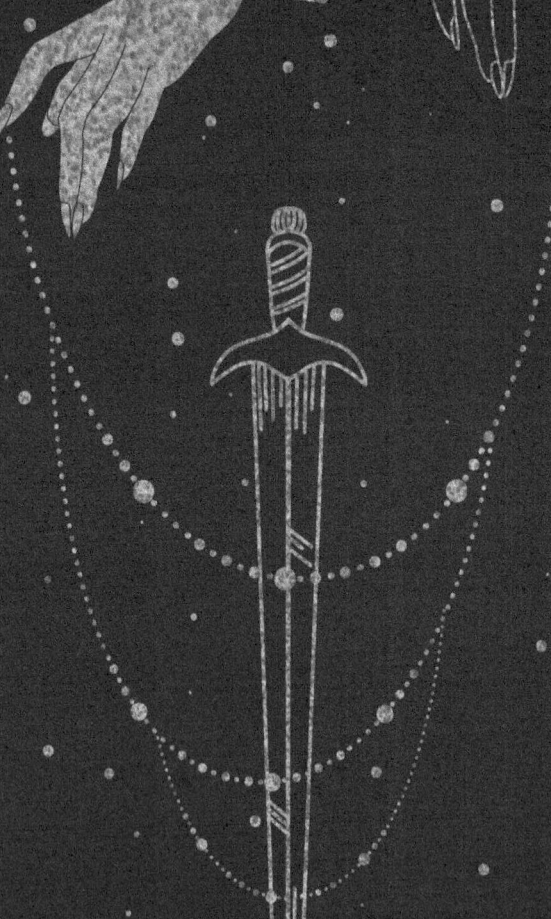

18

MOX INHALED DEEPLY, looking up at the twisted townhouse that defied all logic and physics. It sat between two others that stood up straight like they were supposed to, and yet somehow—a trick of the eye, some might assume—the derelict middle house seemed to tilt to the left then back over to the right as it went up further. Five floors total.

It was strange, and if Mox didn't know it was home to a demon, she'd probably have avoided it at all costs. It screamed *stay the fuck away*.

Normally, Mox would have listened. She was a risk taker, sure, but she didn't fuck with whatever was going on with that. Yet, here she was. Standing in front of the crooked house that somehow sat on the edge of three different gangs' territories but belonged to none of them. As if they all met at a point right on the front lawn.

Mox could imagine the sections Eventide was separated into if she focused hard enough. Could see the exact way that they all parted like the bay for a boat around this bit of property. It didn't sit right with her, this unclaimed land, but no one was stupid enough to cross Lucy to try to take it. She'd been there for far longer than any of them, maybe even before Eventide was built.

And what was that saying about demons? *Never cross a settled demon, for you are flammable and tasty with ketchup.* Maybe that was dragons.

"What is with you people and just standing there, staring at my house?" Lucy's voice carried across the yard as if she'd shouted the words, but she hadn't. And like magic—because it was—one second the porch was empty, and the next Lucy was leaning against the crumbling railing like she wasn't afraid it would give under her weight. A blunt hung between her lips, smoke coming from her nostrils, a brow raised high on her face. "Does it make y'all nervous or something?"

"You ever think maybe it's you, not the house, that makes people nervous?" Just like bothering a settled demon was unadvisable, it was probably equally unwise to snark at one right before asking to make a deal with them. But Mox had never been good at keeping her inside thoughts from becoming outside thoughts when she was nervous. And nervous she was. The happiness of her family depended on this deal. The weight of it sat heavy on her shoulders. She'd do anything to make sure Mal and Chuckles kept smiling. Anything at all. Her arrival on Lucy's doorstep was more proof of that.

"What do you *want*, Moxxie Mystral Tamesis Senka?" Lucy tilted her head, letting smoke trail from her lips lazily before she took another long drag off the blunt, the cherry turning crimson. It cast a red glow on her face in the shade of the porch that made her look . . . demonic.

Mox swallowed, the sound loud in her ears, every muscle in her body tighter at the use of her true name. Was she really going to do this? *Again*? Make a deal with a fucking demon for the sake of her family? Yeah. Yeah, she was. "I'm here to make a deal."

"Another one?" Lucy's brows lifted and the blunt disappeared, her posture straightening so she was standing tall behind the railing.

"Yes. Another one." This was such a stupid idea. One of the stupidest she'd had lately, but Mox didn't have a better one. So here she was.

"Do you even have anything left to offer me?" Lucy's lip curled upward, mocking. She could be a real bitch when she wanted to be, and Mox fucking hated her. "I mean, after you gave me your—"

"Are we going to do this or not?" Mox snarled. She didn't want the reminder of what she'd traded away four years ago. It wouldn't help anyone. It wouldn't change anything. All it would do was make her ache on the inside. An ache she couldn't source, because she didn't have the fucking—

"I suppose you may as well come in." Lucy shrugged. "I can't make any promises I'll do what you want, not if you can't pay. But we'll at least work out the cost."

"I *can* pay."

"Sure you can, babycakes." Lucy's voice floated across the yard again, but the demon herself had disappeared, leaving behind not even a whiff of smoke.

The door to the crooked house creaked open loudly and sat gaping like a maw. It would swallow Mox whole, she knew it would. Just like it had that night so many years ago. The one when she'd traded . . . so much more than she'd meant to.

Mox could still smell the blood, thick and metallic, and when she glanced down at her hands, she was dragged kicking and screaming back to that night in her mind.

She was shaking all over, every single cell in her being trembling with what she'd seen, what she'd had to do. The blood, Mal's blood, thick in her nose. She drew in a breath through her mouth to try to bypass the smell, but then she tasted it on her tongue.

Her brother . . . Her stupid, foolish, beautiful, idiotic, strong, chaotic, amazing brother, had tried to kill himself.

His grief consumed him, making him despondent, empty. Leaving him a shell of the boy—the man—she'd known. And Mox found him there, lying in the middle of their apartment, bleeding into the rug. Thank the Goddess Chuckles had been in school. Thank the Goddess they lived in a tiny apartment and someone had heard Mox screaming. Thank the Goddess their neighbor was a nurse and a healing witch. If he wasn't, Mal would be dead. Not lying in a hospital bed, asleep and attached to monitors. Dead.

Mox almost lost the other half of her soul tonight. He'd almost left her alone in this fucked-up place.

And all she could focus on was the sound of his voice, broken and fading as he repeated over and over and over again, "They're gone. They're really gone. They're gone. What am I going to do without them? I can't . . . I can't keep that promise. I can't do it. Not when they're—"

Mox didn't have an answer for him when he'd first asked her that. She wanted to say something vicious and angry about how Mal had hardly even known Sage. About how this couldn't be healthy. But one look in his eyes, and she knew she couldn't. It wouldn't change anything anyway. Mares only fell in love once, or so the stories went, and Sage had been it for Mal.

"What do you want, little wisp?" the demon asked, looming over Mox where she'd fallen to her knees in the dead grass at some point. She couldn't remember when, her hands still bloody from trying to hold the pieces of her shattered brother together.

"I want you to save my brother. Please," she begged, unable to do anything else. "Give me the power to help him."

The demon tilted her head, the motion unnatural as her face

dipped below her shoulder, almost swiveling so it was upside down on her neck. "Are you aware of what that will cost?"

"Anything. I'll give you anything," Mox breathed.

"Anything?" The demon's head stayed where it was, but a smile curled up the corners of her lips, far too wide and with too many teeth. "Even your wisp fire?"

"Yes. Take it! If it'll save my brother, if it'll help him get past this . . . this . . . this crushing sadness." She clenched her hands on her thighs, ignoring the way her fire sizzled and snapped at the mere suggestion. It was a living, breathing entity. A part of her, yes, but still its own thing. And it was unwilling to go. She'd make it, if she had to.

"You are aware you'll lose more than just power, correct?" The demon appeared before her, kneeling in the grass, all vestiges of that terrifying smile gone. Instead, her freckled face looked almost soft, caring. "You will have to give up something else too. Something you love. Your fire won't go willingly. It will cut out a piece of you. The piece it knows you care for the most."

"What will it take?" Was there anything she loved so much as she loved Mal?

"I don't know. Not yet. I won't know until it's gone." The demon almost looked apologetic.

"Will I know?"

"No. You won't. You'll forget. And whoever or whatever it is will in turn forget you. It will be as if it never was. Are you willing then, to lose something you care for deeply, something you love, for your brother?"

"Yes."

She stood by the decision still, even if the memory of it rattled her now, even if she didn't know who or what she'd sacrificed. With another deep breath, she crossed the dilapidated porch and stepped through the open maw of the house into a sunlit foyer. Somewhere, a record player was playing Pat Benatar's "Wuthering Heights."

"I like what you've done with the place," Mox muttered, following the sounds of Lucy piddling around with dishes to the kitchen at the back of the house. "You don't have to make me tea."

"I'm making tea, and you'll drink it," Lucy said, not looking up from where she had just put the kettle on the stove. "Sit." She pointed to a chair at the little table in the corner and it pulled out.

Mox supposed she could ignore it, but not if she wanted Lucy to give her a fair price and not gouge her. So she sat. Her manicured nails drummed against the chipping paint on the white tabletop. The kitchen looked like something out of *Southern Home* magazine. Glass-paneled canary yellow cabinets with butcher's block countertops.

"What is it now?" Lucy asked once she'd arranged all the tea things onto a silver tea tray complete with doilies and a matching tea set. It looked like something someone's grandmother would serve tea on. Lucy was no one's grandmother.

"I really don't want any—"

DRINK YOUR FUCKING TEA. Lucy's mouth didn't move, but her eyes blazed red and the words echoed through Mox's head like a hundred voices all screaming in agony.

Mox lifted the offered cup and took a pointed sip, ignoring the burn and the bitterness from a lack of sugar. "Happy?"

"Don't be a bitch."

"You started it," Mox bit back. Whatever kindness might have been between them at the start of their arrangement had soured and died over the years. They needed each other, and they both hated it. Without Mox's fire, Lucy could be sent back to the darkest corners of the dark dimensions. And without Lucy, everything Mox had given up to save her brother would be lost forever. They were two sides of one very fucked-up coin.

"I don't have to fucking help you. You know that, right?" Lucy quirked one red brow over the rim of her daisy patterned teacup, not looking the least bit concerned about Mox and her attitude.

"I don't think that's the case." Mox shrugged. She was probably overplaying her hand here, but she was miffed. And why shouldn't she be? Lucy could have solved this entire thing if she'd just— "Why didn't you tell me Sage Nocturna was alive? All those years ago, when I came to you begging for help, for a way to save my brother from his despair. Why didn't you tell me?"

"They've found each other again. Of course they have," Lucy muttered, shaking her head and running a hand through her burgundy hair. Then she returned her attention to Mox, meeting her eyes head on. "I couldn't."

"You could. All you had to say was, *Hey Mox, you know that person your brother tried to kill himself over? Well, funny story, they're still alive. Run out of town, of course. But they're out there somewhere, living their life.* And had you done that, Mal wouldn't have—"

"He wouldn't have seized control of the Faceless," Lucy finished for her, carefully setting down her tea. "Oh Moxxie, darling—"

"Don't fucking call me *darling*."

"Darling," Lucy repeated, unbothered by the snippy tone. "I may be a creature of unnature, but there are things even I don't fuck with. Eventide's will is one of those things. And if you're smart, you won't tango with her either."

"I'm not sure what you mean." Mox's hand twitched around her cup, her rings clanking against the ceramic.

"The city wanted you and your brother in charge of the Faceless Few. And I'm not about to get in the way of what she wants. If I'd told you that Sage was still alive, Mal wouldn't have stopped until he found them. Correct?"

"Probably, but—"

"Everything happens for—"

"If you say everything happens for a reason, I'm going to come across this table and—"

"And what?" Lucy asked, a sharp smile on her face showing off too many teeth. "Put me out of my fucking misery? Oh sweetie, I wish you would. Because Goddess knows, I've tried. But demons don't die. We just . . . go back." She shivered, as if truly bothered for the first time since Mox got there. "Now what the fuck do you want, Mox? Because this was fun for about the first five minutes, but now I'm bored. And nobody wants a bored demon."

Mox huffed, scooting her saucer across the tray, only a sip gone from the cup.

Lucy's smile twitched at the obvious slight, but she didn't take the bait.

"I want your help protecting Sage Nocturna," Mox said after a moment.

"Why? You don't give a rat's ass about Sage Nocturna." Lucy laughed a little, as if she were delighted by the idea of Mox coming to her to beg a deal for someone she didn't even particularly like. She probably was—Lucy was a bitch like that.

"I don't," Mox agreed. "But Mal and Chuckles love them, and it looks like they're stuck in Eventide for the moment. So they need looking after." Mox shrugged and leaned back in her chair, her hands folding over her stomach as she stared into the ever-smiling face of the demon before her. It was easy to forget what Lucy was sometimes, easy to mistake her for some other folk. She was pretty. Tall, curvy, and elegant, and so fucking pretty. Mox would have gone for her if, you know, she had a death wish. She was exactly Mox's type. "What'll it cost me?"

Lucy hummed thoughtfully, refilling her teacup, although Mox hadn't seen it empty since she sat. "I can protect Sage, yes, but that's not what you're really after, is it?"

"Excuse me?" Mox's fingers twitched in annoyance.

"What you really want is a way to keep them here." Lucy looked up from her cup, her smile a row of sharklike teeth again. "Isn't it?"

Mox jerked a little, her nails digging into the backs of her hands where they were folded together in her lap. "Yes."

"No matter what that looks like?"

"No matter what it looks like." Although Mox wasn't sure what that meant, and she was decently certain she didn't want to know. Lucy was a literal demon, and she almost always had a trick up her sleeve. This was such a bad idea. Her worst yet. But Mox was a fool for her siblings. They were all she had, after all.

"Well, you don't have much worth taking anymore," Lucy murmured, tapping her fingers against the ceramic of her cup as she lifted it to her lips once more. She took a careful, thoughtful sip, then nodded to herself. "I suppose it'll have to be money then."

"Money I can do. You're good with a wired transfer, right? Or would you prefer cash?"

"Who the fuck uses cash anymore?" Lucy scoffed, rolling her pretty mismatched eyes. One so dark that Mox couldn't distinguish it from the black of her pupil, the other leaf green.

"It'll take me a couple of days to get the money together." Mox nodded. She didn't know how much Lucy would charge, but that didn't matter. "I'll have to move some things around."

"Hiding your deals with demons from your baby brother still?" Lucy tittered.

"Fuck off." Mox scooted her chair back from the table, making sure the legs scraped loudly enough on the floors to make Lucy hiss. "Just send me your bill, demon."

"A delight as always, sweetcheeks." Lucy winked and Mox huffed, turning on her heel to make her escape before the demon could cause her any more trouble.

She was in her car by the time the hollow ache in her chest finally died down enough to breathe past. But she couldn't shake the memories of that night. Nor the reminder that she'd sold something to that demon. Something that meant almost as much to her as her brother. And she was beginning to think that it wasn't a something, but a some*one*.

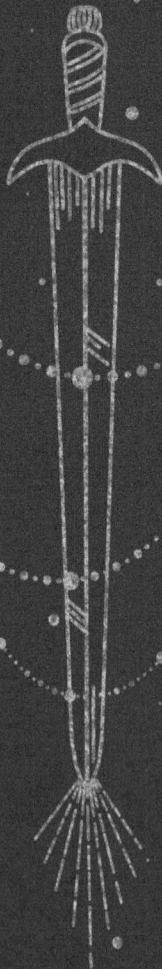

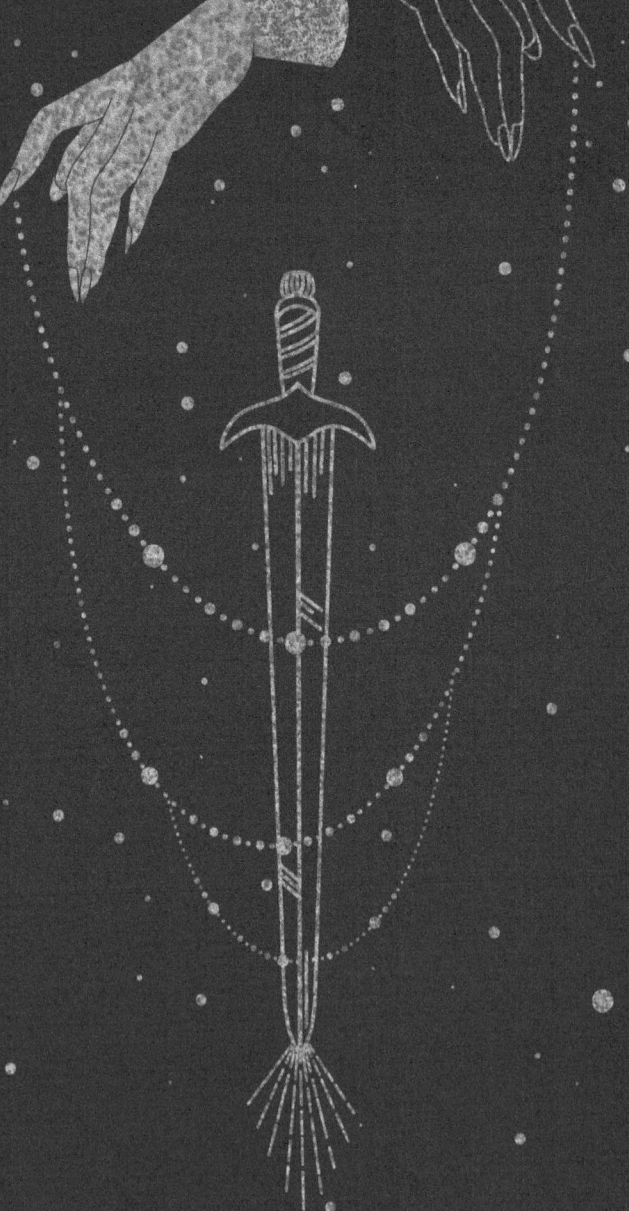

19

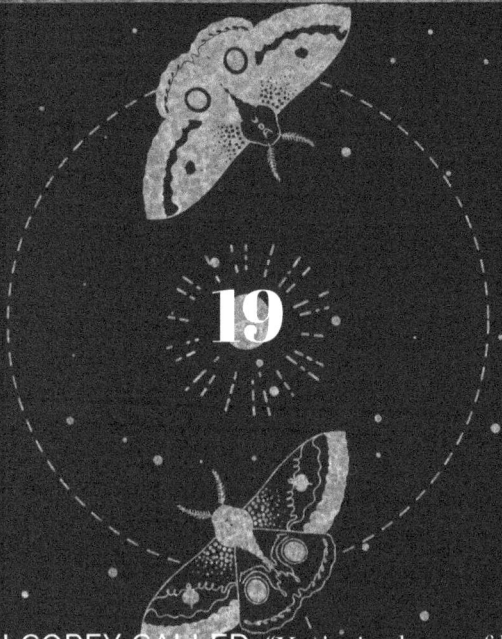

WHEN COREY CALLED, "You're in charge of locking up. I've got a job," Sage didn't even bother to lift their head from the dough they were kneading before firing back a little "mm-hmm" that Corey probably didn't hear.

There was too much else on their mind to be bothered with thoughts of Corey and her side hustle, and prepping dough for tomorrow's loaves was the perfect activity to let their mind wander. And wander it did.

It was silly to walk on air after a single date. To trot the kneaded dough to the proving drawer before grabbing the next ball. To feel like the world bloomed warm and soft around them. All because they'd had a decent night with someone they were just getting to know.

They knew that.

Logically.

But what did logic ever have to do with a person's feelings? Nothing. Nothing at all. And Sage was . . .

Not in love.

Love was definitely too strong a word, and they were definitely too old for the teenage infatuation that was the myth of love at first sight. Not that they'd ever been young enough for it to begin with. Even when Sage was sixteen, immature and free—and not undead—they were too old for it. Sixteen going on sixty, they'd once been told. But that's what happened when a person's only living guardian was a mobster who regularly beat the need for "toughness" into them.

But they were in their early forties now? It was hard to keep track most days, if they were being honest. They knew what year they were born in, but that didn't mean they had the ability to keep track of how many years had passed. Or the desire to do the fucking math every time they forgot.

That was beside the point! Totally beside the point.

The point was, they were seriously *in like* with Ianthe.

He was sweet and even charming once Sage had gotten him to warm up. There had been some awkwardness in the beginning, first date jitters, but they melted away quickly. And once they had, Sage was . . . Well, not to sound like an old Victorian romance novelist, but it was the truth—Sage was very much taken with Ianthe.

He was easy to talk to.

He listened.

There was something strikingly sharp but also gentle about the smiles he kept shooting Sage's way.

And . . . and . . . Oh, who was Sage kidding. This couldn't go anywhere, not really. They would leave when the time came for it. Eventide wasn't their home anymore; they didn't belong there. And falling for someone who clearly had roots in the community wouldn't do.

"Get your head on right, Sage," they muttered to themself, bumping the proving drawer shut with their hip, their hair falling into their face as they shook their head. They knew better. They did. But knowing better didn't change how nice it was to be wanted for the first time in years. It didn't change that soft buzz that went through their limbs at the mere thought of the good night kiss they hadn't managed to get.

It probably would have been better *had* they managed to get that good night kiss. Then it was one less thing to fantasize about. Okay. So that was complete bullshit, and Sage knew it. Had they gotten the good night kiss they wanted, they'd have spent the entire evening fantasizing about pushing it further. That's how these things worked.

"I won't go out with them again," they said sternly, giving themself a nod in the reflection of the wiped-down oven doors. The whole kitchen smelled of the lemony cleaner Corey used to keep things tidy and aboveboard as far as the health department was concerned. It was a vaguely chemically, synthetic scent Sage wasn't overly fond of, but they were getting used to it. The same way they were getting used to working in the bakery. The same way they were getting used to living with Corey.

It was strange how quickly that seemed to be happening. A week. They'd only been here a week.

But . . . It was like settling into a place they hadn't thought they would fit prior to now. Not necessarily cutting off their rough edges to make themself fit into a puzzle where they didn't belong, but more like that thing that happened when a person melted a bunch of different crayons together and watched them drip down a canvas. The colors remained distinct and separate, but they formed a solid block of wax, a work of art. Fitting into Eventide now, into Corey's life, into this whole fucking *place*, was like that.

A beautiful mess.

They could be happy here; they saw that now. If they let themself, they could find a home of a kind in this little life Corey had carved out for herself. A home that would leave them close enough to Tony to help when he needed it, and in a place that was all at once familiar and foreign. They could . . . *belong* in a way they never had before they'd left Eventide.

But danger lurked in that thinking too. Because the fuckers who'd killed Sage four years ago were still out there somewhere. The case had never been solved—not by the Eventide police force, at least. Not that Sage had expected them to solve it, really. They tended to stay out of Eventide's folk-on-folk violence, which was usually better for everyone involved. The police included. But that meant that whoever'd done it—an answer Sage didn't have—was still here in Eventide.

Of course, they thought Sage was dead. But how long would that last with Sage in town? No. It was a risk they couldn't take. They couldn't get attached to anyone here, couldn't make any plans to put down roots. When they'd fulfilled their obligations to Tony and saw he was safe with their own eyes, they'd leave the state. They'd stay in touch with Chuckles, because they couldn't think of a life without her now that Chuckles knew Sage was alive, but everyone else could go hang as far as Sage was concerned.

Even cute, charming, sweet, bumbling men like Ianthe.

Which meant they certainly couldn't—

Sage's phone buzzed on the counter, and they glanced over it, their nose wrinkled, before a tiny, pleased grin blossomed across their lips unbidden.

IA: Are you free on Tuesday??

The smile that had been ever-present on Sage's face to that point, the one they had been steadfastly ignoring while they chided themself on their poor life decisions, seemed to take on a life of its own. It crawled further up their face, making their cheeks hurt.

They rushed through cleaning their hands and scooped up the phone to reply right away.

SA: This Tuesday?

IA: Yes. This Tuesday.

SA: Let me check my calendar

Sage let out a squeal of delight. Because no matter how much they told themself they shouldn't get attached, that they were leaving, they couldn't help the thrill of someone finding them attractive. Especially when that someone looked like Ianthe. Long black hair, with an undercut that showed off an ear full of piercings and parted to the side to allow for a wonderful view of his elegant neck. Full lips. Mismatched eyes—one warm brown, the other cold gray—lined in perfectly smudged liner. A tall muscular frame that looked like it could curl neatly around Sage in cuddles, but also in other things . . .

Sage bit their lip and replied.

SA: Looks like I'm all clear

what did you have in mind?

IA: I'll pick you up at eight.

SA: you didn't answer my question

IA: No. I didn't.

SA: are you going to?

IA: Where would be the fun in that?

A delighted giggle burbled up Sage's throat and surprised them to the point they had to cover their mouth with their hand, lest it echo through the empty bakery. They shook their head, took a breath, and forced themself to finish cleaning the kitchen. It was kind of adorable how Ianthe could be so confident via text, but in person had struggled to start talking. It spoke of a well of thoughtfulness Sage didn't think still existed in this town.

IA: So is that a no?

Because if it's really a problem I'd be happy to tell you where we're going.

I don't want you to feel uncomfortable.

Sage's smile grew again, to a painful degree. How could one person have so many sides? It was amazing.

SA: That's a yes

I'll see you Tuesday at 8

I'm just trying to finish cleaning up so I can get home

IA: Oh. OK. Good. See you then.

SA: Can't wait

With the lights of the bakery shut off and their apron hung on the rack, Sage turned to punch in the numbers that would set the alarm for the night. The glowing alarm box was right next to the back door, and Sage had only made the mistake once of punching the numbers in when they weren't halfway outside. Once was enough to teach them that if they didn't have one foot and one ass cheek hanging out the door when they pushed the enter button and tried to get out before the blasted thing stopped beeping, they'd never make it. Because the back door stuck, and Corey refused to fucking fix it.

So there they were, half their body inside the bakery, the other half out in the muggy summer air, typing in the six-digit passcode for the alarm system. The last number was in and the beeping started. Sage took a giant step into the back alley and let the door shut behind them.

It slammed, loudly, the sound echoing off the buildings that surrounded them, and Sage bent to adjust their messenger bag when something hard slammed into the back of their head.

They stumbled under the force of it, their ears ringing loud enough from the blow to make them nauseous. Their vision began to tunnel, but they swallowed around the swell of hot bile in their throat and forced themself to listen, really listen. A struggle with the ringing.

They heard the next swish of the weapon.

Sage spun away from the blow, putting distance between themself and their attacker. They were disoriented, yes. Their vision swam and their feet caught on the uneven cobbles of the street. But they were Sage fucking Nocturna, and they weren't going down without a fight. Not again.

Their arm disappeared into their messenger bag, reaching for the switchblade that seemed to have vanished into the depths, likely never to be seen again. Fuck. They knew they should have put it into their pocket before leaving the relative safety of the bakery. Too late now.

The swish of the weapon came again, and Sage looked up in time to come face-to-face with their attacker. Or, they would have if the person weren't wearing a mask and a hood to hide their identity. Why hadn't they used a glamour? Were they too weak, too low level of a fae to hold it in place while also doing something strenuous? Maybe they were young. Untrained.

"Can't even look me direct in the eyes when you try to kill me a second time!" Sage shouted, stepping away from the weapon—an aluminum baseball bat. Dangerous, yes, and deadly if used right. But by far not the weapon someone would choose if this were another assassination attempt.

What did that mean? What did that *mean*? Their mind ran a mile a minute. This person didn't want to kill Sage. They wanted to knock them unconscious. What for? To take them somewhere probably. Likely for torture and questioning purposes. Well fuck that.

Sage reached for the panther that had once lived under their skin, praying to the Goddess that for the first time in four years she'd answer their call. But where once there would have been the rage-filled roar of a beast willing to fight to keep them both alive, there was nothing. The hollowness of the place where she'd been echoed in its emptiness. Sage's knees wobbled at the reminder.

They were alone.

Sage's hand caught on something in the bottom of their bag, but it wasn't the switchblade. Fuck it. They dropped the bag toward the ground, stretching out the long strap to wrap it around their hand and use it to protect themself. They just needed a minute. Just sixty seconds to get out of this.

But they were dizzy from the first blow, and they belatedly realized it was low blood sugar. They still hadn't gotten used to the need to monitor that constantly.

And without the panther there to have their back . . .

Their vision cut out for a second.

They heard the bat slice through the air again, headed straight for their head. It wouldn't take three hits to knock them out at this rate. Two would do.

And they couldn't get their fucking feet to—

Another sound came and when their vision cut back in, their attacker had been thrown to the cobbles. A blurry shape clothed in red sat on top of them, shadows writhing around them. They slammed the attacker's head into the ground hard enough that Sage thought they heard a crack.

There was a grunt followed by "You fucking prick. I'll gut you like a fucking fish. How dare you lay a hand on them" in a voice Sage recognized almost immediately. The tone was soft, almost gentle in its brutality.

At another blow to Sage's attacker, blood splattered against the cobbles either from their nose or a cut along their cheek. A grunt, and their attacker fought back. More blood dripping onto the street, the sound loud in the silence of Eventide holding her breath, waiting for the end.

Then the figure in red was rolled off the attacker, who scrambled to their feet and made a run for it. Sage's savior —*Ianthe*, Sage thought breathlessly— held his hand over a wound on his side as he got to his feet with so much ease despite the obvious pain bowing him forward. Shadows writhed around him, dashing after the attacker, but when they caught on the attacker's legs, they seemed to dissolve into nothing.

Ianthe rubbed at his face with his sleeve to clear away some of the blood. He let out an annoyed breath and pulled a phone from his pocket, not even panting from the scuffle.

"I need a runner," he said.

Sage's legs gave under them, and they still couldn't get their vision to clear enough to see Ianthe properly.

"Send five," he replied to the person on the other side. "No, I'm not fucking kidding." Then he looked up and saw Sage melting toward the ground. "Shit." He dropped his phone, heedless of the way it shattered against the cobbles, and dashed forward to scoop Sage up into a bridal carry.

There was a moment when Sage was close enough to make out his face. The mismatched eyes. The long, elegant nose. The ocher-brown cheeks now covered in the blood of the person who had attacked Sage.

"Are you all right?" Ianthe asked, their voice gentler than it'd been a moment ago when it'd been harsh and commanding. Cutting. And oh. Okay. So maybe it was more than the blow to the head and their low blood sugar that had made Sage weak in the knees. There was something undeniably sexy about the man before them, covered in blood, who had been vicious and violent a moment ago, handling Sage with such care. Like they were fragile. Like they were worthy.

"Mm-hmm," Sage mumbled right before the world went dark.

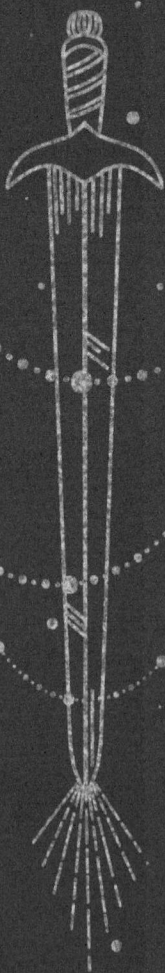

20

MAL'S HANDS were *not* shaking, and if a person knew what was good for them, they wouldn't point it out. Wouldn't mention how even as his arms screamed under the need to put Sage down, he refused to. Wouldn't draw attention to how his face was damp and streaked with tears. How he'd left the scene without so much as making sure that Mox sent people to hunt down the piece of shit who'd jumped Sage. His phone now broken and stuffed into his pocket. The wound on his side pulling as he held Sage impossibly close.

"Fucking cowards," Mal hissed, stopping to readjust his hold on Sage. "Can't even come at you head-on. Have to wait in the fucking—"

"Ianthe," Sage groaned, shifting closer so they could bury their face in Mal's neck, leaving a burning trail of contact along his skin that grew warmer the longer their nose pressed against his pulse. With a deep breath and a hard swallow, Mal forced himself not to act on the impulse to set Sage on their feet and kiss them to within an inch of their life.

Mal was well aware of Sage's cait sidhe nature, and spending the last four years raising Chuckles, he knew that if Sage got a good whiff of his scent then they would be able to point him out in a crowd. That didn't bode well for keeping the other, darker side of who he was hidden from Sage. But then, neither did the fact that he was currently covered in someone else's blood—head wounds had a nasty habit of looking a lot worse than they were, super annoying—nor that he was dressed in his head-of-the-family garb.

It wasn't that he thought he could keep this side of himself hidden from Sage. It had been so nice . . . pretending to be normal. Playing at being someone who could date someone without putting them in danger. Not being Mela Malec Ianthe Senka. Head of the Faceless Few. Ruthless. Evil, some might say. Vicious. Terrifying. If only for a few hours, it had been *nice*.

He had to play this off. Distance himself from the persona of Ianthe he'd been carefully crafting. Sage clearly didn't want to be a part of this world anymore, and Mal wouldn't drag them back in if he could help it. That meant not letting Sage connect the bloodshed they'd just witnessed back to Ianthe. Not dragging the blood and the violence in with him like shit on his shoe.

But with Sage so close, their body warm in his arms, it was hard to think.

"I don't know who Ianthe is," Mal said, but the lie burned his tongue as any lie told by a fae would. Good thing he was accustomed to pain, and even more to the consequences of outright lies. It was all part of the game of being who he was. So what if he wouldn't be able to taste anything come morning? He'd keep Sage away from this life no matter the cost.

"No?" Sage asked, but they didn't sound worried about

the fact that they were being carried off by a violent stranger. Mal would have to address that later.

"No. I'm Mal." They would recognize the name, Mal was sure. Corey had no doubt given Sage the rundown on the twins who ran the Faceless Few gang these days. The ones who had slaughtered all of Sage's kin in a bid for the seat at the head of the family. But even if she hadn't, Mal said, "The head of the Faceless Few."

"I see." But they didn't stiffen where they rested in his arms. Nor did they ask if Mal knew who *they* were. Probably for the better. Mal knew well enough how the more long-winded the lie, the more blistered his mouth would become. Best to keep it simple.

"You're all right," Mal murmured gently, resisting the urge to curl his body more protectively around the precious being in his arms. "I'm taking you home, and I'll have someone come by and check on you. A doctor. From the family."

"Mmm." Sage mumbled against his skin, their breath sending a tingle all the way down Mal's spine. Goddess. Mal was ill-prepared for having Sage this close. For being able to inhale the soft warm smell of them. Cinnamon sugar and petrichor, cut with the metallic bite of blood. Was their head wound worse than Mal had originally estimated, or was Mal bleeding on them? He couldn't tell.

"Yeah, you'll be okay," Mal said to ease his own mind because Sage was drifting again. "Hey. Hey," he murmured softly, giving them a little shake. "Don't fall asleep."

"I'm not asleep," Sage grumbled.

"You might have a concussion," Mal continued, undeterred. "You can't fall asleep with a concussion."

Sage pulled their face away from Mal's neck and shot him a perturbed look. It was undeniably adorable, and it cut him to the quick.

"Sorry." He sighed. "I'm sure you know that. But . . . talk to me. Please? Just so I know you're awake?"

Sage let out a long-aggrieved breath but didn't bury themself in his neck again. A pity, really. Instead, they remained where they were, staring up at Mal with those glowing green eyes. Which was arguably worse. They were undoubtably going to notice something he didn't want them to. But it was too late now. And honestly, he couldn't take it back. Wouldn't. There hadn't been time to throw on a glamour that would hide what he was, and the persona Mal had built around himself was terrifying enough that it had scared their attacker off. If Sage saw the ugly, savage thing that was Mal, then so be it. Maybe it would separate him more from Ianthe even though he'd done little to glamour himself when he *was* Ianthe.

"What should we talk about?" Sage asked, with a slow blink. Like a cat who was undeniably comfortable with the person holding them. Mal didn't deserve that. He wasn't worthy of it. But he'd hold on to it until the day he fucking died, because he might never get another chance to see Sage vulnerable and trusting. If Sage knew who he was, if they knew what he'd done, they wouldn't allow themselves to relax like that.

"I don't know." Mal sighed, shaking hair out of his face. "We're almost there though."

"You're the head of the Faceless now," Sage said, as if they were tasting the information on their tongue.

"Yes." He cut his eyes away from Sage and turned his attention to the apartment building a block up. It had a stone-faced facade, dated looking, although Mal was sure the building was less than a few decades old. Whoever'd built it had been trying to make it fit in with the street, which was lined in cobbles like much of this part of Eventide. Old town.

Sage nodded but didn't scream in terror the way most people would—the way they ought to, considering the implications. "Corey told me about you."

Mal's stomach dropped. That meant Sage had to know that Mal had killed their entire family.

It stung more than Mal would have liked.

He knew how the baker felt about their family, she'd made it clear in her dealings with Mox. Mal should have kept his distance when he wasn't dressed down as Ianthe, but he couldn't seem to. Like a fishing line caught on a log, pulled taut enough to break every time he was too far from Sage, he couldn't leave them alone now that he knew they were alive.

Honestly, it was a miracle he'd lasted the last four years without them.

"All good things, I hope?" he asked, flipping his hair again and leaning into the arrogance that came with the head of a family.

"She wasn't very complimentary."

Mal huffed a laugh. "Well, we can't *all* be right *all* the time, I suppose."

"Code to the door is 10-30-20-20," they said, either ignoring or choosing not to engage with the slight against someone who was clearly a friend. Probably for the best.

COREY WAS FRESH FROM THE SHOWER, HER HAIR STILL wet and in a towel, when she heard the knock on her door. "Sage, I swear to the Goddess if you've forgotten your key again, I'll—"

The words died on her tongue when she opened it to find Mal there, Sage in his arms, both of them reeking of blood, clothes grimy. Sage's eyes turned to her, their glowing gaze glazed and pained.

"What the fuck happened?" she squeaked and was forced to take a step out of the way when Mal didn't wait for an invitation. He pushed in like he owned the place. Neither answered her, and Corey dogged their steps as Mal carried Sage through the house toward the spare room. How he knew where Sage was staying, she didn't think she wanted to know.

The Faceless Few's reach was too far for her liking, but it was better them than Alton, she supposed. At least Mal and Mox weren't likely to try to force her into the family via threatening her sisters. At least they left her alone.

"The doctor will be here in a moment," Mal said, gently laying Sage out on the bed, careful of their injuries. "Let them in."

"You invited a mob doctor to my house?" Corey hissed, but she returned to the door at the soft tinkle of a bell and let the doctor into her apartment.

"Evenin', miss," the man said, taking off his tall hat and dipping forward into a bow.

Corey rolled her eyes and gestured down the hall. He followed the scent of blood that clung to the air like he was a shark in the water. Once he was in with Sage, Mal exited the room, shutting the door most of the way behind himself, and wheeled on Corey.

She'd been expecting to go after him for bringing this shit into her house, but the unbridled fury in his eyes had the words drying up on her tongue.

"Explain to me," Mal said in that dangerously quiet voice of his, "why there was a goon hanging around outside your bakery waiting for Sage tonight."

Corey bristled. "Maybe they were there because you and your sister keep hanging out around my business. I told you you'd draw attention to them like that. I warned you that you were too fucking conspicuous." She stepped forward, poking at Mal's chest hard enough to bruise. "Don't think it escapes my notice that this happened not even twenty-four hours after your little *date*. If you think for once second that—"

"They were Aquarius," Mal said, his eyes narrowing on her, accusing.

Corey's stomach dropped. "What?"

"I know all about you, Corwin." He took a hold of her wrist and pulled her prodding finger away from his chest. "Mox may be happy to play your little game, but I did my research. I know who you are. I know who you used to be. I know your connections to Alton and his people."

"How do you know they were one of Alton's goons?" She . . . she needed proof. She wasn't going to believe it until she saw proof. Why would Alton's people run the risk of stepping foot in Faceless territory? Alton wasn't that stupid, right? He knew if he was caught doing something like this on Faceless territory, it would be war. And no matter how proud and self-assured Alton was, he wouldn't be foolish enough to try to take the Faceless head-on. Not like this. Not after Mox and Mal had single-handedly gutted the gang and rebuilt it in their image.

Mal didn't say anything. He just reached into his pocket and pulled out a lapel pin. It was old-fashioned to use them to signify who a person was with these days. Most gang members only wore them when they were on official business, meaning meetings and such with other families. They certainly never wore them out on the streets, or on hits. Unless they were young and stupid.

"Look familiar?" Mal asked.

The metal burned in Corey's palm, even though it was cold. Of course it looked familiar. She'd had one exactly like this once upon a time. The waves. The statue rising from them like a vengeful Poseidon. The logo had changed slightly in the years since she'd worn one, become more modern looking, but she'd know it anywhere.

Fuck. This is my fault.

"This doesn't prove anything," Corey spat. But she knew better. Alton wanted information from her. Just because he'd let it fall to the wayside for the time being, didn't mean he was going to give up completely. And if he had to force it out of her, he would. This was a warning shot fired across the bow of the ship. It could be a coincidence that the attack was against Sage, or . . . or it could be Alton attacking a former heir because he knew they were alive. "They could have taken it off someone or found a lost pin. This could be—"

The door to Sage's bedroom opened with a creak then shut behind the doctor. "Would you both keep it down out here? My patient needs to rest," the man tutted.

"Apologies, Sirius." Mal dipped his head in respect. "How are they?"

"They need *rest*, as I just said. But they'll be fine." Sirius pulled a pad from his pocket and jotted down something before tearing off the top sheet and holding it out to Corey. "Call me if they're still dizzy come morning."

"All right." Corey nodded.

The doctor didn't even wait to be dismissed. He headed for the door and left Mal and Corey to their seething.

"You were so worried about their safety." Mal rounded on her again. "But from what I've seen, you're incapable of protecting them."

"Well, I guess it's a good thing they have a mobster boyfriend now, isn't it?" Corey hissed, hoping the lowered tone hid the shake in her voice. Mal was right. She'd fucked up. She'd fucked up, and she was going to have to fix this.

Mal snorted then headed for the door. He stopped there and looked over his shoulder to fix Corey with another scathing look. "I sent people after the attacker. If Mox did her job, we'll have answers by morning."

"Let me know what you find out."

"We'll see."

Then he was gone, and Corey was left with the gut-churning guilt of what she'd done. Fuck. *Fuck!* She had to make this right. She had to fix this. The question was, how?

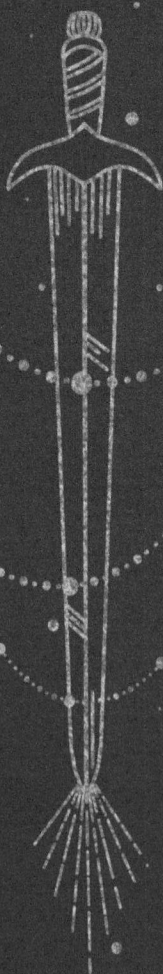

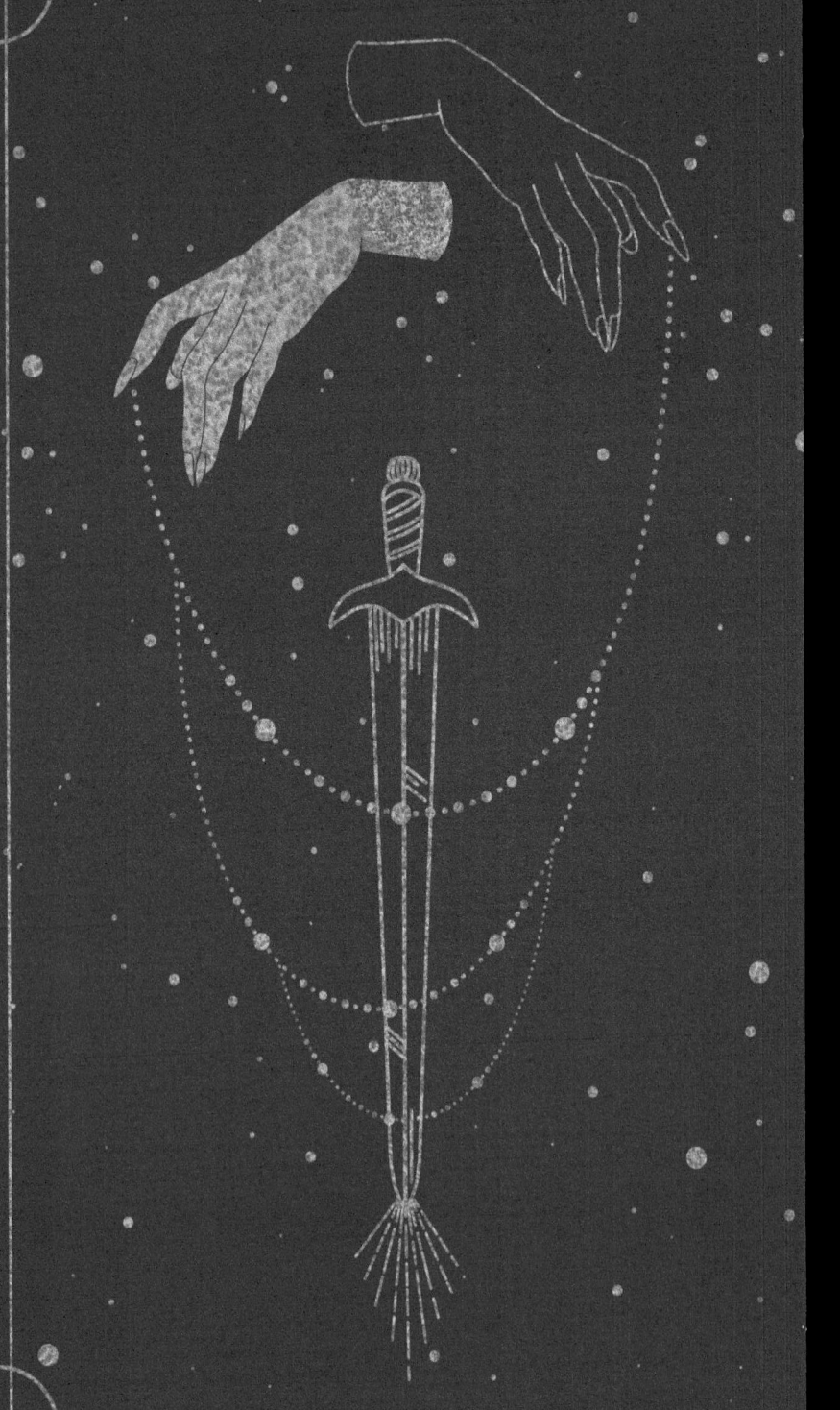

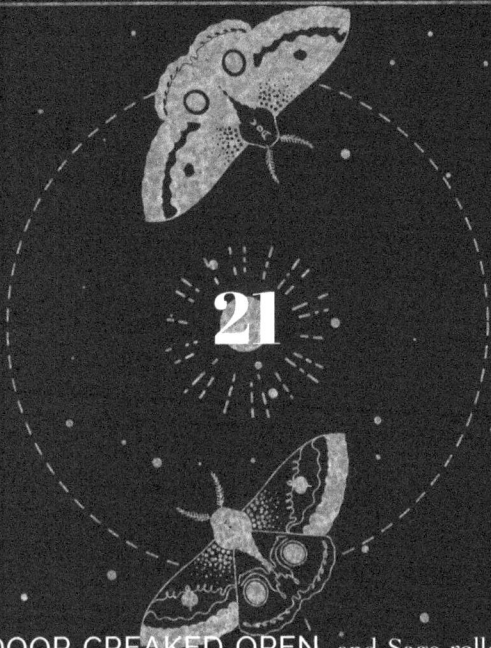

21

THE DOOR CREAKED OPEN, and Sage rolled away from the sliver of light that cut through the darkness of their room. They pulled the blanket over their still-aching head. Who the fuck would have thought that getting hit in the head with an aluminum baseball bat could cause an instant migraine? (Everyone probably, but who's counting? Not Sage.) The blood still in their hair made it stick to the back of their neck, uncomfortable and pulling a little, but they didn't feel like showering.

That was more work—one more thing—they couldn't deal with. Even if it would have made them feel better in the long run.

"I know you're not sleeping." Corey's voice traveled from where she was still standing in the doorway, her figure backlit by the light in the hall.

Sage didn't say anything, didn't even breathe. Maybe if they stayed still long enough, she'd give up and go away. Everything fucking hurt, and they didn't have the energy to deal with her shit right now. They didn't know that they'd *ever* have the energy to deal with her shit again. Maybe they should have taken the doctor up on those painkillers after all. Why had they thought they needed a clear head again?

"Sage," Corey muttered, impatient.

"I most certainly *am* sleeping." The words hurt coming out, pushed through a throat tight with exhaustion and pain. And the sound of their own voice rubbed harshly against their eardrums. They cringed away from it, but it didn't do any good. How could one escape their own voice? They couldn't.

"No, you're not." Corey scoffed.

"How the fuck do you know?" Rolling back over, Sage squinted at her from the darkness of the blankets. A corona of light flowed out around the doorframe like a starburst. It made Sage's head hurt worse, but Corey wasn't going to go away, not until she said whatever she'd come to say, so they might as well give her the attention she wanted. Maybe then she'd leave faster and they could get back to staring at the floating glitter behind their eyelids.

"Because you purr in your sleep." She sounded like she was laughing at them. Which was just plain fucking rude, considering they'd been attacked less than a couple hours ago.

"I do not!" Sage sat up abruptly, instantly regretting the movement when stars burst before their eyes and their head spun. "Fuck me."

By the time their head stopped spinning and they could see past the darkness blotting their vision, Corey had picked her way across the room littered in piles of clothing and dropped into Sage's office chair. She raised her brow as if to say, *You good?*

"No, don't worry about me. I only got hit in the head with a *bat*," Sage grumbled, but they were grateful when

Corey didn't reach out to help them sit. They leaned back against the wall at the head of their bed. They didn't particularly want to be touched right now. Not after they'd been attacked. Something vulnerable and sticky clung to their skin. Something like weakness. It smelled foul. "I don't fucking purr."

"You definitely do. But whatever." Corey leaned forward on her elbows. Her face was lit only from one side by the light of the hall. The rest was in darkness, casting deep shadows on her features. The side of her mouth that they could see was pressed into a serious line. "Do you know who it was?"

"If I knew who it was, don't you think I would have told the mobster who brought me home?" Sage pinched their eyes shut, rubbing them hard enough to cause colors to burst behind their lids.

"No," Corey responded flatly, and okay, yeah, that was probably fair. Sage had made a habit of not trusting people before they'd left Eventide. Least of all people from rival gangs. Not that Mal was technically from a rival gang. And he'd been . . .

"Fine." Sage opened their eyes to squint at her through the dark. "What's your point?"

"My point is, someone attacked you outside my business."

"I'm aware." Why was she restating everything Sage already knew? They were way too tired for this nonsense. "I do hope you're getting to a point soon, Corwin. I'm not at my best right now and—"

"I think they knew you were going to be there." There was no accusation or blame in her voice—likely because she was as much at fault as they were in this. "This was a targeted hit."

"So someone knows I'm alive."

"Someone who would like you to not stay that way." Pushing off from her knees, she leaned back in the chair again, crossing one leg over the other.

"Obviously." Sage still wasn't seeing what she was getting at. Although they were rapidly coming to their own conclusions about this situation.

They'd let someone push them out of their city, their state, their *home* once already. They weren't doing that again.

Enough was enough.

"We need to get you out of Eventide before—"

"No." They shook their head, ignoring the way it made stars flitter around the shape of Corey in the chair.

"What do you mean, *no*? It's not safe for you here. You need to go. I can't protect you, and you can't count on—"

"I'm not going anywhere." Sage lifted their chin, their tone dropping into something deeper, more self-assured, the voice of the heir to the Faceless Few. The last heir. The *true* heir. Born of the bloodline that started the gang centuries ago. They were done fucking *hiding*.

"Sage. Be reasonable."

"I am being reasonable." There wasn't much they could do to make themself look more put together and strong while lying in bed with a concussion, but they tried anyway, meeting Corey's gaze with a hard look. "Someone slit my throat and left me in an alley to die four years ago. I ran then. I let them chase me from my home. I hid. I let them *win*."

"That's not what this is about, and you know damn well it's not." Corey ran her hands through her hair, a frustrated breath leaving her as she sagged in the chair. The determination of a moment ago was gone now. She was tired, just like they were. "It's not about winning or losing."

"No. You're right. It's not. It's about the fact that this

was my home, my life. And some piece of shit chased me out of it, and for what? Because they wanted my seat at the table in the Court?" Sage laughed, incredulous. It sounded stupid when they said it that way. Ridiculous. They had trained for the day when someone would try to overthrow them. Why should they not utilize that training?

And almost before they had realized the decision was made, they said, "I'm *not* leaving Eventide again."

This was their home. And they would not leave it.

Somewhere from deep within Sage's mind, a low rumbling growl sounded, echoing. Pleased.

Hello, old friend.

The big cat living inside of them was silent, but Sage got the impression that she had cocked her head in acknowledgment. It had been so long since she'd been present, relief washed over Sage at her reemergence. They'd thought they'd lost her forever. That she'd abandoned them. She had not, it seemed. Although they weren't sure what had shaken the connection loose from the trappings that had kept her quiet this long.

It's been a long time.

A slow blink of pale green eyes followed the statement.

Once upon a time, the big cat had been black. A panther, ready and waiting for her next meal. So Sage was surprised when they closed their eyes and envisioned the beast, and she had gone gray. Like she had aged several decades since Sage had last seen her.

They wondered if that had happened since they'd been separated, or if it happened when they'd died. They supposed they'd have to do some internal searching to find out. But in the meantime, there was work to do.

"Sage." Corey frowned at them, her eyes drifting to look just over their shoulder as if afraid to meet their gaze any longer. But she seemed to understand that she wasn't going to stop them. Not now. Likely not ever.

"Don't *Sage* me." Sage shifted toward the edge of the bed, ignoring the ache in their joints and muscles. They were tired. So tired. But they were also so very, *very* done.

Done hiding. Done running. Done being scared.

"What are you going to do?" Corey asked, her gaze following them as they rose, stretching out their joints with a series of pops that only slightly relieved the pressure held there.

"I'm going to do what I should have done four years ago." They moved to the clean pile of clothes in the corner. How they knew it was the clean pile when they all looked the same, only they could tell. They squatted and started digging for a pair of black joggers and a long-sleeve black shirt. "I'm going to find the motherfucker who tried to have me killed."

Corey was staring at them, watching as they stripped out of their shirt and sweatpants. "You're not serious."

"Dangerously so." Sage shrugged on the long-sleeve shirt and shimmied into the pants.

"Tonight? You're going to go after them *tonight*?"

"They left a trail. And even if they didn't, we can ask your demon friend—"

"She's *not* my friend."

"—for help. She'll be able to tell us something."

"Why the change of clothes if this is just a fact-finding mission?" The chair creaked under her weight as she rose, but not to stop them, Sage noticed. She'd moved to flick on the lamp by the bed, giving them better light to put on their boots and dig in the duffle they'd slid under the bed for the dagger they had stashed there. The one they'd never thought they'd use again. The metal gleamed in the soft light, and Sage could still hear their father's voice in their head.

"Hold it tighter, Sage. Not like that, it'll slip, you'll cut yourself. Stop that. Hold it like you mean *it. You're never going to get anywhere in this business if you keep being so* soft.*"*

The old bastard would probably be pleased with what Sage was about to do. It was what *he* would have done, were he in Sage's position. But he hadn't gotten a second chance at life when someone killed him. There was no old acquaintance standing by, willing to bring him back and ferry him away in the night. Maybe things would have been different had there been. Or maybe he would have killed Sage himself for being weak. Soft.

Sage shook themself, strapping the dagger to their thigh. "I need the change of clothes because if the trail and Lucy turn up nothing, I have some sources still lingering around Eventide."

"You do?"

Sage turned to fix Corey with the kind of cold, cutting, cruel smile that they hadn't worn in four years. The smile of a person who wasn't afraid to get blood on their hands if it meant getting what they wanted.

Corey didn't say anything, but her eyes widened and Sage thought maybe a shiver raced down her spine. Then she swallowed, lifted her chin, and asked "What do you need me to do?"

WHEN THE TRAIL THEY PICKED UP RAN COLD — EITHER because Mox had found their target, or they were just that good — and Corey refused to see Lucy the demon again, Sage decided to hit up their own contacts.

"Do you know where we *are*?" Corey asked, her voice a hiss from behind Sage, and although they weren't looking at her, they could imagine her glancing around them, searching the thin early morning shadows for a tail. There wasn't one. Sage would have smelled them, the beast's senses keeping them on high alert.

"Yes, Corwin. I can read a map." Not that Sage had pulled out a map when they'd picked their destination and started walking. They didn't need one.

"This is Mata's territory." She was whispering like someone might overhear her and swoop out of the trees to punish them for daring to enter another gang's territory. "The Wildlings' turf."

"No!" Sage gasped and whipped around. "What gave it away?" They widened their eyes, clearly in mockery of Corey's ridiculous reaction to this development. "Was it all the trees, perhaps?" Sage asked, continuing in that tone as they gestured to the forest that surrounded them and the long, winding drive that led through the woods. They knew it wasn't fair to act that way. Corey hadn't asked for them to be cruel and biting. But once they started, it was hard to turn it off. "Or maybe it was the shift in the air when we stepped over the line. The smell of pine growing almost thick enough to choke."

"Sage." Corey kept saying their name like that, like she was tired. Sage wasn't sure what to do about it. It wasn't like they could turn back now. They needed answers, and since Corey had decided she would not go with them to visit the demon again, here they were.

"Corwin," Sage replied, turning back to the narrow dirt road. It was the kind of road a delivery truck would refuse to drive up for fear of getting stuck. But that's how Margau seemed to like things. Tucked away. Hidden. "Don't worry about it. He's not going to tell anyone we're here."

"And why won't he?"

"Because if he does, I'll kill him." Sage shrugged and started at a brisk trot through the trees, their panther rumbling, pleased, under their skin.

Soon.

They would let her out soon. Let her run through the forest like the wild thing she was. Giving chase. Hunting.

The panther chuffed in acknowledgment at the promise.

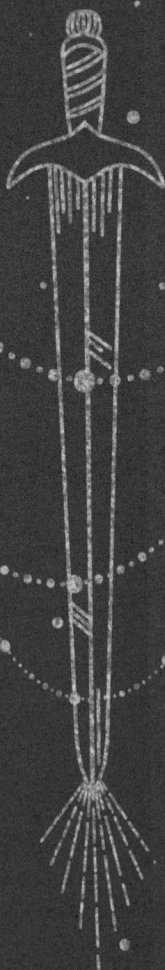

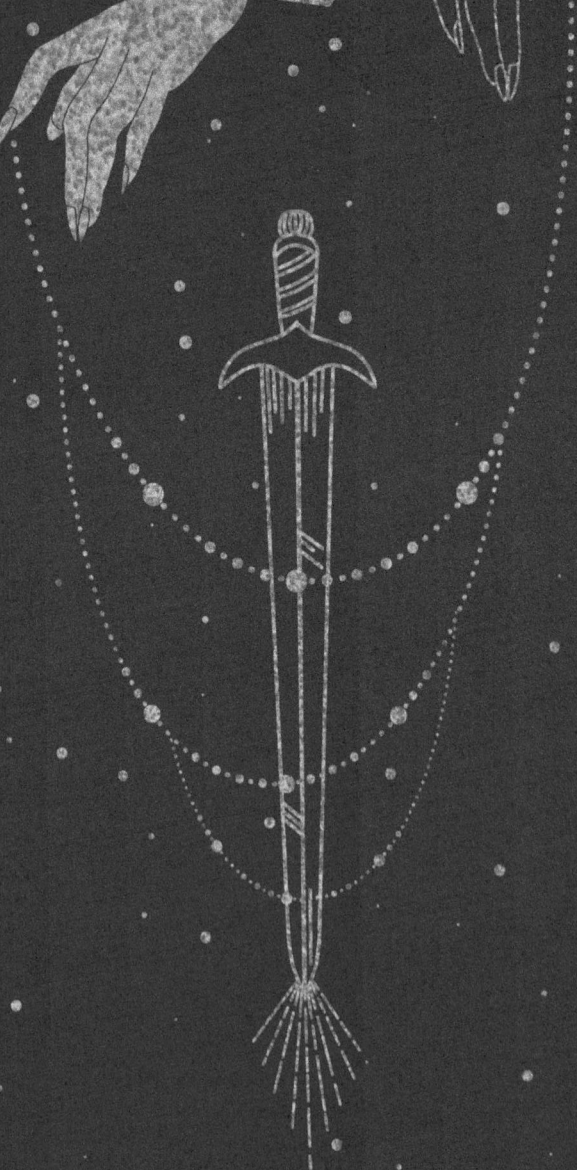

22

"WE TRIPPED some kind of ward back there. I know we did." Corey felt it the moment they'd walked over the invisible line. A shiver of *knowing* ran up her spine. The sounds of the surrounding wildlife, still waking up for the day, faded away along with any sounds from the city that hadn't been eaten by the trees. And there was a smell, something Corey couldn't quite describe. It was almost . . . *rancid*.

"We're fine," Sage insisted, but Corey could see how their shoulders had gone stiffer. They'd felt it too, she had little doubt in that. And it made them nervous. Great. That was just *great*. Now *both* of them were nervous.

"What kind of fae did you say this source of yours was?" Corey's eyes cut to the forest. She swore she saw something move out of the corner of her eye. Something quick and gigantic. Two qualities Corey did not like in adversaries *at all*. Seriously, something she was going to fight needed to pick one of those qualities and stick to it. They couldn't be both fast *and* huge, for Goddess's sake.

"I didn't." Corey didn't like the smile in Sage's voice either.

This was not going at all to plan.

Not that there had really *been* a plan. At least not one that Sage was sharing with Corey. It left her unsettled, anxious. She didn't like not knowing the plan. She didn't like not having some modicum of control over what was coming her way.

And that smile reminded her far too much of how Sage had been before they died. Of how the entire city of Eventide knew their name and was afraid of them. It hadn't been like this that one summer they worked together, but Sage had been young then. Sure, they'd had an edge to them, a sharpness most teenagers didn't, but not like this. Corey could only assume things had changed after that summer. That the Faceless Few had forged Sage Nocturna into something different, something more brutal.

But even if they had, even if Sage had become exactly what everyone expected of them, Corey had seen that scared kid still in there the night they almost died. She'd tried on multiple occasions to shake the image from her head.

Sage bleeding out.

Sage begging for their life.

Their glowing green eyes slowly dimming.

But she couldn't. Corey had seen dead bodies before. Fuck, she'd even been the cause of some of them. None of those deaths had haunted her. None of them had moved her to do the foolish thing she'd done for Sage Nocturna.

She didn't know why—they hadn't been friends in such a long time by that point. She didn't particularly want them to be either. Better not to think of such things.

But now, faced with the razor edge that was *this* Sage Nocturna, she was beginning to wonder if maybe they both would have been better off had she not gotten involved at all.

"Hey," Sage said, brushing her arm with the back of their hand. A familiar gesture.

Corey wasn't sure how she felt about that either, but decided it was better not to make a big deal about it. Not right now. Not when they were sneaking through the woods, coming up on what appeared to be a run-down, abandoned shack. This was the beginning of a horror movie. This was one hundred percent the way stupid kids died. A long stretch of clearly abandoned road. A cabin in the woods. A—

"Hey," Sage said again, and this time they took her hand. They gave it a brief squeeze to draw her attention away from her thoughts before dropping the hold almost apologetically. "You're fine. We're okay."

"I know I'm fine." The words came out too curt, brusque. A lie. It rubbed at her like the seam on a twisted sock, leaving behind a blister. This one would bubble and scar. It wouldn't even have the chance to heal before it popped.

"I've got a plan." And there was that sharp-toothed smile again. If Corey looked hard enough, she thought she might see fangs lining it.

"Well, I'm glad one of us does." She huffed.

"He probably won't even be up yet." Sage shrugged and turned back to the cabin, setting their shoulders into a straight line, the tension making them stand taller. They hadn't looked so like the heir to a Mafia family in the entire week since they'd returned to Eventide, but they sure as shit did now.

"Is that supposed to make me feel *better*? We'll be waking him up, and he'll be grumpy. Because people are always so willing to provide information when they're woken up at the ass crack of dawn."

Dappled sunshine had begun to filter in through the trees, but it didn't seem to touch the cabin. As if a storm cloud hung over top, blotting out any potential light. This was so much worse than Lucy's fucked-up bit of hell dimension on earth she liked to call a townhouse. Especially because out here, no one would hear them scream. And at least Corey knew Lucy was harmless. *Mostly.*

Sage didn't give Corey any more chances to grumble about their circumstances and fret over what was coming next. They crouched, a low growl leaving their lips that Corey hadn't heard in four years. Not since that night. It rumbled through the air, sending a shiver down her spine. Goddess, she did not want to be on the receiving end of that anger.

Then Sage took off at a run so quick they became a blur of black that shifted between one blink and the next into a line of gray. The panther finally free in all her glory.

A breath caught in Corey's lungs. She didn't know when Sage had managed to regain that ability, but seeing the panther again . . . Watching it leap over a downed tree, Corey couldn't help but smile. There was so much joy, unbridled and wild, in the movement. Smiling was the only option.

Corey whipped around to follow them but lost them in the trees somewhere around the side of the house. She ran after them, careful of the roots and fallen logs, her eyes narrowed, searching for Sage between the green.

The blur stopped suddenly, and another growl echoed through the air, followed by a low whimper. Corey rounded the corner of the house to find a large gray panther crouched over an even larger figure that dwarfed them, one clawed paw against the troll's olive-green throat, razor-sharp nails digging in enough only to dent the flesh. But the threat was there. And the troll read it, if the way they held themself perfectly still said anything.

"Call it off! Call it off!" the troll shouted, a warble in their voice.

"No can do," Corey said, pulling on a bravado she didn't quite feel as she tugged a dagger from the sheath in her boot. She might not know Sage's plan, but she thought she was catching on. Hopefully. "We've got questions."

"We who?" Their big black eyes shifted from Corey to the panther looming over them.

Sage blinked once, quick, and shifted most of the way back from cat to fae. The transition was so smooth, it was like they'd simply shrugged off a coat. All except for their right arm, claws still extended. "We. Me."

"Sage!" The troll's brows raised high on their face and their mouth gaped wide, showing rows of mossy teeth right along with their age. This one was more forest than person, and it wouldn't be long before they gave themself over to the trees. How had Sage even met a troll that old? "You're not dead!"

"It would appear not." Sage grinned, sharp-toothed and violent. "Hullo Margau, it's nice to see you again."

"It is?" Margau's eyes flicked from Sage to Corey over their shoulder. Likely looking for some sympathy, or maybe hoping Corey was holding Sage's proverbial leash and she'd rein them in. *No luck there.*

"Don't look at her, look at *me*," Sage snarled.

Corey flipped the dagger between her fingers, a smirk settling onto her face. It felt twisted and false, but she knew better than to back down in this sort of situation. She needed to make their target think she and Sage were on the same page. Needed Margau to look at Corey and Sage and see a duo who would end them before the forest did and ruin all their plans of retirement. It was an easier sell than she would have liked.

"Sorry buddy," Corey said with a shrug, catching the dagger once more between thumb and forefinger by the tip. "This is Sage's show."

"It is." Sage hadn't let up on their grip on Margau's neck yet, and Corey didn't think they planned to. After all, it would give Margau a chance to attack or run and sound some kind of alarm with the other Wildlings. Neither of which they could afford.

"Okay. Okay." Margau held their hands above their head and cut their eyes back to Sage. "What can I help you with, old friend?"

Sage snorted. "Old friend, my ass." They put more pressure on the claws, and Margau hissed.

"Sorry. Sorry. Too familiar. Of course. Of course." Margau was a babbler, it seemed, which could mean one of two things. Either they'd give Corey and Sage fuck all, or they'd give them too much. Corey didn't like their odds, but she didn't say so. "So uh . . ." Margau swallowed, and a relieved exhale left their lips when Sage let up a little. Not enough so Margau could go on the attack or run, but enough so they could breathe easier. "What do you need?"

"Information." Sage shifted, stretching out their neck as if holding their position made them ache. It probably did. They hadn't said as much, but Corey noticed the way they moved slower these days. How sometimes their joints would crackle or they'd have to stretch a grouping of muscles when they held still for too long. A holdover from being dead, she assumed, but didn't ask.

"What sort of information? You know I've got all kinds. I'll give you anything, anything at all."

"Of course you will." Corey scoffed. Anything to save their own ass. Not that she was one to judge. Hadn't she squealed like a pig not more than a few days ago to Alton to get him off her tail as the Phantom? All she could hope was that Sage didn't ask how someone knew they were still alive. Because if they did, she was royally fucked.

"I want to know who put out a hit on me." Sage tilted their head again, this time in a gesture like they were listening, waiting. Corey couldn't see their face, but she could imagine the look — curious in a way that would draw a person in, but deadly all the same. A fine line.

Margau's mossy green brows shot up in surprise and they let out a short, sharp burst of laughter.

"What's so funny?" Corey asked, throwing the dagger so it landed tip down right beside Margau's head in the undergrowth. Her patience was running short. They needed to get the fuck off Wilding territory before Mata caught wind of it, and Margau beating around the bush wasn't helping.

"Just . . ." Margau snorted another loud laugh but stopped abruptly when a snarl left Sage's lips. "I mean . . ." They swallowed, the sound audible in the too quiet of the wood around them. "The list would be shorter if you asked me who *didn't* have a hit out on you."

"Fuck." Sage growled, slashing at the ground to Margau's other side with their claws, tearing up a thick bed of moss, vines, and disintegrating wood.

"But, but, but . . ." Margua went on, clearly worried they'd fucked up. "I do know your cousin survived the purge. And word on the street is, she always wanted the seat for herself."

"Which cousin?"

"Bentley," Corey supplied. "She's the only one who made it out of Faceless territory alive. Where can we find her?"

"I'll text you the address," Margau promised.

Sage fell back on their haunches, and Margau scrambled from beneath them, disappearing into the undergrowth and nearly knocking Sage's significantly smaller form to the ground. Corey swooped in to grab them by the arm. They blinked at the grip Corey had on them, once, twice, slow blinks like they trusted her not to take advantage, then frowned thoughtfully.

"I don't think I like that look," Corey said. "What does that look mean?"

"It means"—Sage took a long, slow breath, the kind that usually signaled someone coming to a decision they didn't like—"I think this is going to be more than a revenge mission for the attack."

"If it's not just that, what is it?" Corey didn't want to know. She did *not* want to know. She didn't want to be a part of it, and she didn't want to know.

"I can't let what she did stand." Sage's shoulders tightened and they lifted their chin. "I think it's time I went back into the family business."

Fuck.

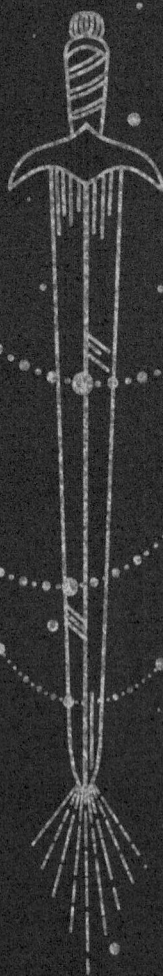

23

BLOOD DRIPPED loud in the ensuing silence. It drowned out even the sound of the bay just outside the back door, the rumble of traffic on the other side of the small grouping of warehouses where the Faceless Few came to *conduct business*. A phrase that meant everything from storing goods for the Night Market to torturing people for answers.

Mal had gone harder than perhaps he ought to. He hadn't been trying to kill the weaselly son of a bitch. Not really. And yet . . .

Said weaselly son of a bitch's head had dropped forward at some point, and at some point later, his breathing had completely cut off.

"Mox is going to have a fucking conniption." Mal sighed, brushing the stray strands of black hair sticking to his face away, then stopped when blood glittered on his skin. The dim light had hidden most of it, but as he looked more closely now, he saw the way it clung to his rolled-up sleeves and the front of his white shirt. Good thing he'd chosen black slacks for this evening's activities and discarded the crimson suit jacket from earlier.

Pulling his phone from his pocket, he winced at the brightness of the backlit screen. All text and apps blurring into mere shapes, even with the magnifying function. Goddess, he missed phones with physical buttons. At least then once he'd memorized the position of the keys, they didn't change. And there was something so satisfying about a flip phone that he could clap closed when he was done with people and their shit. But smartphones, fuck. They were always changing. Apps getting logos with completely different color schemes than what he was used to. Things being added or taken away with each new iteration. Even a function that deleted "dead" apps, which rearranged his home screen occasionally.

Some things about smartphones were a blessing. But others? Well, there was a reason he let Mox set up his phone whenever he got a new one.

With a deep inhale, Mal double clicked the button on the side until the swirling shape of the electronic assistant popped up. One of the few things that made smartphones worthwhile.

"Call Mox."

"Calling Mox," the computer-generated voice responded, and the phone began to ring loudly, finally silencing the sound of the blood staining the cement floor.

"Are you done with him already?" Mox asked when she picked up on the second ring. She couldn't have gotten too far after she'd dropped Mal and his hostage off. He'd only been at this a half hour before his annoyance got the better of him and he finished the fucker.

"Yeah. I need a cleanup." Mal set his phone on the tray he liked to use to hold whatever tools he'd need for the session and picked up a rag to wipe off his bloody hands.

He'd still have to shower once he got back to the house before pouring himself into bed, but at least this would keep most of it out of the car's interior. Something Mox was forever getting on him about.

"Excuse me?" Mox sounded like she was holding herself still, not even breathing maybe. Being her twin came with certain perks, like his ability to know this tone came with a pinched brow. "What do you *mean* you need a cleanup?"

"I mean, I need someone to come dispose of the body." He could do it himself, of course. It wouldn't be the first body he'd cut up and carted off to the incinerator. But what was the point in being the boss if he had to do the messy work himself?

Mox sighed loudly, and he heard her shift. She'd likely leaned forward to press her face to the steering wheel, if she was still in the car. "I'll be there in five. I swear to the Goddess, Mal, we can't keep doing this. Eventually, someone is going to start noticing that—"

Mal didn't wait for the rest of her lecture. He hit the glaring red button and returned his attention to the body still strapped to the chair by writhing shadows. "You shouldn't have pushed your luck," he told it.

No. That wasn't the reason he'd gone too far. He'd gone too far because he couldn't get the image of Sage out of his mind. Couldn't unsee the swing of the bat as it hit Sage in the back of the head and Sage stumbled. How dare this filthy, low-level goon think he could lay a single finger on Sage Nocturna. And in Faceless Few territory, no less? Fuck that. The other gangs had gone unchecked for far too fucking long. Mucking about with the portals to the Night Market. Sending bruisers across turf lines to attack people.

Maybe it was about time Mal started making an example of those who crossed his borders. Fuck the Court. Fuck peace and harmony. He was done with all of it.

"Shit," Mox gasped when she entered to find Mal still glaring at the body, a choked quality to her words, like maybe she was swallowing down bile. "Did you have to"—she paused, stepping closer—"did you have to completely *disembowel* him?"

Mal glanced at the place where he'd cut the body open, the bogie's insides spilling across his lap and out onto the floor. Flicking his gaze back to the face of the fae who had attacked Mal's spouse, he shrugged.

"Was he alive when you did that?"

"Mostly."

A tired sigh, and Mox dropped the duffle bag she'd brought to the floor at the bogie's feet. "Did you even get anything out of him?"

"Some." Mal returned to the tray, still trying to wipe the blood from his hands with the dry rag. He needed a wet wipe or something. Maybe Mox brought—

The crinkling of plastic preceded a pale packet hurling in his direction from over Mox's shoulder. A tendril of shadow shot out to grab it, and Mal swallowed a smile at the packet of wipes. His twin sister thought of everything.

"What kind of some?" Mox pressed more when she seemed to realize Mal wasn't up for talking. He hated it when she did that. Why she couldn't leave well enough alone, he didn't know. But he supposed if she did, maybe he'd never tell her anything. He needed his sister to poke and prod him out of his shell occasionally.

"Apparently, word is going around at that Sage was still alive. He didn't know who spilled the beans first, but it's been circulating." Mal pulled a wipe from the package and started to clean away the thickest globs of blood on his hands. *So fucking sticky.* "Which wouldn't have been an issue, really. No one knew where to find them, and they

definitely weren't going to look for Sage here, in Faceless
territory."

"But?" Mox prompted, not looking up from her work.
The squelching sounds of bloody bits being removed and
shoved into a duffle probably should have some effect on
Mal, but it didn't. It was hard to care at all when the pain
all over Sage's face was still fresh in his mind.

"But," Mal continued, tossing the soiled wipe into the bag
along with the bogie's hands, "it looks like Lucy has been
running her fucking mouth. Corey and Sage went to her for
help with a glamour spell, and for some reason Lucy decided
now was a good time to let her client confidentiality ethics
lapse. Apparently, this morning, she was dealing with a client
and let slip that Sage might be in Faceless territory. From
there, it was almost easy for the Aquarius to track them down."

FUCK. FUCK. *FUCK!*

This was all Mox's fault. She'd gone to Lucy and run off
at the mouth. Asked for a favor. Made a deal with a literal
demon and agreed to Lucy getting the job done by any
means necessary. Clearly, they were going to have to
discuss her methods. But first, Mox had to keep Mal from
figuring out that Mox had fucked up.

"Was that who it was? The Aquarius?" Mox's voice
sounded strange, even to herself. It was too high and shaky.
She knew without even taking her eyes off her work that
Mal heard it. And he wasn't going to let it slide. He was
going to force her to tell him what was going on.

"This time," Mal said, carefully. His heeled boots made
soft clicks on the floor as he came around to stand behind

the chair and looked down at Mox over the bogie's shoulder. "Moxxie-kins, what did you do?"

Mox swallowed roughly and refused to take her eyes off what she was doing. She needed to get the body out of here before it started stinking. Thankfully, Mal had done a lot of the work in taking it apart, but that didn't change how the bogie would need to be carted across their district to the incinerator, hopefully before anyone noticed he was missing. Not that whoever sent him would do anything about Mal's actions. To do so would be to admit openly that Aquarius sent hired muscle into another gang's territory to attack what seemed to be a civilian. It would spell war.

"Moxxie," Mal pressed, his voice gentle.

"You have to promise not to be pissed." Not that it would really do anything. He could promise all he liked. He was going to be positively livid when she told him. But it was worth a try.

"I'll make no such promise."

At least he was honest, she supposed.

"But I *will* promise not to turn you into a new pair of shoes for whatever you did."

"Just use me as crab bait for the pots, right?" The joke fell flat and Mox knew it, but she didn't know what else to do. She needed Mal in a good mood. And while he'd taken most of his aggression out on the poor bogie who'd had the misfortune of taking up a gig that put him directly in Mal's line of fire, Mox knew damn well it wasn't enough.

"And poison the poor crabs? Perish the thought." Mal snorted, shaking his head. Then he let out a slow breath. "Seriously, Mox, what is it?"

"I went to Lucy." She measured the words out slowly, like spoonfuls of medicine that would hopefully go down easier for their relative smallness. "And made a deal."

"What kind of deal?" Mal's voice inched toward a growl.

"Before I tell you, I want to say that I don't think Lucy wants to hurt Sage in any way. I think she wants them here, probably as much if not more than you do."

Mal made a noise in the back of his throat that didn't sound like he believed her, but he didn't say anything to that effect. "What *kind* of deal, Mox?"

"She agreed to make it so Sage stayed in Eventide. That they wouldn't leave. And before you get pissed about it, I did this for you and Chuckles. I know how happy Sage makes both of you, and I just wanted . . . I wanted to see that you stayed happy." She huffed, almost instantly regretting it as the deep inhale that came before it drew the stink of the bogie into her mouth. Fuck, she really needed to hurry this along.

Mal didn't say anything for a long time, but when Mox looked up at him, he didn't look angry. He looked . . . thoughtful.

"Mal?"

"I see," Mal said after a moment, then nodded. "All right then, that makes this a little easier perhaps."

"It does?"

He didn't sound angry. Why didn't he sound angry? It was freaking Mox out.

"Yes." Mal nodded. "I can only assume one of the people coming after Sage is Bentley. She'll want to remove them before they can so much as think about coming for the Court seat."

"And that helps us how?"

"It's going to make her desperate." Mal smiled, the shadows around him writhing in his joy. "And her desperation is going to make her obvious. We just need to get all our eyes watching."

"I'll call Guin."

"Call the Phantom too."

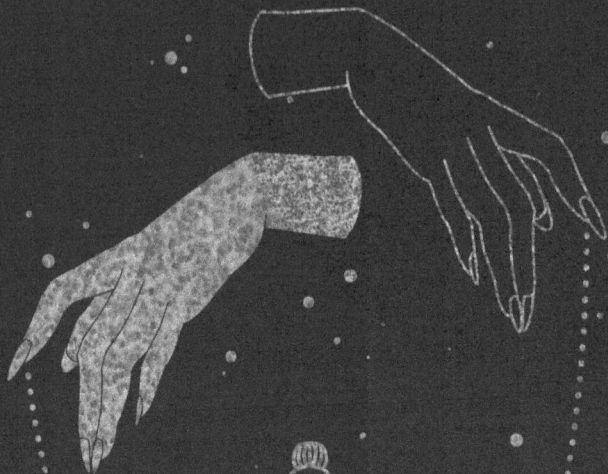

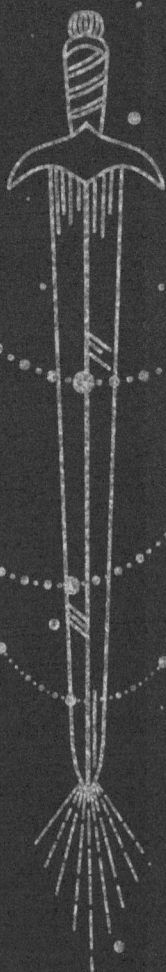

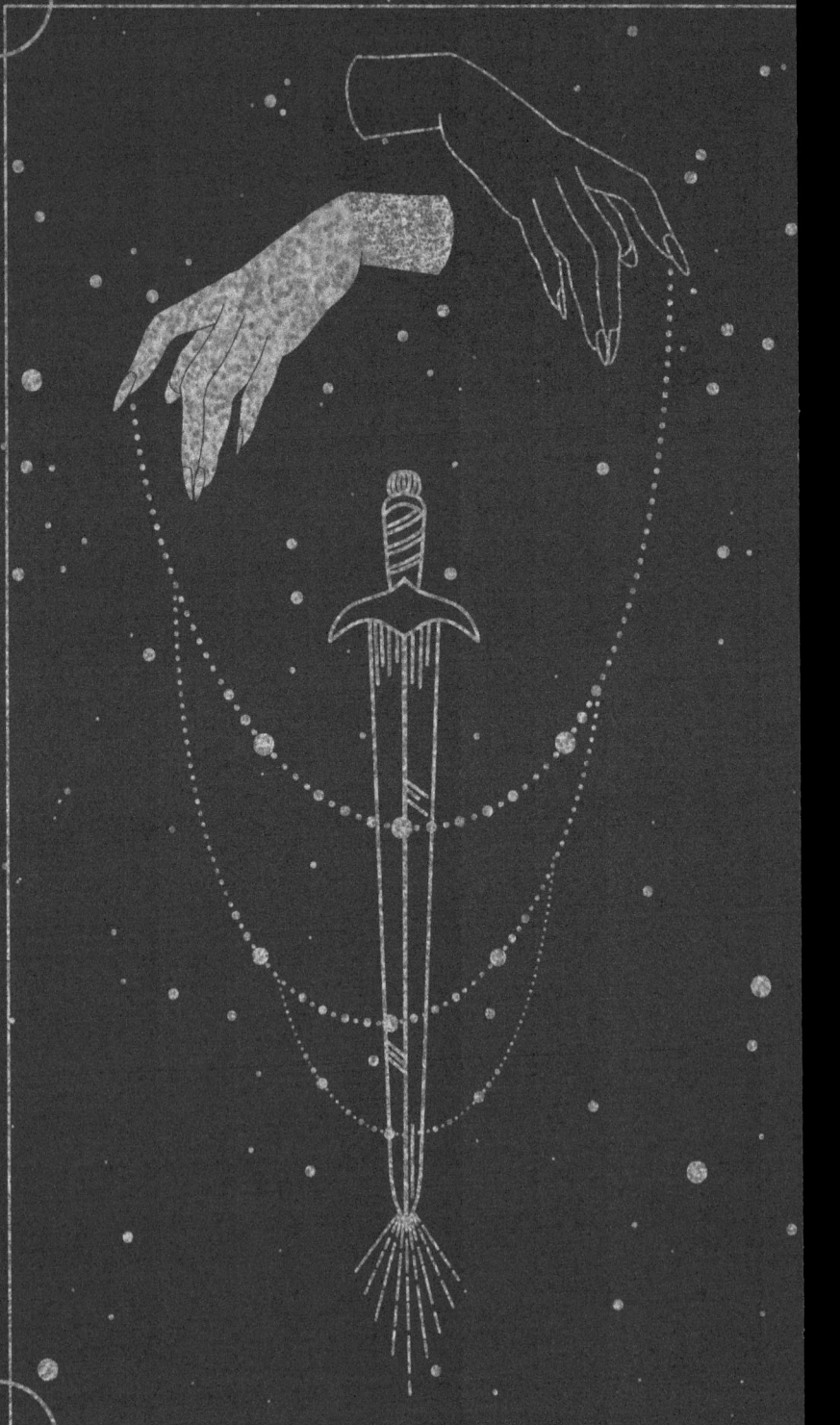

24

SAGE AND COREY had gone back to the apartment
after their little adventure, and Corey had stood outside the
door to the bathroom while Sage scrubbed themself raw
trying to get the greasy feeling of That Person off their skin.
They hadn't been the person who threatened and used their
claws in years. And while they understood the necessity,
they didn't like how easy it had been. How *right* it felt.

But they couldn't think about that now because—

"Bakery opens in ten," Corey called back into the
kitchen, and Sage nearly dropped the tray full of muffins
they were pulling from the oven.

Thank the Goddess Chuckles wasn't there—they didn't
want her to see them like this. It would only make matters
worse.

The door to the bakery chimed with the first customers,
and Sage fell into the steady rhythm of making and
decorating. A birthday cake for someone named Bowie. A
fresh sheet of brownies when they ran out. Dough for
tomorrow's loaves mixed and ready to hit their first proof. It
was exactly what Sage needed to push the evening and the

morning that followed from their mind. But unfortunately, it couldn't last, as most things couldn't.

All too soon, the front door was locked, and Corey returned to the kitchen, a tired sheen to her slowly blinking eyes. "Are you ready?"

"Yeah, let me just grab my pack from the car and we can get changed."

From there, it was almost easy to change into the same clothes they'd been in that morning, slip the dagger into its holster on their thigh, then hunt down Bentley Nocturna.

The apartment building they pulled up outside of looked nothing at all like Corey's. In the heart of Aquarius territory, among the modern skyscrapers of Eventide, built within the last twenty years or so to accommodate the ever-growing population, stood an all-glass building. The windows reflected the bay and the green of the small park that separated the two. Waterview. Expensive. Whoever was paying for Bentley's lifestyle now hadn't skimped. Probably because it was cheaper in the long run to keep her happy and quiet than to have her running about destroying things because she was pissed.

"Are you sure this is the place?" Corey asked as they approached the door.

Sage checked the address Margau sent once more and nodded.

The front door, too, was glass, and unlike Corey's building this one had an easy-to-spoof scanner. Sage could have laughed at the idea that Bentley lived in a building that was technically less secure than the dated three-story they and Corey currently shared.

With a bit of magic, Sage swiped their hand over the scanner and the lock clicked open, letting them push through into the glass and tile lobby. It was cold, and not just because of the air conditioning. Sage had lived a lot of places over the years since leaving Eventide, and they'd come to realize that they didn't care for these modern structures and the way they lacked the humanity built into the those constructed in years prior. There was something nice about brick that had to be laid by hand.

"What floor is she on?" Corey moved on silent feet to the elevator, her voice muffled by the mask covering the bottom half of her face. Sage had opted out of wearing one, as well as out of experimenting further with the glamour stone Lucy had given them now that their panther was back. People seemed to already know they were alive—who cared if they got caught on camera? Besides, they were sure what they were about to do was going to expose them to any of Eventide's underground that didn't already know. There would be little point trying to hide after that.

"Penthouse, probably." Sage waved a hand over the scanner in the elevator, performing the same trick they had downstairs. "No wards," they scoffed, rolling their eyes.

"She's not afraid at all, is she?"

"That's not it." Sage shook their head, sighing as they stared at their reflection in the polished metal of the elevator. Hair sapped of its color, green eyes glowing like a cat's staring back at them. But that wasn't what bothered them. It was the way the black long sleeve washed them out, making them look sickly. Dead. Not far from the truth, really, but that didn't mean they wanted to be reminded of the fact. If they squinted just right, they could see the edges of the scar on their neck that the choker wouldn't cover. If they closed their eyes, they could imagine crimson seeping from below the black velvet.

"Then what is it?" Corey nudged them lightly with her hip, as if maybe she'd asked a couple of times with no answer.

Sage shook themself and frowned, cutting their eyes

away from their own reflection to look at Corey instead. "What is what?"

Corey's brows creased in the center, but she didn't voice her concern about their mental state. Probably for the better—they weren't exactly the heart-to-heart kind. They weren't even fucking *friends*, if Sage was honest with themself. Which made them wonder why Corey was there at all.

"If she's not afraid, what is she?" Corey prompted again.

"Arrogant." That was putting it nicely.

Corey snorted. She looked like she wanted to say something else, but a second later the doors dinged open onto the penthouse, and they both stepped out. "How do you even know she's home?"

The lights in the main living area were off, apart from one in the kitchen over the stove. A clear indication that maybe she wasn't, in fact, home.

"She's probably not." Sage shrugged and dropped onto the big sectional facing the windows that looked out over the bay.

With a grunt of annoyance, Corey wandered further into the apartment, opening doors as she went, dagger at the ready. "Are we going to wait for her?"

"That's the plan." Kicking their feet up onto the coffee table, Sage leaned their head back over the cushions to watch her. "Anything?"

"No. She's probably out at the clubs."

"Like I said, arrogant." To the point of foolishness. Bentley had always been that way. Too enamored with all the bells and whistles that came with the family life to take note of the blood spilled to make that possible. It used to annoy Sage, but now it just made them nauseous.

It was amazing Mal hadn't caught her yet. But that likely had more to do with the fact whoever paid for her lifestyle had restrained her to Aquarius territory, and Mal was still new to this, without the web of contacts Sage had. Given another few years, he'd have found her. Sage just happened to get there first.

"More like stupid." Corey dropped into the armchair on the other side of the room, her dagger balanced precariously between her fingers.

"She's young." Although Sage knew that wasn't much of an excuse. Bentley was only about ten years younger than them and had always erred on the side of reckless. Sage had been there once, so they understood. But they'd grown out of it quick. There hadn't been much choice in the matter, being the Nocturna heir.

"How long do you think she'll be?"

"Take a nap." Sage tilted their head to offer her a grin. "You could probably use it. We've been going, what? Forty-eight at this point?"

"Not quite." Corey pressed her head into the back of her chair, closing her eyes and letting out a soft sigh. "How do I know you won't gut me in my sleep?"

"I've had plenty of chances already, haven't I?" A soft laugh rumbled up Sage's throat, and when Corey opened her eyes to glare at them, they winked.

"I fucking hate you." But she closed her eyes again, and Sage watched as she relaxed, her muscles unclenching as she dropped her dagger into her lap, not releasing it but letting her fingers go lax.

"Keep telling yourself that." Sage wasn't sure *what* they were, but Corey certainly didn't hate them, and Sage didn't hate her either.

Things had changed in the week since they'd been back in Eventide. Which arguably wasn't a long time for Sage and Corey to grow closer, but what was that thing about bonds forming under pressure? They were like diamonds.

That might be sappy for their relationship, and Sage certainly wouldn't say it out loud, but there was some truth to it.

While Corey snoozed, Sage kept watch. They closed their eyes and let the panther do her thing. Let her sniff the cool air, separating out the scents. Lingering traces of takeout. Too much perfume. And beneath all of that, the smell of Bentley. It had been four years, and that smell hadn't changed. Sage tried not to find that comforting, when they were faced with so much change. But it was nice, nonetheless, to know that at least something, some*one*, they'd left behind hadn't changed.

It was also comforting to have the panther back. To feel the way she paced in the back of their mind, always on high alert, always waiting, watching. She seemed antsier than she'd ever been before, likely a byproduct of their death and the years she'd spent wherever she was when out of Sage's reach. Knowing she was there provided Sage some much-needed peace. She'd have their back this time.

Minutes drifted by, but eventually Sage heard the ding of the elevator down below. There was no way to be sure if it was Bentley, but the panther rumbled an unsettled growl and Sage caught the scent of Bentley's perfume.

"She's here," Sage called over to Corey, who blinked awake, rubbing her nose with the back of her hand though the mask and rising from the chair so she could duck into a shadowed corner.

A moment later the elevator dinged again, the light cutting through the dark of the living room, and Sage turned their head to get the first glimpse of their cousin in four years. She looked the same. Another oddly comforting thing.

Dressed to the nines with her long dark brown hair— the same color Sage's used to be before they'd died—pulled into a messy updo. High heeled shoes that looked like they cost more than Sage's entire outfit click clacking across the tiled floor. As she made her way into the living room, she kicked off her shoes, leaving them scattered across the floor before dropping onto one end of the couch.

Sage followed her progress the entire time and waited until she was beside them on the couch before they said, "Hullo, cousin."

Bentley let out an ungodly screech and fell off the couch in a heap, her sparkly skirt sliding up enough that Sage could see the shorts she wore underneath. It took her a couple scrambled seconds of huffing, puffing, and squealing before she righted herself enough that she could fix Sage with a hard glare. It might have been intimidating if one strip of false eyelashes hadn't come loose and was now sitting cockeyed on her face.

"Sage." Bentley blinked at them, her manicured nails digging into the thick carpet of the living room area. Nails. Not claws.

"Bentley." Sage smiled, sharp and feral, all pointed teeth. "Don't act so surprised, you had to know this was my next stop when you heard I was alive."

Bentley barked a laugh, and although she didn't rise from the floor, she lifted her chin, her posture changing entirely. Shifting into the girl who thought being a Nocturna made her a god. Insufferable. "Well of course I did."

"Which is why you tried to have me killed."

"Me?" She gasped, clutching her chest. "Cousin, I'd never."

"Of course not."

"You aren't even worth the effort." A snide smile curled her lip, something ugly coming to the surface that Sage had never seen before.

It struck them then that maybe Bentley wasn't the same girl they'd left behind when they died. Maybe the annihilation of the family had done to her what it failed to do to Sage. Maybe it'd made her hard, nasty, where for Sage all it had done was . . . nothing, surprisingly. They felt numb. What was there *to* feel really? None of the rest of the Faceless had been particularly kind to them. Their father had always fostered an environment of cat-eat-cat. And in the end, it had been what killed his only child.

"Not worth the effort?" The words left Sage weaker than they would have liked, the claws they'd regrown since deciding to go after Margau ripped out in an instant.

"Not at all!" Bentley crowed, slapping the floor. "Why would I bother with you? If I wanted the Faceless for myself, I could just go and get it. I've got the resources now. More than you ever had. What do you think? You can just come home and take over again? You think anyone in this city has any respect for you now that you don't have *Daddy* at your back? You were a useless heir then, and you're *nothing* now." Every word made Sage sink further and further into the couch. "You worthless piece of—"

She continued, but Sage didn't hear her anymore. They heard their father. His words harsh and cutting. Talking down to Sage like they were dirt on his shoe. Echoing the same sentiments as Bentley. Like they were—

"Enough." Corey dissolved from the shadows in an instant, her dagger pressed to Bentley's throat, hardly leaving her room to breathe. "Ask your questions, Sage."

Taking a deep inhale, Sage tried to calm the ragged pace of their heart. It didn't do much, but it did remind them that they were not that child anymore. They were an adult. They hadn't been under their father's thumb in over four years at this point. And they'd made it in the big wide world without him. Without his money. Without his connections.

"Right." Sage nodded, standing from the couch and striding over toward their cousin. "If you didn't put a hit out on me, who did?"

Bentley blinked up at them, her eyes wide, her mouth slightly agape, and then the look of confusion was gone and she was laughing.

Laughing. Laughing.

Laughing so hard that Corey had to pull her dagger away lest she slice Bentley's throat.

"Answer them!" Corey snarled, giving Bentley a hard shove.

It didn't do anything. Bentley started rolling around on the floor, her shrill laughter so loud that if she had neighbors, they would have complained. Corey pulled back her foot as if to kick her, but Sage raised a hand to stay the attack and shook their head. With a huff, Corey stepped back, her arms crossed over her chest.

"Goddess," Bentley said when she seemed to have gotten control over herself once more. She swiped at one watering eye, her mascara running down her face. "I haven't laughed so hard in forever. Thanks for that, Sagey. Had I known you were so fucking stupid, I might not have been so gung-ho to get rid of your dumbass all those years ago."

"So you did put the hit out on me four years ago?" They weren't sure why that hurt. It didn't matter—what was done was done.

"Never said that." She tsked, wagging her finger at them. "But to answer your question . . . Ask yourself, Sage, darling, dear cousin, why ever are you alive?"

"What?" Sage croaked, their throat tight.

Bentley leaned forward, tilting her head to look up at them, her lip curled into a vicious smile. "Never told them how they were brought back, did you, Corey?"

Corey hissed from behind Bentley but didn't say anything, and when Sage looked at her, she pressed her lips into a thin line.

"A life for a life," Bentley said, the words curling out of her lips like a victory. "That's how necromancy works, isn't it? Ask yourself, Sage, who had to die so you could live?"

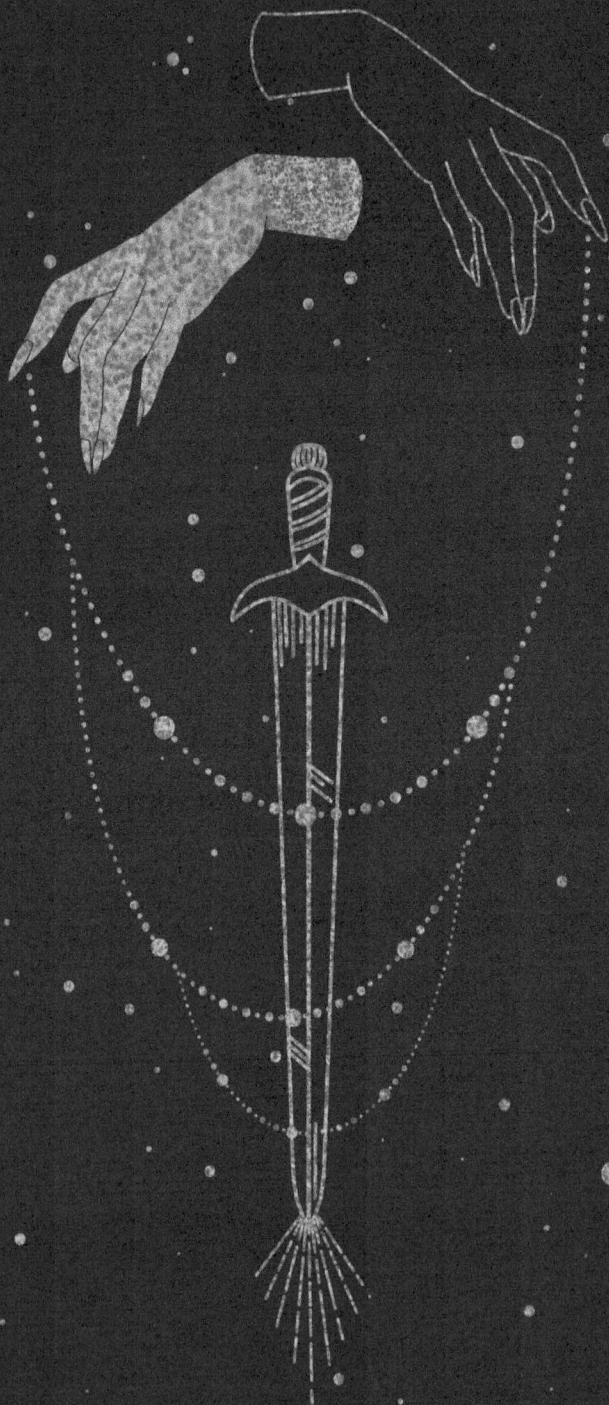

25

COREY'S HEART was going so jackrabbit quick in her throat, she almost choked on it.

They'd never discussed the *how* of the thing. It had never seemed particularly pertinent.

"What did she mean?" Sage asked, their voice so quiet that if the car wasn't silent around them, she wouldn't have heard it.

They'd left Bentley behind, laughing and gloating. There was no talking to her, and Sage wouldn't let Corey cut her down, so what was there to do besides leave? Corey wasn't going to forget where she lived though, and if Bentley caused any more trouble, she'd be making another surprise visit. Alone this time.

Corey took a deep breath, closing her eyes and gripping the steering wheel till it creaked under the pressure. She didn't want to talk about this. But Sage had to know. There was no other option. They had to know.

Sage didn't prompt her again. They waited, their eyes facing forward as if they didn't want to look at her. Didn't want to face what happened head-on. Corey could relate.

"Necromancy is about balance," Corey said, repeating what Icarus Ashthorne told her four years ago, almost to the day now, when she contacted the witch begging for help to bring Sage back. She wasn't even sure how she'd found Ashthorne anymore. A google search. A forum. One person directing her to another to another. It was strange how these things happened sometimes on the internet. Even stranger still how they happened within the witch community.

"Okay," Sage responded, the word drawn out almost like it was a question or was leading somewhere else.

"Balance and opportunity. To save you, we had to take another life. One of similar cosmic value, I guess." Corey shrugged. She hadn't been interested in the math behind what Ashthorne was doing. Or rather, she'd decided that knowing how a necromancer weighed the cost of one person's life against another would do her head in. It would be too much, even for someone like Corey who was no stranger to bloodshed. "We had to find someone of equal value."

"Who did you choose?" Sage didn't sound like they really wanted to know. They sounded like the answer might scare them more than anything else, and honestly, it probably should if what Bentley said was true.

"We tried to find someone that no one would miss. Someone not associated with one of the big families."

"But?"

Corey cleared her throat, forcing herself to release the steering wheel one finger at a time, putting her hands into her lap where she gripped them tight around each other. "Equal value, remember?"

"An heir." Sage hissed, and although it was dark out, although the interior lights of the car weren't on, Corey thought she saw them shake a little in their seat. "You had to choose someone who could be a potential heir."

Corey nodded. She flexed her fingers, open and closed, open and closed, timing her breathing with the movement as if it might head off the impending panic. It didn't, but she wasn't above trying. She'd known when she'd chosen the person that it would come back and bite her in the ass one day. But Sage was leaving and she was going underground, so how would anyone find out? And she was so good at covering her tracks, always had been. There was no reason for anyone to know.

Then Sage came back, and everything went to absolute shit.

"Which potential heir did you choose?" Again, it was like Sage didn't really want an answer, but Corey was going to give them one. They had to know the true danger they were in. They had to know that coming back to this fucked-up city had been a mistake. Not that it would change anything. They were here now, and whatever enemies they'd made weren't going to stop even if they left, so there was no point.

"One of the Blood Moons."

Sage stilled entirely. Corey wasn't even sure if they were breathing anymore. Their body was completely rigid where they sat in the passenger seat. Corey finally turned to look at them. They didn't look afraid, not necessarily. But she wasn't sure what expression they wore. It was as if their face had gone entirely blank.

"Not . . . not one of the upper-level ones," Corey tried to reason, but she knew what Sage was thinking without them having to say it. The Blood Moons weren't just a Mafia family. They weren't just sharp and lethal. They were redcaps. They didn't kill to maintain their position—they killed because they enjoyed it. It brought them pleasure. "That might be why you have some of the . . . some of the side effects. They had a similar level of potential, but we couldn't exactly take out someone like Alton's brother without anyone noticing."

"Right. Of course." The words indicated that Sage understood, but the tone was entirely flat, as if they were still processing what she'd said.

"They were one of the lesser cousins. A second or third cousin, actually. Someone who wouldn't get the seat unless like five people died." She was trying to explain it away, to lessen how bad it was, but Corey could feel herself digging the hole deeper and deeper. Because no matter how she tried to tell herself, and Sage, that the person she'd killed to bring them back hadn't been of any real consequence, the fact of the matter was they were still a Blood Moon heir. Even if redcaps weren't the type to feel strong familial bonds, even if they'd sooner take out their own sister than let her take the seat when they wanted it, the redcaps would use any excuse for vengeance. "Sally, or Suzy, or . . . I don't know. Something with an *s*."

"I see." Sage still hadn't moved, maybe hadn't even blinked, Corey couldn't tell. This was bad. This was so fucking bad.

"Sage . . ." Corey whispered, lifting a hand as if to reach for them but stopping before she did. "Sage, I'm going to need you to tell me what the fuck is going on inside your head."

Sage took a deep breath. It rattled, like their lungs were starved for air, and they relaxed their shoulders. Then they turned to meet Corey's eyes, their own glowing bright in the darkness. "I'm thinking about next steps."

"Next steps?" That was better than panicking, she supposed.

"Yes."

"Okay." Corey nodded, shifting so she could face Sage entirely. "What are you thinking?"

"Well, first I was wondering if we should tell your new girlfriend—"

"What new girlfriend?"

Sage blinked at her for a moment as if debating dignifying that with an answer, then shook their head. "Her and Mal run the Faceless now, and they have some . . . attachment to us. They could help us."

"I suppose." Corey didn't want to bring them into this, not if she could help it, but she could see why Sage would have considered the idea, if only for a few minutes.

"But no." They shook their head. "I don't want to be indebted to anyone else. Plus, their hands are tied, aren't they? If they were seen going after the Blood Moons, it might mean war." Logical. Pragmatic. Corey could see how this version of Sage, the sensible one who was willing to look at things from all angles, would have made a good head of the family. Sensible and brutal when they had to be. Their father had trained them well.

"Right," Corey agreed. They didn't need an all-out gang war, even if Mal was smitten with Sage. "So what are you thinking?"

"I think I need to give it some more thought." Sage wrinkled their nose, frowning. "I need more information. Just because the person you killed to bring me back was from the Blood Moons doesn't mean it's the head of the family after me. It could be someone lower on the food chain."

"It could." She didn't think so, but maybe. "What do you want to do?"

"I want to wait. See if we can draw them out a little more." Sage tapped their foot against the floorboard, chewing on the inside of their cheek. "It's not usually how I like to do things, not if I have a choice. But we don't have the forces we need to combat all the Blood Moons. So if it's a small group, maybe one or two inside the gang . . . Let them come to us. Let us see who they are. Then we can figure out how to deal with them."

"Are we going to kill them?" Corey wasn't sure when she and Sage had gone from a *you* to a *we*, but she thought maybe it was better she not look too closely at the emotion.

"Not sure yet. Let's see what they look like first. I'm not above trying to buy them off over getting more blood on our hands." Sage shrugged, and Corey thought she ought to find comfort in that. It wasn't much but it was something. "In the meantime," they murmured, reaching out to grab their seatbelt and get buckled, "let's go home."

Home.

The word sat heavy and strange in the air between them. Just like *we* and *us*. Corey wasn't sure when Sage had begun to think of her apartment as home. It didn't sit quite right, especially with how they had started, but Corey found she didn't really mind. It was kind of odd. Quirky, not weird.

"Yeah, let's go home." Corey nodded and started the car.

MAL PINCHED THE BRIDGE OF HIS NOSE. THE BRIGHT lights coming through the greenhouse-like windows on the ceiling of whatever mystical structure the Court of Families was held in burned his eyes. He wished he'd been able to wear his sunglasses, but he knew well enough that they made him look untrustworthy to others. Not a look he was going for, not now at least. That, combined with the shouts of outrage and outright fear—silly really, when that fear was directed toward someone who seemed to have absolutely no interest in the Court at all—were giving him a fucking migraine.

There was a reason why just before all of this started about a week ago—fuck, had it only been that long? It felt like fucking months, but Mal figured it had only been about a week after all—Mal had said *fuck the Court*. It was because of this. Because of their inability to see anything beyond covering their own asses.

"They'll want revenge," Alton said, his voice shrill.

"Of course they will!" another voice chimed in, Silva maybe. Mal couldn't tell. At this point, they were all blurring together.

"Do you remember what they were like before?" someone whispered, maybe Flo. Mal hoped Mox was keeping track.

"I remember having to wash blood out of my best—"

"You don't really think it'll be that bad, do you?" That was Evy, her words small, afraid. She wasn't around before Sage *died*; Mal had to remind himself of that. Some of the others were, although not in a capacity to control their own gangs. But Evy hadn't even been a part of the life then. She'd been adopted into this when the former head of the Zephyr needed an heir.

"They have no reason to come for us," Celeste assured, and when Mal finally opened his eyes, he found she'd placed a hand on Evy's shoulder, providing comfort to her family head where she could.

"They have no reason to come for *any* of you," Mal said tiredly. Goddess, he could kill all of them. If he let his control slip for just a second, the shadows lingering at the edges of the room would crawl forward and cut through them better than any blade. It would be so fucking easy. Too easy perhaps. His eyes flicked from Evy to Alton, who looked suddenly as if he'd swallowed something sour. "Unless you've done something to them. It's my understanding that they have no interest in returning to the Court."

"Overconfident as ever." Alton scoffed. "You're just saying that because you don't want to think about what it would mean if they did want to return."

Mal's eyebrow twitched. "I'm unclear on what you're trying to insinuate, Alton, but I can assure you that the heir to Nocturna poses me no threat. My position as the Head of the Faceless is set in stone."

Not really though. If Sage wanted the position, Mal would happily step down. Cede the seat to the rightful heir. *Best not to let the Court know that though*.

"Then why is there word going around that they confronted Bentley in her home?" Alton asked, his tone snide.

Mal heard Mox shift behind him, her attention suddenly homed in on Alton the same way Mal's was. How did Alton know about Bentley? Were they in touch? Did that mean Alton was the one hiding the little rat? Of course Sage would be able to hunt her down, when Mal failed for years. They were just that good. They always had been.

"Bentley has nothing to do with the Faceless anymore," Mal responded, tone calm, detached.

Alton harumphed, his arms crossed over his chest in obvious petulance.

"That may be so," Mata spoke up. She hadn't been yelling with the others. There was something too put together about her. She knew something. One thing at a time. "But you cannot deny that the appearance of this Phantom and the news that the Nocturna heir didn't really die four years ago does make for . . . suspicious circumstances."

And they were off again. Speculation and conspiracy running a mile a minute. Mal made a mental note to ask Sage about that at some point—how they'd survived the attempt on their life, and where they'd been all this time. Maybe during their next date. The thought buoyed Mal, making the meeting more bearable.

He tapped the back of his chair, a signal to Mox. When she leaned down to listen, Mal whispered to her, "After this is through, don't let Guin disappear. I'd like to have a chat with her. Alone."

Mox squeezed his shoulder in acknowledgment and returned to her position at his back, taking in the things he might miss.

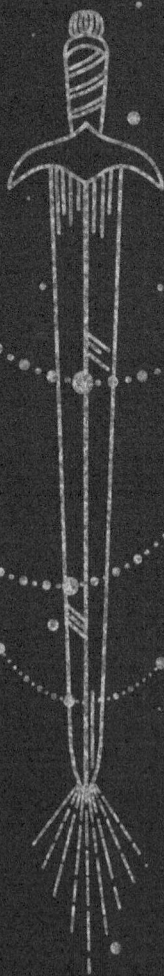

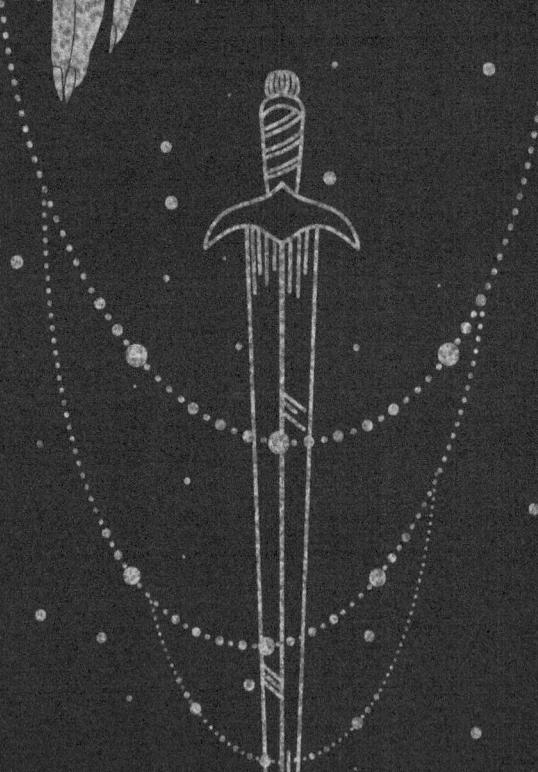

26

THE CAR RATTLED under the force of Mal's anger.

Goddess damn it. Mox winced. Mal had probably just fucked up her paint job by slamming another family head bodily into the side of it, because of course her twin brother couldn't be bothered to ask questions calmly and reasonably. And she couldn't tell yet what damage he'd caused as he still had Guin shoved up against the door, his hands fisted in her lapels.

How they'd gotten Guin away from her second, Mox still wasn't sure. Not that it mattered at this point. But they really needed to take this shit elsewhere. They shouldn't be seen shaking down another family head in the middle of the fucking day out on the street where anyone could overhear their discussion.

She sighed, resisting the urge to pinch the bridge of her nose, and eyed Guin over Mal's shoulder. "Just tell him what he wants to know so we can get this the fuck over with. Before he scratches my car any more than he already has."

"I would if I could," Guin hissed, her nails growing

longer and sharper where she held on to Mal's wrists. Mox thought she heard dripping water, the threat of Guin calling on her magic. She wouldn't push it any further than that, not if she knew what was good for her, but it was a reminder what she was capable of. What they all were capable of if they let their emotions run riot on their sense. "But I know fuck all about where Bentley is hiding."

"In Aquarius somewhere. *Clearly*," Mal insisted, giving her a shake and no doubt dragging her clothes against Mox's paint again. All she could hope was that Guin didn't have any rivets or anything on the back of her pants. The body shop was going to have a field day when she took it in to have it looked at. Mal had probably already left a dent. Asshole. "You've been playing the part of Alton's kid brother long enough that you should—"

"Shut the fuck *up*, you idiot." Guin's head twisted around, looking for any indication that someone might have overheard, her dark blue eyes wide and wild with fear. "If anyone finds out I'm doing that, Alton will skin me alive."

"Well maybe you should have thought of that before you convinced Glyn to run off with his boyfriend." Mal only seemed to tighten his hold on Guin's jacket.

Mox sighed. They weren't getting anywhere like this.

"Maybe I should just let it *slip* that—"

"Yeah. Okay. We're not doing that." Mox nudged her brother lightly, carefully unfurling his fingers from where he held Guin in a death grip. "Are we, *Mal*?"

She cut him a warning look. He might be head of their family, the more powerful of the pair of them, but Mox wasn't fucking with playing that hand this early on. They never knew when they'd need something like that. And keeping it to hang over Guin's head was far more useful than letting the rest of the Court know what she was up to and turning everyone against her.

"Fine," Mal said through clenched teeth. "You don't know where she's hiding, then what *do* you know?"

"I know *Sage* turned up at her apartment with the Phantom and scared the absolute piss out of her. That's what's brought on this shitstorm. She came crying to Alton saying Sage was back from the dead and almost killed her." Guin rolled her eyes with a scoff, clearly as disbelieving as Mox was that if Sage intended to kill Bentley, she'd still be alive.

But something about that news struck Mox in her chest. Sage had been there with the Phantom. Granted, she'd clocked the Phantom as the baker right away, but did this mean they were going into business together? Or were they a couple?

They were living together. Working together. Shaking down relatives/enemies together. They could just be friends, business partners, Mox knew that logically. But something ugly and green curled in the pit of her stomach that screamed of jealousy. What if it wasn't just that? What if there was more to it?

Fuck, when had her stupid crush spiraled this far out of control?

"Focus, Mox," Mal hissed under his breath, and she shook herself before turning her attention back to the discussion.

"If Bentley is so freaked out by Sage and didn't know they were alive until they showed up at her door, who put the hit out on them?" Mal turned his attention back to Guin, who had stood and was smoothing out her clothes.

"That is the million-dollar question, isn't it?" Guin lifted her head to fix them both with a shark-toothed smile, another reminder of what she was and what she was capable of.

"Tell me you don't know, and I swear to the Goddess, Guin, I'll—"

"Of *course* I know." Guin scoffed, affronted. "What do you take me for?"

"An asshole," Mox muttered under her breath, and Guin cut her a dirty look that only made Mox snicker.

"I can't tell you who," she said.

"Why the fuck not?!" Mal launched himself at her, his shadows following suit.

Guin quickly sidestepped him. The shadows slammed into the car, leaving deep gouges in the paint.

"Goddess damn it, Mal, not my fucking car!" Mox shoved him again.

"Fuck your car! I want answers!"

"My car can't give them to you, so stop beating it up." Mox leaned down and tried to buff away the scratches with her sleeve. But all she managed to do was snag the fabric of her blazer on the rough paint, pulling a thread loose. Fucking fabulous. Now she had the beginnings of a hole in her suit jacket along with a fucked-up paint job. Mal's crush was starting to get expensive. "You're paying to have that fixed."

"As I was saying," Guin continued. She had the good grace—or maybe the good sense—not to roll her eyes at the bickering siblings. "I can't tell you who because if I do, the leak of that information will one hundred percent point to me, and I can't have that. I know you don't give a flying fuck what enemies you make, but I do. And I have no desire to go to war with anyone."

Mox noticed she carefully didn't mention *who* she might have to go to war with if the information slipped. Unseelie. Seelie. No hints. Probably not Alton. And not Evy. That left the Blood Moons and the Wildlings. Which of them was up to something that could destroy the careful peace the Court of Families had built?

There was something more Guin wasn't saying, which wasn't terribly surprising, but it nagged at Mox.

"What *can* you tell us then, Guin?" Mal snarled, the shadows around him writhing. Even with the sun high in the sky and the light softened by the mists of Eventide, he was a fearsome creature. Ready to rip his enemies limb from limb, but only when it came to the people he loved. Mox had little doubt he'd do just as much for her or Chuckles. A thought that might have scared some but delighted Mox. This was how he showed that he loved them. And Mal loved *deeply*.

"I can tell you that someone has put a price on Sage Nocturna's head."

"What kind of price?" Mal's face twisted, morphing into the terrifying rictus of a death mask. Even Mox stepped back, a cold sweat trickling down her spine. He didn't do this often—pull on the nightmares. He called on the darkness regularly, it was a second limb to him, but the nightmares were something else. Not even the sunglasses he wore to protect his eyes could hide the way they glowed *black*.

"The kind that gets people's attention." Guin stuffed her hands into her pockets and leaned back on her heels, but Mox could see it for the act it was. She was doing her best to look like Mal wasn't scaring the living shit out of her, but her shoulders had hunched forward, her jaw ticking as if she was swallowing a scream. "A *lot* of people."

She cleared her throat, her eyes cutting to the street around them. It was one of the less traveled ones of Eventide, but there was still some chance that they could be stumbled upon this early in the day. It set Mox's teeth on edge, but she didn't say so.

Then Guin stepped in closer, lowering her voice. "Word on the street is they're looking to nab your Sage. Their little friend too."

"What for?" Mox whispered when Mal was quiet for too long, standing as still as a statue as the weight of what Guin said likely sunk in.

"From what I heard—And this is just rumor, you understand?"

"Get on with it, Guin," Mal growled.

"Right." Guin cleared her throat, doing another quick sweep of the side street where they were parked. "Word is that Sage and the Phantom killed another heir shortly after Sage's funeral, right before their disappearing act. No one is sure why. Some say it was to get a little extra cash, to make a clean break. Others think it's because the heir found out about Sage's plan to run off. I heard someone say something about necromancy, but that's just talk."

"Which heir?" Mox pressed.

"One of the lesser Blood Moons."

"Fuck." Mox hissed, and Mal didn't wait for anything further. He grabbed the passenger side door and climbed into the car, then motioned for Mox to follow.

SAGE SNEEZED, THEIR ENTIRE BODY SHIVERING WITH THE movement.

"Are you all right?" Chuckles asked, peeking into the walk-in where Sage had gone to get eggs. She looked even younger now somehow, dressed in one of the bakery's frilly aprons, her hair tied up in a tight ponytail. And she worried, Sage noticed, almost constantly about them.

"Fine. I think the cold just got to me." Sage pulled the

sleeves of their thick sweater over their knuckles in a bid to keep their fingers warm as they gathered the eggs. "Did you get all the bowls out I told you we needed?"

"Yup!" Chuckles grinned, then swooped in to take the jars of preserves Sage had stuffed under their arm. "Let me help you with that."

"I'm perfectly capable of—"

"I know." She laughed, her smile too big for her face, making her look ever younger. Sage's heart gave a hollow pang. They'd missed that laugh. Missed that smile. Missed so much. They wouldn't miss anymore. Not if they had a choice. "But I'm an assistant, right? Let me assist."

"Fine," Sage huffed. Their jaw ached from the grin that had settled onto their face and refused to leave for the remainder of the workday.

"I'm sorry I'm early," Mal offered when Sage opened the door, a charming smile spreading his lips that didn't itch as much as the glamour he'd had to slip on before leaving home. It would be all too easy to fall into the part of the clumsy-but-doting new boyfriend. Mainly because it wasn't just an act, it was who Mal *wanted* to be. He wanted their lives to be that straightforward and simple. But they weren't. Never could be. Not so long as they lived in Eventide, and Mal couldn't imagine living anywhere else.

"It's all right." Sage's smile was less forced, less a mask. Something in Mal's chest relaxed.

They stepped away from the door, allowing Mal inside where he found that Sage had turned off the overhead lights. The lamps from the living room and over the stove cast the apartment in a soft, warm glow that made it far easier to see. Mal leaned his cane next to the door and followed Sage further into the apartment.

"I was just getting everything together for dinner."

"Oh, are you cooking?" Mal's eyes cut about the room, always looking, never settling. Cautious, and careful. Mal didn't trust Corey and her wards. Didn't for one second think that someone couldn't be hiding in the shadows of the apartment, ready and waiting to rip Sage from Mal's hands all over again.

"I am." Sage had their back turned to him, sliding something off a cutting board into a pot on the stove.

"What is it?" After inspecting the room, Mal moved to the kitchen to peek inside the pot over Sage's shoulder. Whatever it was bubbled like a cauldron, turning from clear to a muddy brown color much more quickly than Mal thought anything edible should. But who was he to judge? He could cook, but he'd much rather survive on takeout and frozen dinners because cooking was too much of a hassle.

"Oh, I uhh . . . It's a stew?" Sage looked over their shoulder at Mal. "It doesn't really . . . I didn't follow a recipe."

"Well, whatever it is, I'm sure it'll be great." Mal stepped back then spun to drop into one of the chairs at the two-person table against the wall and watch Sage as they piddled around the kitchen, stirring the pot occasionally, their slippers scuffing against the worn linoleum.

"I thought we could watch a movie after dinner."

"That sounds nice." Mal glanced at the plaid couch in the living room again. It was small, cozy. They'd have to cuddle close. That was all right by him. "Anything in particular?"

"I love a good Mafia movie, so I thought maybe we'd watched *The Godfather*."

Mal coughed, choking on his own spit. "Really?"

"Sure." Sage glanced at him over their shoulder again, and he thought maybe they were looking for something. A test. "Speaking of gangsters, I met Mal."

"Oh?" Mal didn't want to lie to Sage, but it wasn't a lie. Not really. It was . . . a misdirection. He'd have to be careful.

"The head of the Faceless Few."

Mal wasn't sure where they were going with this. He shifted uncomfortably in his chair, hoping it didn't creak too loudly beneath him. He almost didn't want an answer, but he needed to know what kind of impression he'd left, if he'd left any at all. So he asked, "And what did you think? Were you scared?"

"Not scared at all. I found him rather interesting," Sage said in a tone like they were confiding in Mal.

Several emotions crossed through Mal at once. Jealousy. Pride. Embarrassment. Anger. Sage found the head of the Faceless Few interesting. Did that mean this other persona—this Ianthe—he was putting forward *wasn't* interesting? Which did Sage like better? And which of these two people was the real Mal? Even he didn't know at this point.

"You've been in Eventide for a while, right?" Sage pressed, covering the bubbling pot on the stove and throwing a dish towel over their shoulder as they leaned against the opposite side of the counter. "What do you know about him?"

"Not much really." Mal shrugged. Also not a lie. It was hard to know himself from one moment to the next with the life he led.

Sage tilted their head, a piece of gray hair falling into their eyes, making them look impossibly soft. It was a struggle not to reach out and brush it back behind their ear.

Not to let his fingers linger, sweet and loving, a caress. He hadn't earned that yet. But oh, how he *wanted*.

"I know they say he came to the Faceless Few and challenged the execs to an honest-to-Goddess duel, like in the old days." Mal sat up a little straighter, a slow, proud smile creeping onto his face as Sage leaned forward more. He had their attention, and it was heady. "They accepted, thinking him just a street rat."

"How many was that?" Sage asked as if they didn't know.

"Thirty-three. It would have been thirty-five but there were some holdouts. Bentley Nocturna and one other heir who later was found dead in his bed."

"What happened?"

"He won, of course." Mal's grin turned vicious, stained in blood. He couldn't help himself. He remembered those days all too well. Remembered how they all thought him just a stupid kid. Remembered how he told each and every one of them before they died who he was doing it for. Some of them had laughed, and some had cried. Their faces were plastered to the backs of his eyelids and would stay with him for the rest of his life. "And when they were all gone, he took over the organization and rebuilt it from the ground up."

"Impressive," Sage breathed, and Mal swore his heart would leap from his chest and fall at Sage's feet like an offering. "Did he ever say why he did it?"

Mal hoped the lights were dim enough that Sage wouldn't see the way his cheeks heated at the question. He had to tell the truth, he couldn't lie. Swallowing roughly, Mal shifted in his chair again. "Revenge. They hurt the person he loved."

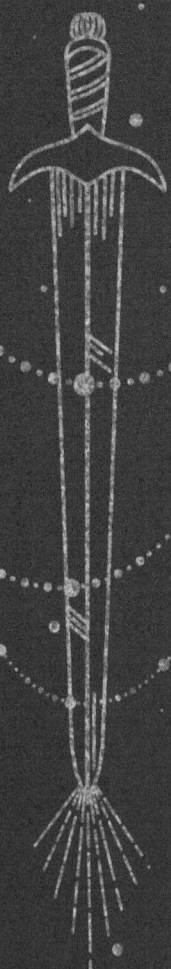

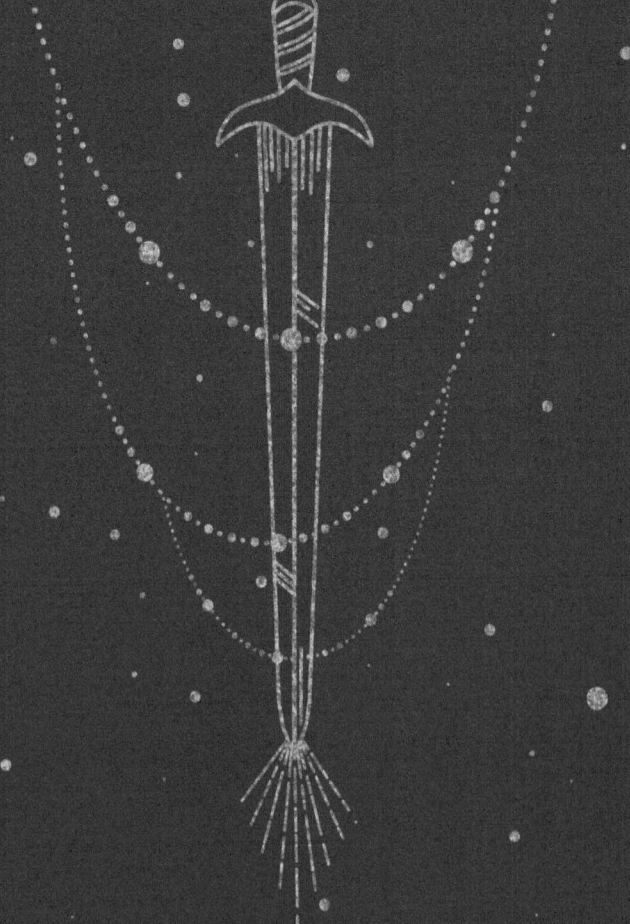

27

SAGE'S FINGERS tingled where they brushed the dish towel still over their shoulder. Ianthe's words echoed in their head. The execs died because they'd hurt the person Mal loved. Warmth spread through their veins, settling into their skin in a way that raised the hair on their arms.

They'd never been loved like that before, not even by their own kin, not even by their own father. Yes, if their father had been alive, he'd have punished those who had a hand in Sage's death. Sought vengeance, but not because he loved Sage. It would be purely a means to maintain order. He couldn't be seen letting people hurt his heir.

This felt . . . different. Although Sage wasn't sure why. Maybe it was the memory of how Mal had held them, like they were something precious, something sacred. Of the way Mal's heart beat a steady rhythm against their ear as he brought them back to this apartment, sending for a doctor and staying with them until they'd been cleared. Sage couldn't remember the last time someone sat by their bedside when they weren't feeling well. Maybe not since before their mother died. How long ago that'd been.

There was no reason for them to think that when Ianthe said Mal killed the Faceless execs for hurting the person he loved, he meant Sage. After all, as far as Sage knew, Mal didn't remember them. Yes, after seeing his face more clearly, not glimpsed through a heavy glamour, they recognized him as the boy they'd saved once upon a time.

Not more than a child, starving on the streets with his sister. Face bloodied from another member of the Faceless beating him after he'd picked their pocket. It had taken time to connect the dots, but now that they were there . . . Sage remembered making that boy promise them he'd find happiness one day. That he wouldn't stop until he did.

That didn't mean Mal had avenged their death.

But . . . there was no shame in hoping, was there?

They must have lost track of time, staring into Ianthe's mismatched eyes, wondering at the enormity of what they'd just heard. Because what seemed like no time at all later, they smelled burning. "Shit."

"Is that your stew?" Ianthe asked, a bit of a laugh in his voice.

Sage whirled around and took a giant step across the tiny kitchen to reach the stovetop again. They pulled the lid from the pot and hissed at the smell coming from inside. It was noxious. Their shoulders drooped, and they let out a pained breath as they turned off the heat. "It's ruined."

"It can't be that bad," Ianthe called from the table.

"It definitely is. We should just order takeout." They didn't know why they had bothered trying to make this special. They'd never been good at cooking. They'd been living on cup noodles in Miami for years. But they wanted . . . They wanted a real date. Something with candlelight and actual place settings. Corey didn't have silverware or candles, but the soft warm light of the lamps and the silver plasticware they'd found at the corner store had seemed close enough. Now it was ruined.

There was the soft shuffle of socked feet on linoleum and Sage looked over to watch Ianthe snag one of the shiny plastic spoons from their place setting.

"What are you doing?"

"I'm going to taste test it." Ianthe smiled, broad and charming, and Sage lost all control of the situation as he swooped in, dipping the spoon into the pot.

"Oh, please don't—"

But it was too late, he'd already put the bite into his mouth. There was no outward indication of how terrible the stew clearly was, and it *had* to be based on the smell alone, just a head tilt as if Ianthe were considering something. Probably how best to beg Sage to *please for the love of all that was good in the world* never cook again.

"Well?" Sage didn't want an answer, but they asked anyway.

"It's not too bad." Ianthe shrugged. "A little heavy on the onion, but definitely serviceable."

"No way." Sage snatched the spoon and took a bite for themself. They promptly gagged at the flavor of char, garlic, and something chemically. "We're ordering out."

"All right. I'm buying."

"Oh no, you don't have to."

Ianthe ignored them and pulled his phone from his pocket, turning his back on Sage so he could presumably find someplace for them to get dinner. "Is Thai all right?"

"Thai is fine," Sage murmured, curling more around the pot. It was ruined now, the stew burned to the sides and crusting over as it hardened. Corey was going to have a fucking fit. She'd told them not to cook. She'd even set a bunch of menus out on the counter before she left that they'd quickly stuffed into the drawer next to the fridge, vowing to do it themself. "The peanut noodles."

Ianthe murmured his agreement, then returned his attention to the person on the phone so he could place their order while Sage dragged the ruined pot to the sink. Maybe if they ran enough water in it and let it soak . . .

"Corey is going to lose her shit when she sees this. She only has like three pans." Sage scrubbed their face, coughing at the smell coming from the pot. The water sat on top of the ruined stew as if it had turned into a solid in less than two minutes. How was that even possible? Sage hadn't had it on the stovetop for that long.

"I'll get her some new ones." Ianthe leaned over Sage's shoulder, seeming not even a bit upset by the smell or the obvious wreckage that was their dinner. "She should have more than three pans anyway. What kind of chef only has three pans?"

"Someone who's a baker, not a chef." Sage couldn't help but laugh, shaking their head as they cut off the water. "You don't have to buy her new pans. I can do it."

"Nonsense, it was my presence that ruined this one." He took a step back as Sage shut off the water and leaned back against the sink, their brow raised in question, but he didn't move far. Sage could feel the heat of him through their clothes, his chest nearly brushing Sage's back. Goddess, they hadn't been so close to another person since all of this had started.

"How's that work?" Sage tilted their head, teasing, for lack of something better to do as they fought tooth and nail against the flush crawling up their neck. *Down, Sage. You cannot jump this guy in the middle of Corey's kitchen right after ruining one of her pans. She'll definitely never forgive you then.* But it didn't make the want lingering under their skin go away.

"Clearly, my good looks were too distracting." Ianthe grinned, boyish and guileless, his mismatched eyes sparkling in the low lights of the kitchen, even through the glamour. Sage had the sudden desire to ask him to dance, to see how they moved together.

"Clearly." Sage laughed softly. "Well, if that's the case, by all means, replace my roommate's pots and pans so she doesn't try to skin me in my sleep."

"It will be done." Ianthe dipped his head, and when he lifted it again, his mouth opened as if he wanted to say something else, to make another quip, but Sage didn't leave him any time. They lunged forward, cupping his jaw with both hands, and pulled his lips down to theirs.

Ianthe let out a soft, muffled protest, and Sage pulled back, eyes wide and worried. "I'm sorry. I should have asked. I just . . . you looked so cute, and I just . . . I've been wanting to do that all night. Since you walked in, in fact. Is this . . . is this okay?" Their eyes flicked all about Ianthe's face, looking for any indication that he was angry, disgusted, upset—any number of terrible things. But all they saw written on his face was shock. "Ianthe, is this okay?"

"Goddess yes," Ianthe gasped and dipped forward to capture Sage's lips again. He didn't touch Sage anywhere else, but Sage backed further against the sink, the counter digging into their back. They looped their arms around his neck and pulled. He wobbled, hands flinging out to grip the edges of the counter to either side of their hips for balance, getting closer.

Not close enough. Not close *enough*. Not *close* enough.

Sage swiped their tongue along Ianthe's lower lip, searching, seeking, and he opened for them, letting them press in further. Their tongue brushed against his, flicking along the roof of his mouth, drawing a soft groan. Their fingers tangled in his long dark hair, giving it a firm tug that had Ianthe breathing so hard, he had to pull away for a moment.

Ianthe bumped his forehead against Sage's, a rich, warm, startled chuckle on his lips, his eyes closed tight. "You have no idea how long I've wanted this."

Sage thought maybe they had some idea, but it didn't matter. Nothing else mattered apart from capturing his lips again and picking right back up where they left off. Nothing else mattered apart from taking a step forward, forcing Ianthe back, and back, and back. All the way across the kitchen, into the living room, right to the arm of the couch.

With a soft yelp from Ianthe, Sage pushed him up and over it, onto the cushions, and followed closely behind.

"If you want to stop, just say stop," they assured, their knees on either side of Ianthe's hips. He had yet to touch them, like maybe he was scared to. But that didn't keep him from kissing back, from releasing soft, strangled noises that egged Sage on.

"I hope to die with you on my lips," Ianthe gasped, lifting his head off the couch, the only indication that he was seeking more contact, and Sage complied, diving back in, pressing their hips down against his, rubbing against the slowly growing hardness they found there.

Reaching down to thread their fingers together above his head, Sage bit gently at Ianthe's lower lip, tugging it softly when his lips parted for air.

"Let's not talk about dying," Sage panted against his mouth, then dragged kisses across his sharp jaw, down his neck.

"Anything. Anything you ask for." It was a promise, a vow, and Sage felt it to their toes.

"Touch me" was Sage's only request, and just as Ianthe

was finally relinquishing his hold, the buzzer went off to let them know the delivery person had arrived with their food. "You've got to be fucking joking."

"Maybe if we wait, they'll go away."

Sage's heart hammered against their chest, and they panted hard against Ianthe's neck. He had tilted his head, seeking more, begging for Sage to sink their teeth into the thin skin. "You already paid for it."

"It doesn't matter."

The buzzer went off again and Sage groaned, dipping forward more to press their forehead into Ianthe's shoulder. "Hold that thought. I'll go down and get it and be right back, and we can continue."

Ianthe nodded and Sage rolled off the couch, almost crashing into the coffee table in their hurry to make it to the door and down the stairs to get their food. They could have taken the elevator, but it was too slow and they wanted to get back. They hadn't even put on their shoes, just skidded down the steps in slippered feet and slid across the tiny lobby lined in mailboxes to get to the door where a delivery person stood outside, buzzing the apartment continuously.

"I'm coming!" they shouted, and ripped open the security door covered in metal before pushing the glass one open and stepping out onto the front stoop. All while keeping both doors open so they wouldn't get locked out. It was a precarious dance, and although they'd done it a handful of times since returning to Eventide, it was distracting.

"Sorry about the wait." Sage grinned. Their wallet was already in their hand. They didn't have much cash on them, but if they had to throw a tip at this person to get them to fuck off so they could get back up to Ianthe quicker, so be it.

Only, when they finally focused on the delivery person, they weren't . . . carrying any . . . bags?

"Where's the food?"

The only answer they received was a face full of powder, the scent heavy with iron, sending their ears ringing. Their throat went tight with the allergic reaction, their breath coming in small sips. Their vision tunneled

Speckled.

Darkened.

Went black.

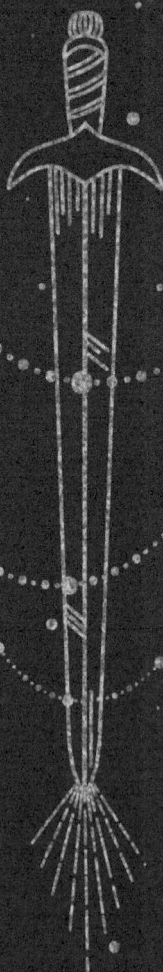

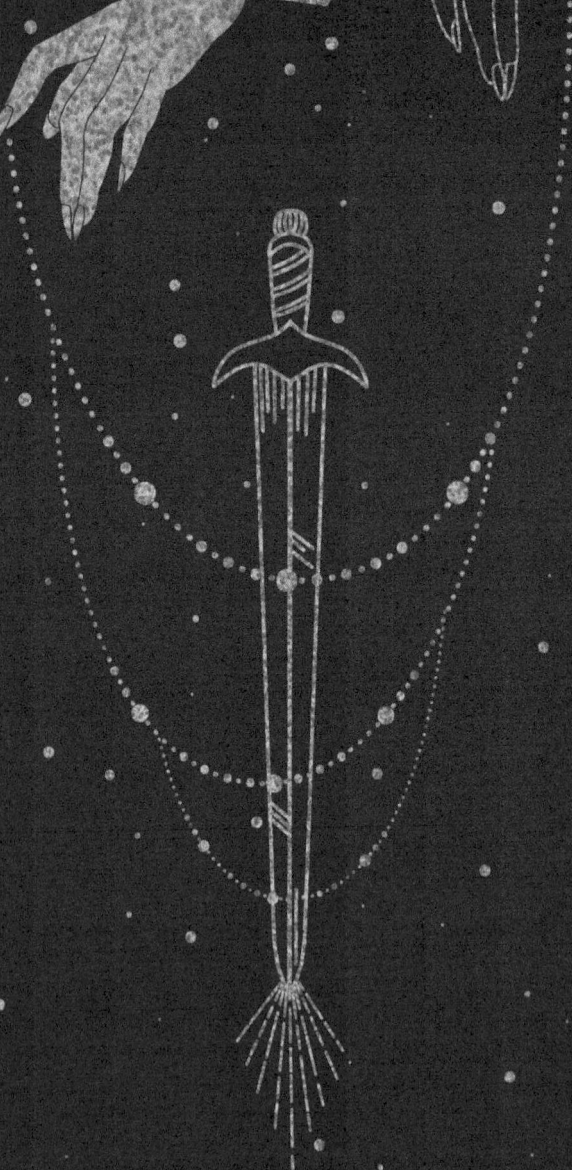

28

PAIN PULSED in Sage's elbows, their arms contorted in a way that was decidedly uncomfortable and would no doubt have their joints aching for days to come.

Had they fallen asleep in their office chair again?

That couldn't be right.

When had they moved to their room? When did Ianthe leave? When had their date ended?

They shifted, lifting their hand to—

Not lifting. Something burned at their wrists, and when Sage blinked their eyes open, the room around them was blurry. Their glasses had fallen off in the—

In the attack.

They remembered now.

Kissing Ianthe on the couch.

The delivery person.

The face full of powder.

"Not again," Sage groaned, tilting their chin back for a moment to roll their neck around, assessing the state of their head. They must have hit it when they'd fallen, the sticky coldness of blood seeping down from their hair. If this shit kept happening, they might need to invest in a fucking helmet.

All right, so their glasses were gone, probably broken on the pavement somewhere, but that didn't account for the double vision. That was the concussion, likely.

Beautiful.

Then there was the burn around their wrists. They couldn't turn to see what had been used to bind them, but . . . it wasn't rope, and the sizzle of their skin under the metal indicated iron.

Super.

Using their magic to escape this was out then. That didn't leave them a whole lot of options. Their best bet would be to sit tight and wait to see who had attacked them. No doubt they'd come to interrogate Sage at some point, and when they did, Sage could talk their way out. They were practiced at that. Get their abductors talking, get them arguing, get them close enough to get something off them that Sage could use to escape the restraints. It wasn't ideal, but it was their best option at this point.

It was fine. They could wait.

Letting out a long, slow breath, Sage pinched their eyes shut and tried to quell the nausea churning in their belly from the concussion. A little water wouldn't go amiss.

"All right, so long as I'm stuck here." Tilting their head down again so they could look around the shadowed room, they squinted into the dark.

Shipping crates. A warehouse or a basement, probably. But they couldn't tell what gang it belonged to. Because, of course, the captors hadn't conveniently left anything to give Sage any clues of their identity lying around.

Narrowing their eyes further, Sage could just make out two doorways along the back wall. One obviously led into the rest of the building, either to a set of stairs or a hall or something, but where did the other go? Outside? That would make things too easy. They wouldn't leave Sage someplace with an exit so close.

Footsteps echoed loudly through the space, coming from above them. Accompanied by muffled voices. Basement then, most likely.

Okay, so they were in the basement of some rival organization, strapped to a chair with iron restraints.

They could make this work.

THE SECONDS TICKED BY INTO MINUTES. FIRST ONE. Then two. Then four.

Mal's heart, which had been hammering when Sage was on top of him, had slowed. The blood racing through his ears, pounding there, calmed while he waited for Sage to come back.

At first.

But as four minutes turned to five, panic set in.

It shouldn't take that long for Sage to get their food. Should it? It shouldn't. Even if the delivery person was chatty.

Mal rose from the couch and headed for the door, grabbing his cane on the way out into the hall. He'd be locked out once he left the apartment, but that didn't matter because he was sure he wasn't coming back. Not if the sinking feeling in his stomach was correct. Something had happened to Sage.

His phone was already out of his pocket, although he didn't remember grabbing it while he waited for the elevator, his mind running a million miles a minute as he thought of all the things that could have happened to Sage. And right under his nose!

"Call Mox," he murmured, his voice strangled by a throat gone tight with anxiety. With shaking hands, he pushed the button for the first floor and waited, his phone ringing, his heart hammering hard enough against his ribs that he swore they'd break.

"I thought you were on a date," Mox said when she picked up. "Or did Sage send your dumbass home already? What did you say—"

"Mox," Mal gasped.

"What is it?" Mox's entire demeanor changed. Gone was the teasing twin sister, and in her place was the second of the Faceless Few, ready and willing to burn down the world at her brother's behest. "What happened?"

The door screeched on its hinges, and Mal stumbled out into the dark, humid night. No one. There was no one there. No sign of Sage. No sign of who had taken them. No one. Nothing.

His foot came down too hard off the stoop, and something crunched under his weight. "Shit. What was that?"

"Mal." Mox's tone dipped further into concern. "Mal, answer me."

"I think I . . . hang on." He stooped down and picked up whatever had been under his boot. Moving toward the light of the yellowed bulb, he squinted at the mangled metal and glass. Glasses. Sage's glasses. They looked so small crushed in his hand, the lenses cracked to the point where pieces had chipped off. "They took them."

"Took who?" Mox asked, but there was a sound in the background, a soft *beep beep beep*. The safe. She was opening the safe and pulling out weapons. She was preparing to come to him and help him get Sage back. Goddess, Mal had the best sister in existence, even when she made stupid deals with demons and threatened to turn him into a fashionable accessory.

"Sage. They . . ." Mal swallowed sharply, the feeling like glass shards in a throat gone raw with upset and rage. Juggling his cane, he pulled a handkerchief from his pocket and settled the broken pieces of Sage's glasses into it, wrapping them delicately. "They came down to get our food, but someone picked them up."

"Do you think it was the restaurant?"

It was a fair question. The more information Mox had, the more likely she was to figure out who'd taken Sage and where. But Mal was struggling to focus on anything outside of the bent metal frames in his hands. He needed better light to see if there had been a struggle, if there was blood. Better light or a second set of eyes.

"Mal," Mox pressed again. "Do you think it was the restaurant?"

"No." He shook his head. "It was one of ours, they have no reason to go against us."

"But was the food ever actually delivered?"

Mal frowned, his brows pinching together, and he clutched the ruined glasses tighter. The sharp metal dug into his palm. "No. It wasn't."

"Okay." Mox was moving again, and Mal thought he heard the car in the background. "I'm on my way."

"What does it mean that the food wasn't delivered?" He was almost afraid to know the answer. Afraid to find out that this had been his fault in some way. That he'd invited whoever was after Sage to them, exposed them to their enemies. He should have been more careful than that. He should have had one of their people bring the food. But he'd been so caught up in the act. In pretending to be Ianthe so

Sage wouldn't think less of him. In being *normal* for once in his fucking life. He'd let his guard down.

"It could mean nothing." She didn't believe that. He could hear it in her voice.

"Mox," Mal pressed, hoping she'd understand that he needed to know. That she couldn't pussyfoot around this with him. If this was his fault, he needed to face it and fix it.

"It could mean someone put a whammy on your phone while we were at Court."

"They're listening right now then?" Mal snarled, the shadows around him hissing with his displeasure.

"If they put a listening charm on your phone, then yes, they are."

"Then I hope they hear me when I say that if they harm one hair on Sage's head, I will burn their entire neighborhood to the ground. Their headquarters. Their businesses. Even the businesses that pay them protection money. Anyone that flies their flag will suffer, and from the ashes, I'll expand the Faceless. Fuck the Court if they think they can stop me."

Mox laughed, soft and threatening. "I'll be there in a minute, Mal. We'll find them."

"Good."

He dropped his phone to the cobblestone walkway and slammed his cane down onto it over and over again.

SAGE DIDN'T KNOW HOW LONG IT HAD BEEN. IT WAS hard to tell time in a windowless basement, but the way their head was starting to feel fuzzy and their hands were sweating told them that their sugar was dropping. It had been too long since the last time they'd eaten. If they weren't careful, the concussion was going to be the least of their problems.

"What is taking them so long?" they mumbled, opening and closing their fingers to try to keep circulation in their arms. This wasn't the longest they'd been held captive like this, but it was the first time since they'd died and been brought back. That made things more complicated, more dangerous.

A door creaked on the floor above and footsteps started down the stairs, getting slowly louder. Whoever it was stopped at the door to the right—that must be the one that went upstairs, although that didn't answer the question of where the other led—a key sounding in the lock, then they came inside.

Sage squinted, trying to get their vision to clear as the person stepped into the light. Fuck, they weren't wearing anything to cover their face. No mask. No glamour.

"You're probably wondering why you're here," they said, stepping closer. A redcap. Not one Sage recognized, but definitely someone from the Blood Moons. So Bentley had been correct, this was about revenge for killing their heir.

"Not really." Sage shrugged. They lifted their chin, doing their best to not let the fear show. They knew what it meant when their captors weren't bothering to hide their faces. When they weren't doing anything to disguise who they worked for. They didn't plan to let Sage walk out of there. "But if you feel like monologuing, I don't suppose I can stop you. I'm a little tied up here."

They jiggled their restraints to illustrate, and the redcap snorted. "Cute."

"I mean, my boyfriend thinks so. But do go on." They

batted their lashes, but despite their best efforts, the redcap didn't seem rattled by the bravado.

"Your cousin told us all about you."

"Oh yeah?" Well, at least Sage was getting somewhere now as far as information went. Bentley was hiding on Aquarius turf but feeding information to the Blood Moons. How many other organizations was she in bed with? And how had it not gotten her killed yet? "What did Bentley say?"

"She said you're undead," they hissed, leaning in closer, their smile knife-sharp.

Sage couldn't restrain their wince. "I guess we're just telling *everyone* that now, aren't we?" they muttered to themself, shaking their head. "Actually, we prefer the term *reanimated.*"

"Whatever." They kicked Sage's chair and it spun, adding to Sage's dizziness. Yeah, the not eating was definitely more a concern right now than the concussion. "She also told us that if we kill you, we get our heir back."

"Ah. Okay." Sage nodded, flexing their fingers again. They needed to get the fuck out of this before the redcap made good on that idea. But how? They didn't have their lock pick on them because they'd been at home, on a date. Why would they have needed the lock pick? Dislocating a thumb would maybe get them out, but then they'd be injured and unable to fight. If only they had access to their panther claws . . . but with the iron that likely wouldn't be possible. "See, there's where you went wrong. Bentley has *no* idea what the fuck she's talking about. Never really has. That's a bunch of horseshit."

"I guess we'll just have to bleed you out and see, won't we?"

The glint of a dagger being removed from a holster

kicked Sage's heart into their throat. Panic settling in. They couldn't panic, there wasn't time for it. They needed to stay calm. They needed to think.

"I mean, you could." Sage swallowed roughly and took a deep inhale, calming their racing heart. "But that's going to be *so* messy. Wouldn't it be better to just—"

"It's a good thing your little friend Corey told us where to find you."

"Wait. What?" Corey wouldn't. They weren't friends, sure, but she'd never . . .

"Sold you up the river to save her own ass, is my bet." The redcap shrugged. "That's what people around here do, isn't it?"

Sage's heart sank in their chest. It *was* what people did in Eventide. It was what everyone had ever done in Sage's life. And even as Sage recognized that that was the pattern, it still . . .

Corey. Corey had ratted them out.

The blade scraped across their skin.

The panther snarled.

Blood flooded Sage's mouth as their fangs cut into their lower lip.

Huh.

The iron wasn't enough to keep them from accessing their cait sidhe nature? Sage would have to give that some thought later, come up with a theory as to why. There wasn't time now.

The white-hot burn of a dagger slicing into skin only made Sage's concentration sharper as they focused on their hands, their nails. They winced at the bite of razorlike claws along their forearms as they adjusted. Shifted.

Another cut of the dagger, deep enough that their captor didn't notice the extra blood being spilled behind them as Sage sawed at their bonds with their claws.

A *normal* panther's claws might not have cut through the iron, but Sage wasn't a normal panther. They were undead. They were cait sidhe. And they had spent their entire life whetting their nails until they were sharp enough to cut steel.

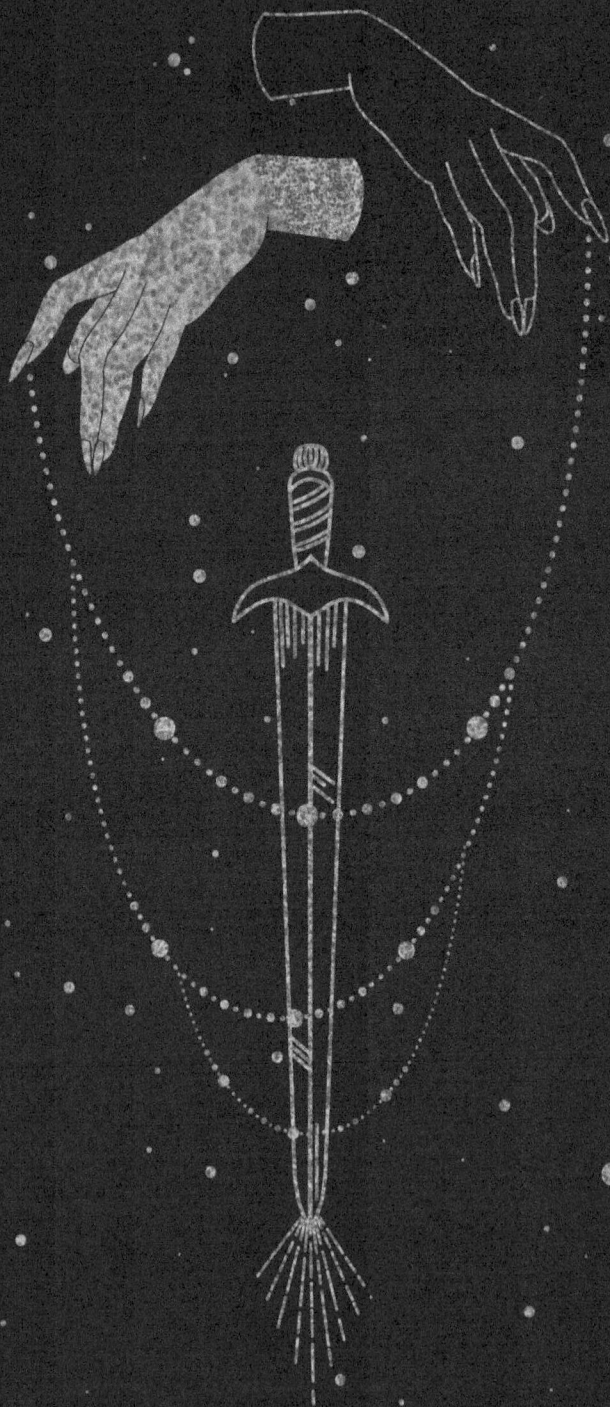

29

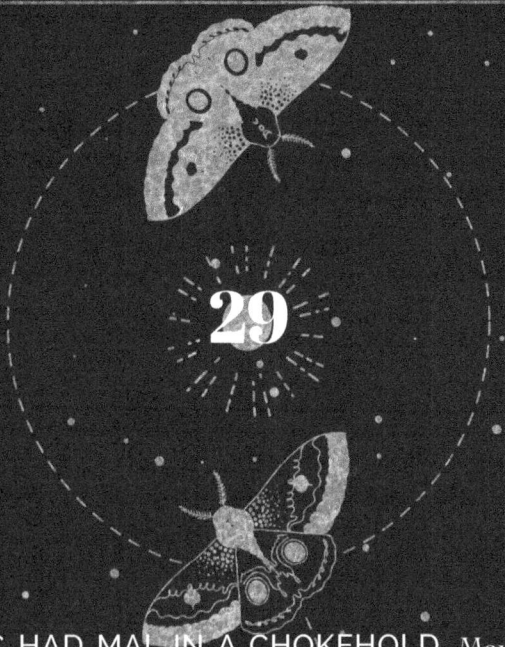

PANIC HAD MAL IN A CHOKEHOLD, Mox could see it. He hadn't been this scared since the night they found out Sage was dead.

"We'll get them back," Mox said from where she stood at his side, handing him one, two, five daggers that he loaded into the holster around his shoulders. She didn't know that for sure, but she tried to keep her tone careful, steady. Mal needed that of her right now.

The number of weapons she was handing him was overkill, probably, but she wasn't taking any chances. Not when Mal had just gotten Sage back. Not when it seemed they were finally getting somewhere in their weird situationship. Mox knew better than anyone that if Mal lost Sage now, he probably would succeed in killing himself this time. And she wasn't willing to play Russian roulette with her family. Not now. Not ever.

Mal had vowed to burn those who took Sage from him to the ground, and she knew he meant to keep that promise. The best thing she could do for her brother was supply him with everything he needed to do just that.

"I want you to stay with Sage's roommate," Mal murmured, his eyes cutting to where Corey was pacing in the kitchen. She hadn't sat down the entire time since she arrived back to the apartment to find Sage missing and Mox and Mal suiting up to go after them. Normally, Mox would think she was just worried, but there was a twinge of guilt around her mouth that Mox couldn't ignore. Corey knew something, and Mox couldn't afford to overlook any hints on where Sage might be. Not when it might lead to her own family paying the price.

"You think she knows something." Not a question. A muttered statement of fact and agreement to do what she had to all in one. It wasn't said, but Mal knew that he could trust Mox with this, despite her crush. She wouldn't let him down.

Mal hummed a confirmation, and Mox nodded in understanding. "Start in a circle," she said as if Mal hadn't just given her silent orders to torture the woman she was attracted to. "They couldn't have gotten far."

"Unless they had a portal," Corey cut in. Her hands were in tight fists, the nails likely cutting into her palms. She looked like she wanted to go with Mal, to help tear the city apart looking for Sage, but something was holding her back. Mox needed to find out what.

"The only organization allowed to create portals in Eventide is the Faceless." Mal growled, his anger flaring more at the insinuation that someone had gone against the accords, but that shouldn't have surprised him. It certainly didn't surprise Mox. They were gangs. Their entire existence was illegal, and yet they continued doing business. Yet they survived. It wasn't surprising to her that one of the other families would act against the ruling of the Court and open a portal in Eventide, but it *was* annoying. An added complication they'd have to think about.

Another thing Mox would have to track down and snuff out.

Corey shrugged and returned to pacing the kitchen.

Another shared look between the twins, and Mal slipped from the apartment into the night to search for his spouse.

IT HURT LIKE SHIT.

It hurt like shit, and Sage's head was going light with blood loss. They didn't know how long they could keep this up. Hold on to their consciousness as pain and wooziness threatened to take them under. But they needed to get out. Preferably before the redcap finished the job of eviscerating them.

"We'll do this slow," they said, leaning in closer, their breath stinking with the tang of metal. Blood. Blood on their teeth. Blood on their tongue. Redcaps soaked themselves in it, a holdover from the traditions of the past that they refused to let go. Even as they adapted and modernized.

"Is that a requirement for the spell?" Sage asked through a clenched jaw, their fingers still working furiously to cut at the metal cuffs on their wrists. If they could just get one free. If they could just slip their right wrist through the shackle. They could swing the cuff at the redcap like a bludgeon, level the playing field by knocking them silly. Set their ears to ringing and make their vision blurry the way Sage's was. They wouldn't be weak from blood loss and low blood sugar like Sage, but it would be something at least.

"No," the redcap confided, "I just like to watch people suffer."

"Of course." Sage resisted the urge to roll their eyes because they knew if they did, the motion might make the dizziness worse. They couldn't afford that. Not when they were almost there. Not when the panther set a low rumble in their chest, a consistent reminder that she was there too. That the moment she was free of the iron, she would burst forward, protect them both. Sage just had to get to that point.

But how much longer could they last?

"I THOUGHT YOU WERE GOING WITH HIM?" COREY ASKED, her eyes narrowed on Mox. She didn't like having either of them in her home. There was too much chance they'd discover something about her that she didn't want them to. Plus, she wanted to go after Sage herself. With her extensive knowledge of the underground of Eventide—from years of cleaning up Alton's messes—she was sure she could get them back faster than Mal, who had been a real player for only four years.

"No. I'll let him handle this." Mox settled at the two-person table against the kitchen wall, her hands tight around a mug of something Corey didn't remember her fixing.

"You're awfully calm for someone whose brother's partner was just kidnapped." Corey was worried about Sage, but she was also worried that her reaction to this situation wasn't right. Was she giving too much away? Was Mox going to realize she wasn't a simple baker? No one knew she was the Phantom, and she couldn't afford for anyone to find out. It would seriously derail any hopes of keeping herself off the radar of the other gangs. And what would Mox do with that information? Would she tell the Court? Or would she use it to blackmail Corey into being her own personal lapdog? Neither would surprise her.

"Mal has it handled," Mox said again, sipping from her mug. "I thought I'd stay behind and comfort you."

"Is that what you thought, huh?" Corey narrowed her eyes on Mox, a glare that would make most people cower, but Mox just smiled back, her body language loose and impassive. What the fuck? Why was that so hot? "Well, I'm fine."

"You definitely look it," Mox agreed easily. "But what if they come back? What if they want to take you as a means to force Sage to do or say what they want? We can't have that. Someone needs to be here to protect you."

"I don't need protection. Least of all from a *mobster*."

"Oof. You wound me!" Mox clutched her chest, leaning back in her chair as if she'd been hit with a bullet. "How can you say such hurtful things to someone as pretty as me?"

"Easy. I just look at your face, and the words come out." She should sit down. She should try to pretend she was calmer than she was. But every second she spent fucking around with Mox and her whole *thing*, Corey felt less and less in control of herself. She was going to slip. She knew it. It was too easy to banter with Mox, to find her reactions almost amusing.

"Are you sure you don't need my protection?"

"Positive."

"Why not?" Mox tilted her head and that stupid smile ticked up more at the corners of her lips, as if she'd caught Corey in something.

Corey stopped, her slipper catching on the linoleum. She pitched forward, stumbled, caught herself, but not before Mox had risen and taken a hold of her waist to keep her from faceplanting. The touch sent something warm and electric through her veins. Something similar to longing, but not quite that. It had a whiff of something more, something like heartbreak that she couldn't explain and didn't want to examine too closely.

"Why not?" Mox pressed again, almost breathless. Her face was too fucking close. Her brown eyes rich, and soft. Corey wanted to—

She shook herself, realizing belatedly that she'd more than just stumbled in her kitchen. She stumbled in her speech. She'd slipped up, just like she knew she was going to. Because she didn't have an answer for that. She couldn't tell Mox that she didn't need Mox's protection because she could protect herself. Or because she knew that they wouldn't come for her. So instead, she said, "Maybe you're right. Maybe I do need you to look after me."

Mox's cheeks turned a little ruddy, her hands flexing against Corey's waist as if embarrassed but unable to let go. "Well, good thing I'm here."

"Good thing." Goddess, why did she want to lean in more? Why did she want to move up onto her toes and close the distance between them? Kiss Mox like she'd never kissed anyone before. She shook herself and took a step back, out of the strangely familiar embrace. "I'm going to make myself some tea."

"Capital idea!" Mox said in what sounded like an embarrassed imitation of Gomez Addams before she slunk back to her seat.

HAD SAGE BLACKED OUT FOR A MINUTE THERE? THEY couldn't tell.

The panther growled at them as if asking if they were all right.

We need to work faster.

A rumbled agreement was the panther's answer, and Sage swore their claws grew another half an inch. They'd lost track of the cuts along their arms and chest by the redcap. Lost track of the redcap's delighted giggle. Sage's focus narrowed down to the thin bit of metal still holding them hostage. Just a little more. Just a couple centimeters, and they'd be free.

Just a little—

There!

They gasped, lifting their chin from where it had lowered as they tried to focus.

The redcap stopped, eyes wide as they stepped away from their captive, and Sage smiled, teeth sharp and bloody. "All right. That's enough. It's my turn."

"What did—How did you—The iron!" The redcap stumbled backward, the dagger swinging wildly.

"Perks of being a zombie." Sage shrugged, then they launched at the redcap, swinging their still-manacled hand out at their captor and landing a blow hard enough to make them wheel backward with a yelp. They got their feet under them a moment later, and Sage took another swing, opening the wound on the redcap's jaw even further.

The redcap groaned, the dagger clattering to the floor, then they went down hard enough that if the floor weren't cement, it would have shaken with the force.

Sage stood still, breathing deeply to regain their balance. They were dizzy with pain, and muzzy with blood loss. *The iron has to go.* Balancing their wrist on one of the shipping crates, they cut through the other manacle. A task that went far quicker without having to do it behind their back, unable to see.

The manacle jangled open, and they pulled their wrist away, taking another deep inhale.

The panther rumbled in pleasure in their chest, and when they reached for her, she answered. Lending them her strength, their breaths came a little easier and the cuts on their wrists started closing.

Huh.

That was new.

It didn't do much for the wooziness of low blood sugar or the cold sweat dripping from their forehead. But it would be enough to get them out of there.

"But first—" They turned toward the door next to the stairs and squinted at it in the darkness. "Where do you go?"

There were no symbols or characters lining the frame, that they could see, to indicate what kind of magic had been used to create it. And when Sage reached for the knob . . .

"That was anti-climactic." They laughed.

The metal was cool under their hand. What magic sizzled there was young, energetic but weak. Whatever the Blood Moons used to connect this door to someplace else was either minimal or they'd somehow managed to borrow it from somewhere else. They turned the knob, pushing the door inward, and peeked their head through.

What they found on the other side was a small dusty alley. The cobblestones uneven and worn from time. They debated for about half a second before stepping through the door and into the alley. It was only a couple of steps from there to the end.

Then they were faced with a sight they never thought they'd see again: the long row of the Night Market. Bustling. Full of tables and shoppers. The sky overhead sparkling with starlight. The air crisp like the mountains. It had been home once upon a time. A place so intricately intwined with their being that they couldn't remember a time where they hadn't visited at least a couple of times a week. One of their first memories was holding their mother's hand as they strolled the aisles while guards from the Faceless Few trailed them not so subtly. Another was the day they'd saved Chuckles.

"Oh, you *are* in trouble, aren't you?" Sage asked, their smile feral. If the Blood Moons had created their own connection to the Night Market, Mal was going to want to know about it. The Court of Families would need to know too. And when they found out? The Blood Moons were going to be fucked.

Sage had no choice but to step back through the door into the basement. One always had to exit the same way they came with pocket dimensions, or risk being lost to the void.

Then Sage spun and found three more redcaps waiting for them in the dimly lit room, one of them crouched beside their fallen comrade.

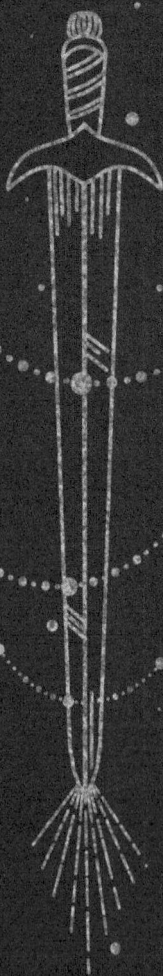

30

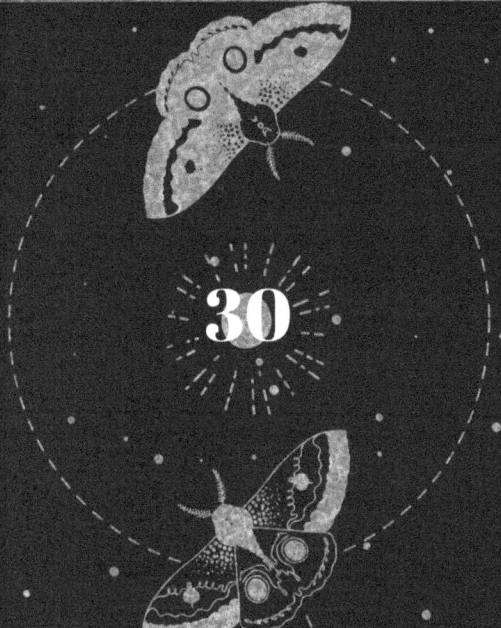

"LONG TIME, NO SEE." Dam rose from where they crouched beside the redcap Sage had slain. Their hands were deceptively loose at their sides, but Sage knew better than to let their guard down. They'd fought Dam enough in their youth.

"Dam." Sage smiled and forced their tone into a light cordiality, almost chipper. "What a coincidence seeing you here."

"Is it?" Dam tilted their head, dark brows raised high on their large forehead. "You had to realize you were in a Blood Moon safehouse."

"Nah." Sage shook their head, their eyes flicking from Dam to the other two redcaps, then subtly over their shoulders. Could they slide from the Night Market door to the one that led up the stairs? What if it was locked? It would require them to turn their back on their potential attackers, and that was something they couldn't do. It had been drilled into their head since they were a child: You never turned your back on the enemy.

One of the others snorted, rolling their eyes. "As if you didn't check the crates."

"Why would I bother?" Sage's grin turned sharp and cutting, their fangs biting into their own lip, drawing more blood. Then they said something more likely to get them killed. "I was just checking out your little Night Market portal here."

Dam shook their head, clicking their tongue softly in chiding. "You really shouldn't have said that."

"You weren't going to let me out of here alive anyway, were you?" It was a genuine question, Sage was curious. But they already knew the answer. Because it was exactly what the Faceless would have done in this situation.

"No. Probably not." Dam grinned, their pointed teeth glinting in the low light of the basement. They didn't give Sage more than a moment to breathe before they launched themself at them, fingers tipped in iron gleaming as they slashed out at Sage.

Sage met the swing with an arm half shifted into the panther, the iron burning and cutting into their fur. They hissed, barely holding off the attack, blood and saliva dripping from their lips with a snarl.

The next attack was a blow to their side with something blunt. A bat. A rib cracked and reformed in seconds as the panther took more control of their body. Sage slipped behind the wall of protection she provided. With a deep, rumbling growl, they shoved off from their back foot, letting Dam's nails cut to the bone where they couldn't cut any further.

Dam yelped, stepping back and away, giving Sage room to duck under the next incoming blow from their other side: the swing of a straight razor headed for their neck. Sweat trickled down from their hair. That had been too close—

much too close—to the injury that had killed them four years ago.

The panther took hold then, leaving Sage no choice but to let her do what she needed to protect them. She burst from their skin, all fur and teeth, and ripped into their attackers. Flinging blood and viscera around the room. First slashing Dam's cronies to pieces, then backing the Blood Moons' second into a corner.

Dam grit their teeth, their hands held in front of them to protect themself, nails at the ready.

"You can't kill me," Dam said, but their back hunched into the narrow space between two joining walls, trying to make themself as small a target as possible. Fear painted across their face. "I'm the second of the Blood Moon clan. If you kill me, it will mean war."

"War with who?" Sage asked, the words coming out garbled and guttural past their fangs and panther throat.

"The—the—" Dam swallowed. A thin sheen of sweat dribbled from their hair, slicking down their neck. "The Faceless."

"I am not a part of the Faceless Few." The panther delighted in the shiver of terror that shook Dam at the reminder that Sage was no longer beholden to the Court and the gangs. "I am a free agent."

Sage wondered for a moment if the best thing that ever happened to them was their death. It freed them from the responsibilities of being the Faceless heir, from the oversight of the Court. What they would do with this newfound freedom, they didn't yet know. But they would relish it.

"And you, Dam of the Blood Moons, are at my mercy." Then they lunged, slamming their entire body hard enough into Dam that they crushed the redcap against the wall, shattering bones and cracking their head against the cement. The panther wanted more. Carnage. Viscera. She wanted to paint their fur in it, to go from gray to crimson. Leave what was left of the Blood Moons who had dared to threaten Sage in pieces so small, not even their family would recognize them.

But Sage pulled back, leaving Dam breathing, although it was in broken gasps, stilted and wet from what might have been a ruptured lung. Listening more closely, the panther could hear the way Dam struggled against a catch in their breath.

"This—" Dam gasped, clawing at their pants to pull their phone from their pocket. "This means war."

"So you've said." Sage leaned down, bumping their snout against Dam's arm to inspect their injury. "You'll live."

"You will—" they gasped. "Not."

"A little late for that, I'm afraid." Sage settled back onto their haunches and the panther let go, leaving them squatting in front of Dam. Blood coated their arms and hands, splattered their once-goldenrod-colored sweater. Gore clumped in their hair. "I died once already," they offered, tilting their head curiously, wondering how long before Dam lost consciousness. "It didn't take."

"What"—another wet gasp—"the fuck"—their eyes fluttered—"are you?"

"Supremely annoyed." Sage smiled, all teeth. "And very much done with people trying to kill me, thanks for asking." Then they pushed to their feet, gave Dam a nudge with their toe, and snatched their phone. They sent off a quick text to Dam's sister before dropping the phone to the floor so it cracked against the cement. "Tell your friends."

The door to the stairs wasn't locked, and the rest of the house was empty as they stumbled through it—the adrenaline had worn off, leaving them shaky and muzzy again. Likely because Dam hadn't wanted anyone apart from their closest and most loyal followers to know what they were doing. That might mean Flo wasn't in on it, or it might mean she was feigning ignorance. Either way, Sage wasn't going to let the Blood Moons get away with this shit. They'd already decided. They were done running. Done letting others try to kill them. Done lying down and playing dead. They would take this to Mal and before the Court.

But first, they had a bone to pick with Corey.

EVERYTHING HAD BEEN WITHIN REACH. IT WAS ALL *RIGHT* there. So close, Mal could stretch out his hand and pull it in —*had* pulled it in, in fact. He'd had the person he'd always wanted pressed up against his body. He'd tasted them. They were right there. Exactly where he'd always dreamed of them. His person, his whole life. The reason he'd done all of this. A joy so tangible, it sat like honey on his tongue. Perfect, and ripe, and more real than he'd ever thought possible.

And then he'd let it walk out the fucking door. Like an idiot.

He let Sage walk away without protection. Not that they needed it, really. They were perfectly capable of ripping someone limb from limb. Mal knew that, he'd seen it for himself. But that didn't mean he didn't want to protect them. Didn't mean he didn't want to make it so Sage didn't have to channel their innate vicious streak.

And now all he could taste was regret.

Regret and fear. Sour and sickening. Replacing any happiness that might have lingered so completely that he almost couldn't remember what that joy had tasted like. It had been so brief. There and gone.

What if he'd lost his chance? What if that was all he'd ever get? Just a peek, just a glimpse into what his life could have been. What if Sage was really gone? Forever. What would he do?

Die. Probably.

There would be nothing worth living for, having lost Sage a second time. Especially as this time it would be his own fault. Especially as this time he'd know what he was missing.

His heart was in his throat, threatening to choke him. Threatening to send him into a panic so sharp he wouldn't be able to think past it. Tears pricked, burning at the backs of his eyes. There wasn't time to cry now. Not yet.

He had to save Sage first.

He just had to *find* them. Then he could deal with whatever came next. Then he could . . . he could break down if he had to.

One block around Corey's apartment building. Nothing.

Two. Nothing. Three. Four. Five. Still nothing.

He circled around into Blood Moon territory, his grip tight on his dagger. Being on another gang's turf set his teeth on edge. Mal knew better than to think that being a family head would lend him any protection in enemy territory. There was no immunity from the violence of the Eventide underground.

Being on their turf would be reason enough for them to act against him, could be seen as an act of war. All he could hope was that no one would notice him, but there was little chance of that.

Not that it would matter. It wasn't going to stop him. He would do anything to bring Sage home, to make sure they were safe. Even if that meant putting his own head on the chopping block. It didn't matter. *Nothing* mattered.

Only Sage. Only—

Mal stopped, hardly able to believe his eyes.

Coming out of the fog about a block away, like an avenging angel covered in blood and wobbling on their feet . . .

"Sage!" Mal gasped, then he was running, tripping, stumbling down the road toward them. His dagger forgotten in his rush to reach Sage. The Blood Moons and their territory pushed to the back of his mind. Let them be seen. Let the redcaps come. He would rip them all apart if it meant getting to Sage.

Joy was within reach again. Fizzy and glimmering in the air. The light to Mal's shadows.

"Mal." Sage's voice was a choked breath, their body slumping against his. They smelled of blood. But they were warm, so warm. And breathing. *Safe.* They were safe. Everything else could be fixed.

His heart in his throat again—for an entirely different reason—Mal tugged Sage in close, pressing a kiss to their head. He hid there for a moment, letting the burning in his eyes turn to tears. Choked sobs of relief. Then he pulled away, holding them at arm's length so he could look them over. There was so much blood, *too* much blood. Fear gripped him again and his next words left him in a rush. "Where are you hurt? Let me see it. Let me see. I need to see where you're hurt. I'll kill them. I'll fucking—"

"Calm down. Relax." Sage laughed, the sound a harsh rasp as if they'd been breathing hard or screaming. *Torture.* Mal's mind supplied the word even as he hardly wanted to think it. Someone had *tortured* his Sage. "Most of this isn't mine."

"Most?" Goddess. He was shaking. His hands trembled

so hard, he wasn't even sure how he was keeping a hold of Sage, but he refused to let go. He couldn't. "How *much* of it is yours?"

Sage shook their head, their chuckle growing weaker as Mal took more of their weight. Goddess, how hadn't he noticed? He shouldn't have wasted time tending to his own happiness. He should have gotten Sage out of there. Seen to their wounds. Time was of the essence.

"Enough," they murmured and stumbled entirely into Mal, their face pressed to his chest as they lost consciousness.

Mal bent, scooping them into his arms, holding them close. "You foolish, brave, beautiful idiot." Mal sighed, pressing his face into Sage's head, kissing their hair. "Goddess, but I love you."

Balancing Sage's weight carefully, he started back to Corey's apartment with his precious cargo.

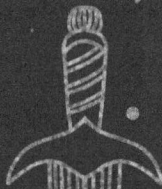

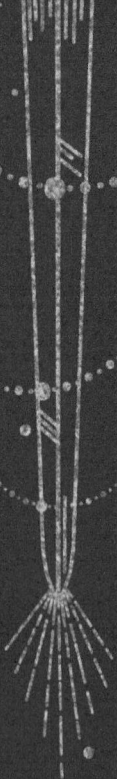

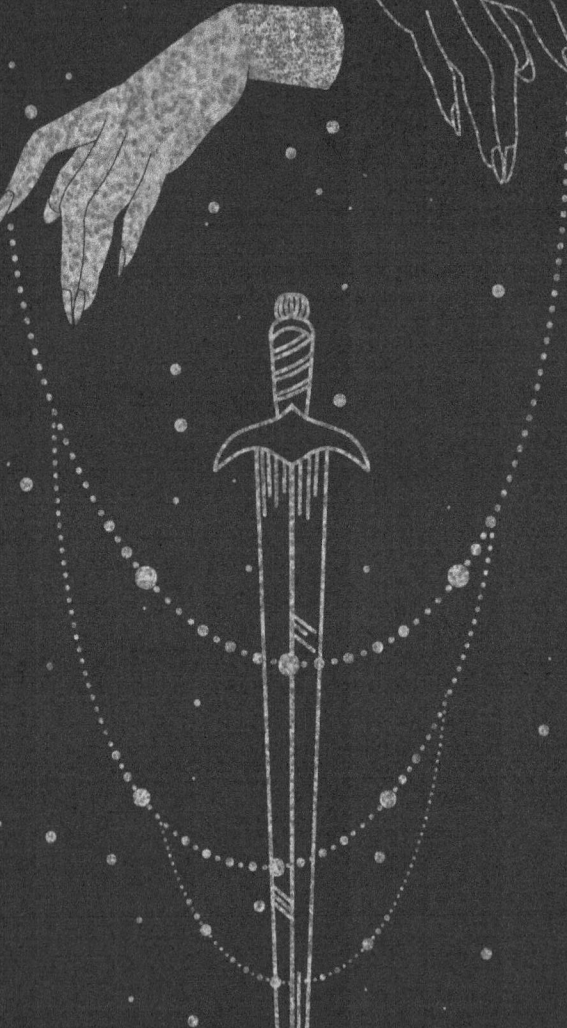

31

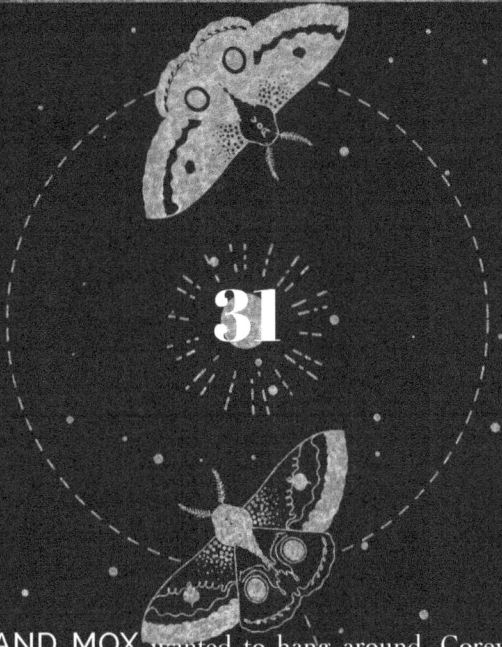

MAL AND MOX wanted to hang around, Corey could tell, and honestly, she would rather not be left alone with Sage. Not when they were following her every movement with anger in their eyes. Their jaw worked as if they were chewing on the words they wanted to say. She wasn't sure why, but she knew that the moment Mox and Mal walked out the door, Sage would let her have it. So maybe it'd be better if the two mobsters stayed the night—or possibly forever.

"I've been checked by the doctor. I've eaten. I've taken my sugar," Sage assured gently, patting at Mal's searching hands while Mal continued to hover beside the couch. Which Corey supposed was better than how she was hovering at the entrance to her own living room as if she didn't belong there. As if this weren't her apartment. But it didn't make this whole act any less awkward to watch. "There's nothing more we can do apart from let me rest. And you need to get home before Chuckles sends out a search party."

"And *will* you rest?" Mal was insistent. Clingy, even.

Not that Corey could blame him. He believed that Sage was his soulmate, and he'd almost lost them for a second time. She wondered how much of himself Mal realized he was giving away by acting this way. And how long it would take for him to realize he wasn't wearing a glamour anymore. As far as she knew, he kept up the farce of Ianthe when they went on dates. But the need for a mask seemed to have melted away when faced with Sage's injuries.

"I will." It sounded like a lie, even to Corey, but she was pretty sure Mal wouldn't call Sage on it. He respected them too much. Idolized them to a point of near worship. At least, that's how it looked from where Corey was standing, but what did she know? She had her own foolish Mafia exec who didn't seem to want to go away.

Corey scoffed. They both ignored her, too wrapped up in each other. Not that she'd expected anything else.

"The panther did most of the healing for me anyway," Sage offered. "There's not much more a doctor could even do."

"Your concussion—"

"Will be fine." Sage shook their head, disgustingly fond. Corey wished she didn't have to witness this. She supposed she didn't *have* to. She could go into the kitchen and avoid this whole scene. But that's where Mox was, and she wasn't going to be cornered into giving answers she didn't want to, again.

"Very well." Mal pressed to his feet, letting out a slow breath and straightening his clothes as he went. He was still in his date outfit, and Corey wondered if he realized that too. Well, if he didn't, she wasn't going to tell him. Let the ridiculous farce fall to the wayside. It wasn't as if he hadn't already dropped a bunch of hints about who he really was. Sage had to know. They just weren't saying anything. Why, she wasn't sure. She didn't want to ask either; it would open a whole can of worms she didn't have the energy for.

"You have things to do anyway," Sage reminded, a rueful smile on their face. Mal must have blinked in confusion because Sage continued, "The Court of Families."

"Ah, yes. The Court!" Mal nodded so hard that he bowed forward slightly, and Corey had to restrain another snorted laugh.

What a dork.

Who would have thought that the leader of the Faceless Few could act this way? From what Corey had seen of him prior to Sage's return, he was as hardened and vicious as any other mobster, but this new version of Mal . . . This soft, almost clumsy man who would do anything within his power to please Sage? It was almost—*almost*—sweet.

"Get some rest," Mal said needlessly, the ear Corey could see because of his undercut suspiciously red. Then he spun on his heel and headed into the kitchen. "Mox! We've got to go."

And then they were gone, leaving Corey alone with one very pissed off Sage. "Are we going to talk about how you told everyone I was still alive?" Sage asked, their hands fisted in the blanket Mal had draped over their legs after they'd settled on the couch.

"I mean, we don't have to." Corey shifted from one foot to the other. Could she run? If she ran, could she actually escape? Even she wasn't sure. "And it wasn't *everyone*."

She was weighing the pros and cons of chancing it when Sage stood from the couch, the blanket falling away. They strode across the living room and grabbed her wrist in a grip so tight, she could feel her bones grinding together. "Corwin," Sage snarled, their teeth sharpened to points, cutting into their bottom lip, "what the fuck did you *do*?"

She supposed she ought to be grateful that Sage hadn't

told Mal. There was little doubt that if they had, Mal would put her at the top of his list of people to skin alive and turn into a patchwork rug for his fancy house in the expensive part of Eventide. Not that she could blame him,. If she were in love with someone the way that he was, she would probably do anything within her power to see vengeance served for that person too. Good thing she'd never bothered with such things.

"I didn't—" She swallowed hard, forced the words out. "I didn't do anything." Panic made her stumble, stutter, sweat. She couldn't lie. The truth sat choking on her tongue, threatening to clog her airways. She couldn't lie. But she couldn't tell the truth either, could she?

"I thought we were friends," Sage gasped, sharp and wounded.

"No, you *didn't*," Corey hissed, snatching her wrist away from them, all the confusion and fear replaced by utter fury. That was easier than facing the fact that maybe Sage was right. Maybe they'd been friends, or almost anyway. "You never thought we were friends. At best we were business partners, at worst I'm just the person who saved your ass when you got yourself fucking knifed. We've always hated each other, Sage."

"No, we haven't."

She wasn't sure why they were so insistent on this. Who they thought they were trying to convince. It wasn't her. She'd never had any illusions of something more between them. They weren't friends, not since they were kids, not since Sage dropped off the face of the fucking earth and left Corey to deal with everything that came after by herself. They weren't even really roommates. Two weeks. It was only meant to be two weeks. And then Sage was supposed to fuck off to Ironport to look after their *actual* friend.

"We *could* have been friends," they tried again. "Had you not fucking betrayed me."

"Fuck off, Sage. I did what I had to. Just like we always do. Just like *you* would have done." She was sure of that. They were *both* the kind of wicked, evil beings more than willing to trade another's life for their own. That's why she was fine killing the Blood Moons' heir. Why she had no qualms about the price she had to pay to get out of Aquarius. It was her life or his, and she'd chosen hers. Just like she did with Sage. Just like she *always* would. "Don't get all noble on me now, Sage *Nocturna*."

They stumbled back, their eyes wide, wild, as if she'd slapped them. "I'm not being noble. I really thought—"

"No, you didn't," she hissed, anger and hurt swirling in her gut, making her nauseous and the room too hot. "You never thought we were *friends*. I was just one more person for you to use. One more goon to order around. You're just like your father." She knew she'd fucked up the moment those words left her mouth. Corey had this habit—this ability, this superpower, really—to say the most supremely hateful thing at the exact wrong time, and she'd just done it. Again.

Sage's eyes flashed a brighter green, the pupils narrowing to slits, the panther living under their skin clearly threatened by the antagonism in her voice. Corey had just enough time to throw herself beside the couch and out of the way of a charging cat. Their gray fur was still stained pink by all the blood they'd spilled before returning to the apartment.

Sage didn't stop. Didn't turn. Didn't bother with the cowering woman. They bolted past and burst through the apartment door, leaving it in splinters in the hall.

Corey curled up then, panic, upset, fear, and sadness all mingling into a solid lump that weighed heavily at her chest as she wrapped her arms around her legs, backing into the corner made by the side of the couch and the wall behind it. She hadn't meant to say something like that, something so obviously hurtful. She had just . . . She wasn't sure *what* she'd been trying to do.

Maybe forestall the inevitable guilt. Maybe push some of the blame onto Sage. But in reality, they hadn't done anything to deserve what she'd done to them. They were just trying to live their life. Take care of their friend. Be good to the people around them. And Corey was . . . she was selfish. Trying to preserve a life that was stolen, not earned. A life she didn't deserve, not with all the blood on her hands.

Her phone rang a moment later, and she struggled to get it out of her sweatpants pocket. She hoped for about half a second that it might be Sage calling to apologize. To work things out when they weren't face-to-face with one another and likely to say something else cutting. But it wasn't.

"What the fuck do you want now, Alton?" she snarled into the phone, her grip too tight on the metal, making it cut into her palm.

"The Phantom. I want them."

"Why? We've talked about this. They're freelance, and I—"

"That was before Sage Nocturna was back in Eventide and they were working together. I want their name, Corey. Or else."

"You know what, Alton," Corey said, sitting up straighter, gearing herself to do something intolerably stupid. But what was one more idiotic decision in a landscape full of them? "Go fuck yourself."

Then she hung up and hurled her phone across the room.

Sage had always been taught that anger made them stupid. And it was true, even if they didn't want to acknowledge it. Some of the most foolish things they'd ever done were done in anger. Running out on someone who had been there for them through some of the worst moments in their life was one of the most recent examples of this. But there were *so* many more.

"You could go back and apologize," they reasoned. But what was there to apologize for? Corey had been the one to betray them, not the other way around. She was the one who told everyone they were alive and exposed them to the limited mercy of the gangs of Eventide. Even if they hadn't come back, there was no way they wouldn't have felt the effects of that. The rival gangs would send someone after them, they had no doubt about it.

But why? Why bother? They'd left all of this behind. Moved on. Why couldn't they live their life in peace? Why did the gangs insist on dragging them back in? Sage didn't understand, but what they did understand was that once Eventide had sunk her teeth into a person, she didn't let go. Not even in death, it seemed.

Their own mother had tried to run once. Put as much distance between herself and the blood and violence of Eventide's underground as she could. She hadn't gotten much farther than a couple of states over before a speeding ticket on the vehicle their father had reported stolen brought her back to Eventide to die.

It wasn't as if they wanted back into that life. They liked how they lived now, even if they had to stay in their apartment most of the time. They liked having their freedom and the room to breathe. And they liked not waking up smelling blood on their skin every other morning.

Their footsteps were slow, deliberate, their mind racing along, trying to figure out how to salvage this. How to fix it. Maybe Corey was right. Maybe they weren't friends at all. Maybe they should leave town, head over to Ironport, and forget all about the gangs of Eventide, all about the beautiful gang leader, all about the possibility of—

The mist grew thicker, blurring their already fuzzy vision further as they pressed on.

Why was the mist so thick in this part of—

No. Not mist. Smoke. Thick and cloying. Something burning.

Ignoring every instinct that might have told them to stay back, to call someone, Sage started running toward the blaze. Down the block. Around the corner. Following the scent. Their feet pounded against the pavement until they could finally see where the sky was lit up. A warm afterglow of the flames below. The flames that were . . .

Oh Goddess. The flames that were swallowing the bakery whole.

The bakery!

There were three figures outside, two large and one small that might have been a goblin or a child. Sage couldn't tell through the haze of the heat and without their glasses. The figures were throwing more fuel on the blaze, making it go up quicker. Sage lunged for one of them, shoulder checking them so hard they stumbled to the ground, then whirled on another. They kicked ash into Sage's eyes and Sage hissed, snarled, and swiped out at empty air as the perpetrators got away.

Now that they were closer, they could smell the sharp bite of fairy fire in the air. This was no normal fire. This was magic. A spell. A charm. Something. And it wouldn't go out by normal means. Not if they didn't find the source.

Rubbing at their still burning eyes with the back of their sleeve, they tore off a piece of their shirt and wrapped it around their mouth. If they could get inside and find the source of the blaze, maybe they could stanch it. Maybe they could save the . . . the one good thing in their life. It could be the one good thing they'd do for the first person to call them friend.

Corey.

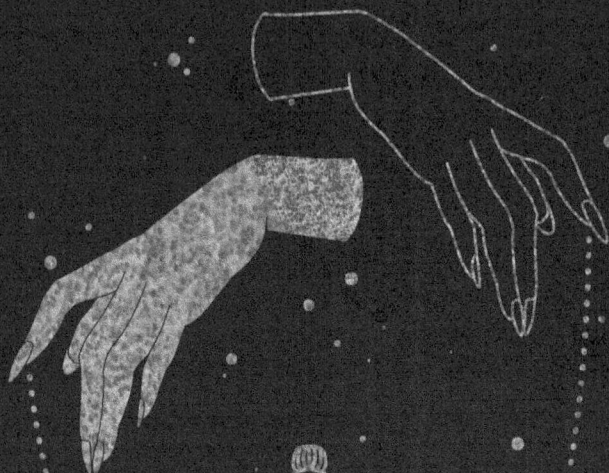

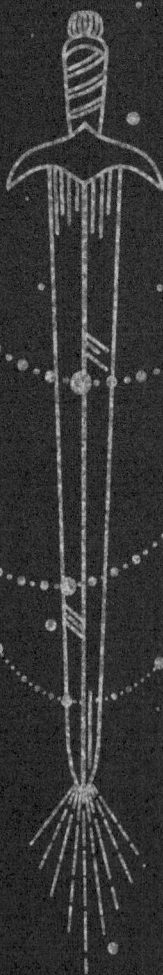

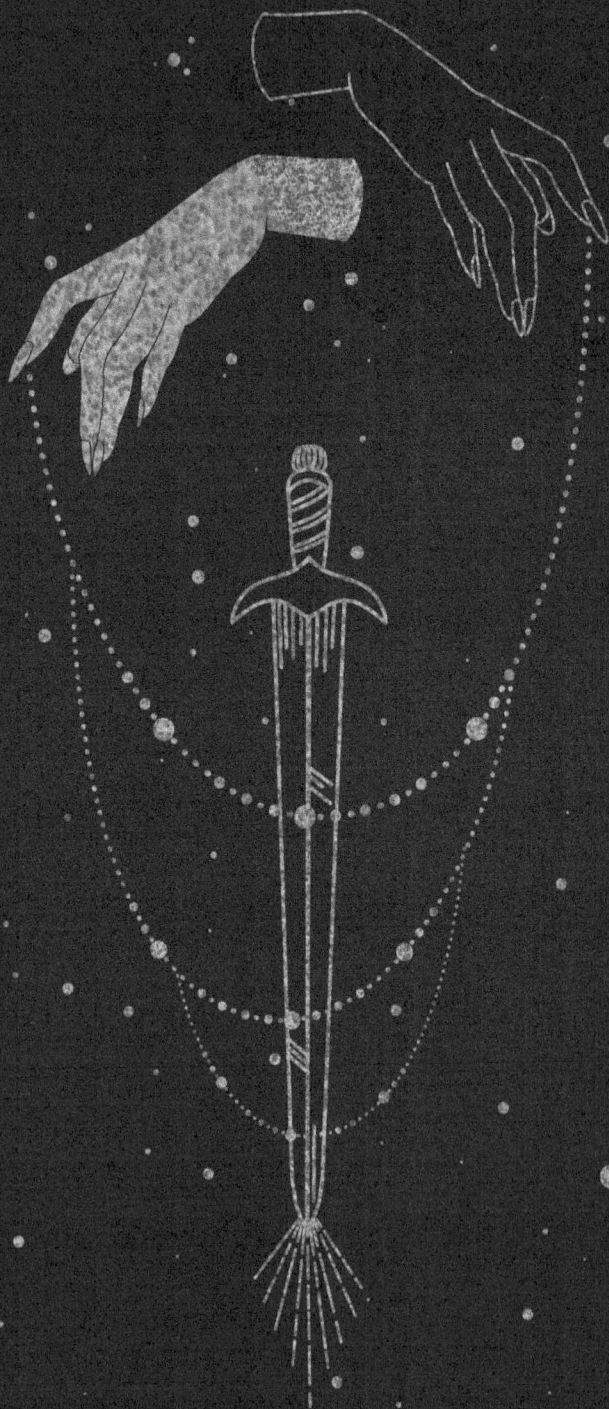

32

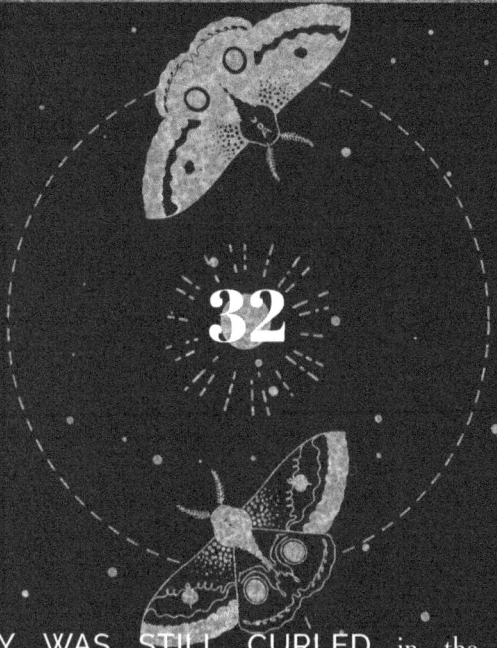

COREY WAS STILL CURLED in the corner, scrubbing at her itchy nose, when the dull ringing of her phone ripped her from her misery.

It was an unfamiliar noise. And not just because it had never gone off before, but also because she kept the damn thing on silent every hour of every day. She pulled her head up from where she'd tucked it against her knees and glared around the room, looking for her phone. Where had it gone after she'd thrown it?

It rang louder, growing increasingly annoying.

Under the coffee table.

She scrambled to her feet and went in search of the device that was now buzzing and ringing so loudly, it threatened to vibrate across the floor until it slid under the cheap red TV stand against the wall. She didn't even need to pick it up to know what had set it off, and the flashing red warning on the lock screen was enough to tell her all she needed to know.

Her heart plummeted.

The alarm at the shop.

She swiped the notification to view the camera attached to the box at the back door, hoping maybe it wouldn't be something terrible. Maybe Sage broke in to throw some shit around. Maybe they were hate-baking Corey a shit cake or something. That, she could deal with. It would suck, sure, but she could make it through that fine.

What she wasn't ready for, what she couldn't make work, what wouldn't be okay, was the blindingly bright wall of flames the camera opened onto. It hadn't melted down yet, surprisingly. But it was close. Lines of static moved over the picture, and the way it flipped over on itself told her all she needed to know about how hot it was there currently.

And then her heart stopped, terror closing over her like a cold vice.

A figure appeared in the flames, their arms loaded down with buckets of steaming water as they tried to put out the blaze. Sage. What the fuck? Why would they—

She shook herself. There wasn't time for that. Someone needed to pull them out before they got themself killed. *Again.*

Corey slipped on the flip-flops she left at the door for deliveries, the phone in her hand already ringing through to the number Mox had slipped her a few days prior. A number she'd added to her contacts under "My Stalker" so she'd know if Mox ever got hers and decided to text her. So she could block it when the time came for that. But she called it now.

"You've reached Mox, Faceless Few second in command," the woman on the other side of the phone said in a tone devoid of any of the emotion she usually layered into her words. Serious. Professional. The second in command of the Faceless Few, indeed.

"Meet me at the bakery," Corey blurted, not bothering

with the elevator, her breaths coming harsh and fast as she tripped down the steps. "There's a fire, and Sage is—"

"We're on our way," Mox cut her off, not even needing to hear the rest it seemed. Corey had to hand it to Mox—she worked extremely well in a crisis. Maybe that came with being the second in command to one of the more violent Unseelie gangs in Eventide. Or maybe it was a consequence of being Mal's twin sister. "Mal, call the fire department," she ordered Mal but didn't hang up. Then she returned her attention to Corey. "Are you all right? Where are you?"

"I'm on my way there. I need to get them out. They're being fucking stupid, trying to put the fire out by themselves. They're using buckets. Why the fuck are they—"

Fairy fire. That was the only explanation. Human chemicals wouldn't work on fire caused by magic. They would only make it worse.

"Okay." Mox took a deep breath that made the phone speaker crackle. "Don't do anything until we get there. Don't go in. If you can't get Sage out without doing that, then you wait outside. Do you understand me?"

"But—"

"No buts." Mox's tone was final, cutting, the kind of tone she used to order her subordinates, and it sent a shiver up Corey's spine.

"Okay. Just hurry."

"We will. Do you need me to stay on the phone with you?"

"No. I don't . . . I don't think so." Running through the streets in flip-flops was a bitch and a half. She stumbled on the uneven cobblestones twice at least, her sandal getting caught on an edge, but she kept going. Pushing herself.

Even as her feet skidded against the perpetually damp street.

"Okay." Corey imagined Mox nodding along with the word. "I'm hanging up now. I'll have some of our people on their way to you too." Then she hung up, just like she'd said.

Corey sucked down another lungful of air. It was starting to smell like smoke now. The scent threatened to choke her, to send her to her knees. But she wasn't going to stop, not until she got Sage the fuck out of there. And no, she wasn't going to think about why she was so dead set on saving someone she insisted *wasn't* her friend, either. Thanks.

The bakery was nothing but a glowing inferno by the time she reached it. Corey's knees buckled under her, slamming hard against the sidewalk on the other side of the street. Her business. Her home. Her happy place. The one thing that was truly her own. The one thing she'd always wanted and had barely allowed herself to have. It was . . . it was gone.

And Sage would be soon too, if she didn't haul her ass up and get them out.

She pushed to her feet, even as her legs wobbled, and raced across the street into the blaze. It was blisteringly hot, and almost immediately she was choking on the air inside.

"Sage Nocturna! You get your ass out here! Right now!" She coughed when yelling meant sucking down more air, but she pushed forward. The last she'd seen them, they'd been in the kitchen, likely trying to put out whatever had started this whole thing. A spell probably. A bit of magic that would keep the inferno going if they didn't get it.

Corey hadn't thought about who could be responsible in the run over, but now that she stood in the center of her shop, the walls burning around her, she was sure Alton had something to do with this. It was his people. A threat and a promise all in one. He'd told her once upon a time that if she ever crossed him, he'd take everything she loved from her. This was just the beginning; the rest would come later.

She'd cross that bridge when she came to it though. Sage first.

"Sage!" Another cough rocked her chest. The door to the kitchen swung inward under her touch but fell off melted hinges a second later, and there was Sage in the middle of the kitchen, throwing water on what seemed to be a sigil of some kind. "Sage! We have to get out!"

"It'll just keep going!" they shouted back through the bit of fabric they'd been smart enough to cover their mouth with while they pointed to the marking burned into the floor. "Will-o'-wisp magic."

"Borrowed?" Not that it mattered. Corey ripped the bucket from their hands and threw more water on the mark, all while her vision started to blur with heat.

"Stolen."

The characters sizzled but didn't go out, and Corey heard something above them groan. The roof. They didn't have time for this.

"Fuck it. We have to go!" Corey grabbed Sage around the waist and heaved them with her out the back door. They both landed hard against the pavement just before the roof collapsed with a crash. Scraping skin, jolting joints. The air wasn't much clearer there, but it wasn't blistering her skin anymore.

"We have to go back!" Sage struggled against her hold. "If we don't, it won't stop until—"

"It's already gone, Sage!" Corey was going to pretend that catch in her throat was from the fire, not from the sudden realization that after the fire had burned itself down to embers, she'd have nothing left. It hadn't touched the businesses to either side of her. More proof that it was targeted.

"The bakery," Sage gasped, but they'd stopped struggling.

"I know. I know." Corey held them closer, unsure anymore of who was comforting who. It felt oddly like they were leaning on each other, a thing she hadn't let herself do since . . . she couldn't remember when. Maybe not since she was a teenager working shoulder to shoulder in a bakery with another kid who was just annoying enough to mean they'd probably be friends for life.

"Who did this?" Sage asked, their arms tight around her middle, their face pressed into her shoulder.

"Looks like you aren't the only one with enemies in this town." Corey wanted to laugh at that. It was kind of funny. But it was also undeniably sad. Alton wasn't going to stop. She'd offended him, denied him, rejected him, and in the end, she'd committed the worst sin of them all: She'd gotten away from him.

"Funny how that happens, isn't it?" Sage asked, and they sounded like they were laughing. When Sage pulled away from Corey's tear-stained shoulder, they fixed her with a watery smile that Corey had to admit she was sort of fond of.

"Not really," Corey said belatedly.

Not that it mattered. The only noise around them right now was the crackling of the fire. It almost sounded merry like this. Cheerful. It made her sick. The destruction of the thing in her life that made her the happiest shouldn't sound like that.

"I MEAN, IT KIND OF IS." SAGE COULDN'T HELP THEMSELF; it was laugh or cry, and they were over crying about things. Crying was behind them. It was time to fight. Time to rail against the darkness that threatened to overtake them all.

"You think having enemies is funny?" Corey sounded incredulous, but Sage could see a smile ticking up the corners of her lips as well. She was coming around. Good. They would need her not to be mired in despair for what came next.

"Means you're doing something right, doesn't it?"

Corey wrinkled her nose, her head tilted in thought. "I suppose so." Then her gaze flicked back to the burning bakery behind them, the blaze reflected in her eyes. She was clearly distraught, but there was steel there too. Strength the likes of which Sage knew well how to harness. "So what do we do about them?"

Sage sat up straighter, brushing their hair from their face, the sweat slicking it back in a style so like how they used to wear it before they left, before they died. It felt right but alien at the same time. Foreign. Just like coming back had felt. Just like this town felt now. And yet, here they were.

"Sage? What do we do now?" Corey asked again, fear lingering at the edges of her voice, but not enough to stop her from asking the question. She was too strong for that.

"Now"—Sage smiled, sharp and feral—"we fight. They've decided to make enemies of us, and we make them regret it the way only we can."

"Together." It wasn't a question. She wasn't looking for their reassurance. Perhaps she could feel the bond forged in fire between them, like the best fae-made blade. Perhaps she knew that there was no going back from this, not for either of them. They were a team now. Whoever had done this had solidified that in ways Sage and Corey couldn't have done on their own. And they would live to regret it.

"Yes, together." Inhaling deeply, they pushed to their feet. Sirens were approaching now. The firetrucks drove fast, but not fast enough to save the bakery. It was all right. They would rebuild it. They would come back from this. There was no other choice. "Do you know who's behind this?"

"Alton wanted the name of the Phantom. He thinks they're helping you, and he wants to eliminate any possible danger you might pose to his power over the Court." Corey pushed to her feet, straightening her clothes. There were ashes on her shirt. Blisters forming on her cheeks from the flames. But she looked almost regal. The kind of person Sage had always wanted as their second, even if they hadn't known at the time that they'd needed one.

"Then I suppose we should make all his worst fears come true. Shouldn't we?" Sage let her look them over for injuries, then they turned as a unit to face the still blazing inferno.

"Yes. We should," Corey agreed readily. "Will we take back the Faceless to do it?"

"No." Sage shook their head. They didn't want the gang anymore; they hadn't wanted it from the beginning. It was their father's beast. Not their own. And if they'd had the choice in those days, they'd have abdicated for someone else, someone who would relish it. Someone more like Mal. "We're going to do this on our own."

Corey nodded, and then Mox and Mal's people showed up, followed by Mox and Mal.

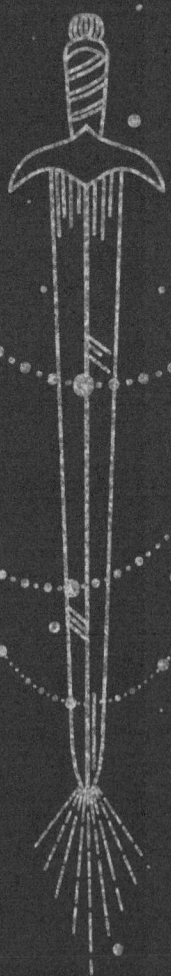

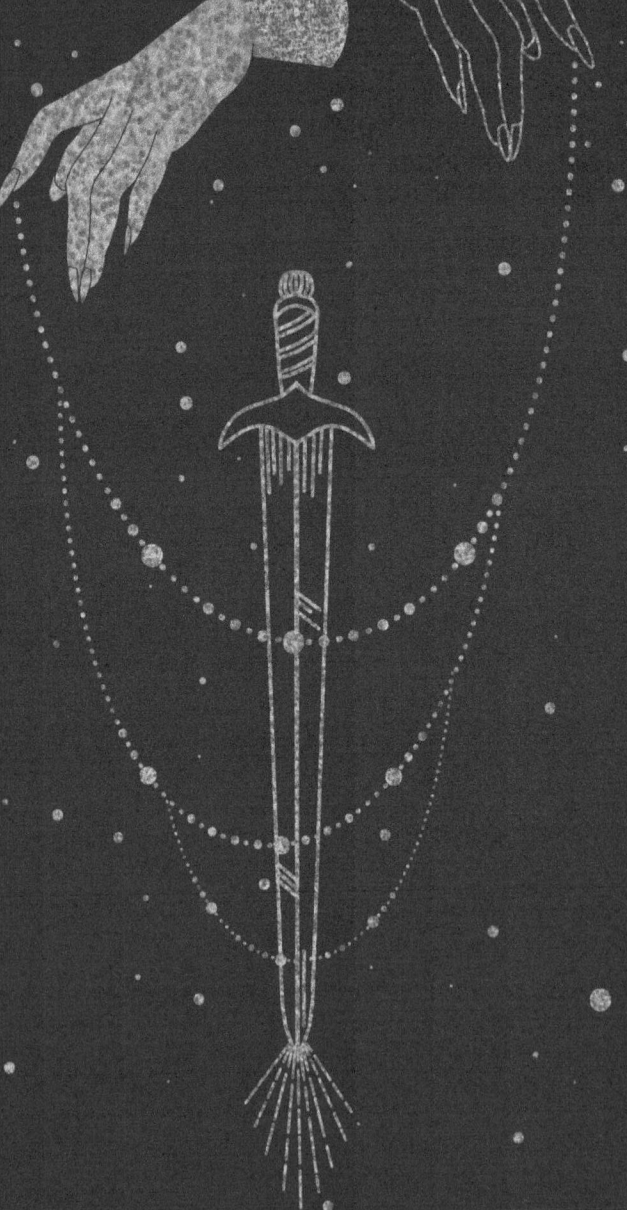

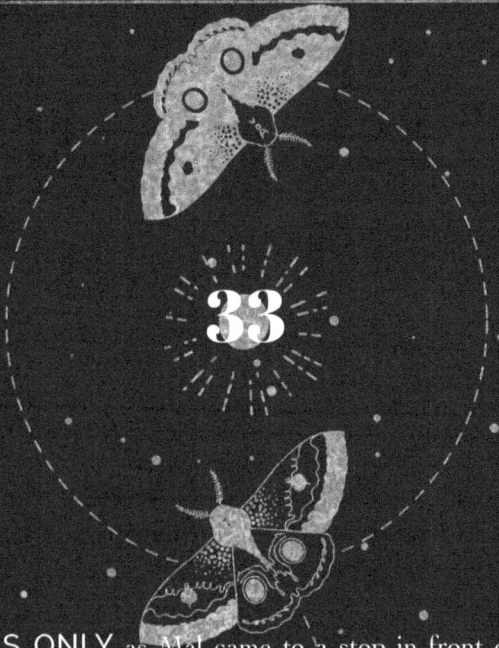

33

IT WAS ONLY as Mal came to a stop in front of Sage that he finally realized he still wore his date outfit. He should have changed when he went back to the house, but there was too much to do. Too much else to think of. And Chuckles was having an absolute fit over the fact that he wouldn't let her storm out right then and there to see Sage. He could only assume no one had told him because both Corey and Mox were assholes. Almost the exact same type of asshole, in fact. They were made for each other.

Maybe Sage wouldn't notice. No. They weren't stupid. They would notice. *Had* noticed already, probably. They had been raised to be the heir to a gang. They were too observant and too smart not to. Fuck.

"Sage," Mal gasped, wanting to reach for them, his hands shaking with fear and adrenaline. They were right there. Why couldn't he reach out for them when they were so close? Why couldn't he pull them toward himself and curl his body around them, protect them? "I uh . . .".

Sage cocked their head for a moment as if they were thinking something over. Maybe deciding if they should even bother with Mal. The answer was no, no they shouldn't. Mal wasn't worthy. He wasn't —

"Ianthe," Sage said after a moment, a sweet, teasing smile playing at the corners of their cracked and bleeding lips as they met his gaze without a trace of fear. Goddess, they were so beautiful, even like this. Even covered in ash and reeking of smoke "Or Mal? Which do you prefer?"

Mal's face burned hot enough to rival the flames only now dying down, his heart stuttering in his chest. Where the fuck had those firetrucks been anyway? Had someone held them up? Someone who wanted the bakery to burn.

But even as the thought flitted through his mind, he couldn't tear his eyes away from Sage to check. Couldn't even blink for fear that he'd miss something.

All the while, words stacked at the back of his throat, choking him. Apologies. Explanations. Excuses.

Sage waited, holding his gaze, and Mal fucking *floundered*.

"As entertaining as this staring contest is," Corey said, breaking the awkward moment Mal and Sage seemed to be having, "the firefighters are here. We should step back."

She tugged Sage by the wrist, and Mox tugged Mal, and they stepped across the alley that separated the back of the bakery from the businesses on the street that ran parallel. It was cold away from the fire, but Mal's cheeks still burned with shame.

"We should get you checked out by a medic," Mox murmured, fussing over Corey, her hands never settling as they jerked around, seeming to look for a place to land all while checking for wounds. "Both of you."

"Right." Mal stood straighter, his tone dipping low as he turned to the small group of subordinates they'd brought along. He'd almost forgotten about them. About *himself*. Thank the Goddess for Mox reminding him of who he was meant to be. "Alfie, direct the medics over here. Earl, I want to have a conversation with one of the firefighters once they're done. I want to know what took them so fucking long. Their response time has never been so bad, and if someone held them up . . . That goes against the accords. The rest of you, canvas for witnesses."

The group nodded before turning to take care of their respective tasks.

"You should also tell the firefighters that this wasn't just a regular fire," Sage offered, stepping in close again.

"What?"

"It was arson," Corey added. "Targeted. Will-o'-wisp fire."

Mox straightened out of the corner of his eye, her expression shifting to something he couldn't quite parse with how little of it he could see in the dark.

"Stolen wisp fire." Sage scrubbed at their face, hissing when the movement irritated the still healing burns.

"How can you tell?" Mox's tone was carefully neutral, but Mal could read it for what it was: fear. A sentiment Mal probably understood too well. After all, wasn't every fae afraid of their power being ripped away from them and used against their will? It was the ultimate perversion of who and what they were. The ultimate betrayal of their nature.

"There are certain binding symbols a person has to use to make something like that work against the fae's will." Sage seemed to be trying to keep emotion from their voice too. Mal couldn't tell if it was because they were angry or scared like Mox.

And he wanted to know how Sage had come by this knowledge. Where they'd learned of these things. Had they done such a thing? Had they performed such a heinous act?

"It was how the first Night Market portals were created

hundreds of years ago. We keep record of every element of magic we ever use in the archives for the Faceless. Or we did, anyway. I imagine that when Father died, and then I . . . Well, much of that was probably lost to the archives that were connected to our magic." The last bit was said with something like heartbreak, sadness at knowing that something Sage had once known was now gone.

Guilt gnawed at Mal's belly, making him shake anew. Because the truth was . . . "I—"

"Were you two in the fire when it started?" a medic asked, his clinical tone almost harsh. Almost as if he blamed them for him having to do his job. Mal spun, jaw clenched, half ready to scream at him. But Sage put a hand on his arm.

"We were," Sage confirmed. They gave Mal's arm an easy squeeze, then they took Corey's hand and both of them followed the medic to the ambulance parked a ways away. Leaving Mox and Mal to watch as the firefighters fought the blaze.

"YOU NEVER DID ANSWER ME," SAGE SAID TO MAL sometime later after they had returned to Corey's apartment, both of them squeezed onto Corey's loveseat with cups of tea warding off the chill in their fingers. Mox and Corey were in the kitchen, talking softly to one another. Mal wasn't sure if they'd decided that he and Sage needed privacy or if they were the ones who wanted to be alone. He didn't care either.

"Answer you about what?" Mal hoped he sounded nonchalant, but he was pretty sure he'd missed his mark. He had never been good at acting like a normal person, and he was even less good at it with Sage. He was, in Mox's estimation, intense. It was why, or so Mox said anyway, he'd attached himself to Sage as he had. Why when he'd been hired to sneak into Sage's room and haunt them with nightmares, and Sage had trapped him, he'd decided they were married. It wasn't just the tradition of the thing—it was also who Mal was.

"Mal or Ianthe?" Sage was smiling at him now. And oh Goddess, he didn't deserve that either. Not even a bit.

"I think"—he swallowed, trying to get control over a tongue that seemed increasingly muddled—"that I rather like the way you say Ianthe. If you don't mind?"

"Very well." Sage nodded and took a sip from their mug, murmuring to themself in what could only be contentment.

"How long have you known?" Mal didn't think he really wanted to know. Whatever answer he was given would no doubt be embarrassing. But what did that matter now? He'd exposed himself and his soft belly to Sage once already.

"Oh." Sage glanced at him from the corners of their luminescent green eyes, then back to their mug. Their ears looked like they might be turning a bit red as well. "For a bit now."

"Why didn't you say anything?" Goddess, he was such a fucking moron, wasn't he? He'd actually thought he could fool Sage into believing he wasn't the worst possible person for them to date.

Sage shrugged. "You seemed rather attached to the act."

"I had a glamour."

"Oh yeah, those don't work quite right with me anymore." They didn't expand on that thought, and Mal wasn't going to ask. Sage hadn't pushed for answers when Mal essentially lied about who he was, and he owed them the same courtesy to let them keep their secrets. But that didn't mean he wasn't curious.

"Then . . . But I'm a mobster. I killed most of your family to pave the way to take over your father's gang. I hold his seat at Court, the one meant to be yours." They had to know that, Mal was sure, but he also felt it bore repeating. If they knew all of that, why would they offer him such grace? He was so clearly undeserving. "I put your cousin in the hospital, drove her out of her home."

Sage seemed to think on that for a moment as they sipped their tea. It couldn't still be warm, but they didn't seem to mind. Or maybe they were looking for a distraction, something to give them a moment that they wouldn't otherwise have. Mal wanted to tell them that he'd give them all the time in the world to think. They just had to ask for it. He'd give them anything. Everything.

"You must have had your reasons," Sage said neutrally. "And as for Bentley, she got what she deserved, all things considered."

"She tried to have you killed."

"Oh yes, I'm very much aware of that. Hence, she got what she deserved. And as for the rest of the family?" Sage shrugged, but they weren't looking at him. They were staring off into the distance, thoughtful, maybe a little pained. Those had been people they had once cared about, or Mal had thought so anyway.

"It wasn't all of them," Mal rushed to assure, because he didn't know what else to say, what else to do.

"No. I know that." Sage nodded, sipped from their mug again, and took their time, careful. Mal couldn't remember if they'd been this way before they left four years ago. Was this new? If it was, Goddess, Mal wanted to learn all the other new things about them that had developed in their time apart. "But none of those that are gone were particularly kind to me in the years before I di—left Eventide. My father encouraged competition among the family, and even the lowest exec was convinced that all they had to do was show him that they were tougher, badder, more vicious than I was. Then they could take my place."

"Was it true?" He wasn't sure he wanted the answer to that question either.

"No. It wasn't." That was worse. That meant Sage's father had sewn discord among his ranks just for the sake of it. Just for— "He thought it would toughen me up. Turn me into the kind of heir he could be proud of. They weren't too bad when I was a child, but once I hit about . . . oh . . . fourteen? They all turned cold, bitter, nasty toward me. I was in a fight at the rings every other day."

"I remember." Although Mal hadn't known why at the time. He'd assumed that Sage felt they needed to assert themself, to prove that they were worthy of the position they'd been born into. Maybe there was even more kindness and heart to Sage than he'd originally thought. They had saved Chuckles, after all. What the beating must have been like for that . . .

"So no, I'm not bothered by the fact that you've taken my father's seat at Court. Or that you're running the Faceless. And I'm not here to take it back from you." Sage shook their head, but they were finally looking at Mal, a rueful smile on their face. "It might seem silly, but I never really wanted it."

"Oh." Mal's heart stuttered in his chest. Was it the smile? Or was it the knowledge that he'd done all of this for a person who clearly hadn't asked for it, nor cared. "Then I didn't have to—"

"I'm glad you did, all the same." Sage's smile went from rueful to genuine. Shining. Proud almost. "I haven't seen much of the Faceless Few yet, but the people who live in your territory seem happy. Safe. They're not struggling to make ends meet like they were under my father. They're not afraid of every backfiring car. I don't think any of the execs who were under my father could have done that."

And now Mal was breathless for a whole different reason. "Okay."

"Okay," Sage repeated.

"Are you—" He knew he needed to ask. He'd never sleep again if he didn't. "Are you angry that I lied about who I was?"

"Well," Sage said, taking another sip from their mug, "I don't approve, and I'm not happy about it. But I wouldn't say angry exactly. Even still, Ianthe." They sighed, tilting their head back to look at the ceiling for a moment before meeting his eyes again. "You know that was a breach of my trust."

"I do. I'm—I'm sorry."

Sage nodded, giving a thoughtful hum. "We'll just have to work to rebuild it."

"On our next date?" Mal was pushing his luck and he knew it, but every time he'd ever gambled before, it paid off.

"We'll see. I want to get to know you a bit before we jump back into that with both feet."

"Okay." Mal's shoulders slumped, his lower lip poking out. "Whatever makes you comfortable."

Sage snorted, rolling their eyes. "I didn't say no to another date. I just said we'd have to work back up to it. We're starting over, square one." They took a breath, leaned forward to set down their mug, and then held out their hand to Mal. "I'm Sage Nocturna. My pronouns are they/them. And I don't like spinach."

Mal blinked for a moment, shocked, then practically leapt forward to take the extended hand when Sage raised their eyebrows at him. "I'm Ianthe. My pronouns are he/him. And I run the Faceless Few gang."

"Nice to meet you." Sage's hand was soft and warm in his own as they shook. Mal didn't want to ever let go, but eventually he had to. Sage reached for their tea again. After a moment, their smile fell away, their hands tightening until the knuckles were white around their mug. "We still need to do something about the Night Market portal on Blood Moon territory that I found."

"You can't go before the Court if you're not part of one of the major families." It was a stupid rule, one that Mal had complained about multiple times. But also, one he'd been unable to overturn.

"Hmmm." Sage tapped their nails against the ceramic. "If I come back, you have to know that I won't be under your purview, and you have to take in Corey. She's my partner, my second. It would also only be temporary. Just until we get this mess sorted."

"Would you want to be an exec?"

"No." But their eyes drifted again to the coffee table, thoughtful once more, turning inward, and Mal gave them the time they needed to consider. However long it took. Not that long, as it turned out, for Sage was an inordinately quick thinker. "I don't think I want to return to the gangs at all after that, if I can help it."

"You could become my second. My right hand. Mox could—"

"I think I'd like it if Corey and I become a kind of check to the power of the Courts. A means to ensure they're all following the accords." Sage turned to smile at him, their teeth sharp and pointed. "And your partner, eventually, of course."

"I'm not sure what that will entail, but . . ." Goddess, it was all Mal had ever wanted. All he'd ever dreamed of. To have Sage back to stay. To have them close. To be able to reach for them in a way he'd never been able to before. "I think we can make that work. And the partner thing . . . definitely."

"Perfect."

"We'll need proof of what the Blood Moons were up to."

"Ah yes, proof. Because my word won't be enough." Sage laughed. "I think I can manage proof. Somehow."

"Will you need help? I have some men who—"

"No. Leave it to me and Corey."

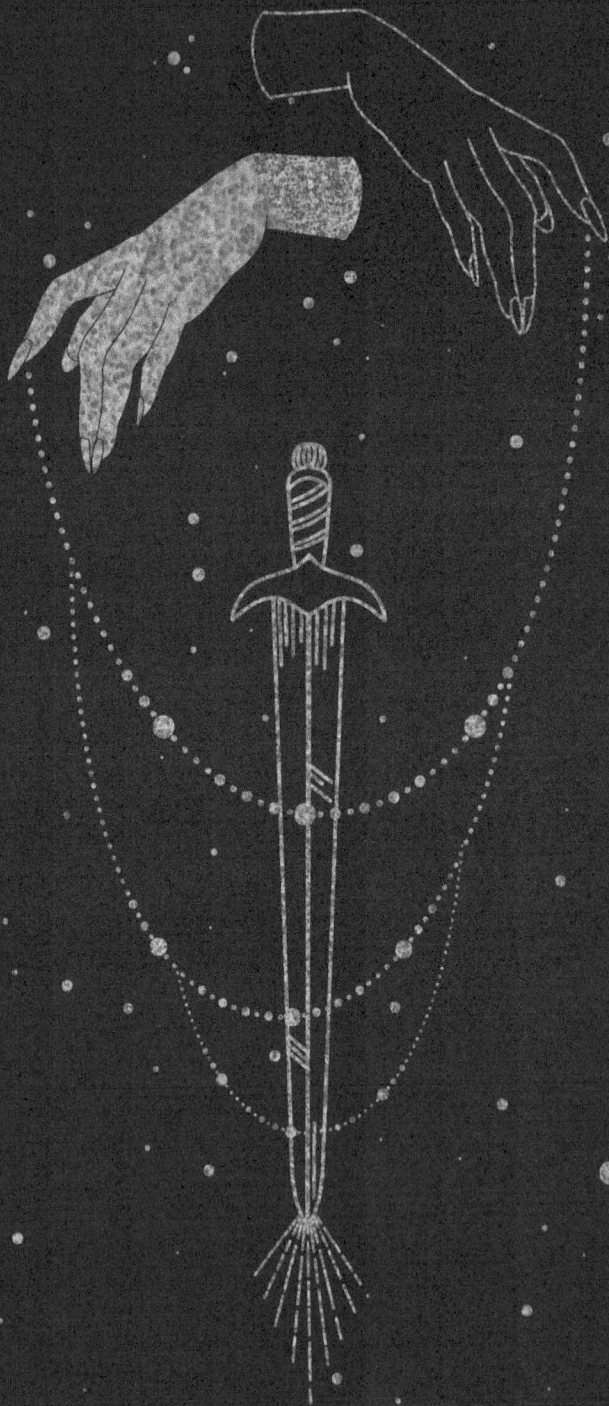

34

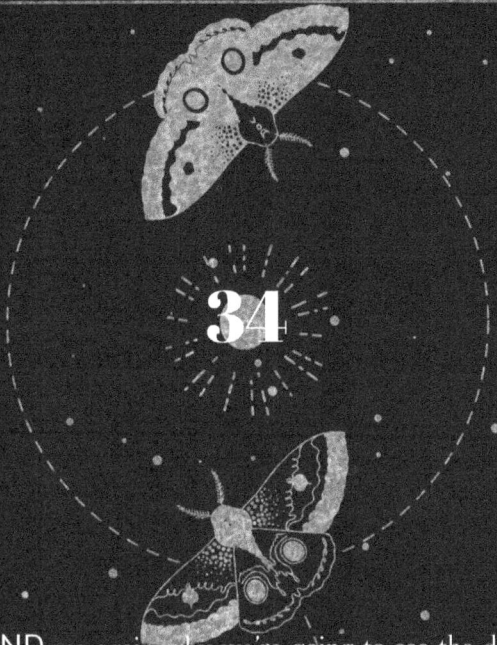

"REMIND me again why we're going to see the demon?" Sage ran a hand down their face, letting out a long, slow, agonized sigh. They were fucking tired. They hadn't slept in what felt like days, and this wasn't anywhere near over yet. Sure, there was a light at the end of the tunnel, but they were starting to wonder if it might be a train.

"Because we need someone who is impartial," Corey said again, sounding equally tired. To be fair, she hadn't had any rest either. From the time Sage had been kidnapped (was that even the right word when they were a forty-something adult? who knew!) to the time Mal brought them home, she'd been under Mox's scrutiny.

Not that Sage felt bad for her. She fucking deserved it after the shit she'd pulled.

All right, they *did* feel bad. But only because someone had gone and set Corey's livelihood on fire. Watching the place burn had been enough to strip Sage of all anger because it wasn't fair that she had to lose that too. Nor was it fair that Sage was being forced back into the family business simply because people couldn't leave them the fuck alone.

They should never have come back to Eventide. But that sentiment didn't hold much water, for if they hadn't, they wouldn't have rediscovered cake decorating, wouldn't have met Mal, wouldn't have reunited with Chuckles, wouldn't have . . . Besides. What was done was done. They'd never been the sort to look back on the past and wish things were different. It wasn't worth it.

"I hardly think a demon who I've paid to do me a favor is impartial." It wasn't really about Lucy, Sage knew. Demons were fine, they'd never had problems with demons before. But they didn't like the idea of including someone else in this. Especially someone who was paid for their services and could likely also be paid for their loyalty. Not that being paid for it really constituted it as loyalty, but Sage—despite having once been the heir to a vast fortune—couldn't afford to get into a bidding war with someone like Dam and Flo.

Corey stopped where she was walking up the sidewalk to the crooked townhouse, wheeled around, and fixed Sage with an expression that could only be described as *I'm-tired-of-your-shit*. It came complete with a clenched jaw, drawn brows, and dark circles around her eyes. Sage tried not to wince. But whatever Corey must have seen on their face made her soften, just a touch—they couldn't expect Corey to soften *entirely*.

"Look, we need someone outside the system of Eventide who has no real stake in the game to come with us and bear witness to what you saw in that basement. Otherwise, it's a they-said-they-said kind of thing going on. And I don't know about you, but I'd rather not have a gang war in my backyard. Would you?"

They wouldn't. That's why they were doing this to begin with.

"This won't stop Alton from coming after you. You're painting a bigger target on your back by going into this with me." There was no love lost between Sage and Alton, not that Sage ever really thought of Alton after they'd left Eventide. But before? Well, before, they'd been rivals of a kind. Two heirs fighting and clawing their way to the top. Alton got there first. He was always going to. He was older. And his father was . . . not gentler per se, but more likely to step down once he came of age. That had never been an option in Sage's father's mind. Seamus Nocturna was going to be the head of the Faceless Few until the day he died, and he had always planned for Sage to be the one to kill him. Someone else just got to him first. "You sure you want to hitch your horse to this wagon? The wagon might be on fire."

"I'll bring a hose." Corey shrugged and turned back around as if there was nothing else to talk about. Sage supposed there wasn't.

"Back again?" Lucy asked from the porch where she sat on the steps, a teacup on her knee that looked like at any moment it might tip over and shatter. Only it didn't, because it knew better. She tilted her head, a long piece of red hair escaping from the messy bun held up with what looked like a yellow pencil and falling into her face. Her eyes glowed faintly as she surveyed them. After a moment of her inspection, she rose—almost forgetting to scoop up the teacup—and turned for the door, calling over her shoulder, "I suppose you ought to come in."

It only took a few seconds to get inside out of the slowly heating day and settle onto Lucy's uncomfortable couch, but when they did there was a tea tray spread out across the coffee table as if Lucy had been expecting them.

"Someone best explain to me quickly what I'll get out of helping you two, other than the chance to see Corwin here in tight black clothing." Lucy lifted her teacup to her lips and took a smiling sip. "Which," she said after swallowing, "is definitely a benefit, but not nearly enough for me to go against a paying client."

"Paying you for what?" Sage asked at the same time Corey said, "Fuck you, Lucy."

"Oh, but I've been trying to, Corwin darling."

Corey responded with a scowl, which made Lucy chuckle softly.

"As for what they paid for, I'm afraid I can't tell you. Client–demon confidentiality and all that." She flapped her wrist through the air. "Would go against the whole code of demon ethics."

Corey scoffed, rolling her eyes. "As if there's such a *thing* as demon ethics."

Lucy's eyes jerked to Corey and glowed brighter, her voice taking on a strange echoey sound. The pencil flung from her hair, embedding itself in the uneven floorboards as her hair floated around her. ONE, DON'T BE RACIST, DEAREST, IT DOESN'T SUIT YOU. TWO, FOR AS SMART AS YOU ARE, *AIDAN CORWIN*, THE SHIT YOU KNOW ABOUT DEMONS COULD FILL A FUCKING THIMBLE.

While Sage shrunk in on themself, intent on putting space between them and the two bickering women, Corey did no such thing. She didn't even move under the demon's furious stare, didn't let her eyes drift. After a moment, Corey merely tilted her head and conceded, "Apologies. You're correct, there is a lot I don't know about demons. Please continue."

This seemed to throw Lucy, whose hair dropped around her, eyes returning to their more mortal-like color, a faint blush staining her cheeks. A pleased smile tilted up her lips. "All right then, what is it we need to do to expose these idiots?"

WAS IT NORMAL TO FIND A DEMON HOT WHEN THEY WENT all . . . demon-y?

Probably not.

Was not being normal going to cool the swell of heat in Corey's belly?

Also, probably not.

So sue her, Corey had a thing for powerful women. It might have been part of the reason why she found Mox so damn annoyingly attractive. Because Mox was insistent, and abrasive, and a busybody, but she was also undoubtably powerful. She was the second in command to the Faceless Few, for crying out loud, of course she was powerful. Which made her more of a bloody nuisance, but that was beside the point.

The point was that Lucy's righteous fury, and the way she wielded her power, was terribly enthralling. Also, very annoying.

"Corey?" Sage asked, their voice low and unsure. "Are you paying attention?"

"Hm?" Corey shook herself and ripped her eyes away from the confident swish of Lucy's hips as she trounced to the door like she owned the place. She focused once more on the house across the street—on where they were. Blood Moon territory. It didn't have any of the old-world charm of Faceless territory, nor any of the modernity of Aquarius territory. The part of the city run by Dam and Flo was for all intents and purposes a mixed bag.

The Blood Moons seemed to have little interest in supporting infrastructure and building up their citizens, instead taking and taking and taking, and ruling by fear. Building up casino after casino, and where there weren't casinos, letting their people live in squalor.

While maybe the Blood Moons would like to tell those who lived under them that it was a consequence of them being given one of the more dilapidated parts of the city, Corey knew enough about the history of Eventide to know that was a bold-faced lie. The Blood Moons had *picked* their territory the same as the rest of the gangs, and then they'd promptly run it into the ground, plain and simple.

"Corey," Sage tried again and Corey sighed, turning her attention to them.

"I know the plan, Sage." It wasn't the most . . . intricate of plans. Or the most complex. Use Lucy as a trojan horse of sorts, come in behind her, get the evidence hopefully before the Blood Moons realized they were even there, and get the fuck out of Dodge. A child could have planned it. In their sleep. The simplicity—to Corey's mind, at least—left way too many holes for shit to go wrong. But this wasn't her circus. She was just one of the monkeys.

The streetlights flickered, and a hush fell over the side street they were on.

Sage pushed open their door and said, "That's our signal" as if Corey didn't already know. But she followed them just the same, if only to keep from arguing.

The front door to the run-down brick duplex was left open a crack, Lucy keeping to her word. And when they crept across the covered front porch—with enough cobwebs that someone might think they were leftover from last Halloween—they found that not only was it left open, but there was no one in the front room either. They had a clear shot to the door to the basement across the hall.

"This is too easy," Corey huffed. She didn't like it. She never had. Sure, having a demon on their side should have made things simpler, but *this* simple? This felt like a trap.

Sage didn't say anything, but they extended their claws, kneading their fingers in the air, a sure indication that they agreed.

Corey turned, giving them her back so she could watch the room as they made their way to the door. Muffled voices filtered from further in the house, and Corey wondered what bullshit story Lucy was giving them. If she was even bothering with lying, or if she'd spun a web of magic that left them seeing only what she wanted. *Could* she do that? Lucy was right—the things Corey knew about demons could fill a thimble.

The stairs creaked under their combined weight. The door groaned closed behind them. But when Corey tilted her head as if in question to Sage, they shook theirs.

No change. No one had noticed them. Not yet.

It was only a matter of time, though. Corey knew that. One couldn't sneak into a safe house from a rival fae gang and go completely unnoticed, even if one had a demon to cover their ass. They had to be quick.

The door at the bottom of the stairs was locked, but Sage grabbed the handle and jammed their shoulder against it hard enough to make the entire frame jolt. It popped inward, creaking on the hinges. Corey ushered them through, then pushed the door most of the way shut behind them. She was turning around to check out the basement when—

"Fuck!" Sage hissed.

"What? What is it?" She spun to where they were standing beside her, facing what appeared to be a destroyed door to nowhere. The wall on the other side of the broken frame was all cinder block, likely the material the basement was constructed out of. And at their feet were shards of wood.

"They've destroyed it." Sage slammed a fist into the wall, uncaring of the pain it would likely cause them, and kicked the discarded boards.

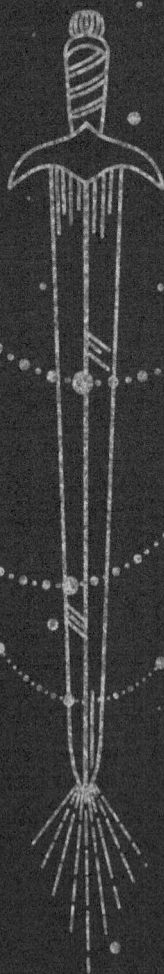

35

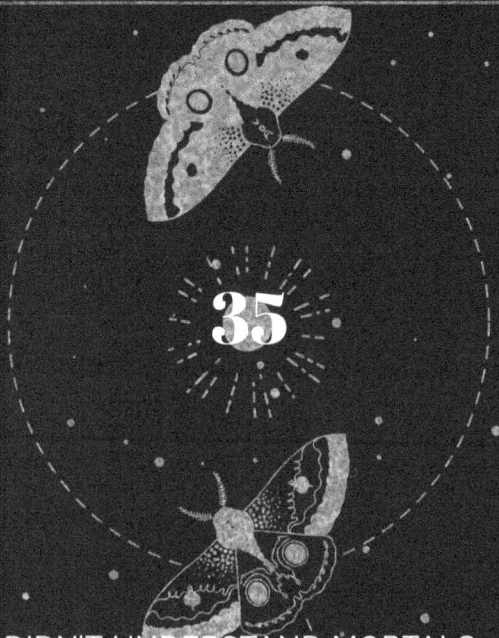

LUCY DIDN'T UNDERSTAND MORTALS. Yes, she considered Sage Nocturna and Aidan Corwin mortal despite their long lifespans. Because they had souls. And having a soul seemed to do funny things to a person. Not that Lucy would know—she'd never had one aside from the strange inkling she got sometimes when she borrowed parts of someone else's. But that was a tangent she didn't have the time nor the patience to go on currently. The point was, she didn't understand mortals.

Which she'd get back to . . . soon.

After she'd dealt with—

"Yes, they've destroyed it," Lucy agreed, stepping from the shadows she'd just melted out of to glare at the shards of wood Sage hunched over. There was something devastated about their face, as if they couldn't see a way out of this now that their plan had been foiled. Oh, how easily the mortal spirit could be broken. Silly mortals. "But there's still proof to be found here."

Sage jerked their head up to look at her, eyes wide with something that could only be described as hope—another mortal emotion she had no context for. They tilted their head in question, and honestly, did Lucy have to do *everything* herself? She'd led them here after all. Tipped the scales in the favor of Sage and their cohorts. Something she *shouldn't* have done. Demons weren't meant to take sides, especially without payment upfront. But Eventide was crying out at the unbalance, and Lucy had learned a long time ago that one didn't ignore a city when she did that. Definitely not if one wanted to keep living in said city and not have it go up in flames. That's what had become of Alexandria, after all.

And . . . Lucy *liked* Eventide. She certainly wasn't perfect by any means, but no city built for and by mortals could be. Not that any place built by immortals was much better, but semantics.

Lucy scoffed, rolling her eyes, and refused to answer. But on her way to the crates tucked further into the basement, she kicked a bit of wood Sage's way that would provide them with everything they needed. Hopefully they were smart enough to fill in the blanks. She didn't particularly want to involve herself any further, not if she could help it. Someone might take notice of her interference then, and only bad things would come from someone realizing that Lucy was hiding out in Eventide, basically a fugitive from her own people.

Fucking demons.

"Oh," Sage gasped, and Lucy glanced over her shoulder to watch as they held the chunk of wood closer to their face, their glowing green eyes narrowing on the symbology carved there.

"Oh?" Corey asked, leaning down beside them to get a look at it herself. She was kind of adorable like this, battle ready but curious, hope glittering in her eyes.

Lucy shook herself. She wasn't sure anymore if those

were her *own* feelings toward the halfling or a consequence of her deal with Mox, and she didn't think she ought to spend time finding out. Best to ignore the strange warm tingle in her fingertips. It'd only get her into trouble.

"Is that a good oh or a bad oh?" Corey pressed when Sage didn't answer right away, nudging her friend lightly with her toe. Yes, friend, even for all they both liked to pretend they hated each other, she knew better. Lucy would like to reiterate: Mortals were strange creatures.

"A good oh." Sage tilted back, letting the light from above cast itself better on the rough grain. "Do you see this?" They tapped on something, and Lucy had to rip herself away as a wrinkle appeared between Corey's eyebrows that was much *too* adorable.

"Yeah?"

"It's a location sigil. Used to tie one location to another magically. It comes in handy when you don't want someone to notice that you've opened a portal into some place they control. You're able to borrow another portal close by without disturbing the magical energy field on that plane. And this . . . You'd use this to steal another's magic to power it so it's not tied back to . . ."

Lucy tuned them out at that point because it was in good hands now, she supposed. Sage and Corey had everything they needed to prove to the Court that at least Dam had been fucking with things he shouldn't have. There was no way to prove that the rest of the Blood Moons had been in on it, but this would be enough to cast doubt and to bring the Blood Moons to heel, at least a little. To return some of the balance.

Eventide hummed around her, pleased with her progress, and Lucy resisted the urge to roll her eyes. As if she *needed* the approval of a sentient city. Foolishness.

There was a smug quality to Eventide's reaction that

said she knew differently, no matter how much Lucy might protest, but she ignored it. Getting into a bickering match with a fucking city—of all sentient inanimate objects and locations—was a recipe for frustration. Frustration she couldn't explain because no one else in this Goddess-forsaken place seemed to be able to feel Eventide the way Lucy could. A fact that should likely be more concerning as it indicated that Lucy had either been in one place too long, or that the city was desperate, reaching out to any being powerful enough within her borders to make real change. Lucy didn't want to think about either of those things.

Thankfully, as she rounded one of the large crates, a distraction was provided.

"Oh Dam, you have been naughty, haven't you?" Lucy murmured as she bent down to the three children covered in dirt and tucked into the corner of the basement. They were huddled together, holding one another as if afraid Lucy would swallow them whole. A reasonable fear. Some demons had a taste for mortal flesh, but Lucy had outgrown that particular phase about a century ago.

"What did you find?" Corey asked. Clearly, she'd finished examining the evidence Lucy had so kindly provided them, and Lucy felt more than heard her and Sage approach. Their presence shifted the air, their movements changing the trajectory of Eventide in ways they would never understand. Butterfly wings making hurricanes and all that.

"Seems Dam has broken more than just the accord that only the Faceless are to create portals in Eventide." Lucy nodded toward the children then shifted out of the way as Corey and Sage swooped in.

"What the fuck were they *doing* with them?" Sage growled, their hackles rising, fur sprouting on the back of their neck. Interesting.

"They must have been using them to power the portal. Come on, let's get them out of here. We've got what we need." Corey moved slowly, telegraphing every motion so as not to frighten the little nuggets. It would be endearing of Lucy didn't find children so . . . sticky. She was glad she'd never been one.

"We could just leave them." Lucy gave a careless shrug. "They're only going to bog us—"

"We're *not* leaving them." Corey leveled Lucy with a glare that could cut diamonds.

And this . . . *this* was where the not-understanding-mortals thing really came in. Many of them had such soft hearts. Bleeding and willing to put their own safety, their own interests, on hold for another. It didn't make any sense to her. Why bother? But she didn't voice another protest, she merely shrugged and stood back to watch as Sage scooped up two of the little things and Corey lifted the other into her arms.

There was another shift in the aether. More butterfly wings. More decisions made. And Lucy couldn't help the smile that cut her face near in half.

There would be blood.

THE BOY CLUNG MORE TIGHTLY TO COREY THAN SHE thought anyone had ever held her, even her sisters. His face pressed into her neck as they climbed the stairs. Fear and probably a multitude of other things made him tremble in her arms so hard, it was difficult to keep him perched on her hip. He couldn't be much older than five, and he was so small.

What the fuck had Dam been thinking? *Kids*? To power a fucking *portal*?

She forced herself to breathe through the rage that lit every cell in her body on fire. It wouldn't do anyone any good. Least of all the children.

But as the door to the basement creaked open again, Corey stilled at the top of the stairs, her entire body going rigid.

"Corey, what is it, what's—" Sage's words were cut off by a deep, rumbling growl. Corey didn't have to see them to know that their teeth had extended into fangs, their bright green eyes flickering to glow more as the pupils narrowed to slits on the group of redcaps that awaited them.

"Did you think we'd let you out so easily?" Dam asked, their head tilted to the side. They stood in the back, several big, burly gang members between them and Corey's group.

The little boy in her arms let out a soft *meep* and held on tighter, his form shaking so much that she almost dropped him.

The answer was *no*, Corey hadn't thought this would be that easy. But she'd *hoped* it would be. So much blood had already been shed, and she'd hoped they could avoid more. Naive, she knew.

"Lucy, I thought you'd taken care of them?" Corey asked, lowering herself slowly to the ground.

"I had." Lucy sounded as annoyed as she did perplexed. Although it could have been an act, Corey wanted to believe her. Wanted to think that Lucy had nothing to do with this development.

"Go to Lucy," Corey told the boy, gesturing to the demon who stood behind Sage on the stairs. This bottleneck Dam and their men had created wasn't ideal, but it would provide an easy way to keep the children out of the fight. Lucy would likely only intervene if she absolutely had to, and maybe not even then. One could never tell with demons. "Lucy."

"Yes?" Exasperation made Lucy's voice even more irritable, if that were at all possible. Corey thought she saw the demon's eyes burning in the darkness of the stairwell.

"Take the car and the kids and head back to your place," Sage said, seeming to read what Corey was planning as they also passed their bundles to the demon. "We'll meet you there once we're through."

"But they're—" Lucy sighed loudly, her shoulders slumping. Corey wasn't sure why she'd stopped herself, what had made her change her mind from arguing further, and she didn't care. "Very well."

Once she had all three children around her on the stairs, Lucy huddled them closer then raised her hand and snapped her fingers. The four of them dropped from view. Corey's ears popped from the change in pressure, and a moment later it was just Sage behind her on the stairs.

"You're fucked," Corey told Dam as she turned toward them, ripping a dagger from her belt and lunging forward into the fray. She took the first blow to the chin, making her stagger, but Sage was there, having used the available space to leave the stairwell, their hands looping under her arms to keep her from falling. They had her back—a strange thought she didn't have time to delve into right now.

"You good?" they asked, their words slurred through the fangs in their mouth.

"Yeah." She nodded, her grip tightening on the dagger, and smirked as Sage used all their strength to launch her to her feet once more, practically throwing her at their nearest attacker.

She stumbled but got her feet under her quickly, the point of her dagger swiping out at the redcap who had pulled a blade from somewhere as well and slashed wildly at Corey. Too erratic. Too slow. Corey cut through their guard, slashing open their forearm from wrist to elbow, and as they jerked back, dropping their blade, she used the hilt of her dagger to beat them on the temple. Once. Twice. With enough force it knocked them off their feet.

Another took their place, but they didn't have the momentum Corey did, and when their blade flashed through the air, she dropped to the ground, sweeping out her leg so they wobbled. As they were catching their balance, Sage planted a foot on their chest and shoved. They stumbled back into the row of Blood Moons behind them, going down like dominos.

Corey didn't know where Dam was. She'd lost them in the ruckus.

"Cut a line to the door," Sage ordered, helping her stand again.

"Obviously." Corey snorted. She spun and cut through the air with her dagger, stopping the arch of another blade mid-strike. She gritted her teeth against the strength behind the blow. It was easier for someone to strike down than to push up. Harder to stop momentum than to keep going. But she'd had practice with this, training. Alton had never let her relax, not for a moment. Pushing off from her back foot, she shoved, and the redcap reeled, their arms cartwheeling as they tried to regain their footing. Sometimes, her short stature was an advantage.

Sage offered no further commentary apart from a roar that would shame any lion as they shifted into the panther. Blood coated their fur as they cut through the surrounding gang members.

Between Sage's claws and Corey's dagger, it became simpler to make it to the door.

"How many of them are dead?" Corey asked as she

raced down the sidewalk after Sage. Her lungs burned from the exertion, and a cut along her ribs made blood soak through the dark top she had on, hot at first, then cooling once it hit the night air.

Sage appeared to be limping, but even that was slowly going the way of all their injuries. It was strange — she didn't remember them being able to heal like that before they'd left Eventide. Was it something to do with their undead nature? She didn't know. There was no time to focus on it as she listened for their pursuers.

"None if they get medical attention soon enough." But Sage let out a whoop of victory as they turned the corner out of Blood Moon territory. It wouldn't stop Dam and their people from chasing Corey and Sage, but a car idled next to the curb as if waiting for them, and relief swept through Corey when she saw a shock of turquoise hair through the window. Mox.

"Lucy told me you might need a lift," Mox said when they climbed in, fixing them with one of those charming, in-control smiles Corey was beginning to realize she actually liked.

In the heat of the moment, the swell of victory sharp on her tongue, Corey leaned over and kissed Mox's cheek. "I've never been so happy to see a mobster in all my life."

Mox blinked, dumbfounded, until Sage cleared their throat too loud in the ensuing silence, then they were off.

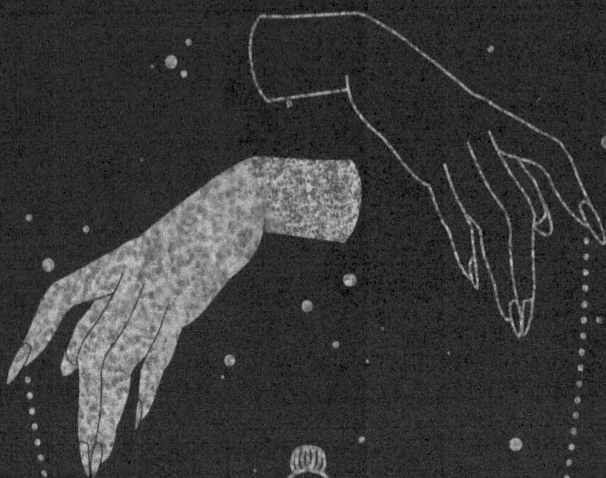

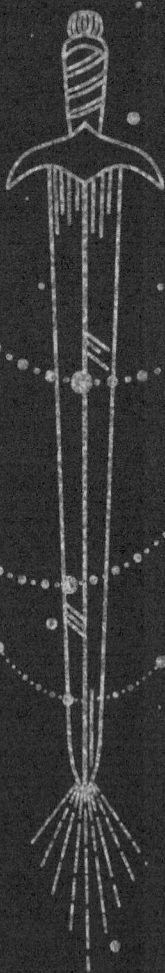

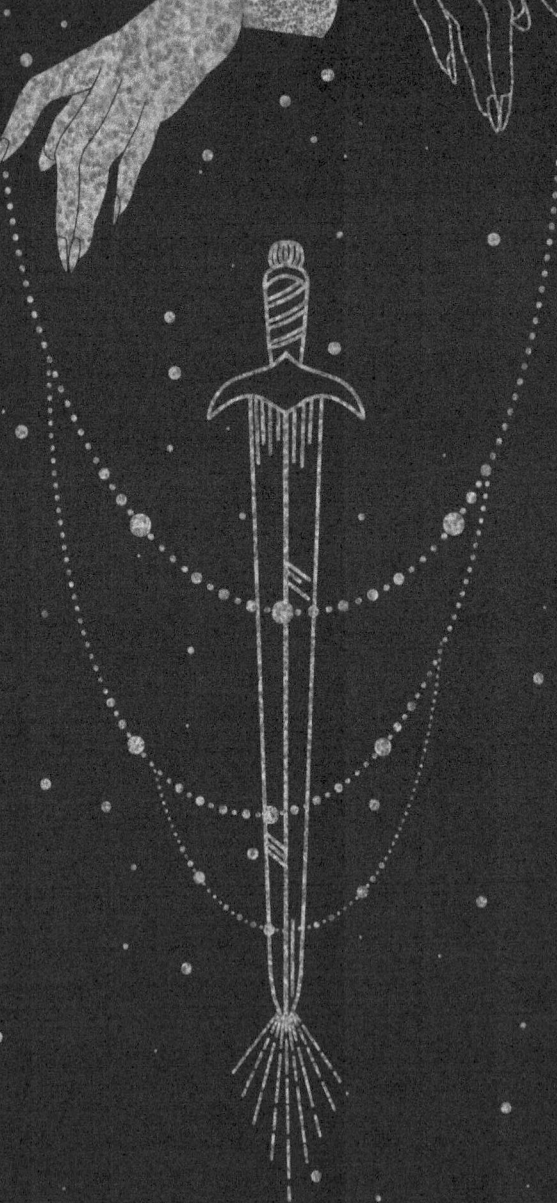

36

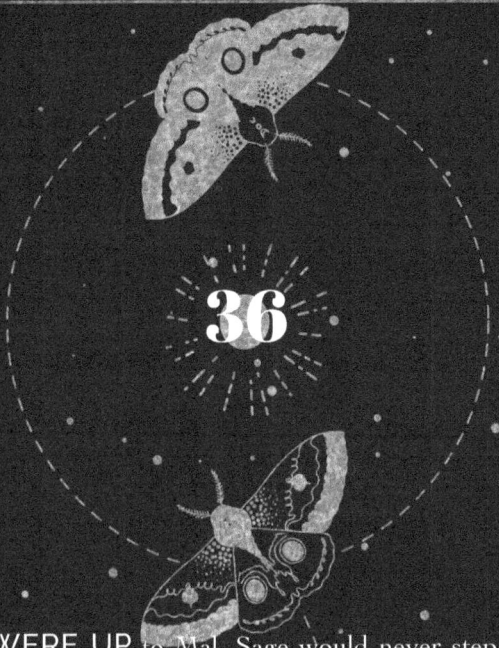

IF IT WERE UP to Mal, Sage would never step foot in the Court again. They didn't belong there. They should be safe. Hidden away from the violence and the ugliness that was the Court of Families. But in the end, he wouldn't stop them. Not if that's what they really wanted.

Still, it scraped him raw to watch the way Sage had to straighten their posture, lift their chin. To see them in a suit like the ones Mal had secretly hoped they'd never have to wear again.

Peace was not for people like Sage and Mal. It was not a part of their lives. But that didn't mean Mal couldn't hope for it, wish for it, *pray* for it. It was foolishness, he knew. People like him—people like Sage—who had been born in the dark, raised in the dark, and lived in the dark their entire lives, weren't meant for the light. They could get glimpses. Brief, shining moments. But ultimately, they would have to return to the shadows.

"How do I look?" Sage asked, slicking back their hair with shaking fingers.

"Amazing," Mal said, and it wasn't a lie. They were

beautiful. They always *would* be, suit or not. But it was less about the clothes, and more about Sage in general for Mal. The way they looked at him. The way they smiled. The way they knew who he was, and they accepted him. It made his breath catch in his throat. Goddess, couldn't he just keep them to himself? Run away from the Court. From the gangs. From Eventide. From the obligations and the blood and the families.

The answer was no. No, he could not.

"You're biased," Sage accused, but it was accompanied by a soft chuckle that made Mal's fingers tingle. He could reach out to them now. Brush his fingers against their throat under the guise of straightening their collar. Smooth his palms over their body under the pretense of flattening out the imperceptible wrinkles in their blazer. Red really was their color.

"I might be." He definitely *was*, but he didn't mind. It didn't matter. Nothing did. Only that Sage was here. Back and ready to let him into their life. He'd gotten lucky. He was blessed. And he didn't deserve it. Not a single moment of it. But he was going to hoard it, hold it close. Selfishly.

"Are you two done making goo-goo eyes at one another yet?" Corey asked, poking her head into the walk-in closet where Mal and Sage had tucked themselves away in the hopes of finding Sage something appropriate to wear to Court.

There had been some small hope on Mal's part that Sage would fit one of his suits. He'd love to see Sage in his clothes. But he was too broad across the shoulders, his arms too long. And while Sage would look absolutely adorable swimming in his clothes, it wouldn't portray the right image to the other families. Sage needed to look polished, put together, and in control. So Mox's closet it had been. Thankfully, she still had some of her suits from before she'd had top surgery, and those fit Sage reasonably well.

Sage tilted their head at Corey, a smile ticking up the corner of their lips. "Not on your life, Corey."

"Ugh." Corey groaned and disappeared again, her own borrowed blazer swishing behind her, sapphire blue.

Once she was gone, Sage turned back to Mal, and he had to suck in a breath again, unused to the way it felt to be the center of his beloved's attention. It was like standing next to a fire after too long in the cold: tingly, warm, and with a bit of a burn that he wasn't ever going to turn away from. Leaving him shivering all over. He'd never get used to it. Never.

"Well," Sage said, straightening up even further—as if their posture could get anymore upright—and taking a deep breath. "Looks like it's time we got this thing over with."

"Looks like." Mal nodded. His fingers twitched when Sage held out a hand for him to take, but after the initial guilt of letting himself have something he'd wanted for most of his life, he took it. Sage's hands were smaller than his own, less calloused, and cold. So very cold. Mal didn't know why. He didn't ask. There was too much else to think of as they stepped through the doorway.

THERE WAS NO GOING BACK AFTER THIS. ONCE SAGE stepped into the Court, showed their face to the heads of the Eventide ruling families, and told everyone they were alive, there was no going back to playing dead.

Sage had to admit, they'd miss it.

Their life hadn't been easier, not by any stretch of the imagination. But it had been quieter, more peaceful. Still, there was always something waiting in the wings, like the calm before the storm. They'd known it couldn't last. There was no universe in which Eventide didn't pull them back like some horrible kind of magnet. No timeline in which they didn't wind up right back where they started.

Maybe that realization should have upset them, made them rage and fume and rail against a destiny they had no say in. But that was kind of the thing about destiny, wasn't it? A person had no say in it. And Sage was too fucking tired to bother.

That and the weight of Mal's hand in theirs as the car parked in a lot just off the walking path that would lead them to the Court entrance was warm, and gentle, and just . . . *nice*. Sage couldn't remember the last time someone had touched them like this. As if they were something that deserved to be protected, cared for. Maybe never.

A soft snort drew Sage's attention to Corey in the front seat. How she'd ranked shotgun, they didn't know nor care. "Looks like Lucy showed up after all."

"Did you expect her not to?" Sage frowned, scrubbing at their face with their free hand. They didn't like the demon either, but they'd figured that she'd keep her promise.

"I don't know what I expected." Corey shrugged.

Sage tried not to notice the way Mox looked over at Corey, a mix of longing and jealousy in her expression as her focus shifted from Corey to Lucy and back. There was something there. Something messy and potentially damaging to all parties involved, but there would be time to deal with that later. After they'd put the Blood Moons in their place. After they'd returned the children to their families. After Sage had cemented their place in Eventide's underground once more.

"Took you long enough," Lucy grumbled as they all

unloaded from the car. She looked worse for wear, which was funny because Sage didn't know demons could be frazzled. Her normally neatly coiled hair was up in a far messier bun. Her glasses seemed to have smudges on them. And the button-up she wore was decidedly wrinkled. All of this, and she'd been taking care of the children they'd found in the basement of the Blood Moons' safe house for less than twenty-four hours.

"Where are the kids?" Corey asked. She deliberately seemed to be putting space between herself and Mox, which made the stormy expression on Mox's face pull tighter.

"Why do you care?" Lucy snapped in a way that was entirely different from all the times Sage had seen her interact with anyone to that point.

"Just answer the question," Mox snarled back.

Sage was relieved when Mal tugged them away from the scene, and they started down the path toward the Court entrance.

"I know the way," they murmured softly but didn't try to pull from his hold.

"I couldn't listen to those three bickering anymore." Mal shrugged, giving Sage's hand a squeeze, his cane tapping merrily against the pavement as they made their way through the dark. "Honestly, if they'd just fuck and get it over with, we could all move on."

"I don't think that's what—"

"I *said* we'd get the kids out of your hair tonight. Honestly, Lucy, it hasn't even been a full day!" Corey hissed, her voice raised so it echoed over the water on the other side of the path. When Sage looked back at the trio, they found them all standing unbearably close. Much closer than a bickering match warranted.

"I see what you mean." Sage laughed, shaking their

head. Would things be different after this? Would Corey, Mox, and Lucy part ways and never speak again? Not likely. Their lives were too intertwined and were about to be even more so after they all stepped through the portal into Court together.

Mal pulled them both to a stop in front of the brick wall, the marble statuary gleaming in the moonlight. A goblin or someone normally stood guard outside the portal, or at least they used to, but there was no one now. Just the brick wall and the broken bits of marble.

"You don't have to do this," Mal said, and Sage thought he meant it. Maybe he would give Sage an out if they asked for it. But they both knew there was no other option. Eventide wouldn't give them one. Just like Eventide hadn't let their mother escape, let *them* escape. She would have things her way, and this was what she wanted.

Sage took a deep breath, the humid air burning their throat. Goddess, was it hot out here or was it just them? They weren't sure anymore. "No." They cleared their throat, trying to dispel some of the stickiness that clung to the inside of it. "No. We've got to do this."

Mal gave them a moment to collect themself then led them carefully over the curb and through the brick wall into the even stickier air of the dimension where Court was held. It was a cross between a greenhouse and a rainforest. Vines crawled across the ground beneath their feet.

It hadn't changed at all. The feeling of stepping through the portal, of it stripping off any potential glamours, was the same—hopefully the one they planned for Lucy to apply for Corey stuck. The thickness of the air on the other side was familiar. And Sage would bet every last dollar they'd saved that the trees hadn't changed either.

With their focus on the moving plants and the uneven earth, it was easier to ignore the way everyone at the big stone table at the center of the space had turned in their chairs to watch Sage and Mal enter. But Sage could feel their eyes on them. Burning a brand into their skin. Letting them know that their every movement was under scrutiny.

When they finally made it to the table and Sage heard Corey, Lucy, and Mox at their back again, they let themself lift their gaze to meet the eyes of everyone in the space. Some of the faces they recognized, others they did not. But it was the furious look from Alton as his gaze flicked from where Sage and Mal were holding hands then up to Sage's face that caught their attention. Sage couldn't parse out the emotion from his look, and they didn't want to either. There had always been something distinctly complicated about their relationship with the only other heir from their age group, and now wasn't the time to consider whether Alton had mourned them.

"Well, this is a surprise," Mata said, but she didn't sound genuinely surprised at all.

No matter. Sage wasn't here for a spectacle. They were here to share what they'd learned at the Blood Moons' safe house and ensure Dam was punished for their actions.

A cold sweat trickled down their spine as they cleared their throat. "Shall we get started?"

"I think that would be best." Mata dipped her head in a nod and settled into her seat as if this were a normal meeting of the Court. Not a conversation where they all came face-to-face with someone they once thought was dead.

The others followed Mata's lead, even Mal, who left Sage to stand alone at the head of the table so he could take his seat. Or perhaps not alone. Not really. Corey moved up to their right side, her shoulder subtly brushing their own, and they caught the bright blue of their glamoured hair from the corner of their eye. She was there with them.

Their enemy, turned friend, turned . . . family? They weren't sure, and they didn't think it mattered, not right now. Not with the thunderous look on Alton's face as he stared down the united front they presented.

"All right," someone said, but Sage had let their vision blur so they didn't have to focus on the heads of the families before them. So they could focus on what they had to do, what they had to say. They'd never addressed this body before, and the nerves made them nauseous. "Tell us what you found."

And then Sage did.

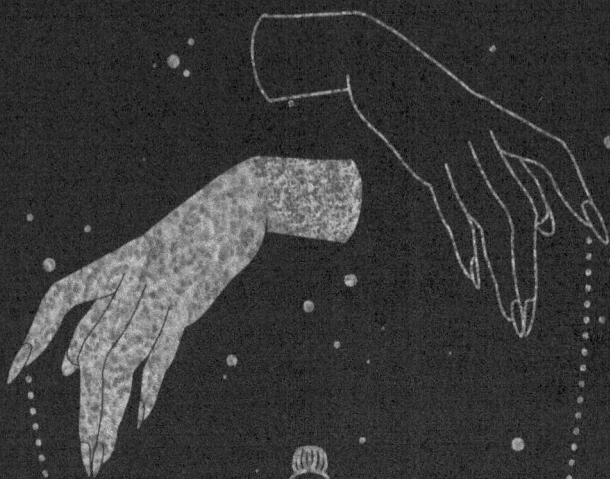

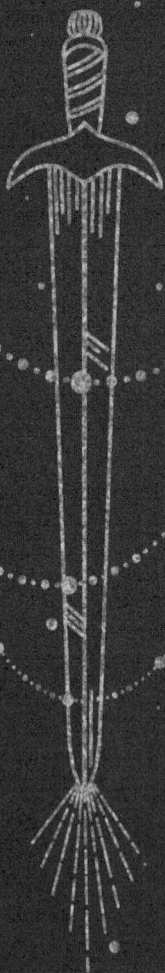

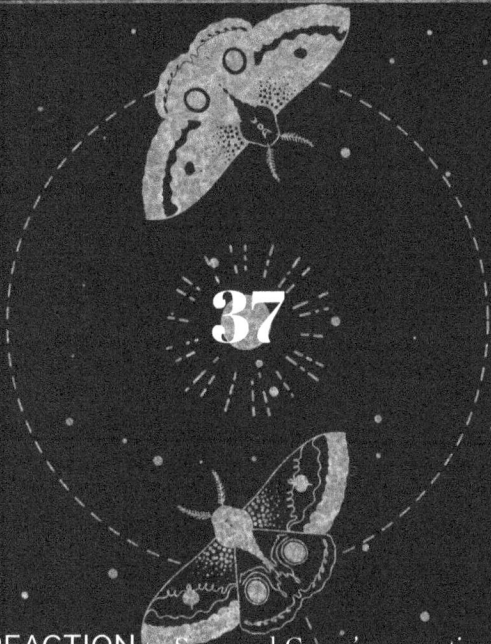

37

THE REACTION to Sage and Corey's accusations was to be expected. There was no world in which the Court would react favorably to learning that they had either been fooled or were now being accused of a willing ignorance to something that went against their accords.

Mox just wished she could have taken a minute to watch each family head react individually. She knew that would have been impossible. This news needed to go live before the entire Court so none of them had time to circle their dragons and hide things. But it was hard to tell with everyone reacting at once who was genuinely shocked by the news and who was putting up a front to cover their own involvement.

Maybe all of them were hiding something.

The affront, the upset . . . It all felt false to her. Maybe they weren't all *involved*, but they'd all *known* or at least suspected the Blood Moons were doing something they shouldn't. The Court was made up of a bunch of criminals, after all, so the idea that one of the organizations was doing something that went against the rules shouldn't have been much of a surprise.

There was no honor among fae.

It was a relief that they'd thought to get indisputable proof before bringing it before the Court. Mox knew that if they hadn't, it would have become a matter of they-said-he-said, and the Blood Moons would get off scot-free. An outcome that was unacceptable, especially when there had been children involved.

They still weren't positive what Dam had been using the children for. Corey and Sage had their theories, but there was no way to prove them. Not that it mattered, but Mox would like to tie Dam to a chair and find out. She could already hear the screams she'd draw forth in her quest for answers, and the hairs on her arms rose with pleasure at the thought.

"Enough!" Mal shouted, cutting through the noise as he rose from his chair, slamming his hands on the table.

The space fell silent, and Mox was intrigued to find that no one looked at all put off by the intrusion, except maybe Alton—who was almost always put off by *something*. Mox wondered if they knew the power they'd just given Mal. Likely not as none of them had gone into automatic panic mode.

"I demand reparations," Mal said, his voice more level than Mox thought she'd ever heard it. Deadly calm, even as he shifted to put himself in front of Sage and Corey, a layer of protection Mox should maybe thank him for, although she wasn't sure why. Corey wasn't anything to her. Just a crush. And not even that with the way she and Lucy were—

"What kind of reparations?" Flo asked, her eyes narrowed. She hadn't moved to protect her sibling. If anything, she'd shifted in her seat away from them, separating herself from what they'd done. She wasn't fooling Mox. There was no way Flo hadn't known what her own sibling and second was doing. No way she wasn't profiting from it. Unless Dam had been trying to stage a coup against her. But if that was going on, Mox had little doubt that Flo would have taken care of it before it ever came to the attention of the Court. It reflected too badly on her that she hadn't.

"Your sibling's head would be a good start." Mal smiled.

Dam hissed from where they stood to Flo's right, but Flo made no move to argue.

"I'll take it myself, if you can't do it." Mal shrugged carelessly.

Sage shifted, their eyes flicking about the gathered group. They'd been quiet since giving their evidence, as if they were trying to disappear into the background again. Likely for the best, considering they still hadn't explained to anyone why they'd come back after faking their death, and what they planned to do now that they had. But now they spoke up. "I'd like to ask them some questions before you—"

"Out of the question," Flo snarled, her eyes glowing red with all the blood she'd taken over the years. The magic had seeped into her veins, there for her to use.

"Then you don't plan on letting us find out what Dam was doing with those children?" Sage raised a brow, lifting their chin imperiously as they moved to stand beside Mal. Mox liked something about that movement. Mal had lived his entire life with only his sister at his side. No one else supported him. No one else cared for him. And he'd loved Sage so wholly for so many years that it had practically consumed every waking thought. To see Sage standing at his side now, as an equal, made a smile twitch on Mox's face. She had to purse her lips to suppress it.

"They will answer to *me*, for that." Flo didn't rise from her chair, but the way she met Sage's gaze would have sent a lesser being scurrying.

Sage stood their ground, and to Mox's surprise, Mal didn't intervene. He didn't step in front of Sage to block the way Flo was looking at them. He didn't snarl at Flo as if to put her in her place. Mox worried when this all started that Mal would be unable to separate his worship from the reality that was Sage. But she needn't have. They were a team. Mal believed in Sage's capabilities and was more than happy to stand by and let Sage take care of themself.

"No." Sage shook their head. "They will answer to *all* of us. They have gone against numerous accords, the least of which is creating an unsanctioned portal into the Night Market without approval of the Faceless. I will not stand by and—"

"Stand by?" Alton snorted. It was amazing he'd been quiet this long with how he tended to be about things. But Mox supposed that since Mal wasn't going after the Aquarius, he'd had no reason to speak up yet. He likely recognized that it was better to keep his nose out of things, to divert attention away from how he was harboring a fugitive of the war Mal and Mox had waged against the original Faceless in their bid for power. Not to mention that Mox was dead certain he'd been behind the burning of Corey's bakery. "You've been gone four years, Sage, what gives you the right to—"

"Justice," Sage cut, their lip curling back from their teeth. "Not for me. Not for the Faceless' lost profits. For the children Dam used for the purpose of opening that portal. For their families. For what they endured. If you're going to make this into an argument of whether I have the right to speak to the Court on the behalf of literal children when we have accords in place to protect the young in our districts, I wonder what that says about Aquarius' practices."

That shut Alton up quickly. A warmth like pride, like respect, bloomed in Mox's chest. Sage didn't belong to her, not in the way they belonged to Mal, but they were a part of her family, and she could take pride in that. Mal had chosen well for himself.

"I propose"—Sage returned their attention to the room as a whole—"that instead of the Blood Moons being in charge of Dam's questioning, all the families will put forth a representative to help in the endeavor. If you feel you must bind them on family secrets beforehand, Flo, you are welcome to do so. But know that should a question arise that goes unanswered, it will be brought to your door."

To her credit, Flo didn't flinch under the implication that she would use the binding to further hide her involvement. Nor did she shy away from the way the rest of the family heads turned to her, following the volley of conversation as one might a tennis match. "I find this solution acceptable."

"Excellent." Mal clapped loudly enough that it echoed through the cavernous space. "Now about my reparations." His smile had twisted into something vicious and cruel, and Mox was glad she wasn't on the receiving end of it. "Your sibling did cut into my profit margins, after all."

DAM'S BREATHS CAME IN HARD PANTS, THEIR HEAD TILTED forward so their chin was pressed to their chest. They had been at this for literal hours, and Mox forgot how fucking daunting it could be to torture answers from someone who was trained to resist.

"We could try truth serum," Celeste suggested, cracking her knuckles. Of the six family members who'd been chosen as representatives for this matter, only she and Mox were still standing. The others had long since settled into the metal chairs set in a circle like some fucked-up version of group therapy.

"That shit never works." Mox tilted her head from one side to the other, stretching her neck. "I think we've gotten all we're going to get out of them, honestly."

"Was it enough?"

A fair question. One Mox didn't have an answer to. "Silva, the minutes?"

Silva stood from his chair, his posture less upright than usual, his clothes rumpled, and pulled a notepad from his pocket. His voice was flat as he read off the pad. "The children were used to fuel the portal. They're not saying where they came from or how they got them. Their aims with the portal were simply to seize control of an import route so they could collect the tariff associated with it. They have copped to the fire at Corwin's bakery but have not answered whether that was a hired job."

"Should we go again?" Glyn—or Guin pretending to be Glyn, anyway—asked.

"No point." Mox wiped her bloody hands on her slacks as she crouched in front of Dam to meet their eyes. "Is there, Dam?" Her voice drifted into a soft whisper for only them to hear. "Your sister's got you locked up better than Alcatraz, doesn't she?"

Dam flinched.

"That's what I thought." Mox nodded, pushed to her feet, and spun to look at the other seconds. "All right, Celeste and I did most of the work, the rest of you are on cleanup."

She left the other seconds to bicker over who was going

to dispose of the body while she dropped into a chair to send Mal a full report.

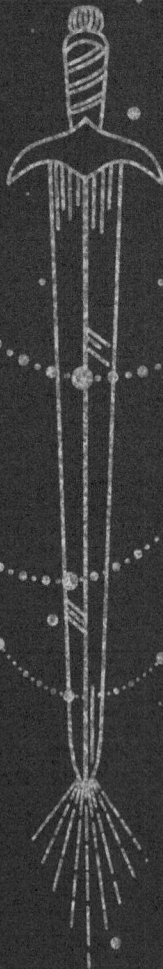

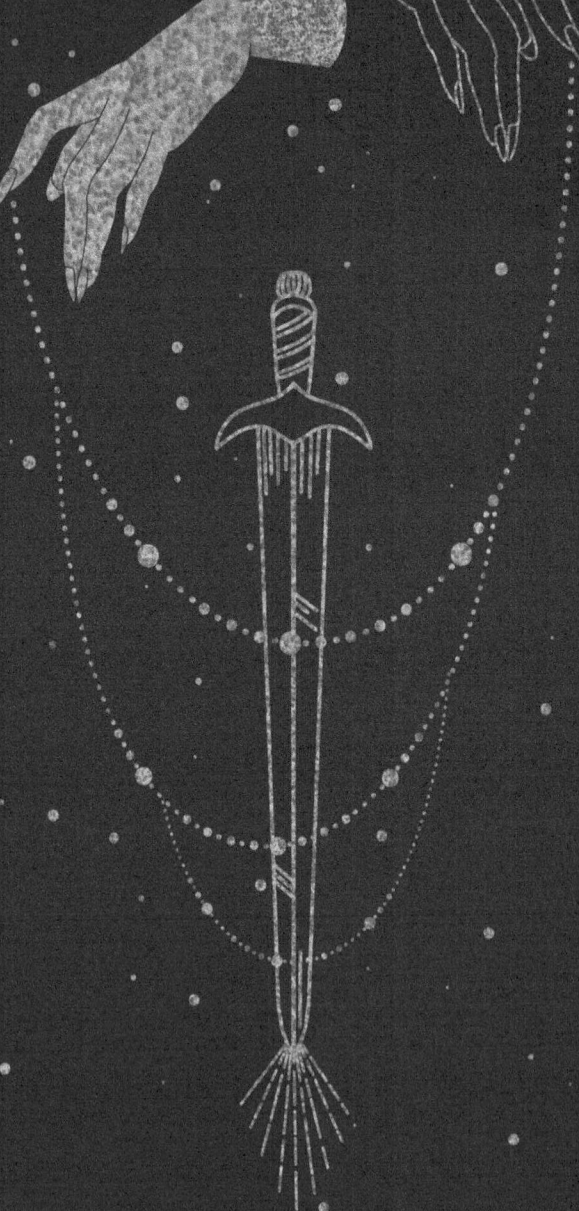

38

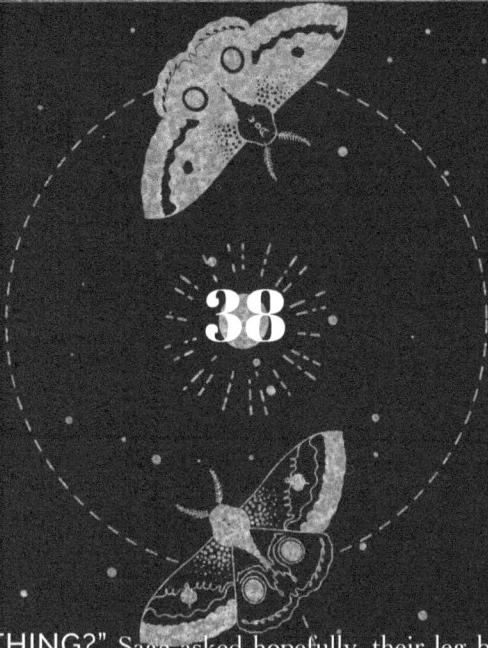

"ANYTHING?" Sage asked hopefully, their leg bouncing up and down on the couch in Mal's office. It had been three days already, and they still hadn't found the children's parents. Dam refused to get up off the information. The longer it took, the more Sage had the sinking feeling that those kids would never get home.

Mal shook his head, his expression apologetic. "He's not talking."

Sage sighed, leaning against the back of the couch, their head tilted to stare at the ceiling. "Well. I guess we'll have to do this the old-fashioned way then. Hand me my laptop."

"What's the old-fashioned way?" Mal asked, reaching for the computer Sage had abandoned on the end table at some point. He set it gently onto their lap, an amused smile ticking at the corners of his lips. He looked good like this. Pleased. And Sage would be lying if they said they didn't enjoy the way he took care of them.

"The internet" was Sage's answer as they pulled open the lid and typed in the password. "Would you mind getting me some snacks and drinks? This might take a while."

"Not at all." Mal leaned in to brush a kiss to their cheek before he rose and left them to their work.

"WHAT DO YOU *MEAN* YOU COULDN'T FIND HIS FAMILY?" Corey asked, looking down at the boy sitting at her two-person kitchen table across from Chuckles. He was a cute kid. Big dark eyes, teal hair so dark it almost looked black. They hadn't figured out what type of fae he was yet, but Corey suspected he might be a halfling like her. Which might have been why he was targeted—because his own parents wanted nothing to do with him. He was easy prey.

"We found where the twins belonged." Sage scrubbed their face, turning the skin a little red and blotchy. They were stressed, maybe more so than they'd been when they were planning how to handle the Blood Moons, but they didn't seem unhappy about it. On the contrary, it was almost like they loved being busy, feeling important, feeling needed. Corey thought she could understand that, likely more than anyone else. "But we can't even find a record of him in the system. No birth certificate. No files with social services."

"He couldn't be Dam's, could he?" Goddess, she hoped not. She hoped Dam was better than to use their own offspring to power a portal.

"I'm not sure what he is, but he's not a redcap." Sage shook their head. A soft huff left them, and Corey knew what they were about to say even before they opened their mouth to say it.

"He could stay here with us," Chuckles said, beating them to it. Which was downright comical because when she said *here* she meant Corey's apartment, the place where all of them, Sage included, were *guests*. And where Chuckles was only spending the weekend while Mal and Mox were dealing with some shit at the Court.

"No," Corey hissed and tried not to flinch when the boy jerked his head up to her, those eyes boring into her like they could see down to her fucking soul. "Absolutely not."

"Why not?" Sage tilted their head. Corey wanted to smack them. *So* fucking hard.

"Because we don't have room for another person here. We barely have room for you and me."

"He's little. He doesn't take up much space," Chuckles argued. Goddess, Corey hated teenagers. What had convinced her to let this kid stay with her and Sage for the weekend?

"And what about when he's *not* so little? Kids grow up, Chucks." She would cave. She could already tell, she would cave. It was hard not to when the boy fixed her with those big eyes. "Plus, if we take him in, Chuckles is going to want to stay too."

"You think?" Sage asked at the same time Chuckles asked, "Can I?!"

They both sounded *way* too excited about that prospect. Maybe that had been the wrong tactic to take to throw them off this idea.

Corey sighed, tilting her head back to blink at the lights in the ceiling as they burned her eyes. They were dated. Older than even her probably. The whole place was, and she'd never put much effort into making it a home for herself, much less for anyone else. It was merely a place to sleep between hours at the bakery. *That* was her real home, and the bastards in Aquarius had destroyed it. Or tried to, anyway.

They would rebuild. They would do it together. A small,

dysfunctional, fucked-up family. Just like they'd raise this kid together, probably.

"I've got some cash stored up," Sage said, their voice soft and leading. A promise. Bastard. "For a rainy day."

"It's raining," the boy said. It was the first words he'd said since they'd found him in the basement. Even with Lucy, he hadn't spoken. Corey couldn't imagine being faced with the frustrating demon and *not* talking.

When Corey glanced back down at him, she saw that he had turned his big eyes to the windows in the living room, and outside it *had* started to pour. The lights of Eventide swam through the glass.

"So it is." She laughed, shaking her head. "Okay, sure. Why not raise a kid with someone I hate?"

Sage snorted, rolling their eyes. "Keep telling people that, and one day we both might believe it."

"A girl can dream."

glossary

While not required, this glossary is intended to offer further context to the world of Eventide.

Fae Terms

- **Bean-nighe:** A sub-species of fae with precognitive abilities.
- **Cait Sidhe:** A sub-species of fae with the ability to shift into some type of feline. Many of the cait sidhe can only shift into common house cats, but some have the ability to shift into larger animals like panthers, tigers, and even lions. Many also have the ability to channel their feline senses while still retaining their humanoid form.
- **Fauthon:** A sub-species of fae that is a cross between a fairy and a ghost. Little is known about these fae, aside from their ability to control water to some degree, and that their glamour hides shark-like teeth.
- **Folk:** The term used to reference all magical

beings of any species or subspecies, including witches, fae, vampires, etc.

- **Glamour:** A magical barrier which works to alter the viewers perception of a place, person, or thing.
- **Halfling:** A child of a human and a fae. These children may retain some of their fae abilities, but often do not. However, they do have the ability to see through glamours making them disliked by most other folk.
- **Mare:** A sub-species of fae with the ability to control shadows, and nightmares. Some even have the ability to use shadows to spy one people. Usually born as one half of a pair of twins, one of which being a wil-o'-wisp, the other being a wil-o'-wisp to balance the light and the dark.
- **Night Market:** The Night Market is a place for folk to buy and trade all types of products that would be otherwise seen is elicit or illegal in the human world. Including, but not limited to, blood, werewolf venom, potions, hexes, fae hair, etc. It exist in a pocket dimension created and run by the Faceless Few gang of Eventide.
- **Wil-o'-wisp:** A sub-species of fae with the ability to control light, and fire. Usually born as one half of a pair of twins, the other being a mare to balance the light and the dark.

mox's court of families files

Faceless Few
UNSEELIE FAE
run the Night Market

Leader: Mal Senka
   Second: Mox Senka

Delta Daggers
UNSEELIE FAE
run the western docks of Eventide

Leader: Guin
   Second: Cas

Blood Moons
UNSEELIE FAE
run the casinos and racetracks in Eventide

Leader: Flo
   Second: Dam

Divinity of Aquarius
SEELIE FAE
run the eastern docks of Eventide

Leader: Alton
   Second: Glyn

Zaphyr

SEELIE FAE
run pharmaceutical production
(including the production of anti-iron)

Leader: Evy
    Second: Celeste

<u>Wildlings</u>
SEELIE FAE
guardians of the forest

Leader: Mata
    Second: Silva

acknowledgments

As always, I want to thank you, dear reader, for picking up the latest addition to the Bay of the Dead 'verse. Whether you're a new reader, or you're coming back to this world after picking up one of the other series in this universe, your support is so appreciated, and so dear to me.

I've always been a big fan of mafia aus, so writing one of my own just made sense. I hope you loved reading about this motley crew of gangsters as much as I loved writing them. If you did, please leave a review, follow me on social media, or give me a shout out. I love hearing from you guys, it's really the best part of writing.

Next I'd like to thank my family—found and blood-related—who support me in this weird journey I'm on to become an established author. They show up to my signings, they listen to my rants about my characters, they look at my covers and tell me when they're complete shit (I design my covers FYI), and they're the best people to have in my corner, no joke.

Then there is the small hoard of beta readers I had look over this to tell me if I had indeed achieved "cozy fae mafia". Turns out I did! Thank you Meg, Val, Nancy, VS, Justin, and Stephanie. You guys provided so much helpful feedback, and I'm super grateful.

And of course my editor, Brenna. Who continues to give The Bay of the Dead 'verse her love, and has dubbed the disembowelment a "cozy" disembowelment.

And last but certainly never least, thank you to my small writing support group. Tiss, Elle, Whitney, Nancy, Meg, and the rest of my MTP family—without you there would be no Lou.

about lou wilham

Born and raised in a small town near the Chesapeake Bay, Lou Wilham grew up on a steady diet of fiction, arts and crafts, and Old Bay. After years of absorbing everything, there was to absorb of fiction, fantasy, and sci-fi she's left with a serious writing/drawing habit that just won't quit. These days, she spends much of her time writing, drawing, and chasing a very short Basset Hound named Sherlock.

When not, daydreaming up new characters to write and draw she can be found crocheting, making cute bookmarks, and binge-watching whatever happens to catch her eye.

Learn more about Lou and her future projects on her website: http://louinprogress.com/ or join her mailing list at: http://subscribepage.com/mailermailer

facebook.com/LouWilham

instagram.com/lou.wilham

also by lou wilham

more books you'll love

If you enjoyed this story, please consider leaving a review.

Then check out more books from Midnight Tide Publishing!

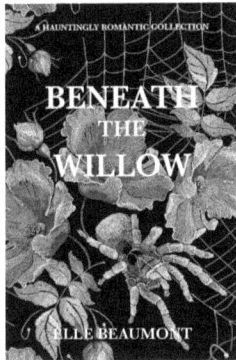

Beneath the Willow by Elle Beaumont

LOVE DESERVES A SECOND CHANCE.

Something lurks deep within the mysterious inn, and when a paranormal expert arrives, so does an unexpected visitor.

A woman pores over letters she discovered in an old bookstore, and every time she reads them, she can feel the presence of the man who wrote them, making her uncertain of her sanity.

A spirit plagues the owner of an inn, but when a paranormal investigator arrives, he requires the aid of the anomaly, or the owner risks losing everything.

After a tragic loss, a man leaves his old life behind. Beginning a new adventure should be easy, but when a friendly ghost appears, he realizes nothing ever is. But with memories of his past haunting him, will he ever be truly ready?

Beneath the Willow is a romantic collection of ghost stories that will haunt you long after reading. From newfound love to rekindled flames, and even healing after loss, these contents are dark, beautiful, and tragic, surely inspiring heart-pounding moments and tears.

Available Now

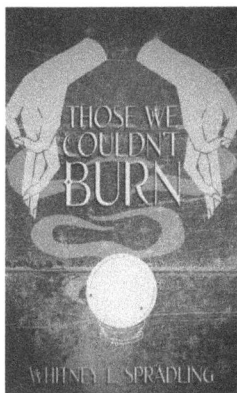

Those We Couldn't Burn by Whitney L. Spradling

WORLDS COLLIDE when an ancient vision brings a witch and witch hunter together.

Prince Tyberius Berkshire, witch hunter extraordinaire, has been set with an impossible task—discover the truth of an ancient vision to keep his family on the throne. His world crashes down around him, when an intricate piece of the vision's puzzle falls into place in the form of a purple-haired witch.

Neave Paker has spent the past ten years quietly taking revenge against the witch hunters. Until the prince of the hunters captures her. Taken to the palace, she's given the choice to either work for the enemy or burn at the stake.

Together, they set out to discover the truth. But difficulties lie ahead as they fight attraction and animosity. When they uncover more than they bargained for, the unlikely duo must determine what is more important to them: their beliefs or their hearts.

Available Now

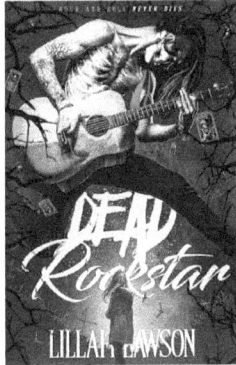

Dead Rockstar by Lillah Lawson

Stormy Spooner is at her wits' end. Careening towards bitter after a nasty divorce, she sometimes wonders what her life is becoming.

After unearthing a cryptic set of lines from a dusty album cover, Stormy tries the impossible: to resurrect Phillip Deville, enigmatic former frontman of the Bloomer Demons. Stormy's love for her favorite dead rockstar knows no bounds...but it was all supposed to be a joke.

When she answers a knock on her door the next day and finds herself face to face with the dark-haired rock god of her every teenage fantasy, her entire world is turned upside down.

Turns out, she's awakened more than just Philip, and Stormy will have to do battle against a cast of strange characters to keep herself and her new undead boyfriend safe.

Available May 15, 2024

www.ingramcontent.com/pod-product-compliance
Ingram Content Group UK Ltd.
Pitfield, Milton Keynes, MK11 3LW, UK
UKHW050405170325
456246UK00023B/54/J